MY

OCTOBER

ALSO BY CLAIRE HOLDEN ROTHMAN

Salad Days

Black Tulips

The Heart Specialist

CLAIRE HOLDEN ROTHMAN

MY
OCTOBER

PENGUIN
an imprint of Penguin Canada, a Penguin Random House Company

Published by the Penguin Group
Penguin Group (Canada), 90 Eglinton Avenue East, Suite 700, Toronto, Ontario, Canada M4P 2Y3

Penguin Group (USA) LLC, 375 Hudson Street, New York, New York 10014, U.S.A.
Penguin Books Ltd, 80 Strand, London WC2R 0RL, England
Penguin Ireland, 25 St Stephen's Green, Dublin 2, Ireland (a division of Penguin Books Ltd)
Penguin Group (Australia), 707 Collins Street, Melbourne, Victoria 3008, Australia
(a division of Pearson Australia Group Pty Ltd)
Penguin Books India Pvt Ltd, 11 Community Centre, Panchsheel Park, New Delhi – 110 017, India
Penguin Group (NZ), 67 Apollo Drive, Rosedale, Auckland 0632, New Zealand
(a division of Pearson New Zealand Ltd)
Penguin Books (South Africa) (Pty) Ltd, 24 Sturdee Avenue, Rosebank, Johannesburg 2196, South Africa

Penguin Books Ltd, Registered Offices: 80 Strand, London WC2R 0RL, England

First published 2014

1 2 3 4 5 6 7 8 9 10 (WEB)

Crown copyright information taken from James Richard Cross's testimonial in the
British Diplomatic Oral History Programme, Foreign and Commonwealth Office, 1996,
is re-used under the terms of the Open Government Licence (U.K.).

Canada Council **Conseil des Arts**
for the Arts **du Canada**

Manufactured in Canada.

LIBRARY AND ARCHIVES CANADA CATALOGUING IN PUBLICATION

Rothman, Claire, 1958–, author
My October / Claire Holden Rothman.

Includes bibliographical references.
ISBN 978-0-14-318867-4 (pbk.)

I. Title.

PS8585.O8435M92 2014   C813'.54   C2014-902412-6

eBook ISBN 978-0-14-319303-6

Visit the Penguin Canada website at **www.penguin.ca**

Special and corporate bulk purchase rates available; please see
www.penguin.ca/corporatesales or call 1-800-810-3104.

For Jacob Holden

Remember you shot a seagull?
A man happened to come along,
shot it and killed it, just to pass the time.
A plot for a short story.

Anton Chekhov, *The Seagull*

I wish there would be no story to tell.

James Richard Cross, 2001

JAMES CROSS, A TESTIMONY

M *y first introduction to the violence that was to come was at the St. John Baptiste Day parade in 1968. This is the Quebec national day and is usually marked by processions and floats through the streets of Montreal. On the reviewing stand that day was Pierre Trudeau, who had just been elected leader of the Liberal Party and who was a convinced and vocal federalist. American consul Harrison Burgess and I attended with our wives. Both of us were to meet terrorism again within two years. The parade was marked by demonstrations against Trudeau, ending with bottles being thrown at the reviewing platform.*

Over the next couple of years, there were a series of terrorist incidents, the most important being the bombing of the Montreal Stock Exchange. In the summer of 1970, I went on leave in England and returned in mid-summer. I learned then that there had been an attempt to kidnap Harrison Burgess, our American consul, but that the police had raided a farmhouse near Montreal, captured the intended kidnappers and seized a quantity of documents, including the demands that they intended to submit. These included the release of a large number of so-called "political" prisoners, the payment of a ransom and the reinstatement of certain workers who had been dismissed under a privatisation contract....

Though Harrison Burgess was protected by police, there was no general warning to consular officials in Montreal that any further incidents were expected. In fact, when the new American consul, General Topping, arrived later that summer, no special protection was given to his house.

October 5 was a typical bright Montreal autumn day. My wife and I were facing a busy week with a number of important engagements, including a visit from the president of the Confederation of British Industries, for whom we were organising certain functions, and we were discussing the week ahead as I walked between the bedroom and the bathroom dressing. I then heard a ring of the doorbell and was surprised that anybody would arrive that early in the morning. My wife suggested that it was probably Hydro Quebec come to read the meter, so I took no further notice. I then heard raised voices but did not pay much attention as our maid was inclined to speak loudly sometimes to her small child. The next thing I knew was, as I was walking back towards the bathroom dressed only in shirt and underpants, a man came through from the opposite side holding a gun and said, "Get down on the floor or you'll be fucking dead."

—from "The British Diplomatic
Oral History Programme," 1996

PROLOGUE

October 5, 2004

*I*t's eight in the morning. The breakfast dishes are done, the kitchen is swept, and the newspaper is already in the recycling bin. I haven't written in my journal yet, or checked my emails. The computer isn't even on. I'm sitting in the pantry with a cup of Japanese tea, doing nothing in particular and enjoying the silence.

Although "silence" is a bit of an exaggeration. The garbage-men are down below in the street, banging cans and shouting at one another. The living room window is wide open. It's like summer today, even though the leaves are hanging from the trees in heavy golden clusters, ready to scatter with the first gust of wind. There is always a lull like this in October, a moment in the grim march toward winter when the foot refuses to fall. It never lasts long. A single day, perhaps two in a good year. But while the moment endures, the entire city seems to pause and take a collective astonished breath, recognizing, as if for the first time, its own beauty.

I'm alone here in the apartment, with no obligations other than to collect my garbage can after it's been emptied and put it back on the patch of yellowing grass beneath the stairs. I'm sitting here, appreciating this fact, feeling the day and all of its possibilities opening before me, when the doorbell rings.

It's too early for the mail. And besides, the mailman usually leaves my cheques and bills and other correspondence in the locked metal box on the ground floor. As I run toward the door, it occurs to me that I am a woman alone, but almost immediately I brush the thought aside. Luc says I should get a spyhole like the one Lyse has in the flat downstairs, but he's overreacting. This is Montreal, after all, one of the safest cities in the world.

The man standing on my welcome mat is not my regular mailman. He's in regulation shorts and shirt, however, a special delivery man from Canada Post. He grins at me, flushed and panting slightly with exertion, and holds out a large box.

"It's heavy," he says in French, and then translates the sentence, just in case.

He's not young, but he looks fit. His legs, which have just climbed sixty-seven steps, are muscular and smooth, marred only by a single protruding vein snaking down one of his calves. He places the box on the floor at our feet, and we stand together for several seconds contemplating it. Then he hands me a chit to sign. I squat, intending to use the box as a writing surface, and see the company's name staring up at me. Beneath it is the logo—a stylized *W* that looks like a bird taking flight.

"What's in there, anyway?" the delivery man asks as I hand

over his chit. We seem to have settled on French, though I haven't said a word. "Bricks?" he presses, smiling.

He's flirting. I smile but don't encourage him.

"Well, whatever it is," he says, nodding in the direction of my many steep stairs, "it made me sweat today."

I laugh in commiseration. I sweated too.

As soon as the door shuts, I go back to the pantry and get my Opinel, the penknife that Luc bought me years ago in France. I break the tape with its tip and make a long slit down the box's middle. The carton flaps spring open. Inside are sheets of recycled brown wrapping paper and, under these, squares of bubble wrap. I pull it all out, and there they are, gleaming up at me in rows.

I pick up one of the books and run my fingers over its cover. The delivery man was right. It's solid, brick-like. Which is a paradox, because its contents are the opposite of solid. But that, I am discovering, is the wonder of this enterprise. This book is made of words, insubstantial, weightless things I dreamed up and strung together to make a plot. Nothing at all really, and at the same time everything.

PART ONE

1

*L*uc stared at the page, or at least the section of the page visible on his screen. The screen he had spent the last fifteen years of his life staring at. The background was blue, slightly darker than the shell of a robin's egg. The blue of the sky at dusk, just as the light begins to fade. Luc had been thinking for some time now about a laptop. He'd mentioned it to Hannah last week, before she'd left for Toronto. He had informed her that he might go on a little shopping spree while she was away. She'd laughed, her eyebrows rising in amazement. Luc Lévesque wasn't big on gadgets. It had taken him years to switch from his old Smith Corona to a computer. And he hadn't gone on the spree yet. If he never did, it would come as no surprise to his wife. She knew him better, in many ways, than he knew himself. He ought to do it. All it required was turning off the screen and getting out of his chair.

Laptops were better for you, apparently, than desktops. Something about the endocrine system. Male rats with reduced libido. Luc sighed and rubbed his eyes. He hadn't had sex in weeks, although the computer was hardly to blame.

He ought to will himself to stand up. He wasn't a gardener or a garbageman or a mailman. Words were his life. And this, unfortunately, was the technology for generating words. At the end of the year, he would turn fifty. Luc had been trying to push it from his mind, but when the work went badly, as it had today, thoughts he normally kept at bay flooded in. The date was October 1, 2001. Luc would be in his forties for exactly three more months.

The signs were starting to appear. An athletic past helped. His chest would always be broad, even if the hair covering it was silver. His stomach was softer than it had been, but it wasn't a complete paunch. The beard was what gave him away. It was thick, like the hair on his head, but empty of colour. Hannah said he looked like the Zeus in the d'Aulaires' *Book of Greek Myths*, which they'd bought in the days when they still read to Hugo. The god's face was proud and handsome, and even though his beard was white, his naked chest was muscled. Hannah had made the remark on one of their good days, a rare moment of conjugal tenderness of the kind they had once enjoyed quite often.

He grimaced. The writing was going terribly. Every sentence came out stiff and lifeless on the virtual white page. Easier to think about loveless rats than deal with a book going sour.

His narrator was too close for comfort: the father of an uncontrolled adolescent son, living in Saint-Henri. There were differences, of course. The character he'd created was a taxi driver with a francophone wife. She was half Irish, though, from her father's side. And their son was showing signs of his mixed heritage. In the scene Luc was at this moment failing to write, the father had just discovered the boy had dropped out of school and was hanging out with members of an Irish gang. The father had observed them as he drove around the city at night. Boy-men from Griffintown. Boy-men who spoke English.

Luc had the ending already. That part would write itself. It was death.

The image of this middle-aged man dragged from his cab and beaten senseless in the freshly fallen snow on a street in Saint-Henri was the reason for the book. Every book has something at its heart: the tinder that ignites. In this one, it was parricide.

There was a knock at the door. Luc sat up from his slouch. He was never to be bothered when he wrote. Everyone knew that. It was the rule.

The knock came again. Too forceful for his mother, Lyse, who would come downstairs only in the event of a true emergency. It couldn't be Hannah. She was in Toronto with her own parents. Luc stood up and strode through the darkened living room and hall. His brother, Rémi, had left some furniture, but the place was largely empty. Not a home, a workspace.

He was dressed strangely, he realized too late, as his hand closed around the doorknob. Silk long johns under baggy black gym shorts, a purple cotton jersey, red Converse high-tops, and fingerless red gloves that his mother had knitted to protect his hands from chafing: the clothes of a writer at work. Or a crazy person, *c'est selon* …

He opened the door and gasped, actually gasped. Then he laughed. "Serge Vien!"

The curly hair was grey, still ungoverned by any comb. The nose was too big for the face, now lined. And the lazy eye was still there, winking behind thick-lensed glasses and aimed disconcertingly at something off to one side behind Luc's head. Vien laughed too. The same honking laugh.

They shook hands, grabbed each other's shoulders—the awkward gestures of middle-aged men who knew a handshake wasn't enough but couldn't bring themselves to embrace. "To what do I owe the pleasure?"

"It is a pleasure, for sure," said Vien, grinning his same old grin. "But actually, I'm here on business."

He stepped aside, revealing a second person standing behind him on the walk, hunched in the neck and shoulders as if trying to shrink out of sight. Squinting in the midday sun, Luc made out the familiar fleshless face. The pale shaved head.

"Hugo? What is this about?"

The boy did not look up. He was staring at a crack in the pavement that had appeared the previous winter and in the spring widened into a hole. Lyse had mentioned it a couple of times, suggesting they fill it in before the frost came and widened it further. Someone could get hurt.

"There was an incident," Vien said quickly. "It's okay now. He's fine, actually." He turned around and gave Hugo a smile that the boy didn't acknowledge. "He was checked by the school nurse. She said everything's normal. But it could have been serious. You were lucky, my man." He gave Hugo a light, awkward punch on the shoulder. The boy flinched and kept his eyes fixed on the hole.

Heat surged up from Luc's chest. "He's talking to you," he said to his son. "Look at him."

Hugo lifted his gaze and looked not at Vien but at his father, with an expression that verged on venomous.

Vien laughed nervously—the honk—and Luc remembered the irritations of long ago.

"It's okay. Really. He's had a tough morning. No harm done. And it gave me a chance to drive down here and see you, *mon ami*. How long has it been? Thirty years? My God, more? Let me do the math."

Luc's eyes had adjusted. It was one of those autumn days that felt like August. Across Laporte Street, the trees in Saint-Henri Park had turned, but the fountain was still flowing. That wouldn't last. The city would turn it off soon, most likely in the next week or so. But for today, there was water. Luc could hear it under Vien's chatter, water flowing through the spout below Jacques Cartier's blackened statue.

Vien stopped for a breath.

"Come in," Luc said. Vien stood on the step, looking uncertain. "This is where I work." Luc pointed at the outdoor staircase leading to the second storey. "We live upstairs."

"Your mother's old place?"

"No, she's still in the middle one. The top one's ours." He started to turn, then paused and said to Hugo, "You. Upstairs."

The boy obeyed.

"I'll be up soon," Luc called after him. "After I'm done with …" He turned back to Vien.

"Monsieur Vien," said Vien, almost apologetically.

"Monsieur Vien."

He led Vien inside, switching on lights as he went. He could feel his visitor looking around, and as he walked, he saw the flat with new eyes. It was makeshift, ugly. Vien sat down on the ratty corduroy couch, which, for obvious reasons, Rémi hadn't taken to the Plateau. Vien was trying to look at ease, but the way he was perched made it plain he would rather be standing.

"Coffee?" Luc asked. "A glass of water?"

Vien shook his head. "I've got to get back."

They looked at each other, shy now in the intimacy of the interior.

Vien was the first to break the silence. "He fainted," he explained, turning the conversation back to the issue at hand. "On purpose. It's a thing they do. In groups, usually in the schoolyard. But Hugo chose to do it differently this time. This time, it was in the classroom, right under my nose."

"Whoa, whoa," Luc said. "He's in your class?"

"You didn't know? I figured you'd seen. My name is on his course list. He's in my homeroom."

Luc shook his head. Hannah handled those things, and she wouldn't have recognized Vien's name. Vien looked vaguely hurt—but just for a moment. He resumed the story. He had been at the blackboard, writing notes with his back to the class, when he heard a thump. When he turned, Hugo was on the floor.

"Blacked out?" said Luc.

"For a few seconds, four or five at most. Everyone in the class turned when he hit the floor. We all heard it. By the time I got to him, his eyelids were already fluttering open. The rest of the kids didn't even have time to react. They only did that after, when Hugo was sitting up. He was sweating, but he knew where he was and everything. No worries there. The nurse shone a light in his eyes and checked his skull."

"Easy skull to check." Luc hated the concentration-camp look.

"Unlike ours." Vien took a fistful of his own grey curls and shook them, smiling like a clown. "The nurse also gave him a lecture. Brain damage. Death. Told him in no uncertain terms how lucky he was."

"How did he make himself faint?"

"There's a whole procedure. You hyperventilate, basically. Then empty the lungs. Hugo can tell you the steps better than I can."

"Right." There was a pause. "You got kids, Serge?"

"Fifteen hundred of them."

In other words, no. Luc frowned. "They're overrated."

Vien honked again. He was wearing shiny black shoes and a cheap tie. His sports jacket was rumpled. He was what passed for authority at the Catholic school where they had once been friends, and now he was teaching Luc's son. A small world: too small for words.

So Hugo had pulled a prank. A stupid one, but stupidity was the essence of pranks in high school.

"You shouldn't have taken this trouble," Luc said. "You should have sent Hugo back to his desk and given him a detention. You probably won't get any lunch now."

"There's a protocol at the school," Vien explained. "If a kid faints, he gets sent to the infirmary and then home. No one picked up when we called your number. We were going to leave it at that, wait for you to call back, but Hugo told me you never pick up when you're working."

Luc reddened. "My wife usually answers the telephone."

"But she's out of town, Hugo said."

"In Toronto. Visiting her parents."

There was a pause while Vien digested this, but Luc wasn't

going to indulge him with any more personal information. Yes, his lifelong companion and helpmate was an Anglo. Yes, her parents lived in Toronto. Life was a bowl of paradoxes. Surely Vien had lived long enough to understand that.

"You do that every morning—unplug?"

"All day, sometimes," said Luc. "Depending on how it's going. Otherwise, I don't get anything done. If someone needs to get in touch, they can do it through my agent."

Vien laughed, nodding as if impressed. If he felt guilty about his intrusion into Luc's working day, it didn't show. "I love your books," he said. "I've read every one of them. It's amazing."

"What's amazing?"

"That you did it."

"Wrote books?"

"Not just books. *Tanneur tanné, La mort d'un rêveur.* You're the voice of Quebec, Luc. That's what they call you. The voice of a generation. Our generation. *Les boomers.* And I grew up with you. I knew you way back when."

"You did," said Luc, smiling magnanimously. This type of talk used to make him want to run. Now, he just let it wash over him. Water off a duck's back. He had a talent, that was all. He could tell a story. But he still woke up at four A.M. worrying about money and the health of his prostate gland. His hair, formerly thick and black, was still going grey. The muscles of his stomach were still thinning and turning incrementally into fat. It wasn't as though writing saved him from anything. At one time, he'd thought it might.

This had changed when Hugo was born, so tiny and dark, so utterly foreign, that Luc had actually felt a shiver of revulsion. It shamed him now to remember. The birth of his son had shown him how little control he had, not merely over extraneous things, but over intimate ones as well. Writing, he'd once thought, sharpened the sensibilities. It rearranged the interior world, making space for empathy and love.

As he watched Hugo emerge from between Hannah's legs, covered in blood and wax, he hadn't felt anything even approaching love. After the doctor had cut the cord and the nurses had cleaned him, after Hannah had taken him in her arms and held him, crooning, against her breasts, Luc was offered the chance to hold him too. Hugo had looked up at him with enormous, worried eyes. His brow was mottled yellow and pink, the skin wrinkled like an old man's. He had resembled in that moment the poster of Franz Kafka hanging above Hannah's desk: saucer-eyed and Semitic. Not a trace of the Lévesque bloodline to be seen.

Vien's chatter brought Luc back to the present. He was describing the details of his life: the house in Longueuil on the South Shore; the daily drive over the crumbling Champlain Bridge; the wife who had walked out a year ago. He still lived in the bungalow by the river they had owned together.

"You're lucky to have this," Vien said, motioning at the room with both hands. "Not the office," he clarified, following Luc's eyes. "I mean Hugo. Your wife. A family."

Luc didn't answer. Vien had always been a sentimentalist. Playing father to a fourteen-year-old son and husband to a woman you'd lived with for over twenty years wasn't unadulterated bliss, not that he was about to go into it.

"Well," said Vien, as the silence grew uncomfortable.

They walked to the door.

"He's a good kid," said Vien.

Again, Luc said nothing.

"Boys go insane at that age."

Luc shrugged and shook Vien's hand, which felt surprisingly spongy. Too many years at a desk marking papers. He watched him walk to his car, a Toyota with a rusting hole above the rear wheel. Vien's back was slightly bowed, his step small. At fourteen, he used to bound down the stairs, taking them two at a time, kicking at the chestnuts that littered the front walk. Life had done its work. Vien was freighted now, slow. He walked by the chestnuts without even seeing them. Luc tucked in his chin, threw back his shoulders, and pulled himself to his full height. He hoped to God he didn't look like that from behind.

Vien's horn tooted twice as he drove off, back to the Collège Saint-Jean-Baptiste. Where he worked, teaching Hugo. It was hard to fathom.

A memory came floating to the surface, a cellular memory of the scratchy ill-fitting uniform Luc had been forced to wear for five years. Luc had not liked high school. He'd had reasons, not all of them related to Collège Saint-Jean-Baptiste itself. The face of his old principal, Monsieur Hervé, rose up in front of him. A fierce, pockmarked man. Or was the fierceness, like Vien's lazy eye, like the honking laugh, just a distraction from the good man underneath?

Luc put away his notes. Too bad it was Monday—a short day might set the tone for the whole week. Where was Hannah, anyway? It had been four days, but it felt longer. If she'd been here, he would have been spared all this. Or maybe not spared, not utterly. He would have wanted to see Serge Vien again, even though it made him sad. Those soft fleshy hands. He took one of his own hands in the other and squeezed. He could still feel his bones.

His wife should be here. This was her responsibility: Hugo, school, health. Especially health. She would have reacted strongly. Dragged Luc into a long, unnecessary discussion about the risks Hugo had just taken, with her father skulking in the shadows behind every word. Maybe it was best she was away.

Nothing bad had happened, after all. Hugo was his usual sullen self. He seemed fine. It had been a stupid, juvenile prank, that was all. Luc put on his outdoor shoes. He wouldn't get angry at his son, even if the boy had cost him a day of work. He opened the front door and stepped outside into the blazing sun. As he climbed toward the second floor, where Lyse lived, the rays felt good on his shoulders, and he chastised himself for his indoor life. It was like summer. He should get out more. Just above him was the flat that Vien had once known so intimately. Vien had practically lived with Luc's family during his unhappy years as a boarder at the school. Lyse had procured a letter from Madame Vien allowing him to have dinner with the Lévesques on weeknights. And most weekends too, Vien would be there, sleeping on an inflatable mattress beside Luc's bed.

At the second-floor landing there were two doors, one to Lyse's place, one to Luc's own home on the top floor. He opened the latter and took the indoor staircase two stairs at a time.

Hugo's scuffed shoes lay upended on different steps. Luc collected them, placing them neatly next to one another, removed his own shoes, and arranged them likewise. You have to stay calm, he told himself. And be firm. He turned his head sharply to the right and then to the left. Sometimes he could get it; there would be a satisfying little pop right up at the top, where the vertebrae connected with the skull. The axis vertebra. Wasn't that the name for it? No pop today. He tried again. Nothing. He opened his front door and stepped into a din of gunfire.

"Hugo?" he called out. He stood for several seconds, listening. No answer. Only the guns.

The place smelled of garbage. He had forgotten to put it out on Friday in the rush to get Hugo out of bed and ready for school. The truck would come again tomorrow, a fact that Luc had written in his agenda in bold red print. That was what turning fifty was about: writing things down in red ink.

Hugo's door was shut. A green copper cobra fanned its oxidized hood at the level of Luc's hand. Rémi had bought this ancient ornamental door handle in India and given it to Hugo for Christmas. Luc knocked and the guns fell silent. There was some rustling. Luc reached for the snake's head and pushed.

The computer was dark. There was a house rule: Hugo wasn't allowed to be at his computer until evening, and then only after his homework was completed. He was on his bed, scratching the plastic cover off *The Guinness Book of World Records* with his thumbnail. His school uniform—an updated version of the navy shirt and pants Luc himself had once worn—lay crumpled on the floor. He was wearing jeans now, his boxers exposed at the waist. Luc picked his son's school pants up and folded them.

"So you made yourself faint."

Hugo's eyes remained fixed on the book. His right earlobe was puffy and red. That had been their last fight. Hugo had visited a piercing studio on a dare with two of his friends. Hannah had been annoyingly calm about the whole thing. The school had not been so accepting; the stud had to go. Hugo had gotten rid of it, but, predictably, the hole was now infected.

"Your ear's red," Luc said.

The boy lifted his hand to touch it but still refused to look at him. His hair was shaved so close that Luc could see the bony ridges under his scalp. Pinhead pimples dotted his forehead.

"Hugo." Luc turned his head away sharply, then turned it back. The crick still would not release.

The boy didn't move.

Luc grabbed the book. "Look at me!"

Hugo looked up, focusing over Luc's right shoulder.

Luc inhaled and lunged.

His son's bones felt like the bones of a bird in his hands. The boy struggled weakly. This was easy; easy and satisfying. Why was his heart beating so hard? He bunched the loose fabric of Hugo's shirt in his fists and forced him down on the bed. He felt, rather than summoned, the grin on his face—an instinctive grin, a baring of teeth. What was happening? His mouth and hands seemed to have disconnected from his reason. He'd never let loose like this before. Never dreamed it was possible. Hugo went limp. There were tears in his eyes.

Luc released him. A mistake, it turned out, because instantly Hugo scrambled to his feet.

"Prick!" he yelled in English. "Dirty prick motherfucker!" He was crying now in earnest, but the words were still clear. Luc watched in stunned silence as he screamed them, again and again, hateful, foreign things that moved through Luc's ribs and lodged, painfully, dully, in the centre of his chest.

2

*L*uc was staring at his screen again. Today was no better than yesterday, though so far it had been quiet. He had plugged in his phone—he couldn't in good conscience do otherwise—but thankfully there had been no calls. He had slept poorly and woken up sweating, with a vague memory of bad dreams. Hugo had risen late, of course, his surliness magnified by the fight. Too late to eat breakfast if he wanted to catch the bus for school. And he'd left on the kitchen table the lunch Luc had taken guilty pains to prepare—a ham sandwich, miniature carrots, the last of the chocolate chip cookies, an apple.

Hannah had a mantra. *"Ne prends rien au plan personnel."*

Luc pictured her shaking her head, accusing him with her big, unhappy eyes. He stretched in his chair. His eyes stung and his head kept sagging against his chest. He should probably take a nap. Instead, he leaned forward, forcing himself back to chapter five.

His narrator was looking for a home. It was a literal search, like Rose-Anna's quest for an apartment in *Bonheur d'occasion*.

How he loved that book. People said he wrote well, but he had never come close to *Bonheur*. Had Gabrielle Roy known how good it was? Could you ever know that about your own novel, or did you have to take other people's word for it?

His narrator felt like a stranger to his half-Irish wife and their mongrel son. He believed his wife was unfaithful. She was distracted, absent, all but oblivious of their son's recent downward spiral. There was no tender talk between them anymore, no talk at all, really, except recrimination. Life in the four-and-a-half on Lacasse Street had become close to unbearable. Art imitating life. Luc's hero was now an avid reader of the classifieds; he watched for rental signs as he worked the streets of Saint-Henri, retracing his route after his fares got out if he spotted anything promising. It had begun innocently, an idle pastime. But it soon turned into a conscious search. He jotted down numbers, knocked on people's doors, took note of every chance. A real home, a place where a man could lay his head in peace: was that too much to ask? Buildings were being bought up by developers all over Saint-Henri. Luc planned to introduce a character inspired by Rémi, a contractor who purchased cheap properties in the southwestern section of the city, fixed them up in a hurry, and flipped them at exorbitant prices. Rémi had renovated this triplex, which their family had owned since 1950. The market value was now twenty-five times what it had been the year it was bought.

Good places were hard to find. Students and artists had discovered Saint-Henri decades ago and displaced the truly poor, but now even they were being forced out by the speculators. Rents were many times what Luc's protagonist could afford.

Luc was searching for a place too.

He enjoyed walking the streets, especially after dark. He had always liked looking through the windows of other people's houses. It was astonishing how few of them had blinds or, if they did have them, how few were pulled down. He had watched a girl dance topless in front of her mirror, so thrilled by her own gaze that she failed to notice his. He had heard couples shouting insults at each other, wives screaming. At least Hannah wasn't a screamer. That he could not have endured. He'd seen plenty of other things on his walks. Love scenes, for instance, trysts in the alleys, men embracing men. But mostly he'd seen people alone, skin tinged with the blue flicker of a multitude of luminescent screens. Because of Hugo, he hadn't been out on his nocturnal rambles in a while. He wanted Hannah to come back. The clock was ticking. Rémi had said December, and that didn't leave much time.

Until Rémi moved out, Luc had worked upstairs. One of the bedrooms had always been set aside as his office. Hannah claimed not to need one. She was fine in the pantry, she said, and he didn't press the issue. Then Rémi met Catherine and moved to the Plateau. And Luc's life went from good to perfect. For three glorious years, Luc had paid Rémi rent and enjoyed complete peace and comfort in the bottom flat.

But now Rémi and Catherine were splitting up. Rémi was returning to Laporte Street and Luc had exactly two months to find a new refuge.

The telephone rang. "Luc?" The voice was young, melodious. "I thought I'd get the answering machine."

"Well," he said, "you got the man. Sorry." Only he wasn't sorry at all. The voice belonged to Marie-Soleil. He was alert now, the hairs on the back of his neck tingling pleasantly.

"I thought you unplugged in the mornings."

He looked at his watch. Eleven thirty. "Actually," he said, "I'm done for the day."

"I didn't mean to disturb."

"You're not."

But she was—if *disturb* was the word for it. He could picture her lips, which were the colour of plums. Luc's agent, Frédéric Axe, had hired her as a personal assistant two years ago. She accompanied him to literary functions, travelled with him to book fairs in Paris and Frankfurt, sleeping, Luc hoped, in a separate hotel room. Frédéric had told Luc with a straight face that he was teaching her about foreign rights.

Luc had left it at that. But recently there had been a shift. Whenever Luc visited the office, Marie-Soleil came out of her cubicle to greet him. She had taken to kissing him familiarly on both cheeks and laughing at his witticisms. And now she was calling him in the middle of the morning at his desk.

"My good luck," Marie-Soleil said, and laughed. She laughed often. "Yours too. I have news."

He heard something in her voice, something erotic. Or was it just youth, amplified by the excitement in his own body?

"I've found the perfect place."

Five minutes later he had hung up the telephone, changed out of his long underwear, and was walking down Laporte Street in the direction of the canal. His teeth were brushed. He had checked his beard for breakfast crumbs. He regretted the grey in it. Beards for men, hands for women: the infallible indicators of age. Marie-Soleil was not yet twenty-five.

The day was bright, surely an auspicious sign. Yet he mustn't raise his hopes too high. Mustn't make a symbol of the weather.

This wasn't a scene from a novel. At Saint-Jacques Street, he turned right and walked west to du Couvent, then south. Not a long walk. Saint-Henri was surprisingly small. Its streets intersected and bifurcated in strange, not altogether logical, ways, often punctuated by parks and squares, but the actual geographical area was not large. Luc quickened his pace. It was good to be walking.

Only people who didn't know him well envied Luc Lévesque. He led a largely interior life, bent over a keyboard, his peculiar form of monasticism that didn't preclude the right—the obligation, even, since as an artist he felt compelled to explore every stage of a man's life—to procreate as well as to create. But solitude suited him. He was a slow maker of sentences. He compared himself (never out loud) to Flaubert. A hesitater, a chronic victim of second and third and fourteenth thoughts, a perfectionist who, unlike Flaubert, never came near perfection. He often worked through dinner and into the night. He and Hannah could spend a whole day within a few steps of each other and not exchange a word.

He walked past the Cinéma Cartier on grimy Notre-Dame Street. It was no longer a cinema; Dawson College owned the building now. In *Bonheur d'occasion*, Jean Lévesque had brought Florentine Lacasse here on their first date. Two doors away, looking every bit as rundown and forlorn as it must have looked in the forties, when Gabrielle Roy was walking these streets, was the Deux Records bar, where Florentine's father, Azarius, had made beer-fuelled speeches about the war. This stretch of Notre-Dame held little charm. Even in sunshine, it remained grey and shabby, with a few shrubs or bits of grass to enliven it.

Luc reached Saint-Augustin Street. The discount store with the diner at the back where Florentine Lacasse had served meals—les 15 Cennes—crowned the north end of the street where it intersected with Notre-Dame. Les 15 Cennes was a dollar store now. *Plus ça change ...*

Luc didn't like this area. Sometimes, he went to Distribution Alimentaire Aubut for cheese—the parmesan was good—but in general the southern half of Saint-Henri depressed him. Most of the factories had been turned into pricey lofts, which made him angry. It was only recently, after Frédéric Axe moved his office into the district, that Luc had started visiting with any regularity.

Marie-Soleil had instructed him to meet her at the last building before the railway crossing. He knew the house, of course. It sat a few steps from the tracks, a wooden structure tapering at one end like a boat's hull, "twisted, as if to brace itself against life's shocks." A brilliant phrase, which Luc surprised himself by remembering whole. Gabrielle Roy had compared the house to a sailing vessel, a clumsy one, cleaving waves of industrial dust and debris.

It certainly was a singular sight, squatting there precariously. A perfect place for surly, ambitious young Jean Lévesque, the character Gabrielle Roy had created to inhabit it. Perfect, now, sixty years later, for another Lévesque. Marie-Soleil was right.

He looked across the tracks, but Saint-Ambroise Street, which lay on the other side, was empty. The way street and rail converged here was vaguely nightmarish. As a boy, Luc used to dream about trains at night. Trains coming at him with not even a whistle, and the tracks placed so close together there was barely space between them to stand. Just the thought of it twisted his stomach.

At the moment, a real train was approaching, its horn blaring. The white barrier swung down. The horn gave a second mournful blast. These were the sounds of Luc's childhood: horns blasting, bells clanging, wheels banging, louder and louder as the train drew nearer. The train wasn't long—a snub-nosed engine pulling twenty or so freight cars the colours of a children's paint set. How many times had he come to these tracks with his father to watch the trains roll by? It had been a sport, when he was small, an outing for father and son.

Hot air and noise pushed him backward. He could taste grit in the air. He held his breath and shut his eyes. A man younger than himself was behind the lids, a visibly unhappy man, holding the hand of a child. And then it was over. The hot rush of air subsided, the bells stopped clanging, and the train rolled west, its horn dwindling. The flimsy barrier rose.

Luc looked at the house again. How could he possibly get any work done here? Romance was nice, but he had obligations: a manuscript to finish, bills to pay. He surveyed the modest clapboard houses that lined the western side of the street. How did people deal with such noise? Turn up the volume on their TV sets? Plug their ears? How could they bear it? But in truth, there wasn't that much to bear, was there? Trains were less frequent now than in the forties. Constant, rumbling freight on the rails, ships on the canal: these were things of the past. In *Bonheur d'occasion*, Jean Lévesque had risen each morning to the lonely cries of ships' horns.

Beyond the tracks, a figure came into view. Dark hair in a pink kerchief, a slender body in a tapered pink skirt. She was waving.

Luc watched Marie-Soleil pick her way over the debris and

gravel. "Salut!" she called out. As she approached, he saw that her lips were smiling, moist.

"I know I should have waited until this afternoon," she said. "But I couldn't. I had to tell you immediately." She had moved up close enough that he could smell her. She was wearing something musky and spicy. The muscles of his belly tensed. He turned to look at the house.

"Noisy," he said.

"That didn't bother Jean Lévesque." She smiled up at him, obviously enjoying his look of surprise. "Frédéric told me," she explained.

He could picture her standing here with Frédéric Axe, gazing up at him in exactly the same way she was gazing now— as though Frédéric were such a genius.

"But I'm the one who saw the *À louer* sign," she went on, "and of course I thought immediately of you. It's fate, Luc. What else can it be?"

At the sound of her speaking his name, he felt that pleasant tingle again. Fate. He was willing to forgive whatever she had done with Frédéric Axe.

He was choosing the words to tell her how pretty she looked when she rose up on her toes and squinted at something behind him.

"Good," she said. "He's here."

A corpulent man in a suit was fighting his way out of a blue Chevrolet Cavalier. Once on the sidewalk, he came toward them, walking gingerly, as if his feet hurt, stopping now and then to grimace at the sun. Jowls hung over his shirt collar. Buttons strained. He was probably not much older than Luc.

"Monsieur Lévesque," he said, sticking out a hand. His

grip was stronger than Luc had anticipated. He nodded at Marie-Soleil.

The man's name was Gagnon. They followed him up the broken concrete walk to the door, where he stood jiggling the key, trying to turn it in the lock until his face went red. Eventually, he got it open. The house seemed to exhale, releasing the mixed and not entirely pleasant odours of industrial cleaner, paint, and something under the chemicals—something stale and dark. Dampness? Mould? Luc turned his face away, looking over at Marie-Soleil. She didn't blink. If she smelled anything, she was too polite to show it.

The walls were an atrocious hospital green. He would have to whitewash the whole first floor, pretend he was a student again, purchase rollers and a tarp. Gagnon sensed Luc's disappointment. "The previous tenants left this place in a terrible state, I am afraid to say. I was glad to be rid of them. Indians or Pakistanis or something. So many of them crowding in here all at once, I couldn't keep track of them. They do that, you know," he said, stopping midway up the stairs to the second floor and turning to Luc. "You rent to one in the morning, and by nightfall there's half a dozen of them camping on your property, waiting for the government to tell them they can stay for good. They get medical care. School for their kids. Free French lessons for themselves and their wives. They're not stupid, *non, monsieur*. They know a deal when they see it."

Luc and Marie-Soleil exchanged a glance. Slurs like this were commonplace, not that this excused them. Back in the fifties and sixties, when Gagnon would have been young, like Luc, Montreal had been predominantly white. Now it wasn't.

Gagnon probably had no clue how ignorant he sounded. Luc watched as he turned his big body forward and wheezed up the remaining stairs.

The staircase had no runner, which was probably a good thing if the previous tenants had been as unhygienic as Gagnon claimed. The floor in the hall upstairs was oxblood red, but at least the walls were white.

The bedroom was the only room with more than one window. Luc had seen enough by then to deter any rational prospective tenant. If the appearance weren't enough, the smell ought to have been a warning. But he swept these impressions to the back of his mind. He was standing inside a place he had imagined in loving detail, had never failed to mention to every class in a decade of teaching. A place of legend. Physical ugliness was appropriate here. It ought to smell and look like poverty. The place was exactly as he had pictured it when he'd opened the novel for that first, magical reading years ago. It was exactly as Gabrielle Roy had described. He glanced at Marie-Soleil, trying to telegraph his gratitude, but she was busy tapping the walls and testing the light switches. He imagined his desk pushed up in front of the larger of the two windows, the one looking east over the tracks. There would be morning light in his workroom. He would watch the sun rise, the beautiful fragile first glow. The corner was not big, but he was certain his desk would fit. It had to. Yes, it was perfect.

"You did an excellent job cleaning up," Luc said, to be agreeable.

Gagnon held up fat fingers. "I had to hire three guys. Three guys—can you imagine?—to get it into shape. Top to bottom, paint, exterminators, the works. I even installed a new toilet."

"Fine job," said Luc, tapping the bedroom wall. Exterminators. He looked more closely at the crack separating the floor from the wall. There didn't seem to be bugs, at least not in daylight. He hoped to God there was nothing bigger.

The oxblood floor tilted. Drop a pencil and it would roll. The rent Gagnon wanted was criminally high. But Luc Lévesque was in love.

Marie-Soleil had not said a word. She was pacing now, hands clasped behind her as if forcibly restraining herself from joining in the men's conversation. Monsieur Gagnon glanced at her, mildly amused.

"There will be just the two of you?"

Marie-Soleil stopped mid-step. Then she laughed.

"Just me," Luc said quickly. "I'll be using it as an office."

Monsieur Gagnon frowned. "This is a residential space, monsieur. Not commercial."

"That's perfect, then. I'm not a commercial man."

Marie-Soleil laughed again. "He's a writer," she said, taking his arm and giving it an appreciative squeeze. She was flirting with him, verging on proprietary, but Luc didn't mind. He drank in the warmth of her touch.

Monsieur Gagnon stared.

"You've heard of him, I'm sure." She pronounced Luc's name again, in full this time, for the fat man's benefit, her tongue darting and pink, like a cat's.

"Forgive me, Monsieur Lévesque! What an honour this is!" Gagnon said, speaking fast. He confessed that he hadn't actually read any of Luc's books, although he certainly would, now that they had met in the flesh. He didn't read books as a rule, you see, not fiction at any rate, just newspapers and magazines, but he had certainly heard of Luc Lévesque. Seen him on television. Luc had won a prize, hadn't he? Refused it? Monsieur Gagnon couldn't remember why, but it had been in the papers. What an honour it would be to have him as a tenant ...

Gagnon was talking about the Governor General's Award Luc had refused on nationalist principle. Luc wouldn't go into it now, wouldn't say anything to jeopardize this deal, although Gagnon was probably a nationalist himself. But maybe not. People surprised you.

Marie-Soleil interrupted Luc's thoughts. Since Monsieur Lévesque would be on his own, she said, writing his books in peace and quiet, surely Monsieur Gagnon would consider lowering the rent.

Monsieur Gagnon looked from her to Luc. "She is your daughter, Monsieur Lévesque?"

Luc reddened and shook his head.

Gagnon chuckled as though he'd just been clever. "Whoever she is, you must keep her."

He reduced the rent by ten percent, and Luc wrote him a cheque to cover the first month. After Monsieur Gagnon had reinserted himself into his Cavalier and driven off, Luc had the inspiration to give Marie-Soleil a victory kiss. They were standing together on the sidewalk outside the house. He felt happy, more vigorous than he'd felt in years. Marie-Soleil had put on her sunglasses. He leaned in, aiming for a cheek, but she turned unexpectedly and their noses collided. Luc pulled back, but Marie-Soleil didn't. She was a head shorter than he was and had to stand on her toes to reach him. And reach him she did, planting two moist, dark plums on his mouth.

Something chirped.

"Sorry, sorry," she said, pulling out her cell phone. She pressed a button and held it close to her face. "*Allô?* ... Yes, yes," she said. "He's right here." She pulled out a notepad and scribbled something.

The street was deserted. Luc was glad no one was around to notice his semi-hard-on. In twenty years, the only woman who had kissed him like that was Hannah, and it had been a while.

"Frédéric," Marie-Soleil said, snapping her phone shut.

The semi-hard-on vanished.

"Apparently, someone has been calling the office all morning trying to reach you. It's urgent." She looked down at the notepad. "Serge Vien," she said. "Mean anything to you?"

3

*H*annah stepped back to avoid the spray. She was standing on a patch of soggy grass across the street from Sunnybrook Hospital. Beads of water shimmered like sequins on the sleeves of her suede jacket. The hems of her jeans were spattered with mud. She had just emerged from the ravine, damp with rain and her own sweat, but pleased. It had worked.

She'd walked here from her parents' home in the posh neighbourhood of Lawrence Park in just over an hour.

It was October 2, a warm, wet, windless day, her fifth in Toronto. The path through the ravine had started off as dirt, which the rain was turning into mud. As Hannah walked south, the surface had changed occasionally to gravel or asphalt, with patches reverting to dirt. The last bit had been an intricate system of boardwalks constructed over a marshy tract called Sherwood Park, a lovely and unexpected artery of green running through the bituminous heart of Toronto. Just now, she had spotted a pair of pheasants. She had also seen cardinals, a woodpecker, flocks of chickadees, and everywhere Toronto's plump black squirrels, less rat-like, somehow, than their thin grey cousins in Montreal.

The walk had been calming. For a time, Hannah had forgotten her troubles, the most pressing of which was her father, who was waiting for her in the narrow white hospital room where she had left him the previous evening. She had also managed to forget her mother, Connie, who was probably sitting in the visitor's chair beside him, reading the newspaper, making comments about Hannah's lack of punctuality and general level of inefficacy compared to Benjamin, their super-organized son, who had flown in to help them the week before. And then there was Luc, back in Montreal, with whom she barely spoke anymore. She wasn't sure what was happening, but for months, now, they'd been in some kind of trouble. And, of course, there was Hugo.

For much of the walk, she had been alone. At one point, she'd spotted a man with a schnauzer some distance away on the path, but as soon as his dog urinated, he had scuttled back to street level. He'd looked vaguely afraid, as though the ravine might swallow him and his little pet whole.

A breach opened suddenly in the traffic on Bayview Avenue. Hannah steeled herself and stepped into it.

SUNNYBROOK HOSPITAL was a small city of newly built and renovated beige pavilions, some squat, some several storeys high, separated by sprawling parking lots. City buses drove through the grounds, stopping at the front doors of each building. Hannah passed the Sunnybrook Regional Cancer Centre and walked purposefully toward the main building, or M-Wing as it was called, which housed the Emergency Department, the Intensive Care Unit, and rooms for patients like her father, recovering from recent trauma. She hoped she looked like she belonged here, like a good and dutiful daughter come to visit, and not some strange, dripping creature, hair full of twigs and leaves, recently crawled up from the ravine.

The guard sitting inside the entrance did not even give her a glance as she entered. She kept her pace, striding with a steady stream of other people down the wide, well-lit corridor. Her father was out of intensive care. He had been moved to the fourth floor and assigned a private room. Hannah didn't know whether that was good luck or the residue of Alfred Stern's past prominence.

She passed a snack shop with the snappy name of Bistro On the Go, and inhaled smells of coffee and sugar-laden pastries. She was hungry. And she had to pee. She stopped at a washroom. Over the door, a mural of water lilies hung: a failed attempt at good cheer.

The elevator was brand new and made of glass, ascending a see-through tube in the middle of the courtyard separating the old hospital building from a recent addition. As part of the renovations, immense wooden butterflies had been suspended from the ceiling. They were supposed to make you think of nature, but to Hannah they looked menacing, a squadron of pterodactyls waiting for the signal to attack.

By the time she reached the fourth floor and stepped out of the elevator, the muscles of her back and neck were tense. She walked quickly down the hallway to her father's door. It was closed. The handwritten sign Connie had put up yesterday was still taped to it: Family Only. The *F* was lopsided, dwarfing the other letters.

For several days, there had been trouble with visitors. The news of Alfred Stern's stroke had travelled fast. People came at all hours. Former colleagues and clients, judges, professors from the law school at the University of Toronto, where he'd lectured, old friends, and two women who identified themselves as former secretaries.

Family only. Connie was worried about hands. She could control her own hygiene, and Hannah's too, to a certain extent. But other people were impossible. The day before Hannah arrived, a judge had pranced in (Connie's words) and proceeded to blow his nose before taking Alfred's hand in his own and clutching it with great feeling.

A woman in a pink pantsuit came down the hall pushing a meal trolley taller than she was. Hannah watched in alarm as she moved quickly and sightlessly toward an orderly wheeling an empty bed in the opposite direction. At the last minute, the orderly called out to her and disaster was averted. A bell rang in the nursing station. A monitor beeped in a neighbouring room. The names of doctors boomed over the public address system.

Family only. In other words, herself and Connie, now that her brother had gone back home. It had been years since Hannah had felt anything more than a perfunctory connection to Alfred and Connie. They kept in touch. She dropped by when she had business in Toronto, and occasionally she called from Montreal. But was this what *family* amounted to? It had been four years since her parents had last seen Hugo. Seven or eight for Luc.

She opened the door. The room was bathed in soft grey light. The curtains were closed, and all the lights were off save the one at the head of the bed, for which there was no switch.

Her mother was not there. Alfred Stern was alone, propped on a heap of pillows, his mouth open, snoring.

He looked shrunken, smaller than yesterday even, when they had moved him here. His eyelids trembled and his skin was yellow.

Hannah moved closer to the bed. Her father slept in snatches now, day and night. Connie had hired a night nurse, who wasn't technically a nurse but was skilled enough to sit beside an old man until the sun rose. "He doesn't sleep much," the woman had told Connie, who repeated it to Hannah.

As Hannah reached for the clunky green visitor's chair, her father's eyes opened.

"Good morning," she said, smiling. It was afternoon, long past the hour at which she had told Connie she'd be here.

He didn't respond, just looked at her with wide brown eyes. They reminded her of her son's eyes, direct and unwavering.

Hannah opened the curtains. She couldn't be still, not here, not with her father staring at her. A cloud of mist had descended on the building and parking lot over which her father's room looked.

She was hot. She unzipped her jacket and removed it, followed by her sweater. Her hair clung to her neck in damp strands.

"Warm today."

Alfred Stern had never liked small talk. Before his stroke, he'd made remarks about people who had nothing more interesting to discuss than the weather. Her eyes moved quickly to his face, but it was empty of expression. "I walked here," she said, her voice louder than she had intended. More words followed, more drivel: the ravine, the rain, and again the unexpected warmth for October.

Alfred Stern did not blink.

Her father had always been good with words. There had been a time when the thing she'd hated most about him was the flow of them.

His eyes were still on her. She busied herself by hanging up her jacket in the locker at the foot of the bed. She sat down in the visitor's chair. She picked up his bad hand, focusing on it to avoid his stare. The fingers were curled in on themselves. They clenched tighter at her touch. Hannah managed to get her thumb up under the pinkie and work her way inside to the palm. The muscles there were hard, as densely solid as bone. One of the nurses had said massage would help. She pressed into the hollow of his palm, trying to loosen things, feeling his resistance.

Her father observed her closely as she did this, but his face remained blank. It was as if he'd detached himself from every-thing—the room, his daughter, even his own hand, which he was now eyeing as if it didn't really belong to him. He didn't seem upset that she was holding it. This was both relieving and astonishing: the angry words that didn't come.

The hand began to warm and loosen. She kept kneading it, looking up now and then to check his face. It was a habit, this checking. Trying to catch the atmospheric shifts. He seemed content enough, but with Alfred she could never be sure. Despite the blue hospital gown, despite his shrivelled old man's body, there was still vigour in him. Plenty of strength. She must not underestimate the strength.

The previous evening, for the benefit of the night nurse, Connie had referred to Alfred Stern as a *shtarker*. Connie liked Yiddish expressions and used them often, with varying degrees of precision.

Alfred Stern had spent his life refusing to acknowledge any acquaintance with the language in which he was fluent. Like many survivors, he had done his best to erase the signs of his Jewishness. Only the accent had betrayed him. He had come to Canada at sixteen, too old to rub out this mark of a Viennese childhood.

Alfred's hand jerked from her grasp and fell onto the sheets. Hannah stared. It jerked again, like a netted fish. She bolted out the door to find the nurse. By the time she returned, her father was lying quietly, his hand inert beside him, clenched once more into a fist. The nurse had stayed at her station, explaining to Hannah in a bored, somewhat condescending voice that it was nothing to get excited about. It was just the random firing of disconnected nerves, a common occurrence in stroke victims.

Hannah looked warily at her father, not quite trusting the nurse's words. He looked like a sleepy child, not threatening in the least. She took his fingers up again and recommenced the rubbing, gently, watching his face for signs. His eyelids, purple-veined and thin as rice paper, fluttered for a couple of seconds and closed. His breathing grew deep and even.

This new post-stroke father was an enigma. Neither his face nor his body betrayed anything. And without words, she had no compass anymore, no map, no road into the sudden desert that was Alfred Stern.

What, really, did she know of him? In the hazy light from his window, she stood and tried to summon memories. What she recalled most clearly were the fights. They were stamped into her in a way the good times were not. There had been good times in the Stern family, plenty of them. Her childhood had been happy, overall. But the face that came up in the happy memories was her brother's. Benjamin was two years older than she was and, until she turned nine, her closest ally and friend. He was the person she'd played with, the one who'd taught her all the important things—how to draw, how to read, how to ride a two-wheeler. Their father had been around, but not intimately involved.

The fights had been intimate. They'd started when Hannah was older, the year she turned ten, just before puberty. They were not physical. That was not her father's way. Nor were they loud. Despite the disadvantage of age, Hannah could not claim she'd been an innocent victim. Most of the time, she was the one who provoked them. It was easy. All you had to do was disagree.

She disagreed often, for no matter how painful crossing him was, it forced an acknowledgment. It was a way of seeing her own small self reflected in his eyes.

Benjamin never did this. He was no fool. He had seen what Alfred did to people who contradicted him. Early in life, he developed a survival strategy. On the outside, he looked like a regular boy, playing sports and goofing around, but if you observed him closely, you saw it. He only spoke when spoken to. He kept his views to himself. Eventually, he even stopped sharing them with Hannah.

Their father was just the opposite. Full of opinions. Constantly airing them. Arguing, forever arguing.

Hannah didn't look like her father, but as a child she'd shown signs of his gift for words, and also of his combativeness. People had predicted she'd follow in his footsteps professionally. But in the end, it was Benjamin who had become the lawyer, although he'd had to move three thousand miles away to do it.

Hannah lowered her father's hand, still clenched though he was asleep, and laid it on his chest. The contraction was permanent and would grow worse unless they worked on it every day. She gave the hand a final caress and pulled the sheet over it.

Connie arrived several minutes later. "I was beginning to worry," she said, and covered her mouth when she saw that Alfred was asleep.

She was wearing a tailored brown suit and looked younger than her seventy years, although the strain of the last ten days was starting to show. She turned and smiled at the nurse who had followed her into the room. "Annie," she said, "this is my daughter, Hannah."

Hannah looked at the pretty young nurse. Her name tag said A. Syjico.

"Hannah is our youngest," Connie said to the nurse. "Her brother, Benjamin, is a lawyer in Vancouver."

Nurse Annie smiled. "A family of lawyers." She flattened the vowel, turning *lawyers* into *liars*.

"Not all of us," Connie said. "Hannah's a translator. She does her husband's books."

Annie nodded pleasantly. She looked young—too young to tell people to be quiet and let her work. She was carrying a meal tray, waiting for Connie to finish. But Connie was now onto the subject of Luc. She told Annie how he'd won the Governor General's Award. "He writes in French. In Montreal, he's a celebrity."

Hannah glanced at her father, who was still asleep.

Connie also looked at him. "Alfred's a celebrity too, of course. He comes from a family of celebrities. His grandfather was a renowned rabbi in Vienna. This was before the war."

Hannah rolled her eyes.

"There's an old Hebrew saying," Connie said. *"Le dor va dor."* She paused, letting the foreign sounds hang in the air before giving the English translation. "From generation to generation."

"Oh," said Annie. "I like that. Can you repeat it?"

"Le dor va dor." They were among the very few Hebrew words Connie knew, not that she would admit this to an audience as appreciative as Annie.

"I'll have to remember that," she said sweetly. "For my other Jewish patients." She rolled Alfred's table close to the bed and swung it in front of him.

Alfred's eyelids fluttered open.

"Well, hello there," Annie said.

His lack of affect didn't bother her. On the contrary, it provoked a stream of talk, which Annie kept up without pause as she moved energetically around the bed, plumping pillows, straightening sheets, pulling Alfred out of his slouch.

"Lucky man," Annie said cheerily, "with your daughter here to visit from Montreal." She bent over him, fussing.

He wasn't looking at her. He wasn't looking at anything, really.

"Feeling better without the tube?" Annie asked.

Hannah realized why he had looked so shrunken. The long blue feeding tube was gone.

"We can see your face now," Connie added.

It was true. His face was more visible. But there were still no emotions to read there.

Lunch that day was butterscotch pudding. Nurse Annie took the top off the pudding cup and spooned a dab into Alfred Stern's mouth.

He swallowed and immediately opened his mouth for more, like a baby bird.

"Good," said Annie in the tones of a nursery school teacher, her face amplifying each emotion. "This is great," she said. "Some stroke patients never manage to swallow again."

Connie frowned. "How do they eat?"

"With tubes. Short term, down the throat, like your husband had. Long term, right through here." She tapped Alfred's belly.

Alfred swiped at the pudding cup with his good hand. "You are hungry," Annie said, laughing and gazing down on him like a favoured child.

When at last Nurse Annie took the tray away, Hannah followed her out of the room. She felt lost, suddenly, unwilling to part with the woman's cheery faith, the energy that made Alfred Stern eat butterscotch pudding as though it were the thing he most cherished in life.

They stood between two large hampers overflowing with soiled laundry. "What can we expect?" she asked. "I mean, is this ... is this the way it's going to be?"

The nurse put a hand on her arm. "It's still early. Not even two weeks. For the moment, it's best to take it slow. One step at a time."

Hannah waited, hoping for more, but Annie had to go. That was it, then. One step at a time. No compass, no map.

4

*L*uc didn't own a cell phone. Using Marie-Soleil's phone, he checked the messages on his voice mail. There were three from Serge Vien, audibly agitated but saying little, and two calmer, equally uninformative messages from a Monsieur Ducharme, the vice-principal at the school, leaving a private number. Luc tried to dial it and found that he couldn't. His hand was shaking. Marie-Soleil had to do it for him.

There had been "an incident," Ducharme told him, when finally Luc got through. His son was fine, but Luc's presence was required. How soon could he be at the office of the school principal, Monsieur Bonnaire?

Luc asked for details. "Just come to the school, Monsieur Lévesque," Ducharme said in his unruffled voice. "Come now."

Marie-Soleil took the phone and pressed End.

He looked into her eyes and thanked her. Then he ran up the street, awkwardly, worrying inanely how his back would look to those lovely young eyes.

THE SCHOOL'S MAIN DOOR was open. Immediately inside was a second door, locked, and a receptionist's booth. He gave his name to the young woman in the booth and she buzzed him through. She started telling him which way to go, but he ignored her. He already knew. Up the worn main stairs to the second floor. Left. Three doors to the glass-walled waiting room. Nothing had changed. Not even the smell of chalk and ammonia cleaner. Luc looked through the glass into the waiting room, searching for his son. It was empty. The door was locked. He searched for a buzzer, but before he found it a man opened the door.

Principal Bonnaire. Luc had never met him before. He was surprisingly short. The students surely made jokes about it— and just as surely mocked his absurd comb-over. He shook Luc's hand with great formality and led him into the inner chamber, an office with a single small window. A serious-looking man in a raincoat who had apparently been conversing with the principal before Luc's arrival stood up, but Bonnaire didn't introduce him. He simply pointed to an empty chair, and Luc sat down.

"First, let me say what an honour this is," Bonnaire told him. He had crossed to the other side of his desk, an immense laminated structure with a dull grey surface that occupied most of the room, and was now looking down on Luc and the other seated man. "I only wish," he said, throwing back his shoulders and standing to his full height, "that the circumstances were more agreeable."

Luc registered the body language. This would be a bad man to defy.

"What are the circumstances?" he asked, trying his best to be polite. The lights overhead were fluorescent, turning everything, including the principal's face, a sickly shade of greyish green. The air was hot and dry.

Instead of answering, Bonnaire sat down. With excruciating slowness, he opened the top drawer of the immense grey desk and pulled out a dark object.

Luc stared.

"You recognize it?" Bonnaire asked, holding the gun out so that it glinted in the artificial light.

Of course Luc recognized it. The long, cruel snout was unmistakable. It was a Luger. But *the* Luger? Could that be?

Bonnaire waited.

"Yes," said Luc, unable to avert his eyes. "No, I mean."

Bonnaire was watching him closely. "Yes or no?" he said. "It cannot be both." He put the gun down on his blotter, which was green, with wide borders of brown leather. The desk was spotless. No papers to be seen, no little yellow Post-its curling with age, their glue dried out and ineffectual. No paper clips or piles of earplugs like the ones cluttering Luc's desk at home. More significantly, Luc thought, no photographs of anyone near and dear. The messy details of life seemed entirely foreign to this officious little man.

"I know that kind of pistol," Luc said, for he had to say something. "It's a Luger. My father used to own one." He closed his mouth, already regretting the statement. Why had he divulged that, of all things?

The man in the raincoat leaned forward, resting his elbows on muscular thighs. He was tall, beefy under the coat. Definitely an athlete in his youth. "Used to?"

"My father is dead," Luc explained.

"Where is his gun now?" the man asked, his chin lifting.

His gaze, which was trained on Luc's face, was uncomfortably direct.

"How should I know?" answered Luc. "The last time I saw it was in the 1960s." He looked away. A single plant sat on Bonnaire's metal computer table. The leaves were two shades of green, shaped like arrows.

"What was your father doing with a Luger?" asked the man.

Luc turned, unable to hide his annoyance. "May I ask who you are?"

The man glanced at Bonnaire. There was something going on here, some plan being followed.

"This is Detective Sergeant Audet," Bonnaire said. "Of the Montreal Police."

Luc's heart started to race. "My father fought in the Second World War," he said, struggling to sound calm. "He brought the Luger home when he returned from overseas."

The detective regarded him with professional blandness.

Luc felt his face redden, as if some ugly secret had been laid out before them on Bonnaire's scrupulously clean desk. His right shoulder began to twitch. He reached over, trying to keep his hand steady, and picked up the gun.

The contraction in his shoulder unwound itself. The Luger was smaller and lighter than he remembered. He pressed his palm painfully into the grip. He had held his father's gun only once, when he was ten years old. It had been kept in a locked strongbox, the only key to which was on his father's key chain. One day, Luc had stolen the key.

"There are quite a number of them in Montreal," Detective Sergeant Audet said, almost casually. "You'd be surprised to learn how many. Collectors' items. Souvenirs."

Souvenirs. A memory of the big dark basement of the Laporte Street triplex sprang up, uninvited, in Luc's consciousness. As kids, he and Rémi had played there with their father's souvenirs: a mildewy gas mask and a canteen that made tap water taste like rust.

"You didn't keep your father's gun after he passed?" asked the detective.

Passed. Luc hated that euphemism. And from a man who had no doubt seen a corpse or two in the course of his career. "No," he said.

"A valuable item like that?"

"Valuable?" Luc looked at the thing in his hands.

"People pay thousands for them."

Luc didn't know where his father's Luger had ended up. He had no desire to know. "I've never had any interest in guns," he said.

Audet was staring at him openly now. "So you don't own one?"

Luc shook his head.

"And your son?"

"You think this gun is Hugo's? Is that what this is about?"

Neither man spoke. Audet's eyes narrowed. He was making his mind up about Luc, and the verdict didn't appear to be positive.

"Look," Luc said, struggling to sound calm, "I'd like to help you, but I can't if you don't tell me what's going on."

Bonnaire finally took pity on him. "That gun was found in your son's knapsack at ten o'clock this morning."

Luc tried to absorb this piece of news. A gun. In Hugo's knapsack. The two things refused to conjugate in his mind.

"So, to your knowledge ..." began Audet.

Luc straightened his back and took a deep breath. "To my knowledge, my son has never set eyes on a real gun, let alone owned one." That felt better. The bewilderment was starting to dissipate. A welcome sense of righteousness had taken its place. Luc was a pacifist. It was implicit in every book he had written. Did this man not know who he was?

"Just to be clear," said Audet. "You yourself have never seen this firearm before?"

"Of course not," said Luc sharply. "And even if Hugo somehow managed to get his hands on a weapon like this, why would he bring it to school?"

"That's the question," said Bonnaire. "That certainly is the question." The little man was smiling at Luc through tented fingers.

Luc met the condescending gaze. "Where is he?"

Bonnaire didn't answer. This was obviously part of some insulting game plan.

Luc felt a prickling heat in his face. He had a sudden comic vision of himself with steam puffing out of his ears. "I want to see my son."

"Monsieur Lévesque. *Je vous en prie*. Hugo is fine. He is with our vice-principal."

"You've questioned him?"

"Oh, yes," said Bonnaire. "Oh, we've questioned him. But he hasn't given us answers. That is the problem." The tone was calm: the calm of a petty sadist. A tiny Bonaparte presiding over a tiny empire. Luc could imagine his son hating this man. Small hating small.

He turned to Detective Sergeant Audet. "We're talking about a crime here. Carrying a gun around in a knapsack. He's underage, but it's still a crime, right?"

"It is a criminal offence, yes," said Audet.

Luc felt the air go out of him. Hugo liked guns. A lot. This was a surprise, but not a shock. Not an inconceivable thing.

Bonnaire retrieved the gun delicately from his hand. "We've brought you in today, Monsieur Lévesque, to try to avoid laying criminal charges."

"As far as we can tell," Detective Sergeant Audet said, "your son had no intention of firing the weapon. It was wrapped in bubble wrap when it was discovered. It was not loaded. There was no ammunition on his person or in his school locker. If there had been, this would be a much, much more serious case."

"How are things at home?" Bonnaire asked.

Luc remembered the fight. The tears and humiliation. His son, fragile as a bird in his grip. He looked up and saw Bonnaire staring.

"Why did you sigh?"

Had he? He felt his face grow hot again.

"Monsieur Lévesque, I know this is hard, but any information you can give us will help."

"His mother's out of town," Luc said, his voice surprisingly plaintive.

"Monsieur Vien mentioned that to me," said Bonnaire, eyeing him thoughtfully. "I gather you and he are friends."

Luc nodded.

"And your wife is an anglophone." Bonnaire's face was neutral, but the remark was so blunt it left Luc at a loss for words.

Bonnaire spoke again. "I only mention it because it seems to be a matter of importance."

"A matter of importance," Luc repeated blankly.

"For your son. He seems very proud of his English heritage."

"His heritage is also French," Luc said, bristling. The language of his wife had always been problematic, but rarely did people push his face in it. "I hope you don't doubt my allegiance to the language of Quebec."

The principal allowed himself a smile. "I'd say you've proven that allegiance admirably to the entire world, Monsieur Lévesque. But not all sons share the attachments of their fathers. I don't know what was in your son's mind this morning when he walked into this building. I only know that language is a sensitive subject for him, as it is for many of us. And I know what we discovered in his bag." He nodded at the gun, now lying between them on the blotter. "This is the first time in the entire history of Collège Saint-Jean-Baptiste that someone has brought a firearm onto school grounds."

"You think it was because of language?"

Bonnaire let the question hang in the hot air. Luc's thoughts were spinning. His own son, engaging in political violence—on the wrong side?

Bonnaire cleared his throat. "Rest assured, Monsieur Lévesque, we're well aware that you are one of our most distinguished *anciens*. You have shown nothing but respect for this school, and we hope we have returned the favour. This could simply be a youthful error of judgment on the part of your son. Energy diverted into an unfortunate channel. Hugo may not be an outgoing boy, but his behaviour has never been cause for undue concern in the past. Still, it's a concern today. I have a thousand students in my charge. Two thousand parents to keep happy. Surely you can sympathize."

He hadn't offered Luc a direct answer. But then, in Montreal, language was, as Bonnaire said, a matter of importance, too volatile to address head-on. Bonnaire was in his element now: a shepherd guarding his flock. "I'm pleased with the way the staff responded when the gun was brought to our attention by one of the students," he said, his face composed and serious. "They acted quickly and with courage. No drama, no hesitation. And thankfully, no one was hurt. But people could have been hurt." He shook his head at this alarming thought. "We have been extremely fortunate."

He paused, scrutinizing Luc from across the table. "What happens now depends on you, Monsieur Lévesque. And on your son, it goes without saying. I will require absolute cooperation from both of you. The alternative is disaster. For you, for Hugo, for all of us here at the school. I'll tell you honestly, I would like very much to avoid a disaster." The shepherd's guise wavered briefly, and Luc saw a small, round, middle-aged man, a tired, anxious man. The sort of man he could find it in his heart to sympathize with.

"There will be a *conseil disciplinaire*," Bonnaire continued. "If this turns out to be worse than it seems, if we find a conspiracy, or ammunition, or any proof of an intention to cause bodily harm, Detective Sergeant Audet will be back and criminal charges will be laid."

Two diplomas hung in black frames on the wall behind Bonnaire's head. Beside them was a photo of the principal shaking hands with Lucien Bouchard, who had resigned the previous winter as Quebec's premier. It was an old picture, taken before the last referendum. Before the amputation of Bouchard's leg. He looked absurdly young and hopeful. Luc stared at the picture. His head felt scooped out, like a melon rind.

There was a knock at the door, and a bearded man poked his head in.

"Monsieur Ducharme," said Bonnaire. "Please come in."

Monsieur Ducharme entered, followed by Hugo, whose school uniform swamped his skinny frame. After they were seated, Bonnaire addressed Hugo. "Your father has been told about this morning's events."

Hugo gazed at his hands. He never glanced at his father—a fact the other men noticed. His expression was sullen, unhappy. His ear was scabbed and red.

"We have shown your father the gun," said Bonnaire. Still no reaction. Luc squeezed his hands together, stifling an urge to reach out and shake the boy.

"For now," Bonnaire continued, "no criminal charges will be laid, although that could change." He leaned forward, pausing for a moment, but Hugo kept staring at the floor. "This is a serious thing you have done, and there will be consequences. At the very least, there will be a disciplinary hearing here at the school. Possibly sometime next week, unless we find that the police must be brought in. In the interim, you are suspended. Do you understand what that means? You have been told about suspensions?"

Ducharme nodded on Hugo's behalf.

"You will not set foot in this school again until you are formally summoned to appear. You have your books and things with you? You have emptied your locker?"

Hugo nodded: his first and last communication of the meeting.

Luc was trembling with emotion. He managed to shake Bonnaire's hand and state more or less coherently that he would take care of things. He shook Detective Sergeant Audet's hand too and, enveloped in shame, led his son out of the principal's office.

As they walked through the familiar corridors, he did not say a word. They descended the worn steps to the main hallway, passed the receptionist, and went out the front door.

On Sherbrooke Street, he finally spoke. "How could you?"

The sun had already started its descent and cast shadows before them. The boy didn't answer. The only sound came from his shoelaces, which flapped undone on the pavement with every step.

5

That evening at her parents' home, Hannah cooked a squash soup, filling the house with familiar, calming smells. Connie had stayed late at the hospital, and Hannah wanted to have something hot for her when she returned.

She had turned on the radio and tuned in to Radio-Canada's suppertime newscast. Hearing the news in French gave her a feeling of the habitual, of being in her own home. A report had just come on about Jacques Lanctôt, one of the instigators of the 1970 October Crisis. Hannah stopped what she was doing. She wanted to hear this. Luc's most recent book, the one she was now contracted to translate, was about Lanctôt. Or rather, inspired by him.

According to Radio-Canada, he had written an open letter to the newspapers condemning the attack on the World Trade Center in New York. A sentence struck her as the news reader quoted the letter: *"Au nom de toutes les victimes innocentes, je crie vengeance."*

She stood there, feeling her blood rise. Jacques Lanctôt was speaking out for the victims of terrorists? The previous year, on the thirtieth anniversary of the October Crisis, Lanctôt had given numerous interviews, visibly enjoying his notoriety, acting as though people had lost their memories. And perhaps they had. Jacques Lanctôt had been transformed, by wilful forgetting, into some kind of prophet.

Hannah switched the food processor on. Good thing Connie wasn't here, or, worse still, her father. Quebec was a forbidden topic of conversation; it had, after all, caused the estrangement. Her father blamed Luc, of course, but Hannah and Alfred had disagreed about Quebec long before Luc came on the scene. Luc may have been the most pressing reason for her decision to stay in Montreal when her father decided to leave, but the conflict had begun years before, in the fall of 1970.

That September, she'd started high school. A month later, life in the Stern household went off the rails.

Outside the house, life had turned equally crazy. High-profile kidnappings were committed by the Front de Libération du Québec, the FLQ. One of those kidnappings resulted in the murder of Pierre Laporte, Quebec's minister of labour. The federal government declared martial law. Five hundred people were arrested.

Hannah's father had been named a special prosecutor and given the politically sensitive job of dealing with the arrested individuals. He became an instant celebrity as the public face of government repression. Those who were arrested sat in jail for days, unable to contact their families or even a lawyer. It was an outrage, an aberration. For Hannah, it was the end of her childhood.

Although he eventually released nearly all the prisoners, Alfred Stern was reviled. Death threats were made. The family took refuge in a hotel. There was briefly talk of sending Hannah and Benjamin to boarding school in the United States. It didn't happen, but when the Sterns returned to their home after ten days, they found that soldiers had been assigned to guard them, camping in the garage at night, alternating shifts as the family slept. These two young men escorted Hannah and Benjamin to school and drove Alfred to his office. Hannah felt like a prisoner.

Her father had always believed that the arrests and his own actions were justified. He and Hannah argued bitterly about it for years. Which was why it was now off limits. Better not to broach it, or to mention the name of Luc Lévesque, the celebrated Québécois nationalist whom Hannah later married.

And so she never spoke to her father about her work as a literary translator. Her specialty was Quebec fiction, although she also liked biography. Her translations had won prizes. She'd rendered brick-like tomes on the lives of Gabrielle Roy and René Lévesque into English, and she'd done smaller works too, on artists like Ozias Leduc and Paul-Émile Borduas. She'd also translated essays and publications about Quebec culture and history. And, of course, she'd rendered her husband's entire oeuvre into English. Besides being Luc's wife, she was his official English voice. None of this was even remotely mentionable in the presence of Alfred Stern. She could speak to her father about her son, provided she restricted herself to his health and schooling, but even school had become a difficult subject after Hugo started attending the Collège Saint-Jean-Baptiste.

Hannah dipped a spoon into the pot and stirred. The soup was a rich orange colour. She wiped bits of ginger skin and sprigs

of coriander off the stovetop and retreated into the breakfast
room overlooking the garden, where her parents frequently ate.
This was where Connie had found him, on his back, wearing
what looked like a grin.

Hannah's laptop was on the table in the breakfast room. Her
screen saver was a photograph of Hugo at age seven on a swing,
his head thrown back, laughing. It was her favourite picture of
him: happiness distilled.

She clicked an icon and a too-familiar file came up: *Death of
a Dreamer*, Luc's most recently published novel. The alliterative
English title pleased her; little else about the book did.

This had never happened to Hannah before. She had always
loved the books her husband wrote. Some more than others, of
course, but every one of them had moved her. She loved Luc's
agility of mind, his intuitive skill at telling stories. It had never
occurred to her that this might change. There were writers you
liked and writers you didn't. Sometimes a writer was uneven, but
mostly it was a question of chemistry. Like love.

She'd been young when she met Luc, not yet eighteen, but
despite her age she'd been neither blind nor stupid. She had
always been a reader. Even as a child, she'd known precisely
what books she preferred. Luc was the first published writer she
had met, apart from an aging poet who had read once at her
high school and tried to grope the girls. Luc was her teacher, so
it was natural she would go to the library in the early days of
term and look up his work. *Tanneur tanné* was the first Quebec
novel she ever read. It told of characters living in her own city,
thinking thoughts Hannah herself had thought. The characters
had troubles like she had. In their lives she discerned the outline
of her own. They were poor. They spoke French. They lived in

Saint-Henri, cultural light years from where she had grown up. Yet she inhabited their skin; they inhabited hers.

She and Luc became lovers that summer, a few weeks after she finished her first year at Dawson College. The following winter, she invited him to her family's annual New Year's Eve gathering. It was the end of 1976. René Lévesque and the Parti Québécois had just formed Quebec's first separatist government. The antipathy between her long-haired nationalist boyfriend and Alfred Stern was instantaneous. The fact that Luc had been her teacher didn't help. Twenty years of marriage had done nothing to mitigate it.

On New Year's Day of 1977, the morning after that first meeting, Alfred Stern coined a nickname for the man who would become his son-in-law: the Pied Piper. He never again used Luc's real name, with its echo of the new separatist premier. Her father was intransigent, and Luc did little to bridge the gap. He made no effort to be sensitive, never toned down his nationalist rhetoric.

Her father had gotten at least one thing right with the nickname. Luc Lévesque had enchanted her. The year they met, he'd just turned twenty-four. To a seventeen-year-old girl, that had seemed outrageously grown-up. Teaching at Dawson College was his first real job. He smoked cigarettes in class, tapping ashes onto the floor, because, of course, there were no ashtrays. The students watched, rapt, all of them loving him, even the boys, many of whom grew their hair and sported beards in emulation of his scruffy style. Privately, they called him Lucky Luc.

And lucky he was. A big man, muscular and well-built. Girls went quiet or else giggled in his presence. But it wasn't his looks that made Hannah's legs go weak that first day. It was his voice.

Tanneur tanné had been published the previous spring and had catapulted his life onto a new path. He was hailed across the province as the literary heir to Gabrielle Roy. When he spoke in the classroom, he was sonorous and self-assured.

He won a Governor General's Award, stirring up a scandal when he declined to go to Ottawa to pick up the prize. A publisher in Paris bought French rights for Europe, and Luc received a wildly favourable notice in *Le Monde*. And then Hannah translated the book. He could have had any translator he wanted, and he chose her. How she had laboured. By that time, of course, she had moved into the triplex in Saint-Henri. People said he was crazy to trust her. She was a child. His English publisher tried hard to dissuade him, but Luc's mind was made up. He sheltered Hannah in the flat and fed her a steady diet of encouragement and praise until the job was done.

Her translation won its own Governor General's Award, which she accepted with gratitude. It helped Luc gain an English readership across North America. And it established Hannah as a literary translator. Luc had gone over every word of the text with her, answering all her questions, alerting her to the slightest nuance of meaning. They were used to the roles of student and teacher. He was opinionated, full of loud certitudes, a lover of argument. Very much like her father, she eventually realized. But by then, she knew how to handle it. She welcomed him into her work as easily as into her bed.

Now she scrolled dispiritedly through the text on her screen. The book was late. Allison March, her editor at the Word Press, had been sending frequent, increasingly uneasy emails. The unease diminished after Hannah explained about her father, but the emails kept coming, incessant pricks to her conscience.

Hannah's resistance to this book had begun long before Alfred Stern's stroke. She'd been slow from the start, limping along, unable to find her stride. She had a reputation for being reliable with deadlines, but suddenly with *Dreamer* she did not care.

And yet. The writing was lovely. The structure worked. Luc's protagonist faced a series of ever-greater obstacles. But there was no pleasure in the book. No lightness. And it ended in death: a suicide. Perhaps Luc had meant the ending metaphorically, but a metaphor for what? When she asked him about it, he shrugged. That was what had come to him.

She read over the most recent paragraph she had translated, days ago, in Montreal. The young Cuban woman had just told the protagonist she was pregnant. Her eyes were radiant. She wanted this child, their child. But the man had turned away. He already had a son. The reality, he told her, would only mock the dream.

Hannah couldn't help taking it personally. *The reality would mock the dream.* She and Luc had dreamed once too—of a marriage that would do away with the old divisions of language and culture, and make for them a space in which to live and work, side by side.

Luc had enrolled in an English class. Every week for a year, he'd walked to the basement of a local school and returned home dutifully to read the English newspaper. He'd asked Hannah to list her favourite novels in English. He had actually planned to read them. Hannah had no idea where that list now was.

These days he was writing nonsense—men turning their backs on paternity and on the women they purported to love. What had happened to the dream?

The story was loosely based on Jacques Lanctôt's life. Very loosely, because Lanctôt didn't have merely one son. He had something like seven or eight kids, maybe more. He had never been one to refuse paternity. The scene with the Cuban girl had little to do with this aspect of his life. It sprang from Luc's own dark fears.

Lanctôt was a man of dreams, in fathering children as in all else. Even now, after all the years, all the failures, he clung to his ideals. Luc admired him for it. So, paradoxically, did Hannah. It took faith and stubbornness after all that had happened. The novel was set in 1995, during the second referendum on Quebec independence, when the province had failed, yet again, to reach nationhood. That autumn, in the bitter wake of that defeat, Luc had lapsed into depression. His sleep had turned fitful. He had spent mornings in bed, unable to get up. He probably should have seen a doctor, but he'd chosen not to. Instead, he spent an apathetic year doing nothing. And when the year was up, he began writing *Dreamer.*

The phone rang. Hannah stood up, startled. She ran back to the kitchen and located her mother's cordless phone.

"Hello?"

"Hannah?" It took her a moment to recognize Luc's voice. "Hannah?"

"Oh," she said, "it's you." She saw herself reflected in the dark panes of her father's liquor cabinet. A thin little person, thin and tired.

"Something's happened."

There was a pause, the pause of a man steeling himself to deliver bad news. And then it came spilling out: the gun, the meeting in Principal Bonnaire's office, the suspension.

She closed her eyes.

"Hannah?"

A gun.

"Are you there?"

The thin little person in the panes of the liquor cabinet had a hand cupped over her mouth.

"You have nothing to say?" His voice was low, clipped. A dangerous sign. She pictured his forehead, the line between his eyebrows deepening till it turned black, the same way her father's did.

"No one was hurt?"

"No. The thing was in his knapsack, in bubble wrap. He says he bought it this morning before school. In a pawnshop on Sainte-Catherine Street. The school is checking the story. Why would a pawnshop be open at eight in the morning?" He sighed. "There weren't any bullets."

Hannah exhaled.

"Hannah?"

"That's good."

"Good?"

"No bullets."

There was another pause. Hannah wasn't sure what Luc was doing on the other end. She couldn't even hear his breath. Was his hand over the receiver?

"Christ, Hannah!" The shout was so sudden she almost dropped the phone. "He brought a gun to school! A gun! They had to call in the police. If he'd been anyone's son but mine, he'd be in jail right now. The detective couldn't have been clearer. It's a crime. There is nothing good about this, Hannah. Are we clear on that? Nothing good at all."

"Luc—"

"Don't make excuses for him."

She wasn't making excuses, not that she would say so now. The little person in the glass had her mouth closed in a flat, determined line.

"There is no good here, Hannah. Not even a drop."

She wasn't about to argue. There was a long silence before Luc started talking again, his voice a little calmer.

He told her Hugo was home for the week. There was a ban on video games. And television. Hugo could do homework, play music, read. He was allowed outside for two hours a day. And if he did go out, Luc had to know where he was going and with whom. Evenings were to be spent in his room. Meanwhile, Monsieur Bonnaire was making arrangements at the school for a disciplinary hearing.

"You will be there," he said.

"Of course I will." Did he honestly think she might decide to miss it?

"When are you coming home?" He sounded suddenly like a child. The anger was spent and now need was calling out. The need for her.

"It's awful, Hannah. I moved my computer upstairs this afternoon so I could watch him. I feel like a prison guard."

"I'll do my best," she said, thinking of what lie she could tell her mother. Hugo had broken a bone. He had mononucleosis. Something serious but not life-threatening.

"It was a Luger," Luc said, interrupting her thoughts.

The little person in the glass looked back at her, startled.

Luc cleared his throat. "You didn't tell him, did you?"

"No," said Hannah, although this was not strictly true. In Hugo's last year of elementary school, he had asked her about it, and she had set out the facts as clearly and simply as she could to a person who was eleven years old. She had mentioned the gun, certainly, but not what kind it was. At least, not that she recalled.

They said goodbye, and for a moment Hannah stood staring at her reflection. She looked so unhappy. Had she somehow been the cause of this? Her eyes ached. Her skull ached. She pulled a phone book from the drawer where her parents kept it. "Metropolitan Toronto," it said on the cover, with a helpful picture of the CN Tower. She was searching for the Via Rail listing when she heard the front door open. Connie.

Hannah had no idea what to say. The pain in her skull was intensifying. She wished she had insisted on speaking to Hugo. She'd gotten so caught up with Luc and his fearful temper that she hadn't even asked. And now it was too late. Her mother appeared in the doorway.

"I saw him," she said, grim but satisfied. Her face was grey with fatigue. "The doctor," she said in answer to Hannah's blank look. She dropped her purse on the floor and took off her coat. "He finally came."

Hannah made an effort to focus. She closed the phone book and put it back in the drawer. "Which doctor?"

"Ufitsky. You know. The neurologist."

"Oh. Right," said Hannah. "Ufitsky." The phantom brain specialist who was said to stalk the halls of M-Wing, although few people ever had the luck to meet him. "What did he say?"

"Nothing. Next to nothing. He's practically aphasic himself." Connie walked over to the stove and lifted the pot lid, sniffing.

"Squash and ginger," said Hannah. "I made it for you."

Connie put the lid back. "You'd think in all those years of medical training he might have picked up some people skills," she said. "But no. He wouldn't even look at me, though I'd been waiting all day. From seven thirty till … what time is it, anyway? God. Thirteen hours. For what? To be insulted." She leaned against the stove, shoulders slumping.

Hannah wanted to reach out to her. But she kept her hands to herself. "Did he say anything about Father?"

"He didn't say anything about anything. He spent thirty seconds with us." She turned as if in imitation of the phantom Ufitsky and left the room, carrying her coat and purse.

There was a jangling of hangers in the vestibule, followed by a groan. Hannah found her mother groping through the contents of her green leather handbag.

"Mum?"

There was a faint smell of mothballs. Hannah gathered her courage and put a hand on her mother's shoulder.

"Goddammit," said Connie, moving beyond her daughter's reach. "I left my wallet at the hospital. Under your father's mattress."

Hannah looked at her with surprise.

Connie caught the look. "Don't patronize me. I hid it. I was tired and needed a nap."

Hannah wished her mother would permit herself to be held, just this once. But that wasn't Connie. "How did you manage to get home," Hannah asked, "without your wallet?"

"Taxi chit," her mother said, as if it were obvious. She waved a little booklet under her nose. "I keep them in my coat."

"I wouldn't worry," Hannah said, and felt herself start to worry. There probably wasn't much cash in the wallet, but there were credit cards, bank cards, her mother's health insurance card. It would mean cancellation calls and replacement forms to be filled out, hours to be wasted over a lost leather pocketbook and its content of plastic.

"It'll be fine overnight. I mean, it's hidden," Hannah said, for her own benefit.

Connie shook her head. There were tears in her eyes. She looked diminished and fragile. Hannah took a step forward, but Connie stepped away. "You don't understand. Anyone could wander in there." She looked at Hannah imploringly.

Hannah felt the old helplessness—wanting to give support but not quite knowing how. "Okay," she said, surrendering. "I'll go."

Connie walked into the living room and sat down in an armchair.

"Is that okay?" said Hannah, following her.

Connie's eyes were closed. Tears glistened in the corners. She nodded.

"Okay," said Hannah. "Sounds like a plan." She smiled cheerily at her unseeing mother and went to get her jacket.

THAT NIGHT, after the wallet had been retrieved from under her father's mattress, after Connie had bathed and drunk valerian tea and been tucked into her bed, Hannah lay in her parents' guest room, watching red numbers blink on the digital clock. They were the only things visible in the darkness. Hannah had said nothing about the phone call from Montreal, about having to leave the next day. Her mother was in no state for more bad news. Hannah would announce it in the morning. Hugo had caught something, she would say. Something that required care; something he wouldn't die of. Something Connie would understand but not fear. Catching the early train wouldn't be a problem. If Connie heard her moving around in the pre-dawn silence and got up, Hannah would be ready with a plausible explanation. Her mother was more exhausted than she had ever seen her. This was how it happened, Hannah thought: illness leading to more illness. Connie was blessed with a steel constitution, but even steel had a breaking point.

6

Hannah had walked to Laporte Street from the metro station at Place-Saint-Henri. She surveyed the park, which was shimmering in sunlight across from the house. Everything was golden and soft today. The only dark spot was Jacques Cartier, pointing northward at the mountain he was about to claim from the Iroquois for his king.

The air tasted sour. A hazy mix of industrial and traffic fumes hung low over Saint-Henri. It was still unseasonably mild; there wasn't a whisper of wind. When the air was this bad, it took a storm to clear it.

Hannah straightened her knapsack so the weight fell more evenly on both shoulders. It was almost noon. Luc would be pleasantly surprised, she thought. He certainly couldn't accuse her of neglect. She'd left her parents' place at five o'clock that morning and managed to get a seat on the first train to Montreal.

Connie had not yet been awake when Hannah crept out into the streets of Toronto. She had left a note: "Hugo has mononucleosis. I should be with him." At least the second part was true. She hoped her mother wouldn't worry, wouldn't feel abandoned. The triplex stood in front of her, reassuring and familiar. At this hour, Luc would be at his desk. Or maybe not. Maybe this drama had turned him upside down too; drained him, at least temporarily, of his creative juices. She took a deep breath. The air tasted like yeast.

She went to the downstairs door first. Usually, he wrote all morning, phone unplugged, door locked against intruders, although no one ever disturbed him. Sometimes he even wore earplugs—bright orange foam bullets, visible through his thick hair. She raised a hand, hesitated, and knocked.

A form loomed up behind the frosted glass window. He *was* down here, after all. A good sign, perhaps, if he felt he could leave Hugo alone upstairs. Her blood quickened as the door swung open.

She smiled broadly, reaching out both arms. How she had missed him. Her mind could forget, but not her body. It always turned to him, like a plant to the sun. Remarkable how instinctive it was, how rooted in the cells. His smell too, especially around the mouth, never failed to arouse her.

He didn't smile. Didn't even meet her gaze.

"I'm back," she said, and instantly regretted it. Luc had a special scorn, as her father did, for people who stated the obvious.

"I managed to catch the early train." Another useless statement. She should stop. What did she want from him? Praise? Thanks? He was probably irritated even before he saw who was at the door. She must have interrupted his work. He was wearing long johns and gym shorts: his uniform. And the lovely soft pullover she'd bought for him last Christmas. His chest hair poked out at the neck. If he hadn't looked so forbidding, she would have stepped into his arms.

"Hugo is upstairs," he said.

"I'll go up, then," she said, as brightly as she could, but she was hurt. After a sleepless night, she had hurried to catch the train, in which she had fretted, dry-mouthed and dry-eyed, lapsing repeatedly into a doze and just as repeatedly being shaken awake. She had left her stricken father and her exhausted, lonely mother because her husband's suffering meant more to her than theirs. He was everything to her. "You okay?" she asked, not daring to touch him.

He looked at her. Finally. His eyes were ringed with blue. It had seeped like ink into the hollows on either side of his nose and up into the lids. His hair looked greyer. Could that happen in the space of six days? Or had their separation, short as it was, opened her eyes and made her look at him a little more closely? His hair was still thick, still beautiful—inviting touch, inviting her to rake her fingers through it—but the colour was definitely fading.

"No," he said. "No. In fact, I'm not."

She took a step toward him, but he moved backward. She could barely see him. It was always so dark down here. As usual, all the curtains were drawn. As her eyes adjusted to the gloom, she saw that he hadn't been working after all. Or at least, not writing. Boxes were strewn behind him on the floor. A couple were filled with books and manuscripts. And he seemed to have dismantled the pine IKEA table on which he wrote. The top of it was leaning against the hallway wall.

Luc saw her confusion. "I found an office," he explained.

"An office?"

He looked at her impatiently, waiting for her to remember what he was talking about. Yes. Rémi was moving back.

"I thought that was for December."

"It is."

"December's in two months."

Luc made an exasperated face, a face that said he'd tried his best.

"Look, I'm sorry," she began, but he held up his hands, stopping her mid-sentence. He wasn't looking at her. Wouldn't meet her eye. He was angry, that much was obvious. But so angry that he felt compelled to move out the instant she got home? His face wasn't giving her any clues, so she screwed up her courage. "What's this about, Luc?"

"Peace," he said tersely, still not looking at her, picking up a dictionary from the floor—his dog-eared *Larousse*—and holding it against his chest. "And quiet. Two things I've never been able to find here."

It was as if he had reached out and pushed her. His laptop was folded up too, she noticed, right beside the dismantled desk, ready to go. Hannah retreated onto the front step, out of the building that for years they'd both called home. Her head felt empty, almost weightless, as if it might rise at any moment and fly off like a balloon snatched by a current of air. There was something going on, something that had nothing to do with offices or writing and that somehow she hadn't seen coming. He was telling her now with his movements, with the defensive curve of his body as he crouched over his books.

"I'll go up and see Hugo," she said quickly. Her chest was aching, physically aching, as though she'd received a blow. Sun flashed in her eyes as she turned away.

She ran up the outer staircase to the second floor, and then the inner stairs to their flat. Her head still felt strange and wobbly on the thread of her neck. She'd known she was returning to a crisis, but she'd had no idea it was affecting Luc like this. Could the fact that it involved a gun have shaken him more than he was ready to admit?

Hugo's school shoes lay on the top stair. She slipped off her own shoes and unlocked the door. Simple gestures. Reassuringly familiar. Inside, the apartment was perfectly still. Another surprise. No gunfire.

The place smelled of rotting citrus and coffee grounds. She went into the kitchen to investigate before facing the more daunting prospect of her son. Luc had forgotten to put the garbage out. Twice. And then he'd just left it there, presumably for her to deal with. Resentment surged. The bin was overflowing. She could barely pull out the bag. She cursed him silently as she tried to create a neck of plastic for the knot, but the ends were too short and slippery with grease. The bag got away from her, disgorging its slimy contents across the kitchen floor.

"Shit!" she said. She always swore in English. Swore and counted. "Shit, shit, shit!" she said to her absent husband and his present mess.

She had to scoop it all up. Hardened grains of white rice from the Chinese takeout place, sawed-off pork ribs that had been gnawed clean, the damp and pungent remains of several grapefruit halves. She closed the bag with a twist-tie this time, and washed her hands in near-scalding water. What a thing to come home to. The smell was appalling.

After putting the garbage out in the shed, where it would rot in peace until the Friday pickup, she mopped the floor and opened the windows, waving her arms to move the stagnant air. Then she opened the refrigerator. The rock-hard remains of a baguette and two cardboard containers of Chinese takeout sat on the bottom shelf. No eggs. Not a vegetable to be seen. Not even a carton of milk.

He wasn't a domestic man. He'd told her so way back when she first knew him. But this was more than disdain for house-work. He was fastidious in his habits. This was not like him.

Her office was orderly and clean, as she'd left it. It was located in a little space beside the kitchen. Before she had claimed it, it had been the pantry. There were two entrances—one from the kitchen, the other from the hallway. It had no actual door, but it was a room. Luc liked to listen to the radio while he ate, which sometimes disturbed her. And Hugo had an annoying habit of materializing when he was hungry and staring at her back until she turned around and noticed him. Still, she'd done plenty of work here over the years. Unlike Luc, she could cook, translate, tend to Hugo, and do a load of laundry all in the space of a morning.

The red light on her telephone was blinking. She walked to the desk and pressed a button. The voice of Allison March filled the room, asking after her father and wondering how Hannah herself was. And where. A wave of guilt surged inside her. She'd told Allison she was going to Toronto, but had neither phoned while she was there nor specified a date of return.

She deleted the message. The idea of working right now seemed absurd. Allison March was in her mid-thirties, single, childless, still young and sheltered enough to know nothing of ailing, mortal parents, brooding husbands, and rebel sons. What she did know about was Hannah's translation. The work that should have been done by now—but wasn't. It wasn't even close to being done.

If Hannah shut herself in her office all weekend, she could finish the third section of the book and send it off. After that, she would have a hundred and twenty-three pages left to translate.

Luc's most recent novel was longer than the other books he'd written: one hundred and thirty thousand words. Although she'd kept the thought to herself, she felt it could have been shorter. But Luc had reached the point in his career when people no longer questioned him. His French publisher treated him like a demigod. His fans were numerous and loyal. Critics' praise was almost reflexive.

Hannah could see Hugo's closed bedroom door. A crack ran down the middle, the result of too many slams. And there was the cobra, its hood open like a fan. She was calm enough now to see him. She walked to the door and knocked.

There was no answer. She could see light in the space below the door. She knocked again, harder.

"Hugo?"

"What."

An English word, spoken without inflexion. Neither question nor answer.

"May I come in?"

When he didn't respond, she pushed the door open. He was at his desk, his back to her, his hand covering a piece of paper he had just flipped over.

He looked terribly thin. A bony little boy in oversized striped pyjamas: not quite a living version of the liberators' photographs of Auschwitz, but not far from it, with the shaved head revealing every ridge and contour of the fragile skull. And the Jewishness. Yes, this boy was undeniably Jewish, with dark, quiet eyes that seemed to reach right inside you. "Honey," she said, and kissed his bristling head, "I missed you."

He had turned slightly and was looking out the window at the neighbour's brick wall.

"How are you?" she asked.

She waited. She had read the books on adolescence, the ones that violated all her instincts with their solemn advice: *Leave space, and words will emerge.* She waited. Hugo stared at the brick wall.

"Dad told me what happened," she said.

His skin was bad. Tiny red pimples covered his forehead. But his profile was beautiful. Regal, almost, under the angry teenage skin.

His hands were small. She had never seen a Luger. She pictured a dainty pocket pistol, a derringer—was that the name? The kind of gun women used to hide in their bodices in cowboy movies. The kind that might fit in the hands of her child.

"You don't want to talk?" she said, shifting her weight.

More wasted words. Luc would have made a sarcastic comment. *She had eyes, didn't she? Ears?*

She wanted to take him by the shoulders and turn him around. Silence could be protective, but this felt hostile, smouldering with aggression.

"Hugo?"

He would not turn. "I'm not asking for a hug," she said. "Or even a hello. But I would appreciate it if you had the decency to look at me."

The stopper was out now, and her own anger began to flow.

She knew, even as it was coming out, that it wasn't strictly about him, but this did not stop her. Out it came. "Your grandfather is sick, Hugo. Life-and-death sick. He's hooked up to tubes. He can't walk. He can't feed himself or take a shit. He can't utter a word. I was beside him yesterday, and now I'm here. Because of you."

Hugo continued staring out the window, but his body had gone rigid.

"So thanks for that. Thanks a lot." She was trembling. On her way out, she slammed the door.

It was only in the kitchen that she allowed herself the luxury of tears. It was stupid even to have tried to speak to him. As a baby, he'd been as clear as water. Long before he could speak, Hannah had known what he was thinking. Or so it had seemed. Luc's mother, Lyse, who lived right below them, nicknamed Hugo "the baby who never cried." She'd said this partly to reassure Hannah and Luc that they weren't waking her up with the night feedings, but also because it was true. Hugo had not cried. He had managed to convey every impulse, every feeling, with a clarity that had stunned her.

To calm herself down, Hannah went to the bathroom and took a shower. She stayed under the spray for a long time, letting the water beat down on her and the room fill with billowing steam. When she was clean, she dropped Luc from her considerations, dropped even her son, and concentrated on what needed doing. She should get to the bank. She had to pick up some food for dinner. It would be good to move her limbs. She couldn't stay here a moment longer. She gathered her tote bags, put a note for Hugo on the kitchen table in the unlikely event that he ventured out of his room, and left the apartment. As she reached the second-floor landing, the door opened and her mother-in-law's face poked out.

"I thought I heard your step!" she said, coming out and taking Hannah in her arms. "Welcome home, my dear one."

Hannah was considerably taller than her mother-in-law. Her chin brushed the top of Lyse's head, but even so, Lyse's small body felt like a haven. "Poor little chicken," Lyse said, holding her close. "You were missed by us!" Hannah stood in her arms, savouring the words.

She allowed herself to be pulled into Lyse's flat, which smelled deliciously of apples. A bowl of them sat on the chest of drawers in the vestibule, red and shiny, their skins only just starting to wrinkle from the heat. Apart from the apples, everything in Lyse Lévesque's flat was white—walls and ceilings, drapes and rugs. Much of her furniture. She had a variety of antiques picked up in pawnshops, or at the Salvation Army on Notre-Dame Street, or from the sidewalks of Saint-Henri.

The floor creaked behind her and a thin, wispy-haired man entered the vestibule. Graeme White, Lyse's good friend. He smiled shyly at Hannah and reached for a jacket on the coat rack.

"Oh," said Hannah, switching to English, "I didn't mean to interrupt anything." She felt herself blush. Why had she said that, of all things?

Graeme White busied himself with his jacket. There probably was something going on between them, not that it was any business of Hannah's. He spent a lot of time on Laporte Street. But he never seemed to stay the night. Lyse called him her "garage-sale friend," because that was their shared passion: meeting every Sunday morning in the spring and fall to pick through the neighbourhood yard sales.

"Well," he said, "I guess I should be off." He bent over Lyse, who chastely kissed him on both cheeks, as she might kiss Hannah herself, or Hugo, or Luc. She certainly wasn't giving anything away. But to protect whom, Hannah had to wonder. Luc? Rémi? They were no longer children.

From the top of a chest of drawers in Lyse's vestibule, the bust of Luc's dead father looked on. The ghost of Roland Lévesque still haunted this house. Lyse had never really let go of him. Nor had Luc. For him, his father was still larger than life, a working-class hero who appeared, again and again, with little alteration or nuance in his books.

"How's your papa?" Lyse asked, in French now that Graeme White had gone.

Hannah tried to smile. "Not bad. He's eating again."

"He can swallow? That's good news."

Hannah nodded. So Lyse knew about strokes. She knew about so many things.

"He's still not talking," she admitted. "Or walking."

"After what? Ten days? It will come, Hannah. Don't you worry. All in good time." Lyse reached out and squeezed Hannah's arm. Human touch. She had been without it for far too long. In Toronto, she'd massaged her father's crippled hand. For the entire visit, that had been the extent of her physical contact with other human beings.

"Do you have time for a tea?"

Hannah shook her head. Who knew what would come out if she sat down with Lyse? "I can't right now," she said, pulling toward the door. She held up her tote bags. "I'm on grocery duty. You should see the fridge. No milk. No eggs. God knows what they survived on."

Lyse's face looked alarmed. "I tried," she said, as though she were responsible. "The night you left, I went upstairs with a *pâté chinois*, but Luc chased me away. Wouldn't take it. I ended up giving it to the woman next door, the one with all the kids. Hugo hasn't gone hungry, has he?"

Hannah shook her head and forced out a smile. She wanted to say something funny and reassuring, but her throat constricted. She tried to clear it, and all that came out was a choking sound.

Lyse reached an arm around her and patted her back. "Are you all right? Here, Hannah, come and sit down."

And that was how she ended up on Lyse's white couch, cradling a cup of camomile tea.

"Now tell me," said Lyse. "What's wrong?"

Luc hadn't confided in her, evidently. He was secretive by nature, particularly with his mother. Hannah knew she should ask him before talking to Lyse, especially about the gun. But surely Lyse had a right to know. She was part of the family, an intimate part, and she was one of Hannah's closest friends.

"Hugo's been suspended from Saint-Jean."

Lyse nodded slowly. "I knew something was up. He didn't go to school today."

Hannah's throat was closing again. She swallowed hard and spoke without looking at Lyse. When she came to the part about the gun, Lyse raised her hands to her mouth.

"It wasn't loaded," Hannah said.

"Thank God," said Lyse. "Oh, thank God."

It took Hannah a second to realize it, but Lyse was crying. She was holding her face in her hands. Her shoulders were shaking.

"It's okay," said Hannah, reaching out to her. She was

beginning to regret this. She was exhausted, emptied of her normal reserves. "No one was hurt, Lyse. He didn't have any ammunition. He didn't even have the thing out. It was in his knapsack, in bubble wrap."

But Lyse was no longer listening. Hannah went into the bathroom to get tissues.

"He's all right, though?" Lyse said, once the crying had finally abated.

Hannah nodded.

"But why on earth …?" Her makeup was running. She looked up pleadingly at her daughter-in-law, unable to finish the question, her face streaked with black lines.

She was probably thinking of Roland. Maybe of Columbine as well. The boys shooting up their school. How could she not? "No one knows."

"Did you ask him?"

They sat there in silence. Luc and his mother had the same half-moon eyes, the same vulnerable brown gaze. At least, it had once been vulnerable.

"There's one more thing," said Hannah. She hesitated, unsure again whether to divulge it. "It was a Luger."

The half-moon eyes grew round. "Does Hugo know?"

Hannah shook her head, feigning more certainty than she felt. She still couldn't remember. If she had mentioned it to him, the guilt would be beyond words.

"No," said Lyse, shaking her head. "No, of course not. How could he?" Her head went on shaking, as though trying to shake off the memories. "Oh, God," she said. "How odd it is. Why didn't Luc tell me? Why didn't he say anything?"

"It happened yesterday."

"Still," said Lyse. "I was here. I always am, you know, for each of you." She shook her head again. "Luc is so ... contained. Rémi is the one who talks about himself. He's the one who tells me stories. Luc keeps all of his for his books." She paused. "He's unhappy, isn't he?"

Hannah averted her eyes. This was the danger of talking with Lyse. She picked up on things. Even when you hid them. She was sensitive, like her artist son. Hannah could picture Luc's face, full of anger, when he discovered that she'd had this conversation with his mother.

"I'm making things awkward for you," Lyse said quietly. "I apologize. But I worry. Luc says so little, and I'm left alone to wrestle with my imagination." She made an effort to smile and dabbed her eyes with a streaked tissue.

She would have been around Hannah's age when it happened. Hannah and Lyse had spoken of it only once, early in Hannah's marriage, when she was still trying to fill in the blanks in Luc's childhood. The experience had marked her forever, Lyse said. Before it happened, she had believed in herself. She had believed in the myth of her own agency. She had believed that if she thought hard enough and put in enough effort and energy, she could make things right, truly right, at least in her own little corner of Saint-Henri. Roland's death had swept that illusion away.

She'd seen it long before it happened. That had been the worst thing, she said. Knowing it was coming. Not when, or how, precisely. Only seeing the image, and knowing it would one day become real. Visions had come to her before, so she wasn't frightened, exactly. Within the family, they joked about her psychic abilities. But her visions had never before been of death.

When the police officers came to the door over three and a half decades ago on that October morning, she'd known why they were there. They had made her sit down before they announced it. She did as she was told, even though it wasn't necessary. She had seen it already, twice in dreams, and a third time when she was awake. A thought, an image of her husband's blue Chevrolet parked at the top of a hill, with Roland sitting perfectly still at the wheel. That was all. No blood. No hint of impending violence. The second time, she watched him from the side; the third, from behind. He was sitting up straight in the driver's seat with the motor idling and the windows rolled up. Each time the vision came, her skin had crawled. For six months, she had been afraid to shut her eyes and sleep.

Lyse got the location right: the lookout in upper Westmount, the quiet green place where lovers went to fondle each other, where Lyse herself had sat with Roland during their courtship, driving up from Saint-Henri in his father's car, navigating streets lined with houses that looked like castles in a fairy tale, one of which Hannah's father would eventually own. Roland had kissed Lyse in that green place, held her tight against him. She had been sixteen, far too young to know anything about love. The lights in Saint-Henri had blinked like fallen stars. She had thought, mistakenly, that she was in heaven.

Hannah's mother-in-law was looking at her, now dry-eyed and serene. Hannah stood up. "I've got to go." She gave Lyse's arm a tender squeeze and reached for the tote bags stashed at her feet.

They said their goodbyes in front of the bronze bust. Lyse had commissioned it at the last possible moment. It had cost her more than the entire funeral. The artist had been forced to go to the funeral parlour to make the mould. There was no back to it, just Roland Lévesque's proud, stern face, and the mouth into which he'd stuck the barrel of his gun.

His Luger.

Once, when Luc was nineteen, he had taken the bust down from its altar in his mother's vestibule and pushed his own face inside. He'd been drunk, he told Hannah years later. It had been late at night. He'd replaced the bust afterward so Lyse wouldn't suspect anything, but although the altar looked the same, Luc himself had been changed by this curious nocturnal act.

"Call on me," Lyse said, pulling Hannah to her for a last embrace.

Hannah tried to smile, but the bronze likeness of Luc's father was staring so fiercely she couldn't manage it.

7

The staircase to the second floor seemed steeper than usual when Hannah got back from the grocery store. She'd bought more than she'd planned, probably because she was so tired. She had a chicken tucked under her arm like a football.

Chickens were on special at the Super C. Five dollars a bird. So, without giving it much thought, in addition to the milk and the bread and the eggs, she had bought a chicken. And a carton of plain yogurt, Balkan style, which she knew she would want the next morning. And cereal for Hugo. Froot Loops, which he still loved. An indulgence. What was wrong with that?

Plenty, she told herself, willing her feet to move faster. She regretted the way she had spoken to him, the assault on his conscience.

She kept thinking about the gun. The Luger. The lugubrious Luger. Heavy, dark, morose. Luc's father, whom Hannah had never met, had been lugubrious. At least, that was how she imagined him from Lyse's accounts. Luc didn't describe him this way. To Luc, he was a hero. But then, he had died before his son outgrew the need for heroes.

Lugubrious. Was it in the genes? Luc and his brother didn't seem afflicted. Oh, they had their moods. No one was spared that. The period immediately prior to *Dreamer* had been a trial for Luc. But his response had been art, not depression. What if it skipped a generation? She pictured her son's affectless face, his strange, empty eyes. She made a mental note to read up on drugs.

Would she notice if Hugo were stoned? She knew what marijuana did to him. His face went chalky and his eyes got dry and red. Besides, she could smell it on his clothes. But he only smoked sporadically, so far as she knew. Weekends mainly, with his friends. She and Luc had spoken to him about it a couple of times, voiced their concerns. The books she had read said it was futile to try to ban it outright. What you had to do was talk.

But what if it wasn't drugs after all? What if it was something else, something internal, something harder to give a name to? What if it was a hidden grandparental legacy, sparing the father the more savagely to strike at the son? An image of the awful bronze in Lyse's front hall returned to her.

She was on the inner staircase now, huffing upward. *I think I can. I think I can. I think I can.* At the top of the stairs, she spotted Luc's shoes. Good, he was here. Maybe the clouds had lifted and they could sit down as a family for once and talk. As she opened the door, however, that thought was dispelled. Luc's voice rang out in the hallway.

"Where were you?"

He was standing in the doorway to Hugo's bedroom, his hand on the cobra's head.

She held up the chicken. "I left a note."

He rolled his eyes. "You just got home and already you're out the door to shop? You might have said something to me." He turned his back on her, presumably to face their son. "Meanwhile, guess what your only child was doing in your absence?"

She put the bags and the chicken down on the floor and stepped forward. She would not mention the garbage, or the empty fridge. Luc was pacing angrily. In his hand was the empty plastic case for *Red Alert*, Hugo's favourite computer game. The game he had played continuously through the eighth grade, to the exclusion of homework and family life, while his parents tried without success to limit his access, to wean him off his addiction. Every day, he would come home from school with the same hunger in his eyes, shut himself in his room, and play.

Hugo was sitting on his bed, his back against the wall. For some reason, he had no shirt on. Hannah hadn't seen him without one for years. Springy black hairs encircled his nipples, which looked vulnerable and pink. She fought the impulse to stare. Black wisps curled from his armpits too. He must have felt her eyes, because he folded his arms over his chest.

"I caught him," said Luc. "*Red Alert*. After all we've been through. Can you believe it?"

Hugo looked up at her then. They both looked at her, waiting to see whose side she would choose. She felt the power of her position, momentary though it was. She felt their attention and their need. She wished it could go on forever, this moment immediately before choice.

"Guns!" Luc said desperately, waving the plastic case. "It sounded like World War Three when I walked in, I swear to you." When Hannah still didn't respond, he turned away from her and threw the case on the bed. It bounced off the mattress, striking Hugo's bare stomach.

"Enough is enough," he said, reaching for Hugo's arm. "Tell your mother what happened." He pulled Hugo roughly to his feet, breathing heavily. She had rarely seen him so upset. "Tell her how you brought a gun to school. Go on," he said, shaking him. "Explain to her. A Luger, for the love of Christ."

Hannah, who was standing in the doorway, tried to intervene, but Luc pushed her aside. The situation felt out of control. He'd never touched her like that before. And he'd certainly never lifted a hand against Hugo.

"What were you going to do, Hugo?" he kept asking. "What was the plan?"

Hannah moved in again, and for a moment the talk stopped and they wrestled with each other. Luc was trying to hang on to Hugo, who was squirming and trying to wrench free, while Hannah tried, unsuccessfully, to wedge herself between them.

"Stop!" she shouted, pushing Luc off with all her strength. But they couldn't stop. Father and son were locked in a strange slow-motion dance, trapped in a panting embrace that only ended when Hannah began to sob.

Four bright finger marks decorated one of Hugo's shoulders. On his neck was the darkened beginning of a bruise. The sight was so shocking that she stopped crying. Stopped even taking in air. He looked like a battered child.

In an instant, he was back on the bed, clasping his arms over his naked chest.

Luc retrieved Hugo's T-shirt from the floor and threw it at him. "Cover yourself."

Hugo didn't move. His back was against the wall. His arms were mottled.

"Put your shirt on," Luc ordered. He stepped forward, but Hannah took his arm.

"Leave him alone!" There it was. She had chosen. From the corner of her eye, she saw Hugo's lower lip start to quiver.

Luc pulled free of her grasp. "All I've ever done is leave him alone. At your urging."

"Luc. This isn't helping."

He held up his hands as if suddenly aware of how he looked. Shame clouded his features. Then he backed away from them, shaking his head, and left the room. A few moments later, they heard the front door slam.

Hannah glanced at her son. He was on his feet now, bending to retrieve the shirt his father had thrown at him. He didn't return her look. As he straightened, she caught sight of his shoulder blades poking out of his back like pitiful broken wings. She felt sick about what Luc had done. Sicker still that she'd participated in the drama and been unable to stop it. She tried to apologize to Hugo, but the words came out false and awkward. He kept his back to her, refusing to move until she left.

She didn't go downstairs to seek out Luc immediately, but went instead to their bedroom and lay down on the bed. When she came out again half an hour later, she happened to look out the living room window, and there he was on the sidewalk, in the bright afternoon sun, loading things into his Peugeot. Beside him were the three cardboard boxes she'd seen earlier in his office, plus his laptop computer and a futon rolled up and tied with a strip of purple cloth. He kept this mattress in his office for power naps. Hannah could see only his backside and legs. The rest of him was hidden inside the car.

8

*T*he Green Spot was empty when Luc arrived. It was Sunday, three o'clock in the afternoon; the brunch crowd had left. Everyone was outside, soaking in the last rays of sunshine. A green banner emblazoned with the restaurant's name hung over the short-order window. The name was a joke, considering that the neighbourhood around here was bereft of greenery. Not a bush or tree in sight. Luc scanned the sea of empty booths and tables. Not a lot had changed.

He hadn't been here in years. When he was small, his father had brought him and Rémi almost every Sunday. It had been their little weekend ritual. Luc had eaten his first poutine here. And his first Pogo. His parents hadn't been churchgoers. Lyse had never prepared a Sunday dinner in her life, unlike most mothers in Saint-Henri. In the Lévesque household, Sundays were Lyse's day off, the day her menfolk dined at the local *casse-croûte*.

It was fun. Luc's father would greet the men he knew from the Imperial Tobacco plant. At the sight of him, they would get up from their tables. Luc's father had been a great talker. A lover of politics, much like Azarius Lacasse in *Bonheur d'occasion*. Not world politics. Local matters, workers' matters. He had been a security guard at Imperial, and before that he'd worked the assembly line. He knew the cigarette business inside out. He lived and breathed it, he used to joke. He knew everybody at the plant, and everybody liked him. He was regarded as a hub in the communal wheel. A union man, through and through.

Dinners at the Green Spot stopped abruptly when he lost his job after nineteen years of service to the company. Luc was twelve years old. They'd steered clear of the restaurant after that. It was only at the end of high school that Luc began to frequent it again. By then, his father was dead, and years had passed since those Sundays of his childhood. Few people recognized him. He went with Serge Vien. They were taking the same classes, both lovers of Charles Baudelaire, both convinced that they belonged to his exclusive club of poetically damaged souls. They came after school and sat right here in the booth at the far back of the restaurant next to the washrooms and gum machines, strategically out of sight of the guy at the cash. They ordered fries in little paper bags that darkened as the grease soaked through. They pushed quarters into the jukebox. "Crimson and Clover." The first time Luc encountered that song, he'd heard it as "Christmas Is Over." Part of it was his English, which hadn't been particularly strong, but part of it was the lead singer swallowing his words. This was what, in his innocence, he had sung for years, until one day Hannah heard him and set him straight.

He flipped through the little jukebox at his table. The Beatles, Bon Jovi, the Backstreet Boys. A bird's-eye view of rock 'n' roll through the ages, and that was just the *B*'s. He found what he was looking for under the *T*'s. Tommy James and the Shondells.

Vien walked in just as Tommy James began to croon. Luc watched his face light up. "Lord," Vien said. "They still have that?"

Luc bobbed his head to the beat, inhaling the comforting smell of refried grease, his own variant of Proust's madeleines.

Vien's head was bobbing to the music now too. He resembled a bird. A beaky, stork-like bird with a jowly wattle under his chin and a silly misaligned eye. "Nothing's changed," Vien remarked, grinning.

"Maybe a bit," Luc answered, his eye on the wattle. "But not a whole lot."

"The waitresses are younger."

Luc burst out laughing. It felt good to be here. Seeing Vien again was the silver lining to all this. He took two menus from beside the jukebox and slid one toward Vien.

As if on cue, a woman with a mop of dyed black hair came over to take their orders. Her arms glowed a strange coppery colour that, Luc supposed, was the product of regular visits to the tanning salon. "What can I get you two gentlemen?"

She was chewing gum. She could still carry off a pair of tight pants, but her cleavage, revealed by a low-buttoned white blouse, was fissured like soil gone too long without rain. The tanning salon had done its work well. She thrust out a hip while she jotted down their orders on a dollar-store notepad.

Luc watched her retreat to the kitchen and sighed. "Not yet forty."

"A child," Vien agreed.

At the kitchen window, she rose up on her toes and gave the cook their order. From the back, she looked a decade younger. The skin was what gave her away.

The last strains of Tommy James's voice echoed as Luc turned back to face Vien. "I suppose you know about the suspension. You've spoken with Bonnaire?"

Vien brought his hands up from his lap and interlaced his fingers, exposing knobby knuckles that looked a little arthritic. "Not just with Bonnaire," he admitted. "The school's had two emergency staff meetings on the subject of your son."

Luc tried to hold Vien's gaze, but it was too much. On the sound system, a new song selection started up: "Come Together," by John Lennon.

Vien unlaced and relaced his fingers, as if he didn't trust them. "What can I tell you, Luc? Everyone's taking this pretty seriously."

A crash came from the kitchen. Silence followed, and then someone swore. Luc and Vien turned, but there was nothing to see. Their waitress was standing by the cash, cracking her chewing gum and staring out at them with unconcerned eyes.

Luc turned back to Vien. "Will charges be laid?" That was the question. The one over which he had agonized all weekend: his son in youth court; the media getting wind of the story and broadcasting every aspect of it but Hugo's name, thus respecting the letter of the law if not its spirit. All of Quebec would figure out who the celebrity father was. He had already warned Frédéric Axe. And Marie-Soleil. This could degenerate into a circus.

The waitress disappeared into the kitchen, leaving Luc and Vien to themselves in the vast dining room.

"Oh, I don't think that's much of an issue," Vien said, raking his fingers through his grey hair.

"You don't?" Luc said sharply. "Why not? A crime was committed. He was caught red-handed."

"You should watch more TV," Vien said, gazing at Luc with his misaligned eyes. "You'd learn that not every crime gets prosecuted."

Lennon's voice was still coming through the tinny jukebox speakers, explaining the eternal mystery of jokers doing just as they pleased.

Luc looked away in frustration.

The waitress had emerged from the kitchen. Whatever drama had occurred seemed to have sorted itself out. The guy who stood by the cash had also resumed his station. Behind him was an old-fashioned glass display case full of pie slices: lemon meringue, apple, and something green. Key lime, most probably. They weren't edible, Luc knew. As a boy, he had liked to get up close to the case and see the layers of dust on the painted plaster. Next to the pieces of pie sat five or six glass goblets filled with green Jell-O cubes. Fake as well. Glowing eerily and topped with grimy plaster cream, the delight of his youth.

Lennon stopped singing. The anthem of a generation was over. Luc turned back to Vien. "The detective said they might prosecute."

"Might," Vien repeated. "Possible, but not probable. I'm pretty sure this thing will stay internal."

"But the police are already involved."

"Bonnaire will disinvolve them."

A couple of kids who had just come in put on a new song. American rap. Angry words spat out to a brainless rhythm.

"Trust me," Vien said, leaning back against the red banquette. "There'll be no formal charge."

Luc reached across the table and took hold of Vien's wrist. "Thank you," he said, his voice cracking. Until that moment, he hadn't known how much he'd needed to hear those words. He withdrew his hand quickly. Wiped his eyes on the sleeve of his shirt.

Vien watched him, surprised. "It's going to be okay, Luc. Really. I have a good feeling here."

Luc suddenly regretted his histrionics. He regretted calling Vien today, regretted laying himself open to another man's pity.

"This is tales out of school," Vien said, leaning in conspiratorially. "But we're *anciens*, right? We're entitled, to some degree. I obviously can't tell you all the details of my talks with Bonnaire. I don't want to play double agent, but the least I can do is reassure a friend."

"Friend" was a bit of an exaggeration. But Vien was at least an ally, something Luc desperately needed right now.

"Bonnaire will do just about anything to avoid the press getting mixed up in this," Vien said. He glanced around the room and dipped his tone confidentially. "Numbers are down at Saint-Jean this year. They've been falling for a couple of years, actually. People in Quebec aren't having kids anymore. Or at least not the kind of people who used to send their kids to schools like Saint-Jean-Baptiste. We're in the red, Luc. It's serious. The last thing Bonnaire needs right now is a scandal."

The waitress picked that moment to arrive with their order: two bags of fries and two large, ice-filled glasses of Coca-Cola.

"You sure you don't want plates?" she asked, depositing the snacks on their placemats.

"No, no," Vien assured her. He smiled sweetly "We're on a trip down memory lane." He took one of the ketchup packets that accompanied the fries, tore it open with his teeth, and squeezed its contents onto his potatoes.

"We used to come here a long time ago," Luc said to the waitress.

"A very long time ago," said Vien, taking a greasy fry between his long, pre-arthritic fingers and examining it. A filament of steam rose into the air. "Now *that* is a *patate frite*," he said, and popped it into his mouth.

Luc and the orange-skinned waitress laughed.

"Are they as good as you remember?" she teased.

"Better," said Vien.

Luc dug into his own paper bag. He hadn't tasted a Green Spot *frite* in decades. Vien was right. They were delicious.

The woman left and they ate in silence.

Luc finished first. "What do you think will happen?" he asked, folding his bag. The fries had improved his spirits.

"Well," said Vien, still chewing, "there is sure to be a disciplinary hearing. This coming week, I would guess. I've sat on these things before, Luc. I can help you prepare."

"Prepare?"

Vien was now digging fragments of potato from between his teeth with a toothpick. Luc averted his eyes.

"The parents have to attend," explained Vien. "The student too, obviously. It's your chance to say your piece."

The bell on the Green Spot door jangled and a big family

group entered the restaurant—grandparents, parents, and a clutch of children. You rarely saw families like this in Saint-Henri anymore. They looked like something out of the fifties or sixties. The waitress led them to a large table at the front of the dining room and went to get a high chair for the smallest child in the group, a little girl of two or three in a frilly party dress. Luc watched the mother settle everyone. They weren't speaking French. Over the traffic sounds coming in from Notre-Dame Street, his ear caught Slavic syllables. Of course. These people were too united to be from here.

"His chances can't be good," Luc said wearily. He and Hannah would have to find another school for him, the kind of school where troublemakers and misfits got dumped.

"Chances?" said Vien.

"Of staying at Saint-Jean. After all this."

Vien surprised him by smiling. "*All this* isn't terribly serious, Luc. Really. Not that I'm exonerating Hugo. But I've seen far worse. He didn't hurt anybody. There was no damage done. His motives don't make much sense to me, but it doesn't look like there was an intent to harm."

A commotion made them turn. The little girl at the front table wanted to sit with her older siblings on the red banquette. She was twisting in her high chair, reaching out to them and whimpering. The mother tried to reason with her, standing up and hovering over her chair, but that only made things worse. The whimpers escalated into shrieks. Finally, the father stood up. He was a short man, solid, probably not yet out of his thirties. He scooped the little girl out of her seat in a single deft movement and carried her, writhing and shrieking, to the back of the room where Luc and Vien were sitting, veering just before he reached their table and disappearing with the child into the men's room.

The shrieking stopped. Vien raised his eyebrows in mock alarm.

Luc ignored him. The man was a good father. When had discipline become cause for alarm? Still, there was something that made Luc listen for sounds from the men's room, something less certain and harder to name than his own tacit approval.

A moment later, the door to the washroom swung open and the man stepped out, leading the girl by the hand. She had stopped crying, although she looked pale and subdued. She held her father's hand and walked with dignity back to her family's table, where the man made her kiss her mother and apologize. Then she climbed uncomplainingly into the high chair.

Luc's approval was complete. He wished Hannah had seen this: the rebuttal of all her arguments. A deep resentment surged.

Across the table, Vien smiled cynically. "Small child, small problems. Give her a few years," he said, and winked his bad eye.

Luc shrugged. The little girl was already laughing and talking with her siblings. "You never know. Some children work out fine."

"They all have to go through adolescence. If they don't act out, it's probably grounds for worry."

"Not all of them bring guns to school."

"No," said Vien. "No, they don't."

"There have to be consequences."

"There will be," said Vien. "But I don't think expulsion will be one of them. Not this time. Think of it, Luc. If Bonnaire kicks Hugo out, how's it going to look? We can't risk that kind of publicity. Not right now, with our numbers so weak."

He sighed and reached out to retrieve the menus again from between the sugar container and their darkened jukebox. He flipped it open but didn't look down.

"If you ask me, the worst is already over. He's been slapped with a suspension. And a disciplinary hearing. Bonnaire will deliver a sermon, make him feel two feet tall. But that will probably be the end of it. He'll get some sort of a punishment—lines to copy or something. A kid who spray-painted graffiti in the schoolyard last spring spent four weekends scrubbing off the damage. That sort of thing."

He searched Luc's face for a moment, then turned to the dessert list. "Can I interest you, perchance, in a bowl of Green Spot Jell-O?" He grinned, but Luc shook his head. His stomach was already burning from all the sugar in the Coke.

Vien replaced the menu in its slot. "Have you talked to him yet?" he asked.

Luc shook his head.

"You should."

Heat flared between Luc's ribs. He gave Vien a sharp look.

"He's not a bad kid," Vien said. He looked suddenly old, a sad, asymmetrical man with uncombed hair. "He's fourteen, Luc. Remember fourteen?"

The heat in Luc's chest was pulsing now. Yes, he remembered fourteen. That was how old he'd been when his father shot himself. That was how old he'd been when he swore to himself he would never, ever fail at anything.

"Has he talked to you about anger? Bullying? Did he ever mention anybody bugging him at school?"

Luc rubbed his solar plexus with his knuckles. He saw where

Vien was going. The teachers would have talked about it. About his son, the boy with a gun and a chip on his shoulder.

"I'm trying to help," said Vien

Luc tried to look grateful. "I appreciate it," he said, but he knew Vien saw right through him. They were back in their old dynamic. Vien meant well, but Luc had always found him irritating. Their years without contact hadn't changed this.

The placemats here were thin grey newsprint covered with the logos of local businesses in pale green ink: a pet store, a dry cleaner, a shop that sold fitness equipment. Luc took an edge of paper between his thumb and index finger and rolled it into a cylinder.

"What's behind the name change?"

Luc looked up.

"Why Stern, I mean?" asked Vien, unaware of how sensitive the issue was in the Lévesque household. "He even asked the school to put it on his transcripts."

Luc tried to compose his face, tried not to think about his burning stomach. "It's his mother's name."

"I thought she went by Lévesque," said Vien, still oblivious.

"She does."

Vien frowned.

"He admires his grandfather," Luc said. "When Hugo was in the sixth grade, he did a project on him. You know the kind of thing they do. A mini-biography of someone close to him. Someone he looked up to. He picked Alfred Stern."

Vien's mouth fell open. "*The* Alfred Stern? That's his grandfather?"

Luc sighed.

"Say it ain't so, Joe," Vien said in English, shaking his head. He frowned again. "I thought your wife was from Toronto."

"She grew up here," said Luc. Hannah's history was the last thing he felt like discussing, but Vien wasn't about to let it go. "Her parents left during the Anglo exodus in the late seventies. Hannah and I were together by then, so she stayed."

"You married Alfred Stern's daughter."

"Yes. We've established that," said Luc. "Fuck you, anyway." He looked up to check that he hadn't offended. This was how they'd talked in high school, throwing punches like tough guys, even though they were both frightened little boys.

"He charged me, you know," said Vien. "In 1970? All I'd done was attend a couple of rallies, and I got slapped with a criminal charge." He paused. "You knew I was arrested?"

Luc had heard about it. The news had come to him second-hand. By the autumn of 1970, he and Vien had parted ways. Luc looked at him now, still proud of his little moment of defiance. If they hadn't parted ways, Luc would long ago have said something cruel.

Vien the rebel. Luc could picture him being mouthy with a cop. He had always been mouthy with figures of authority, even with old Monsieur Hervé, the pockmarked, half-deaf principal. Luc had been more obedient, though in the fall of 1970 he had taken risks too. Everyone had. If you were in Montreal and under thirty, how could you not take risks? Luc had attended the legendary rally at the Paul Sauvé Arena. He had shouted out "FLQ! FLQ! FLQ!" in the same delirium as everyone else. He had felt the rush of tribal belonging. When Pierre Vallières, Quebec's answer to Che, had stood up at that rally to speak, Luc had stood too, whistling and clapping until his hands hurt.

"Alfred Stern's daughter," Vien said again.

"Let it go."

Vien stroked his chin. "Family dinners must be fun."

Luc picked up the edge of his placemat and started rolling again, his irritation rising. Vien had hit a nerve. He hadn't seen his father-in-law in seven years.

"And your son admires him enough to take his name."

"My son can play all the games he likes," Luc snapped. "He's still a Lévesque."

"Listen," said Vien, more kindly. "I can help with this. Smooth things with Bonnaire. We're on good terms."

Luc forced himself to nod. He wasn't used to begging for things. He didn't like it, but he really had no choice.

"Talk to Hugo," said Vien. "We can't do anything unless he cooperates."

Somehow, in the course of an hour at the Green Spot, Vien and he had become a *we*. So be it. Luc nodded to this hapless, childless friend of his youth. Ah, how low fatherhood could bring a man.

9

The Peugeot's windshield was streaming with rain. It was coming down so hard that the wipers were next to useless. Luc leaned forward. Tail lights blinked blurrily in front of him. Beside him in the passenger seat, Hannah unbuckled her belt and rummaged in her purse. They were at Atwater and Sherbrooke, stopped at the traffic light. She extracted a Kleenex and began rubbing the inside of the windshield.

The traffic light was about to turn green. "Your belt," he said, nodding at her. The rubbing wasn't doing any good, anyway. Shreds of Kleenex clung to the wet glass.

Luc stepped on the gas too hard, throwing Hannah back against her seat.

Behind them, Hugo, who was slumped against the door, eyes shut, jerked too.

"Sorry," said Luc, although really he wasn't. Certainly not about rousing his slumping son.

The boy didn't move or open his eyes.

"Sit up," he said, watching in the rear-view mirror.

Hugo needed firmness. Like the child at the Green Spot. Luc had told Hannah about her last night, while they were discussing strategy. Discipline was what Hugo needed. Rules and expectations.

The stone ramparts of the Collège Saint-Jean-Baptiste loomed into view. They dated from a time when intruders—Iroquois, then British soldiers—had to be physically repelled. In the era during which these walls were erected, no man in this place would have married an Englishwoman. They probably never would have met. Luc turned the steering wheel hard and stepped on the gas, cutting across Sherbrooke Street into the school drive. The car sputtered up the little slope to the parking area and stopped. "Okay," said Luc, "let's do this."

He unlatched his seat belt and started to get out of the car, but he could feel Hannah looking at him anxiously. He turned back to her. "What?" he asked, more sharply than he'd intended.

She shrank back a little in her seat, so he reached out for her hand. "It'll be okay. Just let me do the talking."

There was a sigh from the back seat.

Luc twisted around to face his son. "You have something to add?"

The boy looked away.

"Good," he said. "Just remember. You speak only when spoken to. You answer only what they ask. You do not extemporize. You do not justify. And you address the principal as *monsieur*. Got it?"

"It's going to be fine," Hannah said.

She was trying to reassure Hugo, but Luc found it irritating. He wasn't at all sure the boy would get it right. He was irritated all the time these days. It was a precise physical sensation, a feeling of constriction in the centre of his torso, just below the sternum. He couldn't remember the last time he'd taken a full, deep breath. He opened his mouth experimentally and inhaled, but his lungs blocked defensively.

"I know these people," he said, not looking at either of them. "I know exactly how they think."

He did. He knew this place. This institution. This culture. Saint-Jean-Baptiste was the oldest school in Quebec. Men like Louis-Joseph Papineau and the poet Émile Nelligan had studied in its halls. You couldn't get more Québécois than that.

Hannah didn't respond. In the back seat, Hugo stared stonily into the distance.

"Wipe that look off your face."

The boy blinked.

"Hugo!"

He rolled his eyes and muttered, very softly, a profanity.

"It just slips out, doesn't it? You don't even realize you're doing it, and out it comes." Luc slumped in the driver's seat, exhausted before they'd even begun. "If that happens in there," he said, "you're sunk, Hugo. You get that, don't you? This isn't a game. Your future is at stake here."

Rain struck Luc's face and chest as he left the car. Hannah was taking her time, and Hugo was fidgeting in the back with the door lock. Instead of waiting for them, which he knew he ought to do, Luc ran across the asphalt, ran as if he couldn't be touched, as if by will alone he could rid himself of his wife and son and the whole fraught world of choices and coincidences that had brought him back to the imposing grounds of his old school.

After they had made it through the front door and been buzzed in by the receptionist, they were forced to wait outside the hearing room for twenty minutes. Students passed, glancing furtively at them. No one stopped to talk to Hugo, which Luc found strange. He had assumed things were okay at school for his son. Not great. Not fun, but okay, the way high school had been for Luc himself, and for most people he knew. Now he wasn't so sure. Was his son a misfit? One of those kids you never noticed, ticking quietly but lethally away in a corner until some little thing tripped him, releasing the catch? It was harder for intelligent boys. Luc knew that story well enough, although, in his own case, brains had always helped, not hurt him.

After his meeting at the Green Spot with Vien, Luc had decided to get tough. He'd started with Hugo's bedroom, stripping it of anything that smacked of provocation. No more war games. In fact, no more games of any kind until Hugo shaped up. Luc trashed a little clay pipe Hugo had fashioned in art class. It had never been used, but there it was, in plain view on his desk, a reification of insolence. What had he and Hannah been thinking, allowing the boy to keep it? He also threw out a wallet stamped brazenly with a seven-pointed green leaf, and a T-shirt with fifteen different English terms for marijuana. Boundaries. That was what Hugo needed.

Over the last week, Hugo had followed a clear list of dos and don'ts, hand-printed by Luc with a red pen. To Luc's surprise, he'd submitted to it. Not with grace. Far from it. But there had been no shouting matches, no open resistance. Luc had not been proud of the fight the day Hannah returned from Toronto, but perhaps it had been necessary. Hugo moved about the house now with considerably more caution.

The receptionist appeared, finally, and told them they could enter. The room in which the hearing was to be held was spacious and high-ceilinged, with stained glass windows along one wall. Formerly a chapel, surely. Luc wondered whether he had ever been in here before. If so, he had forgotten.

A long folding conference table had been positioned in the room's centre. Six people stood beside their chairs on one side. Vien was among them, Luc noticed with relief, just as he had said he would be. A woman with a laptop was also sitting directly behind Bonnaire, observing him. Luc was taken aback by the scale of the proceedings. He had pictured something more intimate, a meeting in Bonnaire's office, perhaps, with just the principal and vice-principal, Vien, and themselves. Hugo would apologize and Bonnaire would give him a lecture, as Vien had said. End of story, as long as Hugo managed not to scowl or swear. Luc would speak too, express in his most elegant phrasings his regret for a son who had caused such trouble to the Saint-Jean-Baptiste community. He really did feel sorry about it. From the bottom of his heart. Bonnaire would sense the sincerity.

Three chairs had been placed on the table's other side. "Hugo in the middle," Bonnaire said without ceremony, pointing.

Hugo moved to the designated chair. Luc chose the chair to his left, and Hannah walked to the other side of him, directly across the table from Vien. They waited for permission to sit down. Like prisoners in the dock, thought Luc. Across from them, the faces of their judges were uniformly grim.

The gun was in the middle of the table, its barrel pointing straight at Hugo. Was that intentional? A little strategy by Napoléon Bonnaire to shake them up? A label had been affixed to it with a string tied neatly in a bow. Such careful preparations. Three manila folders in different colours—purple, red, and blue—were stacked next to the gun. Each committee member also had a red folder and a notepad and pen. The whole scenario struck Luc as over-serious and vaguely hokey—as one might expect of a high school trial.

Bonnaire did the introductions, starting at his far right with a fat young woman with multiple chins and a sullen glare. She was Hugo's drama teacher, Madame Antoine. Beside her was an older, thinner woman, Madame Laflamme, chair of the parents' committee. Vice-principal Ducharme and Principal Bonnaire introduced themselves next. Then came a big fair-haired man with the flattened nose of a boxer, sitting immediately to their left. Monsieur Groulx, the school security guard. Serge Vien was last in line. He had donned a tie for the occasion and seemed to have combed his hair. Bonnaire thanked them all for their attendance. He made a special point of welcoming Luc. The assembly was doubly regrettable, he said, given the esteem with which Luc Lévesque was regarded by the Saint-Jean-Baptiste community.

A wave of gratitude washed over Luc. He had capital here, and Bonnaire was man enough to acknowledge it. They taught his books in their classrooms, after all. He was on the school curriculum.

After they had sat down, Bonnaire put on his chrome-framed reading glasses. "These are the facts," he said, opening one of the files and reading in a voice much louder and more theatrical than Luc thought necessary. "On Tuesday, October 2, 2001, during the morning recess, Hugo Lévesque, a student in *secondaire trois* at Collège Saint-Jean-Baptiste, was discovered on the school premises in possession of a nine-millimetre Mauser Luger pistol." He looked over the top of his reading glasses, pausing for a beat like an actor in a play.

"The weapon was unloaded and no ammunition was found on Hugo Lévesque's person. The search was conducted by our security personnel, Monsieur Jean-Claude Groulx." He looked up again and nodded at the fair-haired man. "The utmost care for the student was exercised. We had been alerted by another student of the existence of a gun, but had no idea whether it was loaded or what the state of mind or intent of the gun's possessor might be. Hugo Lévesque did not resist when approached. Monsieur Groulx was able to speak calmly with him and then to search his schoolbag, in which the gun, laid out on the table as our chief exhibit, was discovered."

The chair of the parents' committee glowered at Luc, as if he, personally, had committed the heinous act.

"As I have told the offending student and his family," Bonnaire continued, "this school has never, in the two hundred and thirty-four years of its existence, dealt with an issue such as this one. In over two centuries, no one has ever dared to bring a firearm onto its grounds. This is a first in our history, and believe me, I hope it is an act that no one will ever think to repeat."

Such theatrics. Such pomp without dignity. Under his sense of shame, Luc felt the coals of anger catch and glow. He reached for the glass of water that had been set out in front of his seat and took a sip.

Bonnaire asked Hugo to stand and to enunciate his name loudly and clearly for the benefit of the school secretary, the woman with the laptop who was playing the role of court stenographer.

The arms of Hugo's jacket were too short, Luc saw immediately. How had that escaped him? They should have bought something new for him. He looked ridiculous, his vulnerability and adolescent gawkiness on display for everyone to see.

Luc pretended he'd never set eyes on him before. He pretended, for a moment, that he was the pinched woman chairing the parents' committee, the regrettable Madame Laflamme. He used this trick quite often in writing fiction. What would she see as she looked across the table with those ugly eyes of hers? A boy too small for his age in tight clothes, thin and Jewish-looking, with a gaze that shifted constantly. Not good.

"Do you recognize this?" Bonnaire said, picking up the gun. Hugo nodded.

"You must answer in words, Hugo," said Bonnaire, gesturing at the secretary behind him. "Say yes or no. Enunciate clearly."

Luc squirmed. It was hopeless.

"Yes," Hugo said after a pause, so softly they all had to strain to hear.

"Can you tell me the model?"

Hugo nodded.

"You have to speak, Hugo. Speak!"

"You just said it, monsieur," Hugo muttered, addressing the floor.

Luc stared at him. Such insolence. His heart was pounding. Bonnaire's face had flushed a dark pink.

Finally, when Luc felt he could endure it no longer, just as he reached the limit of endurance, the boy spoke. "A nine-millimetre Mauser Luger."

There was a collective release of breath in the room.

"Thank you," said Bonnaire, although he did not look at all appreciative. "You knew the model before I said it, did you not?"

Hugo didn't move.

"You must have. Where did you learn it, Hugo? Please tell us, in a nice, loud voice this time."

Hugo shrugged.

Luc could barely breathe. It felt as if stones, a whole quarry of them, were piled high and precarious inside his chest.

Bonnaire put his hands flat on the table and repeated the question. "How did you learn the gun's make and calibre?"

"At the gun shop," whispered Hugo.

"The gun shop?"

"The pawnshop, where I bought it."

"And where is this pawnshop located? Be precise, now. Give us the names of streets."

Hugo described an establishment on Sainte-Catherine Street, not far from the school. As he spoke, his gaze never once left the floor. He looked guilty as hell, his body all but screaming it.

Bonnaire, for some reason, didn't seem to notice. "I visited that shop," he said, his tone suddenly shifting to conversational. "I had the pleasure of speaking with the owner, a man named Leblanc. Do you know this man, Monsieur Leblanc?"

Hugo went perfectly still. In the light filtering through the stained glass windows, his skin looked yellow, the way it had in the days immediately following his birth. Newborn liver malfunction. An excess of bile.

"I have to tell you, he was surprised when I showed him the gun," Bonnaire continued, ignoring Hugo's silence. "He claimed that he had never seen it before. He said he had no licence to sell firearms." Bonnaire stopped. "Perhaps you'd like to say something now, Hugo?"

Rain had begun to rap on the windows, a light pinging sound against the glass. No one moved.

"We are waiting," said Bonnaire.

The rain kept on rapping. It was disconcerting. It sounded like someone knocking, wanting to be let in. Luc glanced at Hugo, who was looking at his lap. On the far side of him, Hannah was staring straight ahead, her face a stone mask.

"We have two very different accounts here, Hugo. They cannot both be true."

Hugo shifted, making a floorboard creak.

"Are we to conclude that Monsieur Leblanc is lying?"

The floor creaked again.

"It is in your interest to respond," said Bonnaire. "We are offering you a precious opportunity to explain the situation in your own words."

Luc had a sudden impulse to shout. Of course the man hadn't admitted to selling the gun, or even to setting eyes on it. Hugo was underage. This was a lethal weapon they were talking about. Even selling it to an adult would be a crime. It was perfectly obvious. Why didn't Hugo speak?

"I bought the gun from him," Hugo said in a whisper.

Bonnaire brought his fingers together, forming a tent, and pressed them to his lips. "So the man is lying. Is that right, Hugo? You are accusing Monsieur Leblanc of lying." He stood up to ask his next question. "You have also told me that you went to this pawnshop, the one on Sainte-Catherine Street, before school started on the morning of October 2. At eight o'clock. Is this correct?"

"Yes," whispered Hugo.

"And yet the shop only opens at ten thirty."

Across the table, the chair of the parents' committee scribbled something on her notepad.

"He came early for me," whispered Hugo.

"The owner? Monsieur Leblanc?"

Hugo nodded.

"Speak up," said Bonnaire. He turned to the secretary. "That was a yes, Madame Chicoine. You may note down a yes." He looked back at Hugo. "Monsieur Leblanc denies he did anything of the sort."

Bonnaire's questions continued. Why had Hugo bought the gun in the first place? What had he wanted to do with it? What could a boy from a good family like Hugo's want with a gun? Hugo remained silent, not that Bonnaire seemed bothered by this anymore. He was too engrossed in his own rhetoric to pay any attention.

"I am not a mind reader," Bonnaire said, addressing the room like a prosecutor from one of those third-rate TV courtroom dramas that were currently so popular. "I can only guess what was going on in the mind of Hugo Lévesque on the morning of October 2. His motives are a mystery, and will remain as such until the day he chooses to explain them."

The room fell silent. Luc tried to will Hugo to speak. In his mind's eye, Hugo smiled and opened his mouth, but when Luc glanced sideways, Hugo's lips were clamped in a thin, defiant line.

Luc couldn't contain himself. "He meant no harm," he burst out, taking everyone, himself most of all, by surprise. "It was bubble-wrapped in his knapsack, for the love of God. He wasn't waving it around."

Everyone in the room was staring at him. "Please, Monsieur

Lévesque," Bonnaire said. "You will be called upon to speak soon enough. But at the moment, your son has the floor."

Luc was about to answer indignantly that he could speak without being called upon, that he didn't need anyone's permission to talk about his own son, when Hugo turned his way. It was only for a fraction of a second, too short a time for any message to pass, but the sadness Luc glimpsed was enough to silence him. Emotion. Real and unfiltered. He shut his mouth and sat back in his chair. His heart was galloping. He wasn't in any pain, but surely this wasn't normal. *Arrhythmia?* Was that the term? *Tachycardia?* Could a man die of failing to defend his son?

Things were going horribly. Luc had forgotten what this place was like: the rules, the deplorable, petty power plays. How he'd hated it when he was young. He pressed his fingernails into the flesh of his palms and tried to slow his breath. If only Bonnaire would let him speak. He could win them over; he knew he could. He was literary and he was peaceful. Books were his great love. Literature, the only thing he'd ever believed in. What did he know about guns?

Bonnaire had turned to face Hugo. It appeared that the interrogation was not over. "This man," he said, "the pawnshop owner. Can you describe him physically for us?" He was smiling for some reason, but not generously.

Hugo surprised everyone by speaking. In a single clipped sentence, he described a stout person with thinning grey hair.

"And you swear that this person sold you the gun?"

Hugo remained silent.

"Answer in words, please, Hugo. Would you swear to it on the Holy Bible?"

Luc shifted in his chair. Surely this was outside the bounds of a high school disciplinary hearing. Where was Bonnaire going with these questions?

"Answer me," ordered Bonnaire.

Everyone looked at Hugo, but he didn't raise his eyes. A bell rang. Sounds of footsteps could be heard outside the closed door. Muffled shouts and laughter.

Do it, Luc willed.

"Answer me," Bonnaire said again. He was on his feet now, staring at Hugo with his horrid, beady eyes. At length he sat down. "I will speak, then," he said. "You tell a good story, Hugo Lévesque. A story that holds together, that has the virtue of coherence. There *is* a pawnshop on Sainte-Catherine Street, just as you say. And yes, Monsieur Leblanc *does* sell antique guns on occasion. He has a glass case with antique firearms in it. And if, in fact, he *had* sold you a gun, he could never admit to it afterward. You are a minor. He would be admitting to a crime."

Bonnaire paused for a moment, allowing everyone to absorb this logic. Then he leaned across the table and picked up the Luger. "You and I both know, however, that you did not purchase this gun at the pawnshop." He looked from Hugo to the gun, and from the gun to Luc.

"You seem confused, Monsieur Lévesque."

Luc tried to rearrange his expression. Bonnaire was right. He had no idea what was going on.

"I'm glad of it." Bonnaire flashed him a tight, aggressive smile. "It would have pained me to discover that an esteemed graduate of the school and one of Quebec's finest writers would deliberately lead us astray."

What was Bonnaire saying? Was he accusing him of lying too? Luc returned the principal's gaze as steadily as he could. Bonnaire seemed to feel there had been some sort of deception on his part. Did the others think it too? The jury members appeared to be as confused as Luc himself. They were all exchanging bewildered looks. All except for Serge Vien, Luc realized with a start. Vien was sitting very still in his chair, his dark eyes averted.

"Another boy was involved," Bonnaire announced.

Hugo's head jerked up.

"You were seen," Bonnaire said, nodding triumphantly. "New witnesses have come forward." He held the gun out and addressed the entire room. "This weapon belongs to the father of another of our students, who happens to be in Hugo's homeroom class. On the morning of October 2, 2001, the student in question took it without permission from his father's apartment—stole it, to be perfectly frank—and brought it to the school to sell."

Bonnaire turned back to Hugo. "Isn't that right, Hugo? Have I got the facts right this time? I should hope so, since I heard them from the very student to whom I am referring. He told me you paid him seventy-five dollars in cash for it." Bonnaire replaced the gun on the table. "Hugo Lévesque has lied to us, ladies and gentlemen," he said. "Lied repeatedly and systematically, from the start of this inquiry to this very moment. If this were a court of law—" he began portentously, but then stopped, interrupted by a loud scraping sound.

It was Hannah, pushing her chair back from the table.

"Excuse me," she said, leaning in toward the line of judges and fixing her eyes on Bonnaire, "but this changes everything, does it not?" Her voice was much higher than usual and her cheeks were flushed, but she gripped the seat of her chair and continued. "If another student is involved, then Hugo didn't bring the gun onto your school grounds, did he?"

Bonnaire's jaw muscles tightened. "First of all, madame, may I remind you that these are not *my* school grounds. They belong to all of us. To your son. And to you too."

Luc winced. He'd warned her not to speak. That had been a bad slip. Surely, now she'd stop. But Bonnaire's words seemed to make Hannah more determined than ever. She sprang to her feet, her gaze still fixed on the principal.

In her hand was something Luc had not noticed before: a little red booklet. "Your rules," she said, flipping the booklet open and skimming a page of it until she found what she was looking for. "Your rules," she repeated, "refer to 'anyone bringing a gun or other weapon onto the college premises.'" She paused and looked up again at the judges. "Bringing, not having. Not possessing, Monsieur Bonnaire. Those are two different things."

She sounded like a lawyer. Like her father. There was a moment of silence.

It did not last. Madame Laflamme stood up. "This is absurd! Whether your son got someone to bring it to school or brought it himself is irrelevant. It's splitting hairs. The fact remains that a gun was found on the school grounds, within school hours, and it was in your son's knapsack. He's clearly to blame."

"To blame for what?" said Hannah.

Luc shook his head, willing her to look his way and read the message in his eyes: the best thing she could do was sit down and shut up.

She didn't even glance at him.

The chair of the parents' committee was smiling now, moving

in confidently for the kill. "For having a gun. At school," she said slowly, as if addressing a child. She began to describe her daughter, a little girl who had entered the school that autumn. She had just turned twelve, young for *secondaire un*. According to her mother, she had never laid eyes on a gun before, not even on television, which in any case was banned in their home.

Bonnaire raised his hands in a gesture of exasperation. "Ladies, please!"

Madame Laflamme turned on him. "I have a question for you too, Monsieur Bonnaire," she said, clipping her words to show her displeasure. "Why are we even bothering to give this young man a hearing, since all he does is lie? This whole proceeding is a farce."

She folded her arms over her chest. "If you want my opinion, he should be assessed. There are tests that can be done," she said, conspicuously refusing to look at either Hannah or Hugo. "He could be evaluated for ... anti-social tendencies." She stared belligerently at Bonnaire. "I wish I could say I trust these parents to do something constructive, but frankly their contributions to the discussion today have been anything but reassuring."

Hannah was formulating an answer. Luc could see it. Before her mouth could open, however, Luc brought his hand down hard on the table. Now he was on his feet as well.

"Enough!" he said. It came out louder than he'd intended, but at least it had the desired effect. The women fell silent. "I will not be insulted like this," he said. "I will not stand it for another second."

Bonnaire had to call them all to order. As soon as they sat down in their seats, quiet and contrite like schoolchildren, Bonnaire announced that the investigation was ongoing. The second boy would receive a hearing, and, until this occurred, no decision could be made about Hugo Lévesque.

Luc felt exhausted. Hugo had sunk himself. Sunk them all. Luc couldn't have saved him even if he'd had a chance to speak, which he hadn't, thanks to Hannah. He lifted his eyes to the row of stained glass windows along the wall in front of him. It was overcast outside and the colours were dull, but one scene caught his eye. A green hill with three black crosses: Jesus and the two thieves. *Today you will be with me in paradise.*

The chair of the parents' committee didn't apologize for her rudeness. In fact, she kept right on glaring at Hannah while Bonnaire talked, averting her gaze only after the principal bowed and announced, to Luc's immense relief, that the proceedings were adjourned.

As they left the building, Luc couldn't bring himself to look at either Hannah or his son. He felt sick and ashamed. When he had approached Bonnaire to shake his hand before leaving, the principal had made a show of being engrossed in his papers while giving instructions to the secretary. Luc had walked away without forcing the issue. And Vien had hurried off without meeting Luc's eye.

A No Trespassing sign at the entry to the parking area warned drivers that their cars would be towed if they failed to get the requisite permission. Tufts of brown grass pushed through cracks in the asphalt. Luc led the way to the Peugeot, walking beside Hannah but not touching her. Hugo walked a few metres behind.

"I hope you're pleased," he said as they reached the car.

She got in, silent and contrite. Hugo followed.

As he drove them home along Sherbrooke Street, Luc

lowered his window, letting the cool air rush in. The rain had stopped, but a bank of clouds still hung over the city, dark and ominously low. The car passed the Sulpician seminary immediately west of the school, with its row of scraggly poplars over a dry reflecting pool. No one spoke. He accelerated through the turn onto Atwater and drove fast down the hill toward Saint-Henri.

There were no parking spots near the house on Laporte Street, so Luc had to circle the block to the other side of the park. The instant he was out of the car, he walked away. No explanation, no goodbye. He could feel Hannah's eyes on his back, but he didn't care. He was too angry to deal with her right now. Or with her lying son. As he walked, he became aware of something lumpy in his pocket. He reached in and pulled out a dollar-store key ring, a die made of silver-painted plastic attached to a flimsy chain with a single key on it. His new landlord—the fat man, Gagnon—had given it to him with the key. As Luc turned it over in his hand, he felt a rush. Hannah and Hugo were too far behind him to see it, and even if they had, they wouldn't have known what it was. It was small and secret, and that only added to the pleasure.

10

Dr. Mandelbaum's office was on Sainte-Catherine Street in lower Westmount. Hannah must have passed this building a hundred times and never noticed it. An art gallery occupied the first floor. Hannah and Hugo were standing in front of its shiny window, waiting for Luc, whom they hadn't seen since last Thursday's hearing at the school. Five days. They had spoken three times during this period over the phone. Each time, he was the one who made the call—from a pay phone, with an ocean-roar of traffic in the background.

The first call had come Friday morning, the day after the hearing. She had been up all night, waiting and wondering, and then, at ten thirty in the morning, just as she was about to go to bed, the telephone had rung. No explanation. No apology. She had been too distraught to demand either.

The second call had come Sunday night. Luc had learned from Serge Vien that Hugo would not be expelled. He was safe. The school, Luc informed her, would phone her officially with the verdict sometime Monday. The boy who had sold Hugo the gun would be thrown out. It turned out this boy had been in trouble before. He, not Hugo, would pay for the crime.

The final call had come last night. Again filled with traffic sounds and again no indication of where Luc was or why he had left, though this time Hannah asked. She assumed he was bunking at the new office, but he would not tell her. He kept deflecting her with queries about the logistics of their meeting this morning, where the place was located and what time they were expected to show up. She decided not to insist. Explanations would have to wait.

A brass figurine looked at her from inside the gallery window. Barely a foot high, it was by far the most striking piece on display, much more beautiful than the acrylic painting or the geometric Plexiglas sculpture that also occupied the space. The figurine was female. Her breasts protruded generously beneath a garment that covered her from neck to toe. Her belly was a gentle hillock rising from the flat plains of her thighs. Was she pregnant? Hannah bent in for a closer look, pressing her nose against the glass. The moon-like face seemed to be glowing, full of secrets. Yes, thought Hannah. A young woman with child.

Hugo was leaning against the wall a few steps away, his eyes half shut. Earbuds connected his skull to the CD player in his hand. His face was expressionless. He could have been asleep.

Luc's disappearance didn't seem even to have registered with him. Hannah hadn't broached the subject yet. She didn't trust herself to. The thought of discussing Luc with him was, frankly, beyond her. And so she had turned to Mandelbaum—a specialist in teenage boys, a saviour of fractured families. That, at least, was his reputation. On the morning after Hugo's hearing, Hannah had telephoned his office. He had sounded fine over the phone. Calm and reassuring, though not cheap. She had thought Hugo would be seen alone, but Mandelbaum dispelled that notion straightaway. Both parents were expected to attend the initial sessions.

Hannah had resisted, imagining Luc's reaction to this request, but Mandelbaum was firm. It was important, he said, for everyone to be on the same page. The metaphor had made her feel like crying. When Luc happened to call twenty minutes later to tell her he was alive, she explained what she had done. To her surprise, though he disliked psychologists in general and English-speaking ones in particular, he had agreed to attend.

Hugo pushed himself off the wall with one foot, squinting at something down the street. Hannah turned and followed his gaze. Her heart jumped. The blue Peugeot had pulled into a space half a block away. The door on the driver's side swung open and Luc stepped out.

He paused on the sidewalk, checking the address against a slip of paper in his hand. The sun was on him. He threw his shoulders back and stood up straight. He looked like an ad in a magazine—for cigarettes or high-end sportswear—the distil-lation of manhood in a sunlit image. Well-fed but not fleshy, intelligent, slightly bohemian. He looked happy, she thought with a pang. And startlingly young. The opposite, in other words, of her own sad and sleepless self.

It was strange seeing the man you loved at a distance, as if a few feet of concrete on a Montreal sidewalk could give you a perspective impossible to attain in the normal course of events. She wanted to run to him. She wanted to throw her arms around him, tell him how incredibly sorry she was, tell him that she missed him.

He walked up to her and kissed her on the mouth, another surprise. She must not weep, she told herself. Hugo was watching them. She could feel his gaze, although the minute she glanced his way, he looked down at the pavement. Luc tried to pat his arm in greeting, but Hugo stepped away from him and Luc ended up patting the air. The three of them stood like that for a moment, off-balance, silent. Then they trooped into the building in single file, like a cartoon family.

Just inside the front door was a steep staircase. Except for the dusty burgundy runner on the stairs, everything was white—the stairwell, the second-floor landing where they took off their shoes, and the small waiting room beyond it. The place reminded Hannah vaguely of her mother-in-law's apartment, except that into this spartan setting someone had introduced paintings, some abstract, others more figurative, all of them in bright, warm colours, set under glass in expensive frames.

Hannah found herself imagining what Luc must be thinking. His hard-earned royalties going to finance office art for a charlatan. A Westmount charlatan.

Mandelbaum himself came out to greet them, which relieved Hannah somewhat. No added cost of a receptionist. Tall and athletic in a plaid flannel shirt, he looked as if he were welcoming them into a backwoods cabin and not into a shrink's office in west-end Montreal. He was around the same age as Luc, and like Luc sported a beard, though his was more black than white. He had cut his hair short, about the same length as his facial hair, and you could see the thinning patches.

"Hi," he said, sticking out his hand first to Hugo and then to Hannah and Luc. When Hannah addressed him as Dr. Mandelbaum, he gestured at her to stop.

"Call me Manny."

Manny Mandelbaum? It was a joke, surely. She glanced at Luc but could not catch his eye.

When they went into his office, there was some confusion over where they were to sit. Mandelbaum had arranged four leather chairs in a circle, and somehow Luc had failed to note the brown cardigan draped over the one facing the door. He sat down in it, tense and serious, and Mandelbaum had to ask him in a polite voice to vacate it. Luc jumped up immediately, apologizing, but when he sat down in another chair he looked disconcerted and resentful.

Mandelbaum handed them each a pen and a clipboard to which a form had been attached. The form was simple enough, thought Hannah. Requests for four pieces of information with spaces below. He wanted her FULL NAME, her ADDRESS, a PHONE NUMBER where she could be reached during the day, and her REASON FOR VISIT.

Most of the page was allotted to the REASON FOR VISIT. Hannah didn't need all that space. She wrote down a single word—*communication*—and passed the sheet back to Mandelbaum, who gave her an approving smile as he took it, as if she'd accomplished something. Luc was still writing. A dense, scrawled REASON FOR VISIT. A crowd of words pouring out of him onto the page. At last his hand stopped.

"It's in French," he said in English, handing over the paper. A rare concession, though Manny Mandelbaum couldn't know that. He rewarded Luc with a smile.

The only thing Hugo wrote was his name.

"Can't think of anything?" Manny Mandelbaum asked.

Hugo shrugged.

"That's okay," he reassured him. "You don't have to write anything if you don't want to. Maybe it will come later." He reached for Hugo's paper.

To Hannah's surprise, Hugo refused to give it up. He nodded at her, clutching the clipboard as if for protection. "I'm here," he said gruffly, "because of her."

Manny Mandelbaum didn't seem perturbed. "Because she asked you to come, you mean?"

Hugo shook his head. "Because she *told* me to."

"That's fine," said Mandelbaum. "It's a reason." He mimed writing, indicating that Hugo should put it down. Which Hugo, frowning, did.

And then they began.

"First," said Manny Mandelbaum, "I'd like to discuss the language issue." He looked directly at Luc. "I'm American, born and raised in California, where I lived my whole life until I came here nine years ago to join the woman who is now my wife. There is a reason I am telling you this. My French is passable. I can converse with waiters and store clerks. But I learned the language late in life. What I'm saying is, my French isn't good enough for me to conduct a therapy session. I work in English." He paused, looking at each of them in turn. "This may be a limitation that one or all of you are not comfortable with."

"I'm okay with it," said Hugo, surprising them all by being the first to speak.

Hannah nodded and said it was fine with her. They all looked at Luc.

Manny Mandelbaum pulled out Luc's sheet and checked his name. "How does that sit with you, Mr. Lévesque?"

Luc made a face. Not a happy face, but not outraged either.

Hannah wondered for a moment whether the use of the word *sit* had confused him. But he waved a hand impatiently.

"We're good to go, then?" asked Mandelbaum.

"Yes, yes, sure," said Luc. He was still looking disgruntled, but Manny Mandelbaum either didn't register this or chose to take him at his word.

"I'd also like to tell you a little about my practice," Mandelbaum continued. His voice was higher than Hannah would have predicted for such a big man, but it was calm and pleasant enough, and he enunciated clearly, which would be a help for Luc. "This is a safe space," he said, indicating the room. "A space where you can say everything you need to say without fear of interruption or reprisal. My job here is to make sure it stays safe. I am not an expert any more than you are. I am not someone who can tell you what to do with your lives, what is wrong or right, or how to be. All I can do is listen. I'm good at that. I've had years and years of practice. And I can help you to listen too, to yourselves, and to each other."

He had a choker around his neck, a rawhide string with three emerald-coloured ceramic beads. He resembled the boys Hannah had gone to high school with—Jewish boys, sons of dentists and lawyers, with a penchant for dressing like lumberjacks. That had been the style back in the seventies: lumberjacks wearing chokers. Mandelbaum had abundant chest hair, as Luc did. Tufts of it were poking through his open collar, the tips licking at the beads.

"Listening is just the first part of the equation," said Mandelbaum. "The overall focus is communication."

Hannah blinked.

Mandelbaum reached behind him and took a dog-eared paperback from his desk. He held it up.

On its cover, "Communication" was printed in white capital letters over a wash of dark colours from which a yellow flower emerged. Another word in pale cursive script was suspended above it.

"Nonviolent communication," said Manny Mandelbaum. "Otherwise known as NVC."

The layout was bad. Mismatched typefaces struggled for ascendancy against a busy background. The eye didn't know which way to look. The flower was distracting. The effect was kitschy, trite, off-putting. Luc shot her a look. He hated things like this: psychological fads and their accompanying how-to manuals. The books were cleverly marketed. They sold well and were rewarded with ever more space in bookstores. Literature was being crowded into dark corners, slowly suffocating at the hands of self-help.

"This approach was developed decades ago," Mandelbaum explained, as if anticipating Luc's reaction. "A psychologist named Rosenberg came up with it in the sixties. He spent his childhood in a rough Detroit neighbourhood. He had an urgent, personal need to find peaceful alternatives to the violence he saw all around him. In the mid-eighties, he founded the Center for Nonviolent Communication."

Luc cleared his throat. "There has been no violence in our family." He paused. "None to speak of."

Hugo chose that moment to look up. Hannah looked at the rug.

"I am sure you're a peaceful man, Mr. Lévesque," Manny

Mandelbaum said, "but I am using the term *violence* in its broadest sense. I'm not just speaking about the physical kind."

"He's lying anyway," Hugo said quietly.

Luc's eyes hardened. "You're one to talk of lying," he said to Hugo quickly in French. Then, keeping his eyes firmly on his son, as if he could silence him by the sheer power of his will, he addressed the therapist. "We are here today because of him," he said, jerking his chin in Hugo's direction, "not me. I agreed to come here only because of your insistence, Dr. Mandelbaum. My wife has told you, I think, that he bought a gun and carried it inside his school?"

Hugo crossed his arms over his chest.

Once again, Manny Mandelbaum held up both hands. "Look, you are each going to get a chance to speak. I promise you. I just want to finish my introduction, so you know what you're in for. Is this okay with everyone?"

Luc made a show of listening. He folded his left hand into his right, and then he squeezed. Hard, as if cracking a nut. It was an unconscious gesture, a gesture Hannah had seen many times before, a gesture that made her heart sink. Manny Mandelbaum described his method. Basic human needs. The perfectly natural strategies we use to get them. Core values. Hannah found it impossible to take it all in. She was watching Luc's hands. His fingertips had gone dark from the pressure he was exerting. His knuckles had whitened.

Mandelbaum fell silent. He bent forward and pulled something from under his chair. A piece of wood. This got everyone's attention. The wood was almost black, mahogany or something. It looked varnished. It had two blunt ends and a small indentation in the middle, where Mandelbaum held it between thumb and forefinger.

"The talking stick," he said, holding it up for everyone to see. "We'll go around the circle. Only the person holding this stick is permitted to speak. That is the sole rule you have to remember. The others must listen until that person is completely done. Then, and only then, will the person pass the stick back to me."

Luc was no longer even looking at the therapist. His fingertips were still purple. Hannah sat there wondering what she would do if he stormed out. She was caught off-guard when Mandelbaum held the stick out to her.

"You start."

Her face went hot. She really didn't want to—not after the fiasco at the school. But Mandelbaum had pressed the stick into her hands. Her fingers curled around it. It still bore the warmth of his touch. Luc was watching her. His contempt—for this place, for this New Age shaman she had forced him to consult, for her—was palpable. She could feel herself shrinking before it.

"It's okay, Hannah," said Mandelbaum encouragingly. "Safe space, remember?"

Hannah took a deep breath. It didn't feel safe. But she was the one who had put this in motion. She was the reason they had come to this office. She couldn't refuse.

"Why don't you start by telling us why you're here?" Mandelbaum suggested.

She stared at the tufts of chest hair poking out of his shirt. She wanted to cooperate. Truly, she did, but the words were hanging back, cowering like shy children. The last time she'd spoken, Luc had walked out on her. She didn't know if he'd ever return.

"I—" she began, and then closed her mouth. She looked up from Mandelbaum's chest. His eyes were hazel. The left one had a dab of blue. A pretty colour, she thought. A recessive gene speaking out. Without warning, tears were pouring out of her. She hid her face in her hands. She knew without looking that Luc would be mortified. Her son too. Not half as mortified as she was.

Mandelbaum held out a box of tissues. She blew her nose and pulled herself together, then picked up the stick again, gripping it tightly in both hands. She looked again into Manny Mandelbaum's strangely coloured eyes and began to speak. Not about Hugo. Not even about Luc, although she was devastated by what was happening in their marriage. What she found herself talking about was her father, this colossal presence in her life whose words had so recently and cruelly been extinguished.

Mandelbaum listened, never taking his blue-brown eyes off her, holding out the Kleenex box when she needed it.

"Sounds to me like a heavy time," Mandelbaum said when she paused.

Heavy time. What a throwback. She hoped Luc's English was too poor for him to notice. He was looking out the window, probably wishing he was anywhere but here.

Manny Mandelbaum smiled at her, the blue in his eyes gleaming like a little patch of sky. He leaned forward and reached out a hand, and for a crazy second Hannah imagined he might stroke her thigh. But the hand stopped in front of the stick on her lap. "Are you finished with that, Hannah?"

"Oh, yes," she said, giving the talking stick back to him. "Yes, of course. I'm sorry."

Luc crossed his arms, tossing his head when Mandelbaum

held the stick out to him. "I do not need that. I do not need a stick to speak."

Hannah was surprised at how thick his accent was. It was much stronger than she remembered. But in truth, she couldn't actually recall the last time she'd heard him speak English.

Empty-handed, he told the story of the gun, and the suspension, and the disciplinary hearing. No mention of her outburst or her exchange with the head of the parents' committee. It was Hugo who received the brunt of his anger.

"He lied," said Luc. "You want violence in a broad sense, Dr. Mandelbaum? Telling a lie in public to your own father. Bringing shame on him. This is violence."

"Sounds to me," Mandelbaum said, "like honesty is one of your core values."

"It is a value for most people," Luc snapped. "Not for you, Dr. Mandelbaum? Not for my son, either, I think."

"I wouldn't be too sure about that," said Mandelbaum. "In my experience, sons are frequently similar to their fathers. Hugo may very well attach a lot of importance to being honest."

Luc exhaled audibly. "Not my son. I do not think so."

"In this instance," said Mandelbaum, "he may just have valued something else more. You say another boy was involved?"

"Vladimir," said Hugo, taking all three of them by surprise.

Mandelbaum held out the stick, which, again to everyone's surprise, Hugo took.

"Hey," Luc objected. "You ask me the question, no?"

"I did," said Manny Mandelbaum. "That is true. Is it all right if your son speaks?"

Hugo leaned back in his chair, rolling his eyes. "I don't need his fucking permission."

Luc's eyes hardened. *"Voilà,"* he said. *"La violence.* He cannot articulate a single sentence without these, how do you say, *gros mots?"*

Mandelbaum crossed his legs. "Do you mind if Hugo takes a turn? I think it's important, Mr. Lévesque. He has something to say."

Hugo leaned his elbows on his knees and rolled the stick between his palms. Despite his claim about not needing permission, he did not speak until his father nodded.

"I wasn't going to rat him out."

"No," agreed Mandelbaum. "Vladimir was the student who sold you the gun, correct?"

Hugo nodded.

"It belongs to the father," Luc broke in. "The boy stole it. They are alike, this Vladimir and my son. Two drops of water."

Mandelbaum nodded at Hugo's hands. "He's got the stick now, Mr. Lévesque. It may seem arbitrary, but it's important." He turned back to Hugo. "Go on, Hugo. Please continue."

But Hugo had apparently said all he was going to say. He passed the stick back to Mandelbaum. As he let go of it, however, he turned to his father. "I'm not a liar, for your information. I just don't like to rat."

Hannah saw uncertainty on her husband's face. She began to translate: *"Il ne voulait tout simplement pas—"*

Luc gestured dismissively. "I know what he say."

"What I'm hearing," Manny Mandelbaum broke in, turning his clear, calm gaze on Hugo, "is that loyalty is really important to you right now. Loyalty and honour. In some cases, these values might be more important than honesty, especially at school."

Hugo was staring at the rug, but his body language suddenly changed. His arms loosened. His shoulders released and dropped an inch or two.

"He lied," Luc said angrily. "To me. To his father. Not just to some teacher at the school."

"No," said Mandelbaum, unfazed. "The adults he spoke to first, right after being caught with the gun, were at the school, if I understand correctly. From then on, Mr. Lévesque, the story was set. By the time he spoke to you, he couldn't have changed it if he'd wanted to."

Mandelbaum's point was a sound one. Hugo spoke again. "He's Russian."

"Who is?" said Mandelbaum. "Vladimir, you mean?"

Hugo nodded. "He's not French."

Luc made a noise with his throat. "It is not important where he comes from. He is a troublemaker, Vladimir. A thief. And a liar, like you."

"That's enough," said Mandelbaum sharply.

"But it's the truth," said Luc. His face was flushed, his eyes sparking. The d'Aulaires' Zeus, thought Hannah. Lightning bolts were about to fly. "Truth is good, no?" he thundered. "It's better than a lie?"

"Not necessarily," said Mandelbaum. "In Hugo's case, at least, lying was understandable."

Hannah glanced at Luc, who looked ready to explode.

"Understandable?" he cried. "I don't believe what I am hearing! He lied to me. To his own father!"

"Yes," said Manny Mandelbaum.

"It is unacceptable."

"You find it unacceptable?"

"This is what I just say. Yes."

"And why is that?"

Hannah winced. Either Mandelbaum failed to see how angry Luc was, or he had a strategy she could not fathom. She'd rarely seen her husband so irate.

"Do you always repeat the words of others like an echo?" Luc asked coldly.

"And you, Mr. Lévesque," Mandelbaum answered, "do you always speak so loudly, interrupting the words of others?"

There was a pause during which time seemed to stop. Mandelbaum's chin was jutting aggressively. Hannah didn't dare look at Luc.

"I didn't interrupt you," Luc said, his voice cool. Almost nonchalant.

"Not me," Mandelbaum said. "Your wife and son. You've cut them off repeatedly."

"You mean I did not have the stick."

Hannah felt sick. She couldn't take much more.

"I do not care about the stick," Luc said. "The stick is *entière-ment idiot.*"

Mandelbaum's hands made a birdlike movement as if they were wings. He waved them at Hannah. "Aren't you even curious to hear what Hannah has to say?"

"I know what she will say," said Luc. "We are married. We talk all the time. We do not need a third party to help with this."

Hannah shook her head.

"Your wife appears not to agree," said Mandelbaum.

"So you speak for her now?" He turned to her. "He speaks for you? *Vas-y. Parle.*"

But Hannah couldn't. Even with her husband so obviously in the wrong, she couldn't open her mouth.

Luc began to speak in French. Rapidly. Not caring if Mandelbaum could follow; hoping, probably, that he couldn't. He looked straight at the psychologist and in a cold rage let the words fly.

Honesty was one of his foremost values. How could it not be? He was a writer. He had dedicated his entire life to the truth. You couldn't be ambivalent about something like this if you were an artist, but even as a plain human being it was the same. Either it was important or it was not. When a person lied, either that was a bad thing or it was okay. Never both, as Mandelbaum seemed to imply. That was the trouble with the world today. People no longer believed in things. There were no values anymore, nothing was absolute. Luc had absolute values, and honesty was one of them. Always and everywhere, truth was better than falsehood. Any other way of seeing things was contemptible. Dr. Mandelbaum held truth to be a relative value? That was his prerogative as a thinking member of the human race, so long as he kept this thought to himself. But he wasn't capable of that, was he? No, Dr. Mandelbaum felt entitled to share his views with the world. No, not share them, impose them. He had the gall to preach his moral relativism to a fourteen-year-old boy. What kind of therapy was that?

Luc leaned toward the therapist. Nonviolence? Was there not violence in encouraging a boy to lie?

"These are lives you are playing with, Dr. Mandelbaum," Luc said, "not just hypothetical cases. Your words have consequences."

Mandelbaum's silence was like a goad to Luc. Therapists were parasites, he continued. They were the real liars. Fraudsters, all of them, preying on the sick and the troubled, the credulous. They were the false priests of a false god at whose altar weak people knelt down and rose up again relieved of their money, not their troubles.

Hannah knew where this was coming from. In the aftermath of Roland Lévesque's suicide, Lyse had taken her sons to a succession of psychotherapists. All were well-meaning; all did what they could. But none could extinguish the fire of humiliation and rage burning in Luc. If anything, their efforts, like his mother's despair, stoked the flames. That fire had turned him into an artist. She had never pointed this out to him, of course. But in her mind, it wasn't an entirely bad thing.

Mandelbaum listened in silence to Luc's tirade. After it finished, he asked, straight-faced, if Luc would repeat it again for him ... in English.

Luc's jaw went slack.

"I am sorry," Mandelbaum said. "I want to understand."

Luc cleared his throat. "How long have you lived here, may I ask, Dr. Mandelbaum?" He was still speaking French. When there was no answer, he repeated the question a second time, his voice very quiet and low. "How long have you made your life in this city?" Then he stood up, looming over them. His face was pale and composed, deeply regal.

"Did you fail to notice that the language we speak here is French? You are not a prisoner, after all. You can go back to California any time you wish. You can move to New York, or Toronto, or Halifax, or Calgary, all very pleasant locations. But if you stay in this one, if you choose to live in my city, in my nation, you will have the courtesy to speak to me in my language. Or you will not speak to me at all."

Luc nodded curtly at Mandelbaum and then, without a glance at his wife or son, walked out of the room. They listened to his proud footsteps descending the stairs, neither hurried nor slow; they heard the front door open and close. And then there was silence.

"Well," said Manny Mandelbaum.

"It's a sensitive issue," Hannah replied. She was about to say more when Hugo got to his feet.

"It's not sensitive. It's bullshit." He hitched up his oversized pants and shuffled to the door.

Hannah opened her mouth to say something, but Mandelbaum raised a hand to stop her. And Hugo went out, following in his father's footsteps.

"That's that, I guess," Mandelbaum said as the front door shut once more.

"I'm sorry," said Hannah.

"I'm the one who should apologize. That really got away from me."

"I should have warned you. It's an issue right now," she said, thinking of Hugo's recent embrace of all things English.

"I kind of figured that out." He paused to place the mahogany stick on his desk. "How do you guys manage it at home, if I might ask? You're an Anglo, right?"

"Right."

"Hugo too."

"No," she said, and then changed her mind. "He was brought

up in French, but of course he speaks English. It's impossible to avoid in Montreal."

"You'd want him to avoid it?"

"No," she said. But the truth was too complicated to reduce to a simple yes or no. She saw Mandelbaum waiting for her to explain, but fatigue seized her: deep fatigue that made it impossible to think, let alone explain something as complex as being an English-speaking woman married to Luc Lévesque.

She gazed at him hopelessly. The real truth was that she was feeling sick with regret. She'd come here hoping to set things right again. Or at least to take a stab at it. To reopen communications with her husband, to patch up relations with her son. To undo, in other words, the damage she'd caused at the hearing. Instead, she'd made it worse.

"Hannah?"

Her eyelids opened. Manny Mandelbaum was kneeling on the floor beside her chair, a concerned expression on his face. What had just happened? Had she drifted to sleep?

He repeated her name, his voice strangely slow, as if he were distorting it with one of those gimmicky sound-altering machines. "Are you okay?" He got to his feet and went to fetch her a glass of water. After a few sips, she surprised herself by talking again. She talked about the hearing, recounting her version of what had happened, including all the bits Luc had left out.

"So you stood up for your son," Mandelbaum said when she stopped for air. "Sounds right to me. Entirely appropriate."

"But you don't understand," she protested. "Luc was supposed to do the talking. That was what we'd agreed. He knows the school and the religious order that founded it. He used to be a student there himself, and besides, he's good at that kind of thing. I'm not. And this was in French, don't forget."

"Well, your speaking out doesn't seem to have done any harm," Mandelbaum observed. "Hugo was accepted back, wasn't he?"

She nodded, sniffling. To her embarrassment, her tears had returned.

"I don't understand," said Mandelbaum. "What's so wrong with what you did? A lot of parents would have done the same."

An image of Alfred Stern flashed before her, not old and shrunken as he was now, but the way he'd been before, back when they'd been living under the same roof. She shook her head, trying to chase the spectre away.

Mandelbaum shook his head too, his eyes full of questions. "What is it, Hannah?"

She looked away.

"If ever you want to …" he said, but he let the sentence trail off, searching her face. "I don't just work with teenagers, you know."

She hadn't known. But she was feeling more solid now, solid enough to know that certain stories must stay where they belonged. She reached for her purse. "Don't take this personally, Dr. Mandelbaum, but I've got to leave now too." She scrabbled at the purse's bottom in search of her chequebook. "Eighty dollars, right?"

Mandelbaum waved his hand. "Forget it."

"What do you mean?"

"Under the circumstances."

"No," said Hannah. "We've taken your time."

"It's really okay."

She put the chequebook away. He felt as bad as she did, just as responsible. Luc had been wrong. Despite his funny-sounding name, this was a good man.

"I could refer you to someone else," he said as she got up. "A francophone, if that would help with Luc. She also practises NVC. She's very good."

Hannah took down the name of the French-speaking therapist, knowing she'd never call her.

"Listen," Mandelbaum said as he walked her to the door, "if you ever need to talk—you alone, Hannah—you have my number." From his cluttered desktop he picked up the book he had held up earlier. "And please take this along," he said, pressing it into her hands. "There's stuff in here that might help."

Hannah slipped it into her bag. She didn't have the energy to refuse.

PART TWO

11

The corridors were empty as Hugo made his way up from the lockers in the school's basement. Bits of paper and debris littered the floor. He swung his foot and kicked a brown paper lunch bag that someone had scrunched into a ball. It flew down the corridor and rolled along the tiles as far as his homeroom door. He sighed. School was a weird place at this time of the day. An urge to shout rose up in him, but he repressed it, pursing his lips and forcing his feet to move.

The door to the classroom was partially open—Vien's sign that he should enter—but Hugo didn't do this right away. He peeked through the crack. He knew he was late, he knew Vien would be pissed. Vien didn't notice him right off. He was totally engrossed in a mural he was making out of spray-painted cornflakes. In it, a gigantic Iroquois hunter was holding out a fur pelt—a real one—to an equally gigantic coureur de bois. All the kids in Hugo's homeroom had joked about the cornflakes today. The mural looked impressive, though. The cornflakes actually gave the figures texture and substance. Open House was coming up on Friday, and this bizarre breakfast-cereal creation was the history department's contribution. The whole event made Hugo sad. All these hopeful little kids swarming through the school while Bonnaire (Boner, in Hugo's private lexicon) and Vien and the rest of them smiled their fake smiles, trying to entice them to enroll. It was all such a show.

Vien finally turned and saw him. He frowned. "I've been waiting for you," he said, walking to the door, his eyes gazing in two directions at once. "I almost left."

Hugo glanced up at the clock. Classes had ended over an hour ago. He'd made the mistake of stepping outside for air. A guy from his homeroom had offered him a smoke.

"You're lucky I had things to do." Vien pointed at the mural. He had glued the pelt to the Iroquois hunter's hand.

"You can touch it if you want," he said.

Hugo reached out, but the glue hadn't dried yet and the pelt came off in his hands.

"Damn," said Monsieur Vien. "It's too heavy, that's the problem." He began rummaging in his desk while Hugo stood beside the mural, clutching the animal skin. The fur on it was long and surprisingly coarse. "It's goat, not beaver," Vien said. "Don't tell anyone."

His tone was friendly, at least.

"It's the only skin I own," he said, and then smiled. "Except this." He pinched a fold of his own hairy forearm below his rolled-up sleeve. "My ex's uncle has a farm near Rigaud," he explained. "Goats and maple syrup."

He had found a box of tacks, the kind with round coloured tops resembling Smarties. "White's best, I guess. Less eye-catching." He took the pelt and tacked it to the wall, and once again the hunter held it out to the white man. One of the fluorescent tubes on the ceiling began to flicker. Hugo and Monsieur Vien both looked up.

"Got to fix that," Vien said, frowning. "I read somewhere that they disrupt your brainwaves." He made a goonish face and laughed—a honking laugh.

Hugo looked away. Vien was trying too hard.

"How's your father?" he asked after a few awkward seconds.

Hugo didn't respond.

"Okaaaay," said Vien. "Clearly, you think it's acceptable to show up an hour late on your first day back. No apology, no explanation. Not even a pretense of manners. You think I'm going to put up with that?" He reached out quickly and took hold of Hugo's chin. Bits of glue that had hardened on his fingertips now dug into Hugo's face. "Think again."

Hugo jerked himself free. Vien wasn't supposed to touch him: another of Saint-Jean's many rules. "What are you going to do?" he said, moving out of his teacher's reach. "Call my father?"

Vien smiled disagreeably. "Good plan. I can say I've washed my hands of you and you've been expelled. Like Vladimir. Would you prefer that?"

Hugo's face reddened. Heat shot upward from his neck to his hairline.

"I thought not."

But part of Hugo wished he *had* been kicked out. Certainly after what they'd done to Vlad. "It isn't fair," he said.

"What? That Vladimir got turfed out and you didn't? There were other considerations with that boy, believe me."

"Right," said Hugo indignantly. "Like his foreign name."

Vien frowned. "You can't possibly believe we're that small-minded."

Hugo kept his mouth shut this time. He wouldn't fall into Vien's trap. He crossed his arms defensively.

"Vladimir wasn't expelled because he was Russian, Hugo. He was expelled because he's a troublemaker. This wasn't the first time he'd been called in for disciplinary action, as you surely know. And you weren't spared because of your father." He paused. "Or not only because of your father. I'll admit that knowing him made it easier for me to vouch for you."

Hugo looked away. The way Vien was talking made him feel physically sick. It was as if prejudice were all right, something Saint-Jean-Baptiste could allow to happen with a clear conscience. He hated this place. Downstairs, near the front entrance, there was a huge crucifix with a plaster Christ hanging off it. A bogus Jesus for a bogus school.

Vien wasn't looking at him anymore. He was rummaging through the clutter on his desk.

He handed three sheets of small print to Hugo, now seated beside him. "For you." It was a *contrat social* in triplicate. "Sit down," he said, motioning beside him at a chair. Finally he found what he was looking for. The contract was one of Bonnaire's clever ideas for improving the school—or at least for making its students more obedient. Whenever a kid was found guilty of an offence, he had to sign one.

Hugo looked over the first copy. A list of don'ts, followed by a list of dos, laid out in bullet form. First, the don'ts. Henceforth, Hugo would have to

- refrain from committing acts of violence of any
  kind for the remainder of his studies at Collège
  Saint-Jean-Baptiste;
- refrain from bringing weapons onto, or carrying
  weapons on, school premises at any time for the
  remainder of his studies;
- refrain from contacting former Saint-Jean-Baptiste
  student Vladimir Petrofsky;
- refrain from getting into trouble of any kind for the
  remainder of the academic year.

And then the dos. Hugo would have to

- complete all of his school work;
- maintain a grade average of at least seventy percent for
  the remainder of the academic year;
- visit Monsieur Vien every day after school for the rest
  of the semester;
- write an essay on the theme of violence to be submitted
  by Christmas break;
- consult an expert and undergo social-psychological
  assessment.

Hugo scowled. Who did Boner think he was, dictating who
his friends could be, forcing him to see a shrink? He folded the
sheets in two.

Vien stopped him before he could shove them in his bag.
"You have to sign," he said. Vien picked up a pen. "Here."

Hugo refused to take it.

"Did you not hear me? You have to sign."

Hugo took a step backward. No way he'd stoop to such indignity.

"Don't be stupid, Hugo."

Hugo pointed to the bottom of the first copy, where the parties to the contract were identified. "That's wrong."

Monsieur Vien stared at him blankly.

"It's not my name."

Vien looked at the sheets, which he'd laid flat on his desk, and then back at Hugo. "It's what's in the register, Hugo. As far as this school is concerned, this is who you are."

Hugo shrugged. The school could go screw itself. They wanted to make him miserable with all kinds of restrictions like he was some sort of little criminal? Then they should be clear on who they were making miserable. "My name's Hugh Stern."

There was a pause as Vien pushed his glasses higher on his nose. "Why are you doing this? Because of Vladimir? Don't be an idiot."

Hugo was not an idiot. Nor was he blind. He'd seen how the Russians were treated in the school—all of them. And the Iranians. Anyone who spoke any language other than French.

"You know," said Vien, his voice a little gentler, "your name's not so bad, Hugo." He smiled, his eyebrows joining to form a hairy arch. "René Lévesque," he said, bobbing reverently. "Your dad. It's a pretty amazing club, if you ask me."

Hugo looked out the window. Darkness was falling, and the glass had turned reflective. Instead of the sky, his own frowning face, yellowish in the indoor light, stared back at him.

"I'm serious, Hugo," said Vien. "It's not so bad."

"Neither is Stern."

"No," said Vien. "Your mother's name is perfectly fine as well."

"Not my mother's. She changed it. My grandfather's."

Vien nodded. "It's a fine thing to respect your grandfather, Hugo. But just think for a moment. Lévesque is the name your parents gave you. The name you've had since birth. You can't just throw it away on a whim."

Hugo bit the insides of his cheeks. He must not speak. Not one more word. This was no whim. Vien was a hypocrite. They all were. Even his mother, the so-called feminist, who had tossed out her entire heritage for a man.

Vien sighed. "This is how it happens. Every time. You've heard of the *Acadiens*, right, Hugo? In New Orleans, people call them Cajuns. None of them speaks a word of French anymore. Well, maybe a word. But not much more than that. Same thing in western Canada. Manitoba, Saskatchewan. Those provinces used to have real French communities. Thriving ones. Now it's just a few old people speaking a language their children couldn't be bothered to learn. Soon they'll be dead, and then it will be over. And the worst part of it is, they have no one to blame but themselves." He paused to wipe his glasses. "Your father loves his language. Is that such a bad thing?"

Above them, the fluorescent tube flickered and hummed.

Vien walked to the door and cut the power to the dud light. Shadows crowded in.

"He and I were like brothers, you know."

Hugo looked at Monsieur Vien's dark face. His anger was fading, just like the light outside. For the first time, he stopped wanting to get away.

"During our first two years at Saint-Jean, we were both day students, but in grade nine I became a boarder. That was when

I started hanging out with your dad." Vien blinked. Without glasses, his eyes looked vulnerable, like a mole's. "Grade nine was the year we both lost our fathers."

Hugo's breath went slow. He did his best to remain still, not that it seemed to matter. Vien wasn't really talking to him anyway.

"My dad didn't die," Vien said quietly. "He just left. We didn't know where. I later learned he'd been living in Maine. A little town called Belfast ... But that's a whole other story. When I was in high school, all I knew was that he was gone. And Luc's father was gone too."

He glanced quickly at Hugo. "You've heard about that, I presume?"

Hugo nodded. His grandfather had committed suicide. His mother had told him the story just after he turned eleven.

"So, there I was," Vien continued, "sent away by a mother who could no longer cope. Living by myself in a tiny bedroom on the third floor of the east wing. You don't really know that part of the school. It's closed off now. Used for storage. The experience could have shattered me. But it didn't, because I had a friend named Luc Lévesque. I kept running away to your grandmother's house. She'd always feed me a hot meal, and your father would set me straight. He didn't have to say anything. It was enough that he knew what I was going through. He was going through it too. Two boys without fathers."

He fell silent. When he looked up, his expression had changed. "You happen to have a father, Hugo. Let's not lose sight of that fact." He pushed the contract across the desk to Hugo. "Sign."

Hugo shook his head. What had happened to his dad thirty-five years ago had nothing to do with this. But his mind hovered for a moment over his grandfather. He knew about the suicide, sure, but somehow he'd never imagined his dad as being part of that event. He'd never stopped to wonder what it had been like.

He would not take the pen Monsieur Vien was holding out to him—a cheap ballpoint, its end chewed into splinters.

"Come on, Hugo. This is ridiculous."

Hugo shook his head. Vien didn't know his dad. Not deep down like Hugo did.

"Okay," said Vien, visibly pissed off. "If I put 'Hugh Stern' in here and delete 'Hugo Lévesque,' you'll sign?"

Hugo stared at him. Was this a trick? He nodded, tentative.

"Once you do, however, that's it. You understand that, don't you, Hugo? No backtracking. No more changes."

When Hugo still didn't answer, Vien got in his face. "Do you understand?"

"Yes."

Without another word, Vien made the change by hand on all three copies of the contract. It looked messy—a big slash with the new name scribbled in a hurry underneath. "There you go," he said, clearing a space on the desk.

Writing a name was not the same as saying it. The new signature felt awkward to Hugo. It looked awkward too—the unpractised scrawl of a child. Not that Vien seemed to notice. Hugo had to sign all three copies. The instant he was done, Vien gathered them up and stuffed them in his drawer.

"Now we can discuss your project."

Hugo looked at him, unsure what he was talking about.

"Two thousand words," said Vien, shutting the drawer with a bang, as if the contracts might run off like bad mice. "On violence. A vast topic. You could do anything, basically. Within reason." He walked over to a filing cabinet beneath his window and raised one of the long metal flaps to get at the drawers. "Does al Qaeda interest you? I've been collecting clippings ever since 9/11. I've got a fair-sized collection on bin Laden."

"I'm not a *mujahid*," Hugo said. It was a term he'd learned recently from CNN.

"I'm not saying you are," said Vien, impressed.

"People died in the Twin Towers attacks."

"Yes, they did."

Hugo looked down at his shoes. They were badly scuffed. He hated his uniform, hated the fact that you could get a detention if Boner caught you walking down the hall wearing the wrong shoes, or even wearing an undershirt under the scratchy school polo.

"I'm not saying it has anything to do with you."

Hugo resisted looking up. He was staring at two tiny letters, an *H* and an *S*, that he had carved into his black leather toes. From over at the filing cabinet, Vien was watching him. Hugo could feel his eyes. "Not necessarily, anyway," said Vien.

Did he think Hugo was violent, one of those misfits who shot up their schools, like Eric Harris and Dylan Klebold at Columbine High? Hugo had been pretty intrigued by that story. He was eleven years old when it happened, just about to enter high school. He'd watched the reports over and over on the news, trying to imagine what he would do if someone tried something like that at the college he was planning to attend.

He sat up in his chair. Vien was still watching him. Hugo scowled.

Vien came back to the desk and busied himself with a fat binder of papers. "I've got to do some photocopying. Look through my files in the cabinet, Hugo. I'm sure you'll find something of interest. I'll be back in half an hour and we can talk."

After Vien left, Hugo continued to sit for a while. Stacks of assignments filled every millimetre of space on the surface of Vien's desk. Vien's papers and notes were strewn about in no discernible order. Hugo flipped a binder open and found pages of lectures written out in Vien's inimitable scrawl. Some were so ancient they'd turned yellow. He'd been at this a long, long time, old Vien. It seemed like a shitty life. Slightly less shitty than being a student, though, because at least a teacher could choose. Monsieur Vien could. He could pack up his briefcase any time and leave.

Hugo looked longingly out the window. He could leave too, of course. Walk right out of here, never to return. Transform himself into a street kid or something. Find an abandoned warehouse down near the canal. The nights were turning cold, but kids still did it. Kids around his age. He'd seen them outside the metro stations with their scruffy dogs and squeegees, begging for spare change.

A picture on Vien's desk caught his eye, the lone photograph sitting among the piles of papers. A young man smiled out at him. It took Hugo a second to recognize Vien. Happy-looking, his arm encircling an equally young ponytailed blond woman. She was not smiling. She was very sexy, though, her breasts bulging out of a low-cut white blouse. His wife? Hugo glanced at the clock. Seven minutes had gone by. He forced himself over to the filing cabinet.

When Monsieur Vien returned, some forty minutes later, Hugo was sitting at the back of the room at his own desk, totally absorbed.

Monsieur Vien deposited his papers and came to see what he was reading. The clippings were from the seventies, many of them as brittle as dried leaves. Vien picked up the article Hugo had been looking at. The photograph accompanying the newspaper article showed a bearded young man with hooded eyes.

"Jacques Lanctôt," Vien said, surprised. Then, proudly, "I met him once, you know." When Hugo looked up, Vien was smiling. "The last of the big-time dreamers. He still believes. After everything he's been through."

Beneath that clipping was another one with a group photo. Lanctôt was front and centre, clean-shaven and looking a little older. The headline was "Off to Cuba." Everyone in the picture, including two women at the edge of the group, was holding a cigar. The article dated back to the early eighties. There had been some kind of literary exchange between Montreal and Havana.

Standing next to Lanctôt, looking serious in a black turtle-neck, was Hugo's father. His hair was black, tied in a ponytail just like Lanctôt's. He was considerably taller than Lanctôt, but with their hair and colouring, the two men could have been brothers.

Vien laughed. "Your dad knows him personally too. Many writers in Quebec do. Lanctôt's a publisher. He published your father's poetry before he became famous."

Hugo felt his cheeks warm.

"Lanctôt isn't violent, Hugo, if that's what you're about to suggest. I did a lot of research on him. This," he said, pointing at the fat file on Hugo's desk, "is from my master's thesis. Lanctôt's group called itself the Liberation Cell. They were kids, basically.

Young intellectuals defending an ideal. Utopians, every one of them. If there was violence in the FLQ, it was in the Chenier Cell: the Rose brothers and Francis Simard." He looked at Hugo. "You've heard of them?"

"They're the ones who killed the labour minister, Pierre Laporte."

Vien shook his head, making a face. "Laporte was found dead," he corrected. "No one's entirely sure how it happened. He was discovered strangled in the trunk of an abandoned car on the South Shore. Members of the Chenier Cell were charged with murder and did time in jail. Paul Rose got life, even though it was later proven that he wasn't present when Laporte died. But Lanctôt? He had nothing to do with all of that. He was a teacher, Hugo. A thinker. A man of dreams. At a certain point, those dreams led him to acts that might be considered extreme, but not to murder. Not to violence. All he did was hold a British diplomat named James Cross hostage."

"Trade commissioner," corrected Hugo.

Vien smiled. "Okay. Trade commissioner. They're just words, Hugo. It amounts to the same thing. Although it was a clever tactic on the part of the British to couch imperialism in the language of commerce. We weren't the only place where they did that, by the way. Ever heard of the East India Company?" He put the article about Lanctôt back on top of the pile, covering up Hugo's father. "Anyway, Cross survived, right? He walked away unharmed."

The radiator behind them banged and then settled, making Hugo jump. Vien didn't actually believe there'd been no harm, did he? Cross had been held at gunpoint for fifty-nine days. All through the autumn of 1970.

"It was a different time, Hugo," Vien said, his upper lip moist from the warmth of the room. "You have to see it in context. You couldn't speak French at work back then, not even to a fellow francophone. We were second-class citizens in our own home."

For the next half hour, Vien tried to convince him that Lanctôt was a victim of history and of the Canadian government, a man who dreamed of a better society. Surely, that was no crime. He wanted to protect his language and his culture. For this, he was exiled and eventually imprisoned. Hugo's father knew and liked him. All kinds of Quebec writers did. There was absolutely nothing wrong with the man. He had the courage to stand up for his beliefs, that was all.

Hugo slouched against the wall, staring at his scuffed shoes as Monsieur Vien expounded. Vien walked over to a dusty bookshelf near the door and pulled out a book, *Nègres blancs d'Amérique*, by someone called Pierre Vallières.

"Read this before you cast aspersions," he said. "The Québécois are a peaceful people. Jacques Lanctôt never had any intention to do anyone harm. And he didn't end up doing harm. James Cross walked out of that room in Montreal North without a scratch. That's worth bearing in mind."

Hugo stopped listening. It was clear that Vien had his theory. And that this theory was not to be challenged. He didn't want Hugo's thoughts on the matter. He wanted his own view of history handed back to him. Word for word. Good luck with that.

Vien talked for several minutes more before dismissing him. Hugo couldn't look at him. He gathered up his things as quickly as he could and left the classroom.

At the school's main door, Hugo stopped to shove the book Vien had lent him into his knapsack. "White Niggers of

America." What a title. He stepped outside. It was depressingly dark. He hated how early the light disappeared now. It must be past five. He thought fleetingly of his mother, who would be waiting at home.

His first day back at Saint-Jean-Baptiste, and now this after-hours session with Vien, had worn him out. Was this what his life would be for the rest of the term? The year? From class to detention. Detention to home. His days as regimented as a prisoner's. He'd speak the language they dictated, write essays on topics they decreed, describe the world not as he saw it, but as they did, so they could tell themselves it wasn't all arbitrary, that there was some kind of meaning out there. It was pathetic. They'd even deprived him of his friend.

He kicked at a pile of dead leaves and swore, thinking of Vlad, missing him. Vlad would have cracked a joke, made him laugh at the absurdity. "Fuck it," he said again, more loudly, right there on the school's front steps. "Fuck it. Fuck it. Fuck it." His fatigue was gone now. His body felt springy, alive. He could have run straight up the mountain. He could have bench-pressed his own weight. *"Fuck it. Fuck it."* He was yelling now, throwing English obscenities into the darkening sky. He wished his father were here. He'd shout in his fucking French face.

He looked around the yard, remembering the crazy man who hung around the Guy-Concordia metro station whom everyone called *l'hurleur*, "the screamer." No one had heard Hugo, fortunately. He walked down the path leading to Sherbrooke Street.

At the gates, he stopped and pulled his cell phone from his pocket. Without giving himself a moment to think, he pressed the speed-dial button.

Vlad didn't sound surprised, although it had been two weeks

since they'd spoken. "Where are you?" he said, as he always did. His substitute for a hello.

Hugo looked behind him at the Saint-Jean ramparts. It was too awkward mentioning school. "Downtown," he said gruffly.

"You with someone?"

"No," said Hugo. "You?"

"Nope. You're timing's good, my friend."

Hugo smiled and announced he was on his way. Screw the contract. How would they ever find out where he'd gone? And if they did, how would they stop him from doing it again? Put an ankle bracelet on him? He wasn't some sex offender in Florida. Hugo hugged his arms and began walking west toward Vlad's place. He'd only taken a few strides when the lamps lit up all the way down Sherbrooke Street, like lights in a harbour guiding ships to shore. He decided to take it as a sign.

Vlad's high-rise was on Fort Street, two blocks from the school. His parents were separated and he lived alone with his dad. Hugo had never met the dad, though, because he was always out working. In Russia, he'd been a math teacher, but here in Quebec the only job he could find was house painting. And he seemed to do it day and night. It was a temporary thing, according to Vlad, although they'd lived in Montreal for over a decade.

Vlad buzzed him in, and seconds later they were grinning at each other in his front hall. For some reason, the lights were off. "Were you sleeping?" Hugo asked in English, squinting, but still unable to see.

Vlad shook his head and wiggled his thumbs, miming a game controller. Then he reached an arm behind Hugo and turned on a light. "Whoa," he said, noticing Hugo's pants. "You're back in?"

Hugo reddened. He'd forgotten he was wearing his uniform.

"As of today," he said, looking at the floor, embarrassed, because Vlad hadn't found a place yet that would take him.

Vlad scratched his head, shaved commando-style like Hugo's. His eyes were like a cat's, half shut and sleepy even when he was alert. He motioned Hugo to drop his bag, and they went into the living room, where *Grand Theft Auto* was on Pause on an enormous flat plasma screen.

"Take a seat," said Vlad, grinning again and offering Hugo a controller before sitting down in an armchair whose shabbiness contrasted starkly with the sleek technological wonder in the centre of the room.

Hugo sat on the sofa, which was as ancient as Vlad's chair. He kept his jacket on, preferring to keep his school shirt covered. Not that Vlad seemed to mind anymore. His cat eyes didn't waver from the screen.

"Choose your weapon." His voice sounded totally normal, no innuendo or even a hint of irony, but Hugo still felt the sting of it, remembering the last time he'd been here.

It seemed like eons ago, although it had hardly been a month. The weather had been warm and humid, the air sour with smog. Vlad had brought him into his father's den, the innermost sanctum of this palace of forbidden pleasures, and given him his first glimpse of the real thing.

Mr. Petrofsky had been in the Russian army. He was a marksman, but now he only shot for sport. Vlad said he'd once clipped a cigarette out of someone's mouth on a dare. And if you tossed a penny in the air, he could hit it easy at a distance of twenty-five metres.

His guns were locked away in a cabinet, but Vlad knew the location of the key. His father didn't mind if he took them out.

He'd taught Vlad how to handle guns and how to shoot. On his days off, they went to the shooting range.

"So?" Vlad said impatiently, eyes still on the screen. "What's it going to be?"

Hugo clicked his cursor on a bazooka.

Vlad laughed. "Blast the hell out of 'em, eh, Stern?"

Hugo nodded. Stern was his screen name, although Vlad knew it meant more than that. Vlad had taken to using it even when they weren't playing.

The cabinet had contained a dozen pistols laid out carefully on a series of trays. On the lowest tray, a gun with a particularly elegant thin black barrel caught Hugo's eye.

"That old thing?" Vlad had said when Hugo asked about it. "It's a Luger."

Hugo had gotten down on his knees for a better look. He knew the word. He'd heard it first in grade six, and he'd looked it up in the encyclopedia. He never imagined he'd see a real one.

"Pick it up," Vlad said, laughing at his fascination. "Go on. Don't be scared."

The grip had fit him perfectly, neither too wide nor too narrow, and the weight was just right. He stood up and held it out, excited, barely breathing, taking aim and pretending to fire.

"My grandfather had one of these."

"The one who defends criminals?" asked Vlad, interested.

"No," Hugo had said. "The other one."

The frame on the screen changed, and suddenly they were in Los Angeles: bungalows, palm trees, a perfect cloudless sky that looked like a movie backdrop. The game began. Vlad's body was so still he could have been sleeping. Only his thumbs moved, jerking periodically in the cool blue light of the screen.

Hugo blasted at everything that moved. His heart was hammering. He regretted the bazooka, which kept bashing holes in the sides of buildings but couldn't seem to hit a target. Within minutes, he lay dead and bleeding in the dirt.

Vlad smirked. "You gotta chill, Stern."

He reached into his shirt pocket and pulled out a crumpled joint. He looked meaningfully at Hugo, nodding at the balcony door.

Hugo hesitated only a second. Hannah could always tell when he smoked, even if he took a single hit. It was bizarre. As if she had some sixth sense. He gritted his teeth, telling himself he didn't care.

They were five storeys above Fort Street. The first stars had just come out. Sounds of evening traffic were drifting up from de Maisonneuve Boulevard and Sainte-Catherine Street. There was only one chair, a chaise longue with a filthy, torn cushion. Vlad threw the cushion on the floor and they sat down on it, side by side. He lit a match, cupped it, and held the flame under the joint. The tip flared and turned a hypnotizing orange as he sucked in the first smoke. He looked at Hugo and held the joint out solemnly. Hugo took it.

Above them, stars blinked. The balcony floor vibrated with the passing cars. Hugo may have fallen asleep, although there wasn't always much difference between stoned and asleep. He forgot where he was. Forgot that Vlad was beside him.

When he next became conscious, the sky was black. Only gradually did he make out the shapes of clouds swirling and mutating above him, the pricks of starlight shining through. Vlad wasn't beside him anymore. He got to his feet, shivering, and crept back into the apartment. Vlad seemed to have vanished. He tried to check the time, but his cell phone had died. He grabbed his schoolbag and left, hoping not to meet Vlad's marksman dad, who might mistake him for a thief.

Down on the street, rush hour had ended. At the Guy-Concordia metro station, he went straight to a pay phone and lifted the receiver. The digital display said 20:05. His mother would be frantic with worry.

For the two stops to Lionel-Groulx station, he rode the train standing right by the doors. The minute they slid open, he jumped out, ran along the empty platform, and up the first flight of stairs. After that, he got on the escalator, dropping his knapsack at his feet. He was shaky with hunger, although what he craved most at that moment was a glass of water.

Two figures came into view above him on the descending escalator. The station was empty now, and Hugo watched them idly, two stick figures, black outlines at the top of his visual field. But there was something about the posture of one of them that caught his eye. It was a man. A big man. And he was leaning over the woman beside him, almost engulfing her while he spoke. Hugo could hear him now, his words and laughter ricocheting off the walls in the long, deep stairwell.

He knew that voice. He knew the way the man leaned. He had seen him leaning the same way a thousand times. Only every other time, the woman he was leaning over had been Hugo's mother.

Hugo half turned. It wasn't that far to the bottom of the escalator. He could scramble back down, but he'd have to do it right now, no hesitation. Below him, stairs kept appearing, one after the other, like waves on a beach. Watching them made him dizzy. As each new one appeared, he rose higher, a step nearer to his dad. He glanced up again. His father and the woman were descending fast. It was already too late. He couldn't turn and start running down the escalator now, could he? He cursed his half-stoned brain, which seemed to be processing in slow motion. If he did make a run for it, where could he go? There was no place to hide in a metro.

He turned and faced them. His father hadn't noticed him yet. He was caught up in saying something to the woman—something he clearly thought was witty. They were close enough now that Hugo could see how young the woman was. Her coat, tightly belted, was the colour of a stop sign. Who was she, and what was she doing with his dad, who was practically groping her on the escalator in the Lionel-Groulx metro station? He shrank into himself.

They were level with him now, so close he could have reached across the shiny metal divide and touched their sleeves. His father finally looked up, and for a second they stared at each other, eyes locking.

There was a cry of surprise. After they passed each other, his father called out his name. Loud, false-friendly, but Hugo ignored it. He felt like he might throw up, except there was nothing in his stomach. He swung the knapsack onto his shoulder, bashing his ribs with the sharp corner of Vien's book, and hurried upward. The mechanical stairs vanished into a crack at his feet, and an instant later he was pushing the heavy glass door at the exit, fighting his way through a deafening wind into the cold, disorienting night.

12

*H*annah had prepared a stroganoff. Hugo's favourite, her way of showing that she cared. She knew he must have had a difficult day. Everyone at school would have heard by now. And he would probably be tarred by the suspension—set apart. Kids had a sixth sense for things like that. There would be lots of catching up to do, not just in his school work.

In the cast-iron frying pan her mother had given her twenty years ago, the little strips of beef were shrivelled and grey. The mushrooms had turned grey too, and the noodles she'd boiled two hours ago were a gluey ball.

She removed the telephone from its stand on the kitchen counter and dialled. Five rings, followed by a generic message. *"L'abonné que vous désirez rejoindre n'est pas disponible actuelle-ment."* The taped voice told her to hang up.

She slammed the receiver down. The table was set for two. She'd picked marigolds from the garden, the last of the season, to add colour. She didn't even like red meat. She was reaching for the phone again when it rang.

"Hugo?" she said, bringing it to her face so fast she banged a cheekbone.

There was a pause and a man's voice answered. Unfamiliar, in English. "No. Sorry. Is this Hannah? Hannah Stern?"

"Lévesque," she said quickly. The voice was low and extremely nasal.

"Yes. Lévesque. Of course. I'm sorry," the voice said. "It's Manny … Manny Mandelbaum?"

"Oh!" she said, relieved. He didn't sound anything like the guy in the lumberjack shirt from yesterday. "Your voice is lower than when we met."

He laughed. "I woke up with a cold. It's made a man of me."

She frowned, feeling guilty about their encounter, the stress they'd obviously inflicted. She was formulating an apology when he pre-empted her.

"I'm a Stern too, you see. Well, not me, actually, but my mother. Stern was her maiden name."

What was he going on about? How did he even know her former name?

"She was from Vienna."

Static crackled faintly in Hannah's ear. "My father too."

"Thought so," the nasal voice continued affably. "I figured it was either that or Berlin. You never know. We could be cousins."

Kissing cousins, thought Hannah, and then she blushed. "I don't think so," she said quickly. She shifted the phone from her sore cheek.

"Same name," observed Mandelbaum. "Same city of origin. It's possible."

Possible maybe, but not very likely. "My father was the only one in his family to leave Austria," she explained. "Summer of thirty-nine, just before the borders closed."

It had been after the *Anschluss*. After the Austrian government had capitulated, after German troops had poured over the border into the capital, home of Haydn, Mozart, and Beethoven, and, for several generations, home also of her father's family of prosperous, assimilated Jewish merchants and scholars. Alfred Stern had told this story the year her brother turned thirteen. Nineteen sixty-eight. Hannah had been ten.

The Sterns had refused to believe what was happening. By the time they opened their eyes, it was too late for everyone but Alfred. On July 25, 1939, barely a month before war was declared, he found himself on a *Kindertransport* bound for England.

Alfred, who almost never spoke German, had used that term. *Kindertransport*. As though what he had endured was so singular it could not be expressed in any other language.

Static buzzed again in Hannah's ear.

"I just got your message," Mandelbaum said. "I didn't make it in to the office today. Figured I ought to stay home."

His voice really did sound scratchy. Hannah pictured the talking stick passing from hand to hand. They'd probably all catch it now.

"You need an assessment, is that it?" Mandelbaum continued.

Hannah had to make an effort to marshal her thoughts and recall what Manny Mandelbaum was talking about. "Oh," she said. "Yes. The school telephoned this morning requesting it. Hugo's back in class, but with conditions. They told me there's a test you can administer."

The scratchy voice did not answer her directly. "Did they actually use the term *psychopathology*?"

"Yes," said Hannah, collapsing into her chair and staring at the marigolds she'd cut from Lyse's garden. The blooms were a little bedraggled, but their smell was still pungent and earthy. An orange ladybug was crouching, camouflaged, on the biggest one. "In French, of course. *Psychopathologie*."

"Well," said Mandelbaum. "I can't assess for that, per se. We use another term these days. Anti-social personality disorder. There's a checklist of symptoms put together by the World Health Organization. We could take a look at that, if you wish."

Besides being scratchy, Manny Mandelbaum's voice was calm and reasonable. He could have been offering to clean her carpets rather than investigate whether her only son was a menace to the civilized world.

"Anti-social personality disorder," she repeated slowly.

"It's an umbrella term describing people who show a pervasive pattern of disregard for the rights of others and the general rules of society. There are usually signs in childhood and early adolescence."

The ladybug was crawling now, trying to hide among the folds of the marigold blossom.

"What kinds of signs?"

"Can you hang on for a moment?" Manny asked.

Hannah heard his chair creak and a muffled sound as he put down the receiver. She watched the ladybug, whose efforts to hide had been futile. It crouched at the flower's centre, totally exposed.

"I'm back," said Manny Mandelbaum, who must have run to a bookshelf. "Here's the list of symptoms. 'Callous unconcern for the feelings of others,'" he read. "'Gross and persistent attitude of irresponsibility and disregard for social norms. Low tolerance for frustration. Low threshold for aggression. Inability to feel guilt for one's actions. Markedly prone to blame others or to rationalize one's behaviour.'"

Almost every symptom was familiar.

"Hannah?" said Mandelbaum after a few seconds of silence. "Look, Hannah, this portrait can sound like any of us on a bad day. Especially any teenager interacting with an authority figure. Psychology is a terrible field, full of arbitrary, limiting labels. Personally, I don't put much stock in them. They tend to hurt more often than they help."

"But he does show callous unconcern for feelings," said Hannah softly. "And he has been irresponsible. Grossly irresponsible."

"Is he there now?" asked Mandelbaum.

"No."

"Good. Because he must never hear you say anything like that. Words have a huge impact, Hannah. That's the problem with labels like these. We slap them on someone, and suddenly they become solid and real. Promise me you won't get hung up on any of this. If the school wants it, we can do it. But you have got to get a grip on this. Hugo's a kid. Things like this can make you think you know who's in front of you. They can replace the person standing there, you know what I mean? They can shut you down. Close your eyes and ears."

"When can we see you?" said Hannah, only half listening.

"When's good for you?"

"Tomorrow," she said. "If you're okay. Not too sick, I mean. He has to meet with a supervisor after school as part of his punishment. We could be at your office around five. Is that too late?"

He said it would be fine. She said goodbye in a regular voice,

but when she got off the phone, her hand was trembling. Her
son was a complete and utter mystery to her. He had not given
the slightest hint of what he was thinking or why he'd bought
the gun. She had asked him directly. So had his father. More
than once. But so far there'd been no answer. Just his opaque
and dull-eyed stare.

Maybe it wasn't just a phase. Maybe something was deeply
and dangerously wrong with him. Hannah grabbed the rag
hanging over the kitchen sink and began scrubbing the counter-
tops. Frantically. There seemed to be spots everywhere. How had
she not noticed them when she was cooking? A grease stain here,
black smears there where she had sliced the mushroom caps.

Hannah's hand slowed. On the counter was the book
Manny Mandelbaum had given her. It had been sitting there
all day where she'd deposited it after returning from his office.
Nonviolent Communication. She picked it up and opened it.

The foreword, she saw with surprise, was written by a
man called Gandhi. His first name was Arun. The grandson of
Mohandas. Hannah skimmed the first paragraph, then leaned
against the counter to read more.

Arun Gandhi had grown up in the 1940s in apartheid South
Africa, a profoundly violent time and place, especially for a boy
of colour, as he called himself. At the age of thirteen, after being
beaten by white youths for being too black, and by black ones
for being too white, Arun Gandhi himself had begun to turn
violent. His worried parents sent him to India, to the household
of his grandfather, who just happened to be the world's most
famous proponent of peace.

One of the many things he learned from his grandfather,
he wrote years later, when he himself had grown old, was how

pervasive violence was, and how everyone committed violent acts pretty much every day. What was needed was not a quantitative shift in human attitudes to violence, but a qualitative one.

Hannah had to reread this section to make sure she hadn't misunderstood. Everyone was violent. She read on.

His thesis was that people failed to acknowledge their own violence largely through ignorance. They thought they weren't violent because they didn't kill, or make war, or beat other people up. Their definition of violence was limited to the grossest acts of physical aggression.

In the 1940s, Mohandas Gandhi had asked his grandson to draw a tree and to paste it on his bedroom wall. Every evening, they reviewed the day's events together—everything that the boy had experienced, said, seen, or read about. Arun Gandhi was asked to write these things on slips of paper and to paste each of them on his tree under one of two categories: physical violence or passive violence. Within a couple of months, the wall of Arun's bedroom was plastered with acts of violence of the latter kind. These acts (taunts, bullying, refusals of recognition), his grandfather explained, generated anger in victims, who then responded explosively with the first kind of violence. Passive violence always engendered a consequence. It was the fuel.

The phone rang. Hannah put the book down on the counter and ran to answer.

"Hello?" she said, in a small, breathless voice.

It wasn't Hugo, which confused her, because his presence had been so strong while she was reading Arun Gandhi's words. It was Connie.

"I've been calling and calling," Connie said. "Didn't you get my messages?"

"I'm sorry," said Hannah. Over the past three days Connie had left five rambling messages. None of them were frantic. None had announced her father's impending death or even a downturn in his health. This did not justify silence, Hannah knew, but it showed she wasn't totally callous. At least she had checked. She just hadn't answered.

"Is everything okay?" Connie said.

The temptation to talk was great, but Hannah resisted it.

"Hannah?"

"I'm here."

There was a long silence. She felt her reluctance giving way, felt the words coming, when Connie spoke. "Well, I'm glad you finally picked up. I was beginning to think there was a real catastrophe down there. How is Hugo?"

"Hugo?"

"I've been worrying all week about him, and when you didn't answer ..."

"Oh," said Hannah. Mononucleosis. Her excuse. How could she have forgotten? She thought guiltily about all the times she'd let the phone ring, knowing exactly who it was. "I'm sorry. He's doing much better."

"Well, that's a relief."

"It's been incredibly busy around here. We were so worried. He had to have all these tests." Hannah winced. There was a tiny kernel of truth in there, but not enough to absolve her. Lying was violence. Arun Gandhi said so.

"And Father?" Hannah said, shifting away from the uncomfortable subject. "How is he?"

"He's coming home."

"Home?" The word dropped out of Hannah's mouth before

she fully registered it. She pictured her father strapped to the surfboard-like stretcher the nurses had used to bathe him. "But he can't even walk."

"Yes he can."

"He can?"

"When the orderly's there," said Connie. "He walked today. Two full steps."

"Mother," she said, leaning on the stove for support, trying not to look at the congealed mess of her dinner. She couldn't say more. Her parents' house with its long flight of stairs flashed before her. The only full bathrooms were on the second floor, none of them adapted to the needs of a man in Alfred Stern's condition. There was no way he could go home.

"He's walking, I said. Two full steps."

"Yes, I heard you," said Hannah. Had her mother come unhinged?

"They can't keep him at the hospital any longer. Two days ago, Dr. Ufitsky said it's time for him to move on."

"But not home, surely?" Hannah took the wooden spoon from the spoon rest and gave the stroganoff a hard stir. There was sour cream in it. She should probably put it in the fridge.

"Look. I'm doing the best I can."

"I know you are, Mother," Hannah said, suddenly weary. "I didn't mean …" She returned the spoon to the spoon rest, abandoning the stroganoff to its bacterial fate. Either Ufitsky was nuts or Connie was wilfully misunderstanding what he'd said. "Aren't there rehab centres?" she said. "Longer-term places where he can receive proper care?"

"He doesn't want that."

Hannah's eyes widened. "He's talking?"

"No," said Connie. "But he doesn't need to." There was a brief silence. "Would you want to be packed off to one of those places?"

For some reason, perhaps because of the conversation she'd just had with Manny Mandelbaum, Hannah pictured a boy in short pants clutching a battered suitcase.

"Well?" said her mother. "Would you?" She didn't leave a space for Hannah to answer, but began almost immediately to talk about Benjamin. "He's very caught up with his work," Connie said. "I just got off the phone with him. He's in court all next week."

So that was it. Her mother would never state a need simply or ask directly for help. Instead, there were hints. Seemingly random facts, finding their mark in your neck.

"Hannah?"

But Hannah remained silent, her fallback position. In silence was safety. She shifted the telephone to her right hand to change ears. Her neck was hurting. She pressed tentatively into the stiff ridge of her trapezius muscle and winced.

"Benjamin can't fly here every other week. He's come once this month already. Vancouver's so far away."

"It is," said Hannah. She leaned her back against the counter and slid down the cupboard door into a squat. "The other end of the continent." She was still working her neck muscle. The pain fanned down her left shoulder and arm. She regretted telling Connie that Hugo had recovered. Her mind began to scramble. "There must be a decent rehab place in Toronto. It would just take a little research."

"No, Hannah."

"What do you mean, no? Have you even looked into it?"

"Your father doesn't want to go. The doctor talked to him about rehab. He said he could get him a spot in a good centre. The very next day, your father stopped eating."

"What?" Hannah sat down heavily on the floor.

"It's been two days."

Hannah felt sick. The guilt was doing its work.

"Dr. Ufitsky says he sees it a lot. People go on strike."

Hannah pictured her thin, wasted father. "Maybe it's a physical thing," she said desperately. "Is he having trouble swallowing?"

"No," said Connie. "Until that talk with the doctor, he was eating fine. He's had enough, Hannah. It's perfectly clear. He doesn't want to be cooped up anymore. He wants out."

Hannah stared up at the ceiling. A shadow darkened the centre of the frosted glass ceiling light. It looked fairly large. Had some insect gotten trapped in there? Or was it just dirt? "It'll never work," said Hannah. "He's sick, Mother. You'll need round-the-clock nursing care. Not to mention physiotherapy, speech therapy, God knows what else. And where will you put him? He can't handle the stairs. You'll need a hospital bed."

"All that can be arranged."

"This is nuts," Hannah said. It was like a bad dream in which everyone was unaccountably blind to looming danger. Everyone but her.

"He's been in hospital almost a month, Hannah. He's had enough."

"And what about you?" Hannah asked before she could stop herself. If her mother was exhausted now, how would she be as her husband's full-time nurse?

"Me? You think I enjoy it there?"

Hannah took a deep breath. "Think about it a minute, Mum. At least now you can go home and sleep. There are nurses to help. Orderlies to bathe him. This is a huge undertaking. Way too big to manage."

"Alone, yes. That's why I've been telephoning."

Hannah held her breath. The kitchen seemed stark and painfully bright as she sat there for several seconds, legs splayed on the wooden floorboards, gazing at the light.

"They can keep him a little bit longer at Sunnybrook while I fix the bathroom and get a bed installed downstairs. This is the issue. I'll need someone to oversee the workmen while I'm at his bedside. The housekeeper is there Tuesdays and Fridays, but it will take someone with authority."

"Mum."

"What?"

But Hannah couldn't do it. Couldn't bring herself to say no. The word jammed in her throat like a stone—painful, cutting off the air.

"It's one week. That's all I'm asking, while I make the preparations. I can't be in two places at once, Hannah. You could work in the house. Bring your laptop like last time. Get that husband of yours to look after Hugo."

"I'll call you back," Hannah whispered.

There was a brief silence, and Connie said goodbye.

It was half past eight. Hannah felt guilty, but not guilty enough to change her mind. Her mother would think her totally callous, but Toronto would have to wait. The marigolds caught her eye. What was that nursery rhyme? *Ladybug, ladybug, fly away home, your house is on fire and your children all gone.*

She sat on the floor, staring at the telephone. There was still no word from Hugo. Be calm, she told herself firmly. Do not panic. She punched in Hugo's number and pressed the phone to her ear. The ringing sounds were hypnotic. She counted them. One, two, three, four, five, nodding her head in the little pause of silence after each one. *"L'abonné que vous désirez rejoindre n'est pas disponible actuellement. Veuillez raccrocher et essayer plus tard."* She pressed the End button and put the phone down carefully in front of her on the floor. She was kneeling now. She covered her face with her hands and bent forward until her forehead touched the floorboards.

She was still on the kitchen floor when, a half hour later, the front door to the apartment opened. "Hugo?" she said in a shrill voice, standing up too quickly. "Where on earth have you been?" For some reason, perhaps because of talking to Connie, she had addressed him in English.

He strolled into the kitchen, not meeting her eye.

"I called your cell repeatedly." Again, in English.

"It was off," he said to the floor. He too was speaking English, as he was doing more and more, in defiance of Luc.

"I know that, Hugo. Believe me. What I want to know is why." His face was preternaturally pale. She took a step nearer. "Have you been smoking?"

He turned away.

"Your first day back. How could you?"

He raised his eyes then, but only to the level of her mouth. "I was with Vien."

"Smoking up? Do you honestly expect me to believe that?" She grabbed his shoulders and held them. He was looking down again, refusing to face her. "Look at me, goddammit! Look me in the eye."

He didn't resist. It was as if he weren't there anymore. As if he'd packed up and gone, leaving this skinny boy's body, the husk of him, here in her desperate hands. Mandelbaum's book was on the counter where she had left it open, face down. Its title stared at her: *Nonviolent Communication.*

Her hands dropped like dead weights. She had earned a place on Arun Gandhi's tree. "Your dinner's cold," she said, ashamed. "You'll have to wait a minute while I reheat it."

After she'd warmed it in the microwave, he took the entire pot of pasta on his plate and all the beef stroganoff. This, too, made her feel guilty. She knew he didn't want to take anything from her, didn't want to give in. But he was too hungry.

She sat across from him at the table she'd set. Neither of them spoke. He looked like an animal, a squirrel or a rat, nervously scanning the room as he forked down his food. His skin was sallow. It was naturally olive-coloured, like his grandfather's, and did best with a bit of sun. Now, it looked sickly, almost jaundiced in the indoor light. And how thin he was. Not an ounce of fat anywhere, no matter how much she fed him.

He'd definitely been smoking. His eyes were far-off and filmy. There was no point of contact or entry. His jaw moved as he chewed like a machine, clenching, releasing, clenching. Mandelbaum's list came back to her: callous unconcern for the feelings of others; persistent attitude of irresponsibility. She shook her head. Not her son. Please, not her son.

"I've booked an appointment tomorrow with Mandelbaum," she said. She was feeling a little more steady, now that he was safe at home, and had switched back to French. "The school wants an assessment."

Hugo laid down his fork and stopped chewing. "The school can screw itself," he answered in English, his mouth full.

"Hu-go," she said in a warning singsong.

"Han-nah," he sang back.

"We can go together," she said, ignoring this provocation. "I'll pick you up tomorrow after your meeting with Monsieur Vien."

Hugo stood up. "Vien's a jerk." He paused and seemed to think. "They all are." There was another pause. "You all are."

"Who's the you?"

"You. And Dad. Vien. Everyone at that fucking school!"

She took a breath. "Language, Hugo."

"Fuck language!"

It was the most he'd said in months. She searched his face, but he just sneered and looked away. His body language was so angry, both hands balled into fists. Something must have happened at school to upset him. Possibly with Monsieur Vien.

Hugo turned on her suddenly, eyes blazing. "Do you know where he is right now?"

"Who?" said Hannah, bewildered.

"Luc," he said. "Your hus-band." He could hardly contain the anger. His face was contorted. "Well?" he asked.

"Well, no. I don't know where Luc is. People don't keep track of their spouses every minute of the day."

"You ought to check, sometime." The tendons on both sides of his neck were standing out. Hannah could actually see the blood in his carotid artery pulsing upward to feed his angry brain. "There's a lot about Luc Lévesque we don't know," he said quietly.

"Hugo," she said, and stepped toward him again. His energy had shifted. His fingers had uncurled. Perhaps now they could talk. "Tell me what's wrong."

But the moment was gone. He looked down, pursing his lips. "Forget it," he said. "It is what it is. Or isn't."

It is what it isn't? What did that mean? What was she missing?

"Why did you stay?"

Her thoughts were racing. What was he talking about? Stay here at home tonight, waiting for him? Stay married to Luc?

"In Montreal," he said, seeing her confusion. "In the seventies. When Alfred decided to leave."

Alfred. When had he begun calling his grandfather that? And the seventies? She stared in utter mystification. "Because of your father," she said finally. "We'd met by then. We were a couple."

Hugo grimaced. "Do you ever wish you'd gone with them?"

Hugo kept turning his face away from her, but even when she could see his expression, it gave no clue to what he was trying to say.

"I mean," he said, "we just about never see your family."

"I do," she said. "I was down there two weeks ago."

"Because your dad almost died."

Fair enough. Some years she didn't make it to Toronto at all. And she hadn't once been out West to visit Benjamin and his family. Not in fifteen years. The extent of their contact was birthday cards and an annual donation of Hanukkah *geld* for her two young nieces.

"I barely know them," Hugo said.

"You want to get to know my side of the family? Is that what this is about?"

He looked away again. "I want to know why we never see them. It doesn't make sense. They're not bad people."

Hannah sighed. "It's complicated."

"It's because of Luc, isn't it?"

Luc. As if he were a casual acquaintance. But it wasn't Luc's face that flashed before her as he uttered the name. It was the face of Alfred Stern, forehead creased in disapproval.

"I'm not a kid anymore," Hugo persisted.

"No," she said, gazing through her vision into Hugo's angry young eyes. "I guess you're not."

13

The little bronze woman with the round belly was still in the gallery window as Hannah hurried into the building. Hugo trailed behind her glumly.

"Sorry, sorry, sorry!" she said, bursting into the waiting room, where Manny Mandelbaum had come to greet them. "I took a taxi to pick up Hugo, but there was an accident on Atwater, and by the time I got to the school he'd wandered into the yard."

Mandelbaum held up his hands. "It's okay," he said. "I have nothing else this afternoon, there's no rush. I'm glad you both made it."

He was quiet and calm. Hannah took a deep breath. And another one. His client base was probably small. This would explain why he was so relaxed and welcoming. Whatever the reason, she was too grateful to care.

Mandelbaum filled two glasses from a water cooler for Hannah and Hugo before leading them into his office. "You can use my desk," he told Hugo, pulling out a coaster with the face of an elephant on it for Hugo's drink. "Ganesh," he said. "The Indian god of students."

Hugo looked at him blankly.

"My favourite Hindu incarnation," said Mandelbaum. He pressed his nose into his shoulder and waved his arm comically back and forth. "Erases obstacles with his trunk."

Hugo sighed.

"You just want to write this thing, huh? Get it over with?" Mandelbaum said, smiling kindly.

Hugo nodded.

"Okay, then. Here's a pencil. I'll be right outside." He took Hannah's arm and steered her out of the room. She was surprised by that. He was more fluid than the last time they'd been here. More in charge. She wouldn't have predicted such a firm touch. His voice was still low, but the scratchiness was gone.

They sat on his waiting room couch. It was leather, like his chairs, but ancient and sunken, covered with small cushions that smelled of patchouli.

"You're feeling better?" she asked, politely, but also out of self-interest, not wishing to get too close.

He said his wife, a homeopath, had plied him with remedies.

"She's a bit of a sorceress," he explained, laughing. "Got all kinds of medicinal herbs up her sleeve. I can pass you her card if you want," he added, eager once again to promote the services of somebody other than himself. He nodded in the direction of his office. "So. He came."

"Barely," she said. "I had to search all over the school grounds to find him."

Manny Mandelbaum smiled. "But he's here."

She nodded. He was here. He was writing the assessment. That was something. "You didn't think he'd do it?"

Mandelbaum shrugged. "I sure wouldn't want to. Write a thing like that? I mean, think about it."

"It's one of the conditions for staying on at Saint-Jean."

"Sure, sure," said Mandelbaum, sticking his legs out in front of him and letting his head fall back against the couch. "But imagine if it was you. Imagine people wanting to find out if you're anti-social."

Hannah grimaced. "I wasn't found inside my school in possession of a firearm."

"True," said Mandelbaum, nodding at the ceiling.

He was a nice man. Too nice, perhaps. Maybe it was beyond him to imagine a person really going off-track. "I've always wondered," she said in a lowered voice, "what was going on in the heads of those boys in Colorado."

Mandelbaum's expression changed. "You're really worried."

She shrugged and looked away.

Mandelbaum drew in his legs and sat up. "It's okay to have fears," he said, looking at her.

Hannah didn't move. She was perched precariously on the couch's hard front edge, the only solid part of it. If she leaned backward even slightly, she would slide down into the cushions. "Ever since you read me that list of signs, I keep seeing them in him."

He nodded. "I'm like that too. I read about some psychological condition or whatever and every symptom seems to fit. It's understandable. Every one of us shows callous unconcern, Hannah. Every one of us is irresponsible, has trouble with relationships. We all get frustrated and aggressive. You have to remember it's a spectrum."

"Oh?" she said, unconvinced. "Well, Hugo seems to have fallen off the end."

Manny Mandelbaum sat forward, not an easy feat on his ridiculous couch. "I don't know your family well," he said, his voice a little less gentle, "but to me Hugo doesn't seem like he's falling off any end. Unless it's the end of childhood."

Hannah closed her eyes. Until that moment, she'd had no idea how much she'd needed reassurance, or maybe just the permission to give voice to her fears. "I looked at your book," she said.

"Marshall Rosenberg's book, you mean?"

"Yes," said Hannah. She was grateful he'd passed it to her. It raised a lot of questions. "I read the foreword by Gandhi's grandson. I didn't realize you were talking about that kind of nonviolence."

Mandelbaum nodded, drawing his feet up and crossing them. *"Ahimsa."*

"You've been to India, I take it," she said, gesturing at the brilliantly coloured little pillows adorning his couch. Hannah's nose had habituated to the patchouli, but she could still pick up the sugary hints.

"I was one of those lost kids in the seventies, wandering the globe, trying to find myself." He smiled. A man who could poke fun at himself.

"And did you?" she asked, smiling back.

"In a manner of speaking. I found out that I was never really lost." He pulled on a pillow that had wedged between their bodies and stuck it behind his lower back. "So, you read all about needs," he said, steering the conversation back to the book.

"Nothing about needs. Only the foreword."

"Rosenberg's thesis is pretty simple," he said, placing his palms flat on his thighs. "Basically, we all have these needs. They're few in number, and they're universal." He glanced at her to see if she was following, and she looked back with what she hoped was a lucid expression.

"All we ever do is try to meet them," he went on. "Trouble is, most of us haven't got a clue how to do that. The strategies we come up with are usually pretty unskillful. But the needs themselves—"

"Are just fine," she offered.

"Right."

He was smiling, visibly pleased that she'd stayed with him. What harm could there be in indulging him? "Give me an example," she said.

"You've got a need, say, to keep silent. Even when your spouse is bullying you."

She looked sharply at him.

"What?" asked Mandelbaum, gazing at her innocently.

She didn't answer.

"Tell me. What?"

"That was unkind," she said.

Mandelbaum nodded. "Do you remember the reason you gave two days ago for consulting me in the first place?"

Hannah nodded. "Communication," she said, picturing the sheet she had filled out.

"So, you've got a need to keep silent, but also a need to communicate."

She felt exposed. As if he could see right through her.

"It's a contradiction, Hannah. When I was rude to you just now and pressed your buttons, you said nothing. I had to ask you, pointedly, if something was wrong. You have a need to communicate, Hannah, and yet you don't speak."

Hannah realized she was clutching one of his little pillows to her chest. She replaced it deliberately in the space between their bodies.

"I have a need," he said, tossing and catching an orange pillow with tiny decorative mirrors sewn into its fabric.

The pillow glittered like a spinning sun. She couldn't turn her eyes away.

"I need to find out more about this father of yours."

The pillow came down and he caught it, holding it on his lap.

"I'm curious," he said, turning to face her. "Even if we're not blood relations. His story sounds remarkable, leaving Austria right before the war broke out. He can't have been more than a kid."

Hannah told him the story of the *Kindertransport*. Or at least, she told him what little of it she'd heard from her father. He had ridden a train for a day and a night along the Danube and then the Rhine, coming at last to Holland and freedom. From there, he had boarded a ferry and made a night crossing to England. He had eventually ended up on a farm in Sussex. It had been, briefly, a happy summer, during which his parents still wrote him letters. They neglected to mention that his father's livelihood and the family home were gone and everyone he had ever known was in mortal danger.

All through August of 1939, on the dairy farm in the south of England, Alfred was kept in ignorance of these details. On

September 3, after Poland was invaded, Great Britain declared war on Germany. The British family with whom Alfred was boarding was kind to him, despite the fact that they'd hoped for a bigger boy, one who could help with all the heavy physical work to be done. When it became clear that Alfred Stern wasn't remotely up to the job, they hadn't got angry. They let him feed the chickens and, when the summer was over, enrolled him in the local school, where he soon mastered English.

His year in Sussex was a time of discoveries and adventures. The biggest worry was his parents back in Austria, from whom he had heard nothing since the start of the war. It was only years later that Alfred learned about the mass deportation of Vienna's Jews by the Gestapo, which began in October of 1939.

In the spring of 1940, Winston Churchill became prime minister. Germany had just invaded Holland and Belgium, and Churchill issued an edict ordering all German and Austrian men on British soil interned. Never mind that Alfred was a Jewish war refugee and barely shaving. He qualified. The British authorities took him into custody and shipped him with other internees across the ocean to a work camp in Canada, a country about which he knew next to nothing.

"He had to wear a uniform," Hannah said. "The jackets were blue, with a large red circle on the back." This had impressed her when she was ten. The circles were there, Alfred had said, to give the guards a target when someone tried to escape.

"How old did you say he was?" asked Mandelbaum.

"Sixteen. Just turned."

Mandelbaum whistled. "That must have left some scars."

She shrugged. "He's got a tough hide."

Manny Mandelbaum nodded. "I can imagine."

Hannah remembered another story, which she also told Mandelbaum. It involved her father's maternal grandfather, whom he'd adored. Alfred's mother had married late, in her thirties, and Alfred had been her only child. Her father, who had lived with her and her small family, had cherished his only grandson. To ward off evil spirits, he'd tied a red ribbon inside the boy's shirt. Alfred wore this ribbon all through his childhood, even though his parents dismissed it as pure cabbalistic superstition. In the year following his bar mitzvah, Alfred adopted their attitude and dismissed it too. He removed it from his undershirt and tossed it in the gutter. Shortly afterward, in the spring of 1938, the Wehrmacht arrived. Alfred remembered standing in the street with his grandfather, surrounded by a cheering Viennese mob and feeling personally to blame as wave after wave of German aircraft flew over them.

"What happened to him?" Mandelbaum asked.

"The grandfather? No one knows. He disappeared in October of thirty-nine, along with all the other Jews. Alfred thinks he died in a transit camp somewhere, or maybe on a train. He never found any record. His parents' deaths were documented, though. Auschwitz. Fall of forty-two."

"What a legacy," said Mandelbaum.

Hannah nodded. "It's why he went into law, I guess. Defending people's freedom."

"I mean you," said Mandelbaum, searching her face. "It's your legacy too."

"I guess," she said. Alfred Stern had never made it seem like her legacy. "My father didn't like to talk about it."

"He told you those stories about England and the internment camp."

"Yes," she said. "But that was exceptional. As a rule, he didn't dwell on the past. I think it was too painful."

Mandelbaum smiled. He seemed more attractive than he had when they first met. "You know what my definition of adulthood is?" he asked, seemingly out of the blue. "I didn't get it out of a book or anything," he said. "It came to me from watching the kids in my practice. When a person can tell the story of his parents, really imagine them as beings with their own complex pasts, well then …" He tossed the pillow into the air.

They both watched it spin.

"Well then?" said Hannah.

The pillow landed with a soft *thud* in Mandelbaum's blue-jeaned lap. "The job's done."

"Okay," she said uncertainly.

He was smiling again. "I like that Hugo picked it."

"Picked what?" she asked, still pondering the definition.

"Your name. I like that he's trying to resurrect it."

"It's not mine," she said, forcefully enough that it surprised her as well as him. "I go by Lévesque now, I told you."

Mandelbaum leaned slightly away from her, causing the mirrored pillow to slip off his legs. "Sorry," he said. "This time I didn't mean to press your buttons."

"How did you even find out about the name?"

"Hugo put it down on the sheet I gave you at our first session. It wasn't French, so I figured it was yours." He paused for a moment. "Changing names isn't always a bad thing, you know. It can be just the opposite. In Japan, for instance, artists used to change their names ritualistically. They did it only once, at a point in their careers when they felt they'd developed into the creator they'd always wanted to be. It was a sign to the world that they'd arrived."

He retrieved the pillow. "I changed mine," he said affably. "My first name used to be Bruce. Manny was a nickname from high school. But I liked it. It made me feel like I was part of the human race."

"Which you weren't as Bruce?"

He looked uncomfortable. "I was pretty alienated in my twenties."

"So you changed it," she pressed. "Legally?" The roles had switched. She was interrogating him now, truly curious.

"Yes. Legally. It was right after I opened my practice. I was thirty."

Hannah shook her head. "But Hugo is fourteen."

Before she could say anything more, the door to the inner office opened. Hugo stood glowering at them on the threshold.

"Hey," said Manny Mandelbaum, putting away the pillow and standing up. "All done?"

There was no answer.

Hannah got up off the edge of the big old couch. She scanned Hugo's face, wondering how much he'd heard. He must have overheard something, because he didn't look at her or at Manny Mandelbaum as he headed for the door.

"I'll call you," Dr. Mandelbaum said hopefully. He raised his eyebrows and seemed on the verge of saying more, but she couldn't stay to hear it. Hugo was already out of sight.

14

The next afternoon, Hugo slipped outside again after the final bell. He had to get air. Couldn't face the stuffiness of Vien's classroom after a full day of sitting inside. He didn't see anyone he particularly wanted to hang with. Without Vlad, the yard didn't look all that welcoming.

He wandered to the back of the school. The basketball court was full of boys playing pickup. No one called out to him, not that it mattered. He wouldn't have played anyway, and basketball wasn't his thing. He stopped and watched a kid take a foul shot. The ball bounced off the backboard, touched the rim, and dropped through the net, hitting the asphalt with a satisfying *thunk*. The kid pumped a fist. Hugo moved on, unnoticed.

"You're late again," Vien said as Hugo entered the classroom. He was sitting at his desk, marking papers. The mural was done now, the paint and glue dry.

"The contract says 'after school.' Your last class ended forty-five minutes ago."

Hugo didn't look up.

"You didn't bring the folder on Lanctôt either, I see. Did you take a look at Pierre Vallières?"

Hugo couldn't restrain himself. "He's a terrorist. It actually says so in the title."

Vien smiled, his eyebrows forming their familiar arch even as his eyes gazed in different directions. "He uses the word ironically, Hugo. The authorities in New York slapped that label on him when they arrested him for staging a hunger strike in front of the United Nations. That's all he was doing. Refusing to eat, trying to draw attention to the rampant injustices in Quebec and the need for political independence. It was nonviolent resistance, Hugo. Just like Mahatma Gandhi in India."

Hugo frowned. "So why does he call for armed struggle?"

"You've got to understand the times. It wasn't like it is now."

Vien kept repeating that phrase like a mantra. You had to have been there. And if you hadn't been, there was no way you could understand. The truth was, Vien just wanted to be agreed with. Hugo remembered seeing a guy in a T-shirt once with the words "You're Entitled to My Own Opinion" printed in bold black letters on the front. Vien should seriously buy one.

He'd never admit it to Vien, but Vallières's book had been a shock. He couldn't believe it had been published, let alone reached cult status among students and so-called intellectuals in Montreal. It was a rant against the people who ran things— the presidents of banks and corporations, the leaders of political parties. In one ten-page chapter, Vallières blazed through three hundred years of Canadian history, reducing thousands of stories to a simple fight between capitalists and workers—referred to by Vallières as "slaves."

The only chapter Hugo hadn't found completely maddening

was the one about Vallières's home life. He had stayed up until one thirty in the morning reading it, but even it rang false. Vallières blamed his parents' failed marriage and his own tortured relationship with them almost totally on their working-class status. Capitalism was to blame for every problem, large and small.

"He did condone some violence," Vien conceded, "but his actions were selfless, political."

"You mean like bin Laden's?" Hugo shot back.

"No, Hugo. Not even a little bit like bin Laden's."

"Or Lanctôt's?"

Vien exhaled. "That's enough."

Hugo fell silent.

"Look," said Vien, making an obvious effort to stay calm. "Lanctôt wasn't violent. But don't take my word for it. See for yourself. I have boxes of material about him. I'll tell you right now, though, you're not going to find what you think. I've read everything that's out there on the man. As I said, he was the subject of my master's thesis."

Lanctôt was obviously a sore spot. It was as if Hugo had slandered a member of Vien's family or something. Not that *slander* was the right word. All he'd done was group him with someone willing to sacrifice anything to achieve a political goal. Lanctôt had kidnapped a man and held him captive for almost two whole months. He'd made repeated threats against the man's life. He had even wired him to a bunch of dynamite and filmed him sitting there like a human time bomb. These acts were established. He'd admitted them, and yet Vien and practically his entire generation defended Lanctôt as if he were a hero.

They saw themselves as victims, that was why. But when you thought that way, it seemed you almost always ended up hurting someone else.

He would write about Lanctôt, Hugo decided. He would lay out the violence so plainly that no one, not even Vien or his own father, could deny it.

15

*H*annah was lying on the couch with a book she had taken out of the Westmount Public Library over the weekend. When the telephone rang, she held her breath until it stopped, and then she shifted her weight, guiltily rearranging the cushions. She would check the voice mail later, she told herself, although for the last week she had stopped performing even this simple task. Numerous messages were waiting, unheard and untended to. This last call was probably from Connie, relentless in her campaign to guilt Hannah into coming to Toronto. Allison March was another possible candidate, with another cartload of guilt. Most days, Hannah managed to repress all thoughts of the translation, her mind busy with the much more pressing concerns of Hugo and her father. Luc's book felt utterly unreal, like the fiction it actually was. It had no substance, no connection to her life.

She checked her watch, which she'd placed beside her on the floor. Two in the afternoon. She should get up. She really should.

Every day, she had these arguments with herself. One part of her wanted to lie here on the living room couch and never get up again. Another part observed the first part with mounting horror. She hadn't eaten breakfast yet. She hadn't even looked at the chores written out in white chalk on the slate hanging on the kitchen wall. Hannah tried to recall what day it was. Monday? No, that couldn't be right. She got up from the couch and went to the window.

The sudden movement left her momentarily dizzy, and she had to lean on the wall until her vision unclouded. She looked out the window. Empty garbage cans stared from every doorway all the way down Laporte Street. Same thing for Agnes Street, on the other side of the park. She had missed the Tuesday pickup—something she'd never done before. And the worst part was, she didn't care.

She was probably depressed. But how could it be depression if all she felt was … nothing? She had no appetite. No interest in washing herself or in keeping even a pretense of order in the house. Her sloth was boundless. Reading seemed to be the only activity left to her. Each night, she read so late and long that the next day she could barely get out of bed. For Hugo's sake she did rise, but the minute the door shut behind him, she sank onto the couch, where she lay until his return nine hours later. The book she was currently reading was on mass killers.

It was a recent publication, a bestseller in the States. Since Columbine, the subject was a hot one. Mass murderers characteristically suffered from personality disorders. There was some speculation that Eric Harris, the instigator of the killings in Colorado, had been anti-social. He had died before anyone could diagnose him, but that didn't stop a deluge of post-mortem hypotheses. He was very bright, the book said. Good in math, a whiz with computers. He'd been in trouble with the law, but he lied with great facility so they kept letting him off.

Marc Lepine, who'd killed fourteen women at the École Polytechnique in 1989, had been another anti-social kid. Like Harris in Colorado, he also had loved video games. And had a thing for guns, just like her own son.

Dylan Klebold had been different. He'd had a conscience, the book said. He wasn't anti-social so much as depressed. For him, the shootings were as much about putting a bullet in his own head as about hurting other people.

Hannah shivered. The assessment results for Hugo had come in, not that they clarified anything. Many of Hugo's responses had been puzzling, Manny Mandelbaum had said, defying categorization.

"He's a complicated kid," he'd told Hannah the week before, when she had still been answering the phone. "More complicated than the average, I mean. No discernible portrait has emerged."

Hannah had tried to read hope into this utterance. "You mean he's not anti-social?"

"Not definitively, but like I said, a number of the answers are puzzling."

"What will you tell the school?" This was the question, of course. The ostensible reason Hugo had been subjected to the test in the first place.

There was a long pause during which Hannah had held her breath, listening to the sound of papers being shuffled on the other end of the line.

Manny Mandelbaum sighed. "I really can't say one way or

another. Some of the answers definitely point to insensitivity. Or anger, or something. Some kind of reactivity. But why wouldn't he be reactive, writing a test like this?

"I hate this kind of thing, Hannah," he said. "I really do. Human beings resist categorization. Who knows? Maybe he just ticked the boxes arbitrarily, and here we are, trying to read meaning into them. People are way too complex to fit into neat little squares. Adolescents even more so than the rest of us. So much is happening in adolescence, on so many levels, that an assessment like this is beside the point.

"There have been studies recently showing that the brain is still growing well into one's twenties. That's pretty outrageous, when you stop and think about it. It takes over two decades for the frontal lobe to operate at full capacity. Hugo is still unformed, Hannah. Not everything is in its place, and yet we expect him to be as rational as an adult. His brain might not be ready for that quite yet. And apparently it's perfectly natural."

Hannah had wanted to believe this. But surely what Hugo had done wasn't natural. Buying a gun and carrying it around with you at school—that went beyond immature frontal lobes, didn't it? The principal had said it was the first time anyone had done such a thing at the Collège Saint-Jean-Baptiste. Mandelbaum was probably trying to protect her, trying to cushion the blow. Hugo was fragile in some possibly unfixable and permanent way. The gun might have been a cry for help. But while Mandelbaum was sympathetic, the school certainly wasn't. It wanted judgment.

In the end, Hugo had been allowed to stay. This was good news, Hannah had to acknowledge, although she felt as confused about her son as ever. He was a black hole, singular and unknowable, into which she was pouring her darkest, most inarticulate fears.

She returned to the couch and slipped the book on mass killers under the cushions so Hugo wouldn't see it when he got home from school. She had thought she might go to the kitchen to see about making some food, but a wave of fatigue hit her, forcing her to shut her eyes.

An hour or so later, the two-toned ring of the doorbell woke her. She jumped up to answer it and became dizzy again. But she kept walking, unsteadily, toward the door. By the time she opened it, her vision had tunnelled. She staggered forward and would have pitched right down the staircase if a pair of arms hadn't caught her.

A muffled, distant voice said her name. Moments later, she looked up into the skewed, frightened eyes of Serge Vien. He seemed so alarmed that she wanted to reach out and reassure him, but her arms were pinned. He was down on one knee, clasping her to his chest like an operatic lover.

"Are you all right?"

Hannah nodded.

"I'm sorry," he said quickly, looking down at their bodies.

She wasn't. She lay perfectly still. Her right ear was pressed against his chest in such a way that she could hear his heart-beat. She lay there, listening to the sound and gazing up into his face. She had no idea how long they spent on the front hall rug. Time stopped, or at least stretched so elastically that it lost its meaning. The sea-swell of nausea receded. Her vision brightened and cleared. She yawned.

"Thank you," she said.

He shrugged. "I couldn't very well let you fall down the stairs."

"No," said Hannah, still gazing up into his face like a child. She shifted, and it occurred to her that she wasn't looking her best. Her hair smelled; her eyes felt dry and gritty. She was wearing her nightgown over an old pair of sweatpants. "I must look awful," she said, struggling to get up.

He released his hold. "*Au contraire.* I was just thinking how lucky I was to have this beautiful woman faint in my arms." The skewed eye surveyed her appreciatively. "You don't look one bit like your father, you know."

Hannah's smile froze.

"We had the pleasure of meeting once. Years ago," he continued, too engrossed in his story to notice her reaction. "The circumstances weren't all that pleasant, unfortunately."

Hannah steeled herself for what was coming. It wasn't the first time a friend of Luc's had made the connection between her and Alfred Stern. Luc hung out with artists—writers like him, painters and singers. Exactly the type that the RCMP would have rounded up back in the fall of 1970. In most instances, they laughed it off. But she knew of at least one acquaintance who had stopped speaking to Luc.

"You were arrested?"

Vien's chest puffed out ever so slightly. He nodded. "I did four days at the Hôtel Parthenais."

"I'm sorry," she said, as if she herself were responsible. Not that "sorry" was enough. Not by half. But what else could she say? She'd dragged this thing around all her life, and she still had no clue how to handle it. The name change helped, but inevitably someone learned whose daughter she was and the whole cycle of questions and guilt began again. *The sins of the fathers.*

Vien, who was still sitting on the floor, noticed her discomfiture. "I was actually looking for Luc," he said, scrambling to his feet. "He's not downstairs."

"No," Hannah said. She must try to keep her voice normal. "He's got a new office."

Vien looked surprised.

"He didn't tell you?"

He shook his head.

"It's been a while now." She paused, trying and failing to count the days. "He hasn't installed a telephone yet," she added. "He's not a big fan of those things. I can give you the address, if you want."

"Would he be there?"

Hannah shrugged. He was watching her, trying to gauge what was up. He sensed something, that was for sure. She knew she looked like hell. She rearranged her face into what she hoped was a neutral expression.

"I have papers from the school," he said, reaching for his briefcase. "Both parents have to sign." He pulled out several sheets covered in print. "Protocol."

He laid them out on the chest of drawers in the hall while Hannah went to the kitchen to write down Luc's address for him. When she returned, he was looking around. The apartment was bathed in afternoon light. The floors and oak door frames that she and Luc had scraped down with such hope and patience at the start of their marriage were a rich, burnished gold. The walls were clean and white with clusters of prints for colour. On the dividing wall between the dining room and kitchen, a collection of emerald bottles gleamed in the sun. Luc had a thing for green glass.

"Lovely place," he said, looking wistful. Luc had mentioned that Serge Vien's wife had left him. Poor man. Did he envy this?

She signed the sheets he'd laid out and then handed him the slip of paper with Luc's address. "Luc's new place."

"Saint-Augustin Street."

"It's not far."

"Thanks," said Serge, folding the papers into his briefcase. At the door, he paused. "Are you all right?"

An odd sound came from somewhere in the back of her throat. She covered her mouth and pretended to cough. "I'm fine," she said, and turned her back until he was gone.

*L*uc was on his back on a grimy blue yoga mat he'd appro-
priated from Laporte Street about a week ago. He'd gone
there looking for Hugo the day after their chance meeting in the
metro, but Hugo hadn't been home. Neither had Hannah, so
he'd unlocked the door and wandered through the empty rooms,
feeling like a home invader. He'd taken none of his things, not
even a pair of boxer shorts, which he happened to need, but the
yoga mat had been rolled up and propped beside the front door
as if waiting for him. He couldn't resist.

He hadn't returned since, hadn't even telephoned, though
the startled face of his son on the escalator still haunted him.

Luc turned his attention back to the task at hand. He was
still damp from his run. At the moment, he was recovering from
the first of two daily sets of sit-ups. The floor of his new house
was more crooked than he'd thought. He pressed the small of
his back into it, resisting the urge to roll. The tilt was almost
comically pronounced, as if half the house had sunk into a bog.
Standing up, you could miss it, but not lying down. It really

was like living on a boat. He lifted his socked feet in the air and crossed them at the ankles. Time for the second set. Each day, he tried to do a total of fifty.

His body was warm, despite the chill. Over the past couple of days, the temperature had fallen quite dramatically, and his new place, for all its charms, wasn't insulated very well. The drywall was cold to the touch, and from under the baseboards Luc swore he could feel a flow of frigid air. If the little house was cold now, he shuddered to think what it would be like in February. For the moment, noontime jogs were doing the trick.

He'd forgotten what a pleasure it was to get out of the house in daylight hours, and to feel endorphins pinging inside his skull. His usual route was along the Lachine Canal to Ville Saint-Pierre and back. Today, he had gone farther, most of the way to the lakeshore. It had felt great at the time, but now his knee was sore.

He did five last sit-ups and abandoned himself to the floor. His body was finally cooling off. He was wearing the new black silk jersey that Marie-Soleil had bought for him. He loved the feel of it against his skin. He closed his eyes, conjuring her. She always came to him lips open, laughing, exposing her pink cat's tongue. Her teeth were like little pearls. He felt the beginnings of an erection. He was young again himself, absolutely shameless.

Last night, he'd slept with Marie-Soleil. Up to the last minute, he'd sworn he wouldn't, but a dinner of grilled sirloin steaks and a smooth Merlot had washed away his defences. He had thought that infidelity might jolt him to his senses, fill him with remorse, or, worse, force him to acknowledge that he was no longer physically up to it. After so many years with Hannah, he'd had no idea whether it would work with another woman. For months, he had fantasized about Marie-Soleil, of course. She'd filled his waking hours. His sleeping ones too: he'd even had a wet dream about her. He closed his eyes, sniffing his fingers where traces of her smell still lingered, and had no idea why he'd ever hesitated.

He rolled onto his stomach and placed both palms on the floor by his armpits. Twenty-five push-ups, he told himself sternly. Then, and only then, could he shower. He lowered his head, brushing the tip of his nose against the mat's surface. Little bits of blue had flaked off and scattered across the floor. The smell of rubber made him think of condoms, which last night he had neglected to use.

He hadn't brought one to her flat. Pure foolishness, and a measure of the strength of his denial. Marie-Soleil wasn't in danger of getting pregnant. He wasn't totally crazy, and, more to the point, neither was she. She was on the pill, something Hannah had avoided all the years he'd known her. No messing with Hannah's hormones, *non, monsieur*, not even if it meant a mess of spermicides and diaphragms every time he wanted her. Marie-Soleil made it easy. Too easy. She hadn't even raised the condom issue with him, which, in retrospect, Luc found worrisome. She was a gorgeous, liberated young thing in her sexual prime, quite obviously not the type to deprive herself. How many men had preceded him—without condoms? Luc took a deep breath and pushed his body off the floor. He refused to let his mind go there.

On push-up number three, there was a knock at the door—a double knock, somewhat tentative. Luc leapt to his feet. It was her. It had to be. She had dropped by twice before in the early afternoon on her way back to the office after lunch meetings.

He dashed down the stairs, his whole body singing. He was wearing the black jersey. He would enfold her in it, let her feel the softness for herself. A vision of him carrying her, laughing, over the threshold rose up in his mind. He would do it. He would literally sweep that girl off her feet.

When the door opened, Serge Vien stood before him, gazing at him with his unnerving eyes. Luc's expression must have been weird, because Vien stepped backward in alarm. "Is it not a good time? I can come back, you know. It's no problem."

Luc shook his head and made reassuring sounds even as his heart folded up like a piece of origami. What was Vien doing here? How did he even know the address? No one besides Marie-Soleil had it.

"I was just at Laporte Street," Vien said, as if reading his thoughts. "Hannah told me where to find you."

Hannah. He'd forgotten about her. He looked at Vien sharply. How casually he'd said her name, as if he considered her a friend.

Vien was squatting now, the flesh of his flabby thighs straining the seams of his flannels. "I've got something for you," he said, rifling through his briefcase. Papers were jammed in haphazardly, some of them creased and torn, with faded pencil scribblings, obviously years old. He found what he was looking for. "It's a contract," he said, handing over a plain brown envelope. "School protocol. Both you and Hannah have to sign it."

There it was again—*Hannah*. Luc took the envelope but didn't open it.

Vien's attention shifted. "So this is the new space," he said, smiling politely. Dead leaves and the pages of an abandoned newspaper swirled behind him in the street. A sudden gust blew up, sending dust into Luc's face. Vien shivered in his thin suit jacket.

Luc pushed the door open and waved expansively inside. As they walked through the dim and narrow ground-floor rooms, he became aware in a way he hadn't been before that there was no furniture. Not a rug or single ornament. And the colour Monsieur Gagnon had picked for the walls looked atrocious in this light.

Luc had walked through these rooms plenty of times already, but with Vien by his side, he was seeing them with fresh eyes. And smelling them with a fresh nose. He had been habituated to it, but now, coming in from the street, he was assaulted by the close, musty odour. It grew stronger as they passed the kitchen. The strip of counter behind the kitchen sink was black with some kind of growth. The air was probably teeming with noxious spores.

He led Vien up the stairs. There was a chair upstairs—the only one in the house. As soon as they entered Luc's workspace, he regretted bringing Vien in. The yoga mat was still on the floor, but this wasn't the problem. It was hardly a crime to work out in one's office. Luc had forgotten all about the bed, however. It wasn't a real bed, just his futon in the corner, and it was obvious that it had been slept in. The sheets were in a tangle with his soiled laundry heaped on top. It looked like the room of a student.

Luc pulled his chair out from the desk and gestured for Vien to sit down. Another error. The desk was piled high as well. Clearly, not a whole lot of work was going on here. There were two boxes of light bulbs and some plastic hangers Marie-Soleil had brought over when she realized he didn't have any.

There were also tools that Luc had taken from Laporte Street: a hammer, a wrench, a screwdriver with exchangeable tips in the hollow interior of its green plastic handle. At the age of two, Hugo had vomited into this implement. Luc couldn't remember the details of how this had come about, but all these years later the screwdriver still reeked.

Vien picked up a CD from the desk and read the name on the front cover. "David Gray?" he said, breaking into a smile. "Since when do you listen to British pop?"

Luc didn't smile back. "It belongs to a friend."

Vien lifted his eyebrows twice, Groucho Marx–style, his stray eye magnifying the comic effect. Luc ignored him, turning his focus instead on the photograph of the rugged blond man on the CD cover. The shot was in black-and-white, with *David Gray—Lost Songs* printed in purple across the singer's chest and shoulders. He was unshaven. Not an actual beard, just a couple of days' growth. The hair on his head was the same length as the bristles covering his chin. He looked like a thug.

Marie-Soleil was wild about David Gray. She'd played the album for Luc the previous evening over dinner, making him listen to the lyrics and singing along in an accent that was worse even than his own. She'd played it after dinner too, which had been a shock. He'd never made love to music before. It had never occurred to him. Or to Hannah, for that matter. He didn't like it. There was something juvenile about it.

Vien was still reading the cover. To distract him, Luc opened the brown envelope. He pulled out the pages and skimmed them: several copies of a document entitled *"Contrat social."* An echo of Jean-Jacques Rousseau? He groped through the pile on his desk for his reading glasses.

When he got to the end of the document, where he was supposed to sign, he stopped short. "What's this?"

Vien looked up guiltily.

"Hugh Stern?" Luc's voice was hard with anger. Only he tripped over the pronunciation. Did one enunciate the *H* or not? *You Stern* was how it came out.

Vien shrugged. "We had to get him on board."

Luc frowned. Bonnaire used this metaphor too. As if they were a bunch of sailors.

Vien regarded him meekly. "He wouldn't have signed otherwise," he pleaded.

Luc stared at the unpronounceable first name. Part of him felt like raging. Another part whispered to let it go. Marie-Soleil's smiling lips floated into his thoughts. His breathing eased. One thing about infidelity was that it left little room to dwell on other things. Things like his infuriating son, for example, or his wife. The rabbit hole of his marriage opened in his mind, but he turned away before he could fall in. All that remained was the wobbly-sick sensation he used to feel as a boy, spinning on the tire in Saint-Henri Park. He turned away from that too, and closed his eyes.

Marie-Soleil's face was still there. He pictured her body, the delicate red rosebud tattooed on the small of her back. Half an inch below her panty line, in fact, just above the crack of her fine, shapely ass. He released his breath and turned, smiling, to Vien.

Vien's head bobbed. "You're not mad at me?" He looked like a character in a Chekhov tale, a former serf who couldn't break the habit of servility.

Luc waved as if the whole thing were a joke, youthful folly, something unimportant and excusable.

"We're good to go, then?" said Vien, looking hopeful. "You'll sign?"

Luc signed the sheets with a flourish. "Keep a copy," he advised, handing them back to Vien one at a time. "Maybe one day it'll be worth something."

There was a noise below. Vien didn't hear it, but Luc did. He hurried down the stairs, leaving Vien sitting puzzled on the chair.

Marie-Soleil was standing in full sunshine on the doorstep, smiling her luscious smile. She was in pink again, her favourite colour. Luc had watched her get dressed that morning, pulling on little white boots, ankle-high, with heels that made her pelvis jut. He loved her choice of clothes. Loved her smell too, which he breathed in hungrily whenever they embraced: spicy and sweet all at once. His balls clenched inside his gym shorts.

"Come in," he said recklessly, pulling her by the hand. She resisted at first, saying she had to get back to the office, but eventually allowed herself to be led into the little house, down his green corridor, and up his stairs. Her laughter was like music, her hand so soft it made him giddy.

It was only once they were upstairs that he realized she'd thought he wanted to make love again. When she saw Vien, she stopped short and turned to Luc, her smooth brow creasing in surprise and displeasure.

He made the introductions, telling Vien she was his agent.

"Fortunate man," said Vien, staring like a boy.

"I'm the fortunate one," she said, and illuminated Luc with her perfect white smile. "He's our brightest star."

Luc's face went hot. A pleasurable heat.

Vien couldn't stop staring. He blinked his unmoored eyes

and grinned a loopy grin. The three of them stood there, flushed and happy, buoyed by the waves of sex filling the room like a rising tide.

They conversed politely about books and the fate of the publishing industry in an increasingly digital age. Vien said that kids today were illiterate. But Marie-Soleil disagreed: they were literate, just in a way that was different from the past. Usually, this kind of talk bored Luc silly, but he was so busy attending to the happy sensations of his body that he didn't feel irritated. There was a lull in the conversation and Marie-Soleil turned to him.

"I brought you something." She reached into her handbag and rooted among its contents. The bag was large, the same shade of pink as her dress. "Ah," she said after a moment, and pulled out a promotional flyer. "I knew it was down there somewhere." She laughed and handed it to Luc. "My bag's such a *bordel*." She stood quietly beside him, almost like a child, while he took a look at it.

"Oh, this," he said. "Lanctôt."

"You hadn't forgotten?"

He *had* forgotten, as a matter of fact. Completely. Since the move, he couldn't keep the days straight. Earlier in the week, he had missed an interview with an arts reporter from *La Presse*. Wiped the rendezvous clean out of his mind. His publicist had had to phone the guy and sort it out. Now Marie-Soleil was double-checking his bookings and phoning to remind Luc before every event.

"Jacques Lanctôt?" asked Vien.

Marie-Soleil nodded and plunged a hand back into the bag. She extracted another copy of the flyer and handed it to him. "You might find this interesting too."

"Marie-Soleil used to work for him," Luc explained.

"Several years ago," said Marie-Soleil, lifting her lovely thin eyebrows as if she herself could not quite fathom it.

The skin around Vien's eyes crinkled as he laughed. "Several? Did he hire you when you were in primary school?"

Marie-Soleil beamed at the compliment and shook her dark curls.

Vien opened the flyer, then looked at Luc. "Hey. You're the main attraction."

"Hardly," said Luc modestly. "It's a fundraiser," he explained. "Lanctôt's publishing company is on the verge of bankruptcy."

"So his friends have gotten together," Marie-Soleil said. "Everyone's chipping in."

"Marie-Soleil organized the whole thing," Luc said, smiling at her.

She shrugged. "He was good to me. A generous man. Several distinguished writers are attending. Including our friend here." She took Luc's hand and raised it as if he were a boxer, as if she were showing him off. "He's reading from the new novel."

"Thank God you reminded me," said Luc. He really was grateful. His agenda was back at Laporte Street, a place he wasn't about to visit.

"That's what you pay me for." She winked at him, and the wink was so laden with sexual innuendo that Luc had to avert his eyes.

Marie-Soleil did the same, shifting her focus to Vien. "Would you like to come?"

She sounded so young. Like a Girl Guide selling raffle tickets. She began to read the list of "celebrity authors" she had persuaded to take part.

"When is it?" Vien asked, searching the flyer for a date.

"Tonight." Marie-Soleil gave Luc a meaningful glance. "I'll swing by after work and pick you up. We can get a bite to eat en route."

"I like Lanctôt," Vien said suddenly.

"Oh," said Marie-Soleil. "You know him?"

Vien laughed. "No, no, although I did have the pleasure of interviewing him once." He was wearing his serf's smile again, bobbing his big hairy head. "And of course I've seen him often enough on TV. He hasn't given up. It's inspiring."

Marie-Soleil nodded, smiling. "So come," she said. "The event starts at eight, but you should come earlier if you want a seat. We can save you one, if you want."

The two men followed her down the stairs to the door. Her telephone hummed. It was Frédéric, she said, checking the caller ID. She would be in serious trouble if she didn't get her ass back to the office.

At the door, Vien shook Marie-Soleil's hand a moment longer than absolutely necessary, telling her what a pleasure it had been and wishing her good luck with the soirée. Luc stood by and watched. Men must shake that hand a lot, he realized. Anything to touch her.

Luc's gaze slipped unconsciously to her chest and he pictured the breasts nestled beneath her blouse inside an expensive lacy bra. She liked good lingerie, a fact that he found surprisingly exciting. Aesthetics mattered to her. The rituals of arousal. She had a whole drawer full of fine underthings. Unlike Hannah, Marie-Soleil would never dream of wearing torn panties. She kissed him goodbye, two chaste pecks, her lips barely grazing his whiskers. It lasted only a second, but the effect on Luc was incendiary. He stepped backward, and she walked away. He and Vien watched in silence as she picked her way down the cracked front walk.

"Whooo," said Vien when she was well down the street.

Luc laughed, but a bit of dust from the street caught in his throat.

"That's some girl." Vien turned back to face him. "So, you two are …?" He didn't finish. He'd seen his answer in Luc's eyes.

For a moment, neither man spoke. Luc could see his friend was envious, but his expression was also sad.

"I'd be careful if I were you," Vien said.

Luc laughed again.

"Seriously. I've been on the other end. And it was hell. Believe me." He began again to recount the story of his marriage, or at least the end of it. It had been someone at his wife's office. Someone they'd both known for years.

"There's no going back once it's done," Vien said, shaking his shaggy head. "We tried, believe me. You don't throw out ten years of marriage just like that. She broke it off with the guy and we started going to counselling. For months in that therapist's office, she talked about her father, who'd also been unfaithful. She wept over him. I wept over her. I took her to Italy, a trip she'd always dreamed of. Venice, Rome, the works. None of it made the slightest difference."

Luc listened in silence, his sympathy not quite equal to his irritation. He felt bad for Vien, sure, but he had nothing to learn from the story of his silly ex-wife and her middle-aged gropings. This thing with Marie-Soleil wasn't like that. It wasn't just a piece of mid-life craziness. Luc looked out over the vacant tracks. It was far more elemental.

The word tolled inside him like a bell. It sounded dramatic, but now that he had allowed himself to formulate it, he knew it to be true. What was going on between him and Marie-Soleil was elemental. It went to the core of him. It had to do with language and culture, with his identity. He'd felt a profound and instant kinship with the girl, a feeling he had never experienced with Hannah.

Vien was making an irritating snapping noise, flipping the buckle on his briefcase with his thumb. Luc cleared his throat and the noise stopped, but Vien didn't look at him. He kept his eyes resolutely down. Even when they said goodbye, he didn't raise them.

17

*H*ugo made it to the classroom on time for once. He was tired today, fed up with these after-school meetings. He wanted to go home and sleep. He rapped loudly, three decisive knocks, to show Vien he meant business. The sound of his knuckles striking wood reverberated through the empty hallway. He knocked again, then tried the door, but it was locked. He knew how to open it; he carried a small flat comb in his knapsack for just such occasions. All you had to do was slip the comb in the crack below the bolt and jerk upward. They'd done it hundreds of times last year, tormenting Madame Martel, the art teacher, stealing her art supplies and writing obscenities on the board, until finally she took sick leave. He felt bad about that. She'd been too nice, really, to teach in a high school.

The comb would stay in his knapsack this afternoon. Hugo couldn't afford any trouble. He leaned against the wall and slid into a crouch. Goddamn Vien, late himself, after all the times he'd lectured Hugo on the subject.

He reached into his knapsack and pulled out a ball of Kleenex.

It opened like a flower when he gave it a poke, exposing a plastic dime bag stamped with a seven-pointed leaf. Bought today from a kid in his class who had a junior grow-op in his basement. Death if he was caught. Hugo was on parole. Carrying a dime bag of dope into a meeting with your supervisor was courting disaster, but some part of him needed to do just that. Fuck them all.

The door from the stairs opened and Vien stepped into view, huffing and looking more dishevelled than usual. He'd obviously just run up the stairs. He raised his hand.

"Sorry, sorry."

Hugo stuffed the Kleenex back inside his knapsack and zipped the pocket shut as Vien came striding up.

"Sorry," he said again, wiping sweat from his brow. Pathetic. "Give me a minute." He fished in his pocket for his keys, found them and fumbled with the lock. He was a clumsy man, prone to flusters, not at all like Hugo's dad, the master of smooth. Vien grunted and muttered, forcing the key repeatedly until he realized he was using the wrong one.

More apologies. Inside, all the windows were closed; with the radiators blasting, it felt like they'd been closed for months. Vien swore, yanking at his tie. Then he did a quick striptease, ripping off tie and jacket as if they were on fire, picking up his hair to air his neck. His face had turned red. He instructed Hugo to pull up a chair and spent long minutes struggling to open all the windows.

"*Bon,*" he said, coming back to Hugo's side. He sat down, heaved a dramatic sigh, and smiled. "So," he said, "how are you?"

Something had changed. Vien's eyes actually looked interested.

Hugo shrugged.

"Everything okay today?"

Hugo averted his gaze uncomfortably. The tree in the yard out front was clinging to the last of its leaves.

"It's not an easy time, I know," Vien said, his eyes big and receptive. To Hugo's astonished dismay, he reached out and touched his forearm.

Hugo jerked back in his chair. The door was ajar. His whole body tensed, ready to bolt.

Vien withdrew his hand and put it safely on his own knee. "I know what it's like. My dad walked out too, Hugo. I told you about it, remember?"

Hugo stared at him in surprise. So he knew. His father must have talked. Who else had he told besides Vien? Was it common knowledge now?

"I was just about your age," Vien continued. "It was the most painful thing I've ever experienced. Worse than when my wife left me."

Hugo shifted in his chair. Too much information, but Vien kept right on talking. His eyes were slightly unfocused, as if he were in a trance. "I woke up one morning," he said, "and he was gone. Just like that. No warning, no note. He just left." Vien removed his glasses and started rubbing them with great thoroughness.

"That's when I met your dad," he said after a pause that had grown uncomfortable. "But you know all that. We talked about it." He put his glasses back on. "Fathers." He sighed. "They can be complicated."

Hugo was looking at Vien's hands. He'd never noticed how ragged his nails were. The skin between the top knuckle and the cuticle was bumpy and red on nearly every finger. Close-bitten. What a sad, sad man.

"Any more thoughts on your paper?" Vien asked.

Hugo didn't reply.

"I hope you've opened Vallières," he continued. "*Nègres blancs* is critical. Anyone who wants to understand the 1970s in Quebec has to read it."

The air in the classroom was still hot. It pressed in on all sides. And it smelled stale, as though his classmates' lungs had been recycling it all day. Hugo was overpoweringly sleepy. And hungry. His stomach was making noises.

He *had* opened Vallières. He'd stayed up late again last night trying to read it. But he wouldn't admit it to Vien. Thinking about it made him sleepier. He didn't want to discuss Vallières or anything else. When this sad man and Hugo's father had been boys, they had stood by each other. But they weren't boys anymore, and as far as Hugo could tell, neither of them was making any effort to stand by him.

What Hugo wanted right now was food. Nachos and cheese, to be exact. He could picture the melted cheese, which bubbled and then turned rubbery when you poured on salsa from the fridge. Not that the fridge at home usually contained anything half as good as this. Still, he salivated thinking of the salt and spice.

Vien stood up, jolting Hugo out of his reverie. He reached, with some difficulty, into the pocket of his too-tight grey flannel pants. "Here," he said, pulling out a flyer of some sort. "Someone just gave me this. It's a happy coincidence. I thought immediately of you."

It was an invitation.

"It's a benefit event," said Vien, beaming. "For Jacques Lanctôt. He'll be there tonight. So will your dad, by the way. He's one of the readers." His smile widened. "We could go together if you wish. I could talk to your mom, tell her that I'll drive you." He paused to take a breath before pressing on. "Your dad could introduce you to Lanctôt. It's a great opportunity, Hugo. I bet he'd give you an interview, if you asked. The son of Luc Lévesque? For sure he would." He stopped suddenly and frowned, struck by a thought. The frown cleared. "We'll let Luc know you're coming. Best to avoid surprises."

Hugo mumbled something about being grounded. A lame excuse, but there was no way he was going to this thing. No way in the world.

Vien didn't get it. It was as if he hadn't even seen Hugo's sneer. The man was bent over his desk, scribbling down his cell phone number on a slip of paper. Jesus. He was serious about this. Vien looked up as he handed the number to Hugo.

"Try to come. I can convince your mom, if you want."

Like he really wanted Vien telephoning his mother. The skin of Hugo's chest and face prickled with heat. He shoved the flyer and the slip of paper into his pocket. "That's okay," he said, although the situation was as far from okay as he could imagine.

18

All the way home on the metro, Hugo couldn't push Lanctôt out of his mind. He'd kidnapped a man, and yet his dad and Vien and all kinds of other supposedly sane and thoughtful people were throwing a party in his honour? And then there was his dad, revered by all of Quebec, and yet such a prick. The world was a truly messed-up place.

It was rush hour. Hugo got caught in the throngs at the Guy-Concordia metro station. On the train, he was forced to squeeze in beside a guy whose headphones bled music so loudly Hugo felt it shaking in his bones. Most of the riders were students. Somebody had dropped a bottle of iced tea, which rolled back and forth under the seats, splattering the floor with sticky brown liquid. People stepped over the puddles as they entered and exited the car, but no one thought to pick up the bottle.

Hugo's sneakers made faint sucking sounds with every step on the staircase at Lionel-Groulx. Iced tea syrup. He looked at the stream of people on the escalator and remembered the physical shock of seeing his father.

When he got home, his mother was reading on the couch. She was always there now, glued permanently to the cushions. She blinked as if she wasn't sure who he was and spoke his name in a dreamy voice.

He didn't answer.

Her books and some pillows were scattered beside her on the floor. A couple of Kleenexes too. The place was a pigsty. And there was no whiff of food coming from the kitchen. She'd probably forgotten about dinner. Again. The fridge had been empty for days. The kitchen, when he entered it, had a sour smell. He walked to a window and yanked it open.

"Hey, summer's over," his mother said, coming into the kitchen and rubbing her arms. But neither of them made any move to close it.

He made Kraft Dinner. She wasn't hungry, so he took the whole pot for himself, upending it on his plate and dotting the bright orange noodles with splotches of ketchup. She sat across from him, elbows on the table, and watched him eat.

He couldn't stand her long, mournful face, the greasy smell of her hair. This thing with his dad was killing her; anyone could see that. And yet she was the one who had given everything up, handing him her language, her culture, even her name, as if none of it meant a thing. How had she thought it would end? He couldn't even feel sorry for her.

He needed a strong parent right now, not this beaten-down person. He needed to ask her things. About his father. About *her* father.

Vien had said that Alfred Stern had been a Crown prosecutor. Hugo was confused. He'd thought his grandfather had defended criminals, not prosecuted them. And he'd played some kind of role in the October Crisis. An important one, Vien had suggested. This hadn't been mentioned when Hugo had done the project in grade six. Hugo did know that his grandfather had left Quebec shortly after René Lévesque came to power, giving up his house on the mountain and ending up in Toronto with all the other Anglos. *The Exodus.* His mother had told him that soldiers had guarded their Westmount home. There were two of them, only a few years older than she was. Hugo had seen a photograph of her, at age twelve, posing between two guys with helmets and C7s.

So many questions. Hugo was lost in his thoughts when the telephone in the pantry rang. His mother made no move to get up. After five rings, the answering machine clicked on and a woman's voice spoke. "Hey, Hannah. It's Allison at the Word." The voice sounded pissed. She'd already left two messages and asked to be called back. His mother made a face as the woman hung up.

"You could've taken it," Hugo said, swallowing the last of his macaroni, which was now cold.

His mother smiled her weary smile, which he found hateful. He was about to say as much when the phone rang again. And again his mother just sat there. By the third ring, he couldn't stand it anymore. He stood up, but she shook her head. He stayed where he was.

From the pantry came a woman's voice.

At first, Hugo didn't recognize it. "Is that Oma?" It sounded too feeble to be his grandmother.

"Where are you?" it asked.

"I'm done," said Hugo. He pointed at his empty plate. There was a house rule about dinner and telephones. You didn't answer if there was food on your plate. But this, quite obviously, had nothing to do with rules.

His mother sat there, slumped in her chair. Hugo sat down again and the answering machine clicked off.

He addressed his plate. "Vien knows your dad."

She lifted her head and nodded. She was still wearing her nightgown, the same one she'd had on when he left for school that morning.

"He said he was a prosecutor."

She blinked. "That's not quite true," she said. "He was a defence lawyer." She frowned and then continued. "But the government made him a special prosecutor." She pressed her fingertips into old crumbs on the table. "In 1970. To deal with the people who'd been arrested under the War Measures Act."

"Is that why you hate him so much?"

"Who?" She looked up in surprise. "My father?"

"Because he put them all in jail?"

"He didn't put them in jail, Hugo. The police did that."

"But he was part of it, right? Part of the operation. That's what Vien said. His name was in all the papers. They hated him. Is that why we don't see him now?"

She had assembled a little pile of crumbs in front of her. "We do see him, Hugo. I do. I just spent a week—"

He cut her off. "You hate going down there."

Hannah shook her head. "I don't hate it," she said. "And I certainly don't hate him."

She was lying. Treating him like a child and assuming she could still get away with it.

Hugo took a breath. "What did he do to you? Hit you?

Abuse you in some way? You can tell me. I don't need protecting anymore."

His mother's eyes closed. He wanted to shout and make her look at him. But then she started to speak. Very softly. Her eyes were still closed and her face was slack and expressionless. He leaned toward her, holding his breath. "We used to fight," she said. "Not physically. It never went beyond words, but the words were pretty awful. For some reason, he saw me as an enemy." She sighed. "When your dad came into my life, it made things worse."

So there it was, just as Hugo had imagined. His father was at the heart of it. He was the one who had broken up the family.

"Is he why you stayed?"

Seconds passed. Her eyelids were darker than the rest of her face, the colour of a bruise.

"Maman?" he said, but her eyes stayed closed.

Silence. The story of his mother's life. And of his.

He picked up his plate and brought it to the sink. She'd opened her eyes, but he no longer cared. He turned the faucet on so hard that water splashed onto his shirt front. The plate slipped from his hands and clattered against the stainless steel. He left it there and walked out of the kitchen.

He closed his bedroom door and stood there, breathing hard. He hated his life. He hated his fucking father, hated his depressed rag doll of a mother. The floor creaked in the hallway and Hugo's breath stopped. He strained to hear, but the hallway fell silent. He felt angrier, then, at the stupid hope that he couldn't stop from rising up in him. Damn his mother. *It was time to put away childish things*: a favourite saying of his father's. An image of his father materialized in the semi-darkness. Hugo took an experimental swing at it and smashed his fist into its nose. The face looked at him, surprised. He swung again, this time at the mouth, with another satisfying impact. On and on he swung, his heart beating wildly, until the face was a pulpy mess.

He collapsed backward on his bed. He'd once loved his father more than anyone in the world, more even than Hannah. His whole life had been one unbroken effort to please him. That was what being a child was about. You didn't question. You spoke like him, you dressed like him, you ate all his favourite foods. Hugo shook his head in disgust. Childhood was over now.

He picked up a book that was lying on the floor. Vallières. His father must have read it too, back in the 1970s. The story he told of his own father was identical to Vallières's. Both men had worked in factories. Both had had their spirits crushed by evil Anglo bosses. Luc Lévesque had made his name on this cliché: a French-Canadian martyr-father had figured in every one of his books. It was like a trademark. Scholars wrote papers about it. This father figure was always long-dead. He hovered above Luc's plots like a ghost, blocking the way as his son tried to define himself in a rapidly changing world. At least, that was what Hugo's literature teacher at Saint-Jean-Baptiste had said two years ago, when they'd studied *Tanneur tanné*.

Hugo had recognized so many things in *Tanneur tanné*— Saint-Henri's streets, its churches and factories, the train tracks, the canal—that it felt more like fact than fiction. He had never met his father's father. Roland Lévesque had died before he was born, but *Tanneur tanné* had resurrected him for Hugo, if only partially, because in the novel his character was a ghost. But for Hugo, the book had been a first step. Hugo's entire class had met his dead grandfather. They knew him as well as Hugo did.

After reading his father's first novel, Hugo embarked on the others, lifting them one after the other from the living room bookshelf reserved for his father's publications and their translations. That was how he came upon a fictionalized version of his second grandfather, Alfred Stern. He materialized in *Les blues de Saint-Ambroise* as the host of a party into which the young Québécois hero had stumbled, invited by the host's beautiful English daughter. Alfred Stern's last name was changed to Klein, which in German meant "small," but the physical traits were all there. The Westmount home was described in detail, as were the kind of people Hugo's grandfather had invited to his parties, all English, all shaking with fear at the thought that Quebec might become a country one day. *Les blues* was set in January 1977, two months after the separatists had won a victory—their first ever—in a provincial election.

The scene was intended to be comic, with the *petit gars* from Saint-Henri committing gaffe after social gaffe at the table of his wealthy father-in-law-to-be. But Hugo had not laughed. Alfred Stern came across as a bigot, a cartoon of a man, baiting his daughter's French boyfriend without mercy, and then, when the young man finally rose to the challenge, kicking him shamelessly out of the house.

Hugo opened Vallières at the place at which he'd fallen asleep the night before. "Sometimes," he read, squinting in the weak light from the overhead, "one imagines that one's past has disappeared leaving no memory, like a cloud that has drifted apart in the sky. But that is an illusion. One has only to be immobilized for a few weeks (in prison, for example) to find one's past again and relive it in its smallest details." Hugo slammed the book shut and let it fall to the floor. He was in prison too—a kind of prison—and like Vallières he was rediscovering the past. Only it was not *his* past. It belonged to his father, to Vien, to Jacques Lanctôt.

On the dust jackets of his father's books, Hugo had read the claim that his father was the voice of his generation. Which poor sucker, he wondered, would end up speaking for *his* generation? The generation that had watched hijacked planes fly straight into Manhattan's two tallest towers, and for whom the word *suicide* was, as likely as not, followed by *bomber*. Perhaps his generation would be voiceless, condemned to having older men like his father repeat their own stories, thoughtlessly, mechanically, until they finally rolled over and died.

Vallières was a lousy writer. That was the sad truth of it. His sentences were bloated with slogans and terms meant to shock a reader. Words like *nigger*, for example, and *slave*, applied carelessly and wrongly to the Québécois. Monsieur Vien had also talked about a writer named Frantz Fanon. Fanon wrote about Algeria and its suffering under French colonial rule. The political situation in Quebec in October 1970 was totally different from Algeria, yet Fanon's words had inspired Lanctôt's kidnapping plot.

Hugo pulled off his itchy school shirt, scrunched it into a ball, and hurled it across the room. As he pulled off his pants, he remembered the flyer in his pocket and retrieved it. *Une célébration d'un des nôtres.* Hugo made a face. Then he checked his alarm clock.

Screw reading. He wouldn't pick up Vallières again if someone paid him. It would be interesting to see Lanctôt in action. He didn't have to speak to him or anything. He could watch. Anonymously. Consider it a fact-finding mission.

He pulled on his favourite pair of jeans and a hoodie, and fished an old pair of sneakers from his closet. Then he turned the lights off and positioned his pillows under the duvet to make it appear that he'd gone to sleep. His window had a ledge from which, if you didn't mind heights, you could jump onto the fire escape.

The night was colder than he'd thought. He hit his knee when he landed, so hard that the iron bars hummed. He crouched, holding his breath until the noise and the pain subsided. The living room glowed before him. His mother was on the couch, a book propped on her knees. She was thinner than he had ever seen her. Older-looking too. The hair at her temples was turning grey. She raised her head suddenly, and looked directly at him. She couldn't see him, though, he was pretty certain. She sat up and looked at her reflection in the window. What she saw didn't appear to make her happy. She touched her hair and looked away.

Hugo climbed slowly down the fire escape. Lyse's flat was lit up too, but she had curtains and they were drawn. Through the lacy white material, he made out the silhouette of a form. No, two forms. It was probably Graeme White, the English guy she claimed was just a friend.

The ground-floor flat was completely black. The last few steps weren't steps at all but the rungs of a ladder, from which it was a long drop to the grass. For several seconds, Hugo hung as if on a trapeze, swaying over a black void. He landed hard, then jumped to his feet and ran. By the time he reached the street, he felt almost calm.

The party for Lanctôt was on Saint-Joseph Boulevard, not far from Saint-Laurent. That was on the orange metro line. Half an hour later, Hugo was jogging up the stairs at the Laurier station. Saint-Joseph Boulevard was a wide, divided street that seemed to lead straight to the mountain, which crouched to the west, crowned with a glittering cross. Hugo walked toward it.

He didn't have to go far. He spotted the place almost immediately, alerted by the crowd of people crammed into the front yard. Like many of the houses in this part of the city, it had a porch and a little patch of grass. Some of the houses had bushes and flowers, but the garden here was bare.

Hugo slowed his pace. He didn't like crowds. And in this one everybody seemed to be talking at once, laughing and blowing smoke from cigarettes at the pale slice of moon. Hugo was bound to stand out in this gathering. He was way younger than everyone else. And because of his height, they would think he was even younger. A woman unlatched the gate for him, smiling tenderly, the way a mother might. He had a sudden urge to run, but the woman was watching him, so he had no choice but to keep going. People blocked his path. They were everywhere, spilling out of the house onto the porch, hanging over the wooden railing, waving their hands, discussing things. Inside was even worse. There was no air at all. The hallway, which was lightless, led to a bright main room, which turned out to be two rooms. A black man was standing at a podium reading something about Port-au-Prince and making people laugh. Every seat in the place was taken.

Hugo could hardly breathe. He tried to retrace his steps, but people were pushing in from behind him now, blocking his exit. Everywhere he looked, more people kept appearing, elbowing their way forward. The black man closed his book and people started clapping. Then a man in the front row stood up to shake his hand. Hugo stared. He was shorter than in the newspaper photos. Fatter. And his eyes darted. Beside him was another person Hugo recognized, holding his hands above his head and hooting and clapping. His father. And next to his father was the woman Hugo had seen at the metro station. Vien was sitting one row behind them, grinning like a loon.

Jacques Lanctôt stepped up to the podium. "A difficult act to follow," he said, shaking his head with false regret. He looked up at the packed room as the last of the applause frittered away. "Unless, *bien sûr*, your name is Luc Lévesque."

The room erupted again. People weren't just clapping now, they were whistling and stamping their feet. Lanctôt waited until they calmed down. "It's an honour to have this esteemed *auteur* with us. The voice of our people. I cannot tell you what pleasure it gives me." He held out his hands, his gaze briefly direct, his eyes shining. "Come up here, Luc."

His father rose to his feet. Before going to the stage, however, he bent over the woman and kissed her on the mouth. In public. In front of all these people.

His father's mouth now wore a trace of her lipstick. He looked like a stupid clown. Hugo felt ill. He hoped the Kraft Dinner he'd wolfed down an hour earlier would not come back up. He tried to move toward the hall, but the crowd behind him was like a wall, solid and insistent like the Montreal metro at rush hour. He didn't stand a chance.

At the podium, Jacques Lanctôt had put an arm around his father. Lanctôt was grinning, pressing against him as if they were long lost brothers. He gave a speech about the *p'tit gars de Saint-Henri* and how Luc Lévesque had possessed the guts and the genius to set his stories locally, with characters culled from his own *petite vie*. Writers like Luc, he said, significantly dropping his father's last name, gave the people of Quebec a voice with which to address the world.

The room erupted into cheers.

Somehow Hugo pushed his way into the hall. People were staring at him. Some of them swore as well, but to get back out that door he was willing to face their displeasure. He was convinced that he would vomit. His mouth was full of water. It was all he could do to keep upright. But the minute he was out, his panic fell magically away. The nausea was replaced by euphoria. He felt as if he'd scaled a mountain, crossed enemy lines. He'd made it.

The smokers were still in the yard, although the woman who had opened the gate for him was nowhere to be seen. What a relief. He unlatched the gate and slipped out onto the sidewalk, not bothering to close it. And then he took off, sprinting down the wide boulevard, knees and elbows pumping, his boy's body blazing like a shooting star through the night. Only when the downward arrow of the Montreal metro came into sight did his feet slow. He'd done it. He'd broken free. And nothing in this pitiful, two-faced excuse for a world would ever force him to return.

19

*H*annah awoke with the panicky sensation that someone was kneeling on her chest, pressing the air out of her. She sat up, rubbed her eyes, and squinted at the clock on Luc's bedside table. It was a couple of minutes past four. Three hours to go till sunrise.

She needed to talk to Hugo, to explain. Not that she felt remotely capable of doing so. How could she put something as fraught as her relationship with Alfred Stern into words? She had never had a sense of kinship with her father, not even when she was a child. In some dark corner of his heart or soul, he was appalled by her. Her colouring was different from his. Her height and build were wrong, not to mention her opinions. This was the central fact of Hannah's life, the one that had structured the whole of her experience: she had been unable to win her father's love.

At nineteen, she'd given up. When he moved to Toronto, she pushed him out of her mind. It had worked. The distance allowed her to function with something that felt, at least at first, like tranquility. But now her father was back with a vengeance, crying out for attention as he lay speechless in a Toronto hospital. And Hugo was his defender, accusing her of callous disregard.

Why had she stayed in Montreal? Maybe there was no answer to this question. Maybe there were just moments. Memories and scenes. Like the disastrous New Year's Eve party when her father and Luc met for the first time. Luc had immortalized it in *Les blues de Saint-Ambroise*, but her impression of the occasion was different, even if *Les blues* had, inevitably, reshaped her memory. Fiction did that. It solidified things, which was a problem, because life was fundamentally fluid. There were a thousand ways to interpret it, all worthy, no matter how cleverly a writer like Luc Lévesque tried to convince you otherwise. Hannah knew her father more intimately than Luc did, knew his history, his culture. Knew what might, perhaps, lead a man to throw his daughter's newly acquired, semi-famous, long-haired, separatist Québécois boyfriend out of his home on a snowy New Year's Eve in the mid-1970s. Alfred Stern, doubtless, had a different version of his own. Reality boiled down to this in the end: the story you told. Everyone had one. No one could claim a right to the last word.

Now that she'd begun to think about it, there were other stories she could tell Hugo. Stories that went further back, to a time before her birth. The story of her father's escape from Austria, of his arrival in Canada as a potential enemy of the state when he was barely sixteen. She couldn't remember the name of the prison camp where he'd ended up, but she remembered certain details. It was in New Brunswick. And he'd had to wear the uniform she'd told Manny Mandelbaum about, the one with the red target on the back. Her father had slept in an unheated barracks crowded with other Jewish German and Austrian refugees. He'd chopped trees all that winter, freezing his fingers so badly he still carried the scars.

Some of this information Hannah had received second-hand from Connie. Alfred Stern did not like looking back. Once he'd been released from the camp, he had tried to strip himself clean of anything associated with it and with his country of origin. This desire, Hannah knew, lay behind many things.

Was it Aristotle who said man is his desire? Alfred Stern's desire had been to fit in, to take the colours of his new habitat and make them his own. This explained Connie, the blond beauty he'd met at a McGill football game and courted so vigorously that six months later she married him. It explained why he had not insisted on her conversion to Judaism, and why Hannah and Benjamin had received a largely secular upbringing.

The moment he gained his freedom in Canada, Alfred Stern had set about disappearing. With each passing year, he erased a little more of himself, the better to gain entry into a world with little tolerance for people like him. The deeper into that world he ventured, the less there remained of the immigrant child who had arrived alone and friendless in this cold, wintry country. But erasure came at a cost. The more he disappeared, the harder it became to recall essential parts of himself, and to reveal them, even in the safety of his own home.

It was all speculation, of course, a daughter's necessarily partial account of a man whose past was inaccessible to her. But how had Manny Mandelbaum put it? Adulthood was the vantage point from which you could tell the story of your parents, really start imagining them as human beings with their own complex pasts. This much, Hannah had done. Or at least was in the process of doing.

She pulled the sheets up, letting the cotton rest lightly on her lips. She would talk to Hugo at breakfast, she decided, provided she could get him out of bed in time to sit down with her. She pictured the intimate scene, herself and her son in the kitchen eating toast together. Yes, she would start with the story of that family party all those years ago on the last night of 1976 at her father's home on the hill. The memory was still singularly painful.

She turned on the bedside lamp and glanced at the side of the mattress that used to belong to Luc. Folding her knees into her chest, she made a hummock in the flat plain of the bed, and soon she was asleep.

SHE WOKE UP STARTLED. The lamp beside the bed was still on. She was lying on her back with her knees drawn up. She unhooked her fingers and gingerly stretched out her legs, one at a time, beneath the duvet. She had dreamt of her father. He'd looked different, though. For a split second, Hannah had glimpsed another, much younger person when she'd scrutinized his face.

She blinked uncomfortably. The light from her bedside lamp was shining directly in her eyes. She rolled out of bed, suddenly recalling all the things she needed to do this morning. It was past seven, she saw from Luc's clock. She'd have to hurry if she was going to make Hugo breakfast and tell him her story.

The house was silent when she emerged from the bathroom. She knocked on Hugo's door, and knocked again when he didn't answer. After the third try, she grew impatient and opened the door. The duvet had been pulled up crudely over his three pillows. That was the first shock. Hanging from his closet doorknob, just to the left of the bed, were his school clothes. The next shock was the cold. The window was wide open, with the screen on the floor below it.

Hannah rushed to the window. She felt sick and alert at the same time, her senses desperately alive, sucking in every colour, shape, and texture: the cloudless morning sky, the beige paint flaking in shaggy feathers on the neighbour's balcony, the rusted iron railings of the fire escape. Her hands braced themselves on the window ledge and she bent over, sticking her head out into the bracing October air. The gravel in the yard came into view. A pile of leaves raked up against the front of Lyse's shed. A strip of yellowed grass, trampled and dead, awaiting snow.

No body, though. No fallen son. Her knees felt weak with relief.

She lifted her hands from the ledge and held herself, rocking. She breathed in the cold air. He hadn't jumped. Her arms were trembling. She looked out into the day and registered now what in her panic she had missed before. The fire escape. Luc had used it too when he was a boy. He'd told her stories about illicit late-night escapades.

Hugo's hoodie was gone. And his favourite jeans. She slammed the window shut and ran out of the bedroom to the front hall for her coat. She hadn't felt such a rush of pure energy in months. She hurried down the stairs, past Lyse's door, and out into the dazzling morning. Frost had come in the night, covering the cars with a fuzzy skin. It was shockingly cold, and the outside stairs were treacherous. The icy metal railing stung her hand.

She'd left without gloves or a hat. She balled her hands into fists and ran into the alley behind the house. She looked into the yard, the neighbours' gardens. No sign of Hugo. Everything was in its place. She re-emerged from the alley and ran down Laporte Street to Saint-Jacques, her heart pounding. She felt exhilarated, almost happy. Her son was alive. He had done what boys do: he had sneaked out.

She ran through Saint-Henri Square and past the fire hall. The firefighters washing their trucks in the sunshine stopped to watch her—a woman in her forties running hard, the way few women do, with a purpose.

She knew exactly where the house was. Knew exactly what she would find. It was past seven. Luc would be at his desk, hard at work. He would have been there for an hour, maybe more. There would be coffee in the Turkish pot. The place would be full of its dark smell. And he, her husband, would be hammering away at his computer.

It was smaller than she remembered. He had brought her here once—brought his whole class—on a *Bonheur d'occasion* tour. It was the crowning moment of his Quebec literature course: the strange ship-shaped house of Jean Lévesque. There was no bell on the door, so she knocked. When no one answered, she started pounding with both fists. An elderly woman coming out of the apartment block across the street with two small children paused to watch.

There were no windows on the front of the house, so she couldn't look inside. She went down the cracked front walk and was about to go around the back when the front door swung open and Luc stuck his head out into the sunshine. His eyes were small, the skin around them puffy and cross-hatched with fine lines. His feet were bare, and he was wearing a bathrobe. His breath, when he finally said her name, came out in a cloud.

"You were sleeping?" she asked, surprised.

He nodded, his eyes avoiding hers. He looked slightly stunned, as if he wasn't yet fully awake. He didn't seem to notice the cold. Instead of inviting her inside, he stepped down onto the walk and closed the front door behind him. His feet looked white and vulnerable on the concrete.

"It's about Hugo," she said, her voice competing with the traffic. "He's run away. When I woke up this morning, he was gone."

He stared at her stupidly, as if the words weren't registering.

"Did you hear me?" she said. "When I looked in his room, the bed hadn't been slept in. The window was open." She stopped. His face was still blank. It was like a bad dream. "He used the fire escape," she said angrily. "Like you used to, remember?"

When Luc still said nothing, she lost her temper. "What is the *matter* with you?" But even as she formulated the question, she saw the truth. There was someone inside the house, someone he didn't want her to see.

"He's here, isn't he?"

"No," Luc said quietly.

"If he is, you have to tell me. You have to. I need to know he's safe."

He stood there, frozen.

"Luc," she said. "For God's sake."

He lowered his eyes. "There is someone here. But it's not Hugo."

"Oh," she said, as understanding dawned. She could not face this right now.

He looked reluctantly at the door. "It's probably best you don't come in."

"Well, we can't talk here."

They agreed he would come to Laporte Street as soon as he could manage. And that she would contact the police. That was that. She turned and walked back up Saint-Augustin Street, retracing the route she had just taken, blind and deaf now to sights and sounds, unaware even of the wind biting at her face.

The outer stairs at Laporte Street were still treacherous with frost. She climbed carefully, holding the railing. Her fingers were so stiff and cold that when she got back inside she could barely dial 9-1-1.

When the police showed up twenty minutes later, she was waiting by the living room window. They got the address wrong and rang at her mother-in-law's door instead of climbing to the third-floor flat. When they finally came up, Lyse was trailing behind them, pale with panic. "What do you mean, gone?" she kept saying, her voice a high-pitched tremolo.

Luc arrived a moment later, combed and dressed. He'd recovered his composure and proceeded to take charge. There were two officers—a young woman and an older man. He led them to the living room and sat facing them as though his position as head of this household were unchanged, as if he had not been absent and unreachable for the past two weeks. As if he'd given Hugo a single thought during that time.

He answered the questions of the female officer, who did all the asking, in his calm, authoritative way. He smiled at the young woman, even daring to be ironic despite the seriousness of the situation, looking her in the eye when she smiled in response. His voice was deep and sonorous. Everyone in the room was listening, falling under its sway.

"So, you have no idea where he may have gone?" asked the young cop. "He gave no sign of anything last night?"

Hannah had had enough. "My husband wasn't here last night," she said.

Luc reddened. "No, no. That's right. I was out."

Hannah stared at him in astonishment. "You weren't out," she said. "Or strictly speaking you were, but that's not the point. The point is, you don't live here anymore. They need to know that, Luc. It's important."

Hannah could feel her mother-in-law's anxious gaze on her. "You don't live here?" the younger officer asked Luc.

Luc shook his head, but not before giving Hannah an odd look. He wasn't used to his wife speaking out like this. Neither, frankly, was Hannah. But someone had to, for Hugo's sake.

"So, when did you move out?" asked the girl. The officers seemed to have taken separate roles. She was doing the talking while the older one watched.

Luc cleared his throat and admitted it had been two weeks. There had been tensions in the family. The officers listened quietly. They knew they were dealing with a celebrity. The young woman took down his new address in her notebook and then turned to Hannah.

"So, you were with Hugo last night, is that right?"

Hannah nodded. "We ate dinner together," she said, remembering the Kraft noodles.

"And he seemed all right?"

Hannah paused. *All right.* She had no reference points anymore for what that might mean.

"Madame Lévesque?" said the young woman.

"It's been a difficult period," she said. The officer was terribly young, in her mid-twenties. What could she possibly know about faltering marriages and runaway sons? "He's been in trouble at school," she said slowly. "And things at home haven't been the best."

Luc sprang to his feet. "It's not as dire as she makes it sound. He's back in school now. They took him back. He attends a private school. A good one. Saint-Jean-Baptiste," he said, speaking fast. "They are very strict there. Lots of rules and regulations. He's been rebelling. Nothing outside of the normal teenage stuff." He flashed a congenial smile.

The female officer looked at Hannah. "There has been trouble at school?"

Hannah nodded. She told the story of the gun.

The officers exchanged looks. The female officer scribbled something in her notebook, which was small and black and official looking. Her handwriting was large and loopy.

"It wasn't so serious as that," said Luc.

The older officer raised his eyebrow. "Showing up at school with a gun?"

"It wasn't loaded," said Luc. "It was an antique, a showpiece from the Second World War."

The woman kept scribbling. She asked for the model and whether it was registered, and where the weapon in question was now.

Luc began to answer, but the young officer waved a hand. "Your wife," she said. "I'd like your wife to speak."

Luc sat back down in his chair, the big red velvet armchair that had once been his father's. His arms were crossed tightly over his chest and he stuck out his long legs, taking up practically the entire space on the living room rug. Hannah's books were still stacked on the floor beside the couch, and he nudged them with his toe, toppling them.

"Sorry," he said to the officer. He had interrupted her with the noise. But it was obvious he wasn't sorry at all. Lyse watched him with wide, worried eyes.

It was the older cop who asked, finally, if Hugo had ever shown signs of being suicidal.

The room went silent. Luc tried to laugh off the suggestion, but the laugh was odd, a single strained note, like the bark of a dog.

"We have to consider it," the man said. "We have to cover all the bases."

Lyse jumped up, fluttering her arms like a trapped bird.

"It's okay, Maman," said Luc. "Calm down. It's not that, trust me."

But his mother wouldn't be calmed. She burst into tears, and before Hannah could stop her, ran from the room.

PART THREE

20

Hugo stood shivering at the entrance to the Décarie Expressway on-ramp on Sherbrooke Street, holding a handmade cardboard sign. He had no parka or gloves, and his fingers were raw. The sun was up now, a pale yellow balloon without warmth. The real fire, the blazing reds and oranges, had lasted only seconds. He couldn't remember the last time he'd been awake this early. Blink and it was over. The traffic light turned red. He scanned the cars as they slowed. There were lots of them, even though the sun was just rising. He waved his sign and walked up the line, trying not to look scared, bending at every vehicle to look in through the passenger window.

Most people turned away. They were afraid too, he realized. What a strange thought.

As the light changed, a man made a gesture with his hand. It wasn't a wave, exactly. Smaller than that. A flick of the index finger. Hugo ran toward him. The car was an Echo, bright metallic blue. Ontario plates.

"Buckle up," the man said in English after Hugo climbed in. He turned the car onto the ramp and for the next few seconds concentrated on merging and then positioning himself strategically in the middle lane of the northbound expressway. When this was accomplished, he turned to Hugo and stuck out his hand. "Frank," he said simply.

"Joe," replied Hugo, looking away.

"Hey," said the man, "you're English."

His handshake wasn't firm, although it could have been the angle. Frank's hair was brown, starting to grey at the sides. He wasn't fat, exactly, just sort of soft, like his grip. And even though it was mid-autumn, he was wearing short sleeves. His arms were pale and covered with dark hairs. He began talking about himself almost immediately. He had spent the week in Montreal at a convention, he said, not bothering to say what kind. For five whole days, he had spoken nothing but French. Well, that wasn't entirely true, he admitted. His French wasn't that good, but he'd been surrounded by French people trying to speak English to him. He couldn't understand half of what any of them said. Joe, he announced, was the first honest-to-god English person he'd spoken to since leaving Ontario.

He gave Hugo a sidelong glance. "You from out of town too?"

Hugo shook his head. He was from Montreal, he said, but his family was mixed. He regretted it as soon as he'd said it. He had to watch how much he gave away.

"Ah," said the man. "You're a *mélange*, are you, a half-breed? I suppose there's quite a few like that now. The real English left years ago, the purebreds. I ought to know. They're all in Toronto with me."

They were approaching the Trans-Canada Highway, about to merge. Hugo and the man fell silent so that he could concentrate again on the road. Hugo turned his whole body to look out the window, thinking about the man's words. *Half-breed*. Was that what he was? It seemed demeaning, somehow, that a life could be boiled down to this one defining aspect. On either side of the elevated ramp, the roofs of factories and the tops of stunted trees rushed by. Hugo stole a look at Frank, who was hunched over the wheel, following the other cars into the merge.

Once they were on the Trans-Canada, Frank unbuttoned the top of his pants, laughing when he caught Hugo glancing at him. "I ate way too much this week. Steamies. You know what steamies are, Joe?"

He meant *steamés*, those hot dogs they sold on the Main, but Hugo didn't correct him. Frank was chuckling to himself, but not in a warm way, not including Hugo in the joke. Hugo wasn't sure how to react.

"How old are you, Joe?" he asked suddenly.

"Sixteen," said Hugo. He'd been anticipating this moment.

There was a pause as Frank digested this. Hugo couldn't tell if he believed it. He was wearing Ray-Bans. He asked if Hugo had a girlfriend.

Hugo's heart missed a beat. He tried not to glance at Frank's open zipper. Was he angling? He didn't know what to say. There was a girl in his class. Angélique. Her face rose like a moon in his mind, white and ethereal, the way she sometimes came to him in dreams. He shook his head. He'd never said a word to her.

"You're kidding me, right?" said Frank, his face lighting up with amused surprise. "A good-looking guy like you? All grown up?" He paused and smiled as though Hugo were the most interesting person he'd met in a long time. "Sixteen years old," he said, grinning broadly.

Hugo shrugged.

"Haven't met the right gal yet, is that it?" He had put it as a question, but he didn't wait for a reply. "There's no rush, Joe, believe me. You got plenty of time for all of that."

Hugo was warm now. Too warm. Frank's probing was making him uncomfortable. He took off his hoodie and, on Frank's insistence, tossed it in the back seat. He sort of regretted it. He felt exposed in his T-shirt, but Frank had the heater up so high he was starting to sweat. They covered the next few kilometres in silence. Hugo's head began to droop.

"You want to sleep?" Frank said, his voice kind. "Be my guest. It's a long, boring drive."

Hugo pushed his seat back as far as it would go and closed his eyes. He was grateful for the lift. He had spent the whole night on his feet, trying to keep warm. From the reading, he'd walked back to Saint-Henri, taking his bearings from the cross on the summit of Mount Royal. Instead of going home, though, his feet had surprised him by keeping on walking. He'd ended up at the canal, wandering by the water, looking for shelter. Itinerants camped out there. Kids like himself and older homeless men. Someone had lit a fire, and Hugo had stopped to thaw out. But then a fight broke out and he'd left. His breath grew heavy. He felt himself sinking. And then something startled him. Frank's hand was on his inner thigh.

Hugo jerked his head back and slammed his knees together.

Frank pulled his hand away. "Sorry, pal. You were interfering with my gear shift."

Hugo stayed wide awake after that. Frank was a *pédé*. That

was the word they used at school, the casual mocking insult the boys threw at each other—but until this moment, Hugo had never knowingly been in the presence of one. He angled his legs toward the passenger door, making sure no part of him came anywhere near Frank's gear shift.

When a sign for a highway rest stop appeared, Hugo told Frank he had to take a leak. Conversation had stopped some time before, and now the radio was blaring. They had been listening to a rock station, an hour of golden oldies from the seventies and eighties, but it was the top of the hour. The news had just come on.

"Looks like we're going to war," Frank observed after the anchor delivered a report about al Qaeda. He turned on his flashers, and for the first time in thirty kilometres, Hugo felt like he could breathe again.

"Heads are going to roll in Afghanistan," Frank went on, "and they won't be American. You watch. They got drones." He removed his Ray-Bans for a second and looked over at Hugo. "You ever heard of drones? You don't need a pilot to steer them. It's all done by remote control, like a video game. I saw a program about it on the military channel."

He kept talking even once the car was stopped, but Hugo had had enough. He grabbed his hoodie from the back and opened the door. Frank pretended not to notice his haste. He told Hugo he would wait and leaned in the sunshine on the car's hood, trying to look nonchalant.

After ten minutes, when Hugo failed to reappear, he drove away.

Hugo watched with relief from the window of the food court. He marked the event by buying a Tim Hortons coffee and a chocolate cruller. Then he went back outside. It had warmed up since dawn, but not enough to tempt people to eat out here. The picnic tables looked abandoned and sad. He sat down at one of them and licked flakes of frosting off his cruller. He was famished. The dark-chocolate dough was so soft and fresh, he barely had to chew. The coffee warmed him. He'd never had a full cup before, and it wasn't too nasty when you loaded it with cream and sugar. Not far away, there was a parking area with three eighteen-wheelers lined up in a row. *Mastodons*, his mother used to call them. He'd loved them as a little boy.

A man was standing near the front of the farthest one, checking his tire pressure. He was wearing an undershirt even though a stiff wind was blowing. His arms were thicker than Hugo's legs. Hugo finished his snack and walked over.

The man didn't look up. He was shorter than Hugo had supposed, and his legs were slightly bowed. On his right arm, just beneath the shoulder joint, was a tattoo of a man either falling or leaping through the air, his limbs outstretched and flailing. Above the tattoo was a banner with a single word.

"*T'es français,*" said Hugo, walking up to him.

The man looked up, startled.

Hugo pointed at the banner. *Icare.* From the Greek myth.

"Québécois," the man said in French, wiping his hand on his jeans and offering it to Hugo. "Jean-Louis Joncas."

There was a pause. "Hugo Lévesque," said Hugo.

Jean-Louis worked out of Saint-Jérôme, forty minutes north of Montreal. He was a long-haul driver. His pickup this time had been in New Brunswick, and he was on his way to Toronto. After that, he was going to New York and Pennsylvania. Only then would he head home again. A short trip, he said, starting with the 401, which he disliked. It was a dead strip, he told Hugo. Good for nothing but paying the bills.

Hugo screwed up all his courage. "You take passengers?"

The man looked sharply at him. "You are alone?" Unlike Frank, Jean-Louis Joncas waited for an answer, appraising Hugo's face in the bright noonday sun. When Hugo nodded, he asked his age.

Hugo told him the truth.

"I could get in trouble," Jean-Louis said, looking at him with chocolate-coloured eyes. "Big trouble. How do I know you're not a runaway?" He paused for half a second. "Not that that would stop me." He did a quick check to see if anyone was watching, then pulled open the passenger door of the truck's cabin.

Once they were safely on the highway, Hugo discovered that Jean-Louis was a talker. Driving a truck might seem romantic, but the reality was boredom and long hours of solitude. Jean-Louis was like a bottle uncorked. He had been driving trucks for two decades, he said, even though he was only thirty-three. Hugo laughed. Jean-Louis must think he was a complete imbecile. He knew, after all, how to subtract. But Jean-Louis swore it was the truth. "My stepfather did overnight runs on weekends, delivering bread up north to supply the lumber camps. When I was thirteen, he asked me if I wanted to come along. It became a thing we did. Something to share. One Saturday, we were speeding up the highway, and he asked if I would take the wheel. He was sleepy, he said. It would be safer. He could nap. It was supposed to be a short nap, twenty minutes, tops, just to give him energy. But in the end, I drove the whole night through. I had never even driven a car, but there I was at thirteen, driving a fifty-three-foot tractor-trailer."

"No one stopped you?"

Jean-Louis shook his head. "When I pulled in at the end of the run, I told them my stepfather was worn out from the drive and that I would unload the shipment. Truth was, he'd been in the tavern all afternoon with his buddies. So I unloaded the bread, turned the truck around, and drove all the way back to Saint-Jérôme with him snoring beside me in the passenger seat. Just before we reached this coffee shop outside town, I poked him in the shoulder. The sun was almost up. The sky was starting to brighten. When he saw that, he started cursing me. What did I think I was doing? I was heading in the wrong direction. He would catch it big time because of my incompetence. We pulled in at the coffee shop, and he gave me a dressing down right there in the parking lot. I tried to explain, but he wouldn't let me speak. Then this waitress came outside, a friend of his, and she started yelling. At him. I'd *made* the trip, she said. She had seen the truck leave at dinnertime the day before. That wasn't a sunset out there. It was a brand new day."

Jean-Louis threw back his head and laughed. "When my stepfather opened the empty trailer, his jaw dropped, I can tell you." He winked. From that day onward, the route was his. He drove while the old man snored. By the time he was fifteen, he was a seasoned trucker. The following year, when he got his licence, he quit school and started working under his own name.

He turned to Hugo. "You still in school?"

Hugo looked down at his jeans, which were frayed above each knee, the white threads showing through. He couldn't bring himself to talk about Saint-Jean-Baptiste.

Jean-Louis shrugged. "Not that I'm in a position to lecture

you." He squinted into the sunshine, eyes on the road. "I wish I were, though. I wish I had stuck with it."

Jean-Louis offered him some coffee from his Thermos, sweet and creamy, just the way Hugo liked it, and they drove in silence for a while. Hugo's hands were trembling, probably because of all the caffeine he'd had. And his thoughts were jumping around like sandflies. He kept picturing his mother's face. She would like Jean-Louis, and she'd absolutely love his truck. She'd been almost as enamoured of the mastodons in his childhood as he had, making a beeline to any truck they spotted parked on the street. The little boy in the stroller had been her excuse. She would push him closer and closer to the gleaming wheels until he could reach out and touch them. One time, a driver had let Hugo climb into his cab and honk the horn.

"I got a boy your age," Jean-Louis said suddenly. The trucker was facing forward, looking intently through the windshield at the highway, even though the road was as straight and easy as a ruled line.

"Not so old, actually. He's a year younger than you," Jean-Louis continued, still staring at the road. "He'll be fourteen next year."

"Does he drive with you?" asked Hugo, envious.

For several seconds, the only noise was the groan of the motor and the sigh of the eighteen tires. Jean-Louis shook his head. He hadn't seen his son in years. In fact, he admitted, he'd only met him once, right after his birth.

The mother had been a waitress at a truck stop in Sudbury. Jean-Louis had been passing through when a snowstorm hit. She'd offered him a bed for the night and he ended up staying the whole week. After that, he drove up to Sudbury a couple of times and she came down once to Saint-Jérôme. She would have married him, he said. But what did he know about that? He was twenty at the time. "And believe it or not," he said, "that's young."

By the time Jean-Louis learned she was pregnant, it was too late to do anything about it. Their child was born on October 3. His name was Dylan, like the folksinger.

"He's English?"

Jean-Louis shrugged. "I hope he knows a little French. His mother's family speaks it, but it's dying in Northern Ontario. Just like it did in Louisiana." He glanced at Hugo. "You ever been to New Orleans?" he asked. "The Mardi Gras?" He hardened his *r*'s to sound like an American. "No French there anymore. No siree." Jean-Louis turned to him again. "You ever been outside the province?"

Hugo went quiet. He had travelled to Toronto several times. He had vivid memories of his grandfather's house, big as a castle. They'd let him climb a crabapple tree in the huge backyard. His grandmother had been afraid, but his grandfather had cheered him on, confident he wouldn't fall. Hugo gazed out the truck window at the naked trees by the side of the highway.

Jean-Louis kept asking questions. He wanted to know where Hugo had grown up, what school he went to, what had brought him out on the road today. Hugo couldn't answer. He liked Jean-Louis and wanted to be friendly, but he couldn't tell the truth. Not now. Not with so much at stake. He had to reach his grandfather's place. He couldn't risk messing that up.

Eventually, Jean-Louis got the message and began talking instead of all the places he'd travelled to. He was a born storyteller. Once more, Sudbury slipped into the conversation. He had tried his best to forget about Dylan, he said. The boy's mother wanted nothing to do with him now. She didn't even want child support. She had hooked up with someone else and made a new life for herself. Jean-Louis was firmly behind her.

"I dream about him sometimes," Jean-Louis confessed. "And when I do, it's the strangest thing. He's still a baby." He turned in his seat. "What would you do, Hugo? I mean, if you were me? I've only been up there twice in all these years. He has a new life. A stepdad. Maybe some half-brothers and -sisters. Either he's forgotten all about me," he said, pausing to take a breath, "or else he's mad as hell."

Hugo didn't even stop to think. It was a no-brainer. "I'd go," he said. Dylan was waiting. It was obvious. A picture of him began to form in Hugo's mind, a miniature Jean-Louis, built sturdy, with the same bright spark in his eyes.

"Just like that?" asked Jean-Louis. "No warning or anything? You'd pack up and hit the road?"

Hugo nodded. Jean-Louis had an impressive set of wheels. And he obviously still cared about his son.

Jean-Louis kept glancing at Hugo as if he held all the answers. "What if he refuses to see me?" he said, his voice small and anxious. Then he raised his right hand and smacked it down hard on the steering wheel. "He probably hates me, walking out on him like that."

"He might be angry," Hugo said, surprising himself with his certainty, "but if he is, it's not because he hates you." A wave of sadness rose up from his stomach.

WHEN THEY REACHED the outskirts of Toronto, they discussed where to let Hugo off. By that time, Hugo had told him he was visiting his grandfather and that the house was in North Toronto. He trusted Jean-Louis and didn't want him to worry that he had no place to sleep. Jean-Louis couldn't take the truck into the city proper. He would lose too much road time. "I'm sorry, my friend," he said. "I would have loved to drive you to the door."

They pulled off the highway in York Mills, where there was a subway station close to the 401. "It's been a pleasure," Jean-Louis said, coming to a stop near the red-and-gold subway sign and climbing out of the rig to offer his hand. The stubble on his chin, Hugo noticed, was silver in spots. A sort of growl came out of him as he took Hugo in his arms, scooping him up and crushing him hard, chest to chest, the way Hugo's father used to do in happier times.

Then Jean-Louis climbed back into the cab, and the gleaming mastodon rumbled away, leaving Hugo by himself in the Toronto sunshine.

21

York Mills, the stop where Hugo got out of the truck, was near the eastern tip of the U that was Toronto's principal subway line. His grandparents lived one stop to the south. Hugo paid the full adult fare so as not to have to show his Montreal student ID to the ticket-taker. Then he darted through the turnstile and into a purring red-seated train that arrived at the platform at the same moment he did, as if ordered personally for him. The subway trains in Toronto were quieter than Montreal's, and grander. They also came out of the ground sometimes and into the open air. Hugo liked these differences. And all around him, people were speaking English. Another change. The passengers looked more or less the same as in Montreal, the same mix of skin colours and styles, but they sure sounded different.

As the train started to roll, a woman pushing a stroller sat down in the seat beside him. Her little girl, who was around two years old and had been crying, quieted instantly and smiled coyly up at him.

Hugo smiled back and wiggled his fingers.

The child arched her body and pressed her face into a corner of the stroller so that one eye was hidden from view but the other could keep sight of him. "She likes you." The mother laughed—the first words addressed to him since he'd left Jean-Louis's truck. A good omen, if you were into that kind of thing.

At the Lawrence station, he disembarked and followed a crowd of people up the stairs and out onto Yonge Street. The sun was still shining, although it was now starting to sink noticeably toward the horizon. The adrenalin buzz from all the coffee he'd drunk had worn off, leaving him chilled and tired. He wanted to get inside where it was warm, and to eat a decent meal. He had to cross Yonge and walk past a little park to get to his grand-parents' place. That much he remembered. And hopefully, once he did that, he'd remember the rest of the route. But even if he got lost, he knew he'd find it eventually. He'd just hitchhiked five hundred and fifty kilometres. This last bit was the easy part.

The houses in this area of Toronto were enormous, with long strips of lawn hemmed in by geometrically carved hedges. It looked like Westmount, only flat. Hugo tried to rehearse what he'd say once he arrived at his grandparents' door. He couldn't exactly tell them about his adventures with Jean-Louis and the eighteen-wheeler, or with Frank. He didn't want to scare them. And he was guessing his mom hadn't phoned to tell them he'd gone missing. She wouldn't have wanted to worry them, and besides, she wasn't even returning his grandmother's calls.

The house was just where he'd pictured it, beyond the little park on a quiet street directly across from a high school. Finding it had been no problem. This trip had gone pretty smoothly, all things considered, as if the universe had been waiting for him to step out of his safe little home and start exploring.

His grandfather's lawn was like the others on his block, huge and almost too green to be true this time of year, with a walkway of shiny flagstones leading to the front door. Hugo paused on the sidewalk and took it all in.

Though the sun was still fairly high in the sky, the blinds in his grandparents' living room were shut, giving the place a closed-off, unwelcoming look. Hugo took another deep breath. The exhilaration and almost giddy happiness he'd felt in the truck were gone. Cold was seeping in through the bottoms of his sneakers. His feet were numb.

He'd been so caught up with actually getting here that he hadn't stopped to think about how his grandfather might react. He had been here four times in his life. He'd always pictured the old man being happy to see him, but maybe this was optimistic. There didn't seem to be any lights on. He wasn't even sure anyone was home.

He went up the walk to the front door, took the solid brass knocker, and rapped, a little tentatively. What, in the end, did he know about his grandfather? The crabapple tree was, by far, his strongest memory, the reason behind this trip. The incident had left him with an impression of a man who might understand him, who might have faith in him when others, quite plainly, did not. Hugo could picture the chair in the living room where his grandfather liked to sit, listening to Mozart and reading his newspaper. He smoked a pipe. Usually out of doors, because his wife couldn't stand the smell.

To deal with that smell, Alfred Stern chewed Doublemint gum. That was another thing Hugo remembered. He always had a pack on him and would give Hugo sugar-dusted sticks of it, wrapped in tinfoil. His other memories of Alfred Stern were not so positive. He did his own snow shovelling in winter, creating a precise, geometrical path from street to door. One day, when Hugo was small, he'd tried to help. His grandfather had let him, but then he'd done the job all over again because Hugo's lines weren't straight enough.

The door opened suddenly and his grandmother's face looked out. At first, her expression was blank. When she took in his shaved head and grimy clothes, it turned suspicious. He had to say his name before she recognized him.

She clasped him to her chest, and then pushed him away again so she could look at him. "My God," she said, gazing at him with intense blue eyes. "You've lost all your baby fat." She ran a hand over his scalp. "And this? When did this happen?"

She'd transformed too. She looked smaller. The whole house did, in fact, now that they were inside. It had loomed so large in his mind that he must have inflated things a bit. He could actually look Connie in the eye now.

She led him into the hallway and stopped beside the living room door, which was closed. "Your grandfather's new bedroom. He's in there now with the nurse." She squinted at him. "He just arrived home yesterday, so we're still getting used to it. When she's through with him, you can go in there and see him, if you want."

She led him to the kitchen. Something was simmering on the stove. It smelled like his mother's cooking back in Montreal, or at least like the things she used to cook before his dad left. Connie put on an oven mitt and lifted the pot lid, releasing a cloud of steam. "Soup," she said. "You hungry?"

Minutes later, he was seated in his grandparents' breakfast room with a big bowl of the stuff. It was full of carrots and turnips, just like the soups his mom made. And Connie put out a plate of bread—whole grain, with butter. He ate it all.

"My goodness," she said. "It's nice to see someone with an appetite for a change."

By the time they cleaned up the dishes and she'd ushered him back to the living room door, he was feeling almost like someone his grandfather might wish to see.

"Your mum told you, I suppose," she said in a low voice before they entered, "that he's not the same since the stroke."

Hugo nodded. "He can't speak. I heard."

"He can't do a whole lot of things, I'm afraid." She made an effort to smile. "But it's still early in the game, Hugo. And strokes are unpredictable. You never know what will come back."

She knocked lightly and opened the door a crack. "Alfred, my love. We have a visitor."

She turned to check on Hugo, then opened the door wider and moved aside so he could enter.

A bed had been set up in the middle of the room. It had a metal frame and a row of command buttons, like a hospital bed. Because of the drawn blinds, there wasn't much light, but Hugo could see that the back of the bed had been raised. Propped on the mattress was a very small, wizened person who was watching him intently. Hugo blinked. The person looked nothing like his grandfather. If his hair hadn't been white, he would have mistaken him for a child.

For several seconds, they stared at each other in shocked silence. Perhaps it was exhaustion, or perhaps something was seriously wrong with him, but Hugo's brain felt like it was short-circuiting. He couldn't make sense of the picture. In his dreams, the house in Toronto had been a refuge, a place where he would finally, for the first time in his life, find his place. With mounting panic, Hugo watched as the strange, childlike face in front of him jerked, its mouth stretching and opening. Then, without warning, his grandfather turned his face sharply away and began to howl.

22

*H*annah awoke to the sound of a baby crying. She had shut her eyes after Kingston, and now they were passing the beaches of Lake Ontario on their way into Toronto. Some of the passengers on the train had their coats on, ready to disembark. The lake was a dull silver colour, a tarnished spoon reflecting an overcast sky. She glanced across the aisle at the baby, who was now wailing at full throttle. He looked like a newborn, his little face puckered and red. The baby's mother was, of course, trying frantically to quiet him. She looked like a child herself. She was wearing a bright shalwar kameez and was trying to get the child to feed from her breast. But with all the other passengers so close, and with the child writhing in her arms, she was too agitated. Her husband, clad in a suit a couple of sizes too big and a pair of shiny black shoes, sat stiffly beside her, glaring, as if the whole thing were her fault. She had thrown a shawl over herself, which muffled the baby's cries but didn't do much to help its humour. She shifted in her seat, readjusting him, her body, and the shawl, and as suddenly as it had begun, the crying stopped.

Hannah looked out the window. Her neck was sore. As the train rounded a bend, the CN Tower came into view and her eyes brimmed. Had anyone ever cried with joy to see the CN Tower? Hugo was here, in this city, alive and safe.

When her mother had called at around nine o'clock the night before, Hannah had been reluctant to pick up the telephone. The police were still in the apartment. Every officer in Montreal had in his or her possession a description of Hannah's only child. *White. One hundred sixty-nine centimetres. Fifty-two kilograms. Black hair and eyes. Likely wearing dark jeans and a black hooded sweatshirt.*

The search had gone on all day, feverishly, because of the story of the gun. When the call came in, the detective in charge of the case, a large, calm man named Dubois, was asking Luc again about Hugo's state of mind. It was clear where the questions were going, but neither Luc nor the detective would say the word. Could it be that Hugo was depressed? the detective had asked. Had he seemed unusually preoccupied or withdrawn prior to the disappearance? Had he dropped any kind of a hint? Had there been conflicts at school or at home that Luc could recall?

Luc was clearly not going to talk about the fights, so Hannah had been forced to do it. She'd felt awful, especially with Luc sitting across from her looking stricken. But really, she had to. She told of their differences over language. Of the physical fighting that had erupted between Luc and Hugo following the incident with the gun.

"She's making mountains out of molehills," Luc kept saying,

his eyes searching those of the detective. "Conflicts come up in family life. *C'est normal.*"

He had just finished asking the detective, rather aggressively, if he had kids of his own, when the telephone rang. Luc and Dubois stopped talking. Hannah, who was seated nearest to it, leapt up. She stood over it stupidly for a moment, not daring to move, just staring at the Talk button until it rang a second time, shaking her from her trance.

The voice on the other end was instantly recognizable. "What a surprise," said Connie. "Though you might have warned us."

Hannah turned her back to the two men. She had not returned her mother's calls all week, even though four had come in since they'd last spoken. "Mum, I—"

"Not that I'm complaining. You should see your father. He's in heaven."

Hannah glanced over at her husband. He was frowning in irritation and mimed hanging up.

She looked down at the bare wood floor, trying to concentrate. "This isn't the best time," she said, doing her utmost to keep her tone even. She had no idea whether Connie had gone ahead with the plan to bring Alfred home. She had no desire to know. Wherever he was, Connie needed help caring for him. And Hannah could not provide it.

"But really," her mother said, "I think you might at least have given the boy an overnight bag."

Hannah felt her heart stop.

"Which boy?"

Across the room, Luc saw her expression change. He stopped gesturing.

"And those jeans," Connie went on. "You're his mother. God knows, I wouldn't dream of interfering, but honestly, someone should tell him it's inappropriate for a person's underwear to be on display to the entire—"

"Mother. Which boy?"

After she had given Dubois an account of what had happened and seen him to the door, she sat beside Luc on the couch, absorbing the news.

"Toronto," Luc said, as if learning a new word. "I don't believe it."

But Hannah did. Hugo had given plenty of clues. All those questions about Alfred on the night he disappeared. And the name change, which Manny Mandelbaum had immediately recognized as significant. Hugo had been interested in his grandfather for years now. He'd done that project about him in grade six, learning more about him in a single long-distance telephone call than Hannah had learned in a lifetime. In retrospect, it made perfect sense that he would go to Toronto.

"I could come with you," Luc had offered when she said she'd go down the next day. He seemed serious, but when she shook her head, he looked relieved.

The train was on the last stretch before Union Station. People were standing in the aisle even though they had been told repeatedly in both official languages to remain in their seats until the train came to a full stop. Hannah sat obediently. There was a knapsack on the floor by her feet. Her only clothes were on her back, plus an extra pair of underpants and some items for Hugo. She had brought the laptop along, which took up most of her packing space. She would have to visit the Word at some point. She owed Allison March that much.

Before they reached the station, the train stopped and hissed. The lights went out, and everyone, including the baby across the aisle, fell into sudden respectful silence. Hannah sat in the dark, feeling the clutch and release of her heart. She felt calm and strangely united with these strangers waiting around her. And then the moment was over. Outside the train, someone shouted, and seconds after that the lights came up. People started moving again, as if they too had just been reconnected to an electrical source. Women combed their hair and called their children to order. Men buttoned their coats. The train roused itself from its moment of stillness and made the final push down the tracks into Toronto.

She took the subway north to her parents' neighbourhood. Coming up the steps at Lawrence, she noted changes in the landscape since her last visit. Most of the leaves had fallen. Piles of them filled the gutters. Above them, denuded branches swayed in the October wind. In the little park on the far side of Yonge Street, the grass was yellow and dead. Autumn was drawing to a close. That coming Sunday, the clocks would be pushed back.

The walk did not take long. Within ten minutes, Hannah rounded the corner onto Chatsworth Drive. There was the house. She concentrated on the details of its exterior, not daring to let her mind ponder what awaited her inside. Her parents' bushes had been pruned, divided neatly into bunches, and tied with string. The grass was a chemical green, not a fallen leaf in sight. Her mother had once enjoyed tending the lawn. Now a company took care of it, sending a crew each week with a deafening army of leaf-blowers. Hannah turned up the front walk, repaved just last spring with interlocking flagstones.

When the door opened, a smell engulfed her: roasting meat and garlic. Her mother stood before her, wearing an apron and a smile—a happier smile than Hannah had seen for years. "Come in from the cold," she said, pulling Hannah by the arm. "I knew you'd get down here. And I knew it would be in your own particular Hannah style. I just never imagined Hugo would be part of it."

Connie was beaming, as though this arrangement were a stroke of genius, a plan laid by Hannah with her parents' best interests in mind.

She hugged her mother.

"I'm so glad you're here," Connie said. "Things have worked out fairly well with Alfred. For now, anyway. Who knows about tomorrow." In her right hand, she was holding a wooden spoon, which she flourished. "Look at me! A cartoon granny."

Hannah shook her head. "You look great."

Her mother cocked her head toward the interior of the house. "That's because he's doing better. He's eating again."

"I can imagine," Hannah said, inhaling the smell wafting out of the kitchen. *Gigot d'agneau* with rosemary and slivers of garlic inserted under the skin: a Connie Stern classic, and certainly more enticing than anything on offer at the hospital.

As they hung up Hannah's coat, Connie described Hugo's arrival. She didn't seem to realize he'd run away. Hannah hadn't told her, justifying this in her own mind as a protective move, for everyone's sake. Now, watching this agile woman bend down to stow her knapsack under a chair, Hannah felt guilty. Connie was obviously strong enough to handle the truth.

"I didn't recognize him," Connie said, looking up at her. "He's transformed."

"You mean the hair?" In spite of herself, Hannah made a face.

But Connie wasn't passing judgment. "The hair. The body. The lines of his face. Everything," she said, smiling. "His baby fat's melted away. He's left his childhood."

Hannah's throat went tight. Was this what had happened? She was too close to see it.

"Alfred's reaction was even stronger than mine," Connie continued. "He was so upset when he saw him, he started to cry."

Hannah pictured her son's shaved head and sullen mouth. "Did Hugo scare him?"

Connie laughed. "No, no! Not at all. If anyone, it was your son who got the scare." She paused, remembering the moment. "Honestly? For Alfred, I think it was … well, Dickensian. An apparition from the past. Come," she said, taking Hannah by the hand and leading her back into the hall. "There's something you must see."

On the little mahogany table that her parents used for mail and keys lay a small black-and-white photograph. Connie picked it up. "I pulled this out of your father's album last night to show Hugo. It's quite something."

Hannah recognized the shot, although it had been years since she'd seen it. It was one of a handful of surviving photographs from her father's youth. It had been taken by an administrator at the internment camp in New Brunswick just after Alfred arrived in Canada. He was standing outside a wooden barracks in the snow, dressed in a dark bulky prison uniform. His head was bare, presumably for the picture. He had no hair to speak of, just a film of fuzz so thin it could have been a shadow. Hannah let out a cry.

"Amazing, no?" said Connie.

"They could be twins."

"Clones is more like it. They can do that now, you know. They've got the technology, and not just for Scottish sheep."

Hannah turned the photograph over. In her father's faded handwriting were the words "Minto Internment Camp, February 1941."

"Your poor father must have thought he was hallucinating. He kept reaching out to touch Hugo's face as if he didn't quite believe he was real. I had to repeat Hugo's name several times before he would calm down."

"Which he did?"

"Oh, sure," said Connie. "He did more than calm down. You should see them." She took Hannah's hand again and led her to the living room door, which was closed. "They're in there at the moment," she said. "That's his lair."

Hugo didn't get up when she entered. He was sitting on a hospital bed in the middle of the room, wearing his big jeans and hoodie. He did not look suicidal. Or remotely anti-social. Beside him, propped on pillows, was his grandfather, wearing a navy sweater that swamped his thin frame. The sight of them together was striking—like the beginning and end of a single story. Set out between them on her father's bedspread was a chessboard with a dozen or so pieces in play.

Hugo glanced up at Hannah and announced, in English, that he was being trounced. She went to his side. In Montreal, he used English as a weapon. But here, in his grandfather's home, it was just a language. That was all. His language, as much as the other one.

The chessboard was a travel set with tiny magnetized pieces. Her father was leading the black forces, her son the white. Her father's side was indeed winning. The white king stood in a narrow circle of defenders as black invaders swarmed for the kill.

"Wow," said Hannah, kissing the bristly top of Hugo's head. "Trounced is right."

She kissed her father too. Alfred Stern looked up at her with his strange new affectless face. Not a hint of the old judgment or anger, the gaze as open as a child's.

"Chess?" she asked, not quite believing it.

As if in answer, Alfred Stern reached out with his left hand and, with surprising dexterity, took the enemy queen.

23

Hannah got off the subway at St. Patrick and joined the masses of people making their way up from under the ground. She allowed herself to be swept along by the human current, as if her own will had nothing to do with it. And in truth, it didn't. She was moving on instinct now, nothing that resembled reason. She had no idea, for instance, why she was heading at this very moment for the Word, or what she could possibly say to Allison March once she got there. Her eyes rested momentarily on the jacket of the man in front of her. It was navy blue and padded. Flesh-coloured hearing aids were visible behind both of the man's ears. She looked more closely. He must be in his eighties at the very least, possibly nineties, tottering along unaided in the core of this city. There was a story here, as compelling, in its way, as her father's.

At the top of the stairs, she moved past the man. His face was composed, giving none of its secrets away. She lengthened her stride, passing people, pushing ahead. The previous night, she'd slept badly, tossing in her parents' guest bed until two in the morning and then falling into a dreamless sleep from which she awoke hours later than she'd intended. By the time she got downstairs, her mother and Hugo had left the house.

She glanced at her watch. Twenty-three minutes late, and she wasn't even at street level. She should have phoned Allison to tell her, but that would have required a level of organization that was beyond her. It had taken all her energy to come here for Hugo. There was nothing left for anyone else.

Her mother had taken Hugo out shopping first thing that morning, Hannah had learned from Irene, the housekeeper. Her mother, whom Hannah had always thought so confused, so blinkered and unadaptable, was doing just fine.

Alfred's frontal lobe could be thanked for that. So Connie had told Hannah late last night, in confidence, after Hugo and Alfred were safely in their beds. In some ways, she'd said, the stroke was a blessing. It was as though a crust had fallen off Alfred Stern. There was a tranquility about him. He looked at her when she spoke. He listened. At first, she'd thought she was imagining it, reading her own hopes into the silence of this man with whom she'd lived for almost fifty years. But it wasn't just hope. It was Alfred himself, stripped down, his essence revealed.

Dr. Ufitsky had confirmed that such things could happen. After a stroke, people's sociability often changed. Most of the time, it decreased, especially in left-hemisphere strokes that robbed people of their language. They often sank into despondency. But occasionally, as in Alfred's case, sociability increased. Inhibitions were lost.

"He didn't lose all of his inhibitions," Connie had said, resting her hands on the edge of the sink, "but enough to keep me laughing."

Hannah walked west toward Spadina. Traffic was badly snarled. When she reached Spadina, even the sidewalks were crowded. Where was everyone going at ten thirty-three on a Friday morning? She missed Saint-Henri, where at this hour the streets were mostly empty.

The Word Press was on the fifth floor of a renovated warehouse squeezed between two shiny office towers. Over the past few years, a number of warehouses here had been gutted and refitted as offices for designers and publishers and other artsy types. Stylish men and women walked purposefully down the wide sidewalks. Hannah was hurrying now too, caught up in the rush, slaloming toward her destination. She could see the building with its discreet doorway, over which hung the publisher's name with its eye-catching *W* that doubled as a bird. She glanced at her wristwatch. Thirty-seven minutes late now.

As she entered the building, she took off her hat and sunglasses and stuffed them into her knapsack, which was empty save for a brush, a small plastic package of tissues, and her wallet. She was wearing the same clothes she'd worn on the train and looked, she knew, lamentably stained and rumpled.

Allison March didn't appear immediately after the receptionist informed her of Hannah's arrival. This was to be expected. First of all, there was Hannah's lateness. Second, there was the larger pattern of which this lateness was a characteristic part. For several months now, Hannah had played a perverse game of chicken with Allison, failing to meet every deadline the young woman had set. And third, Hannah Lévesque was a translator. Her work might have won prizes, and it was certainly necessary in a country with two languages, but still, it was derivative. *Traduttore, traditore.* She was not a writer. Why should a gifted fiction editor like Allison March make any special effort?

Minutes passed. Hannah studied the spines of recent novels arranged in alphabetical order on the shelves. The Word Press was a class act, well known in literary circles for its sense of aesthetics and for the care it took with its publications. The company had been around since the 1940s. Everything it published was meticulously edited, designed, and printed. In an age of mass production, the Word still managed to make books that looked and felt like works of art.

After ten minutes, Allison March walked into the reception area extending a hand. She was perfectly groomed, as usual. Her nail polish was the light, creamy pink of the interior of a conch shell. She was slightly breathless. "Sorry, sorry," she said. "What a morning we've had." Working for a publishing house, she was necessarily a professional defuser of crises. Always a little short of breath. But the crises seemed never to shake her calm. Not a hair was out of place.

Hannah reflexively smoothed her own hair and checked her sweater for button malfunctions. She noticed that the cuff of one pant leg had somehow got caught in her sock, and she bent to unhook it.

Something about Allison was different, though. Her features seemed less angular than usual. She was still thin, still impeccable, but for some reason her contours looked softer. She led Hannah into a conference room, closed the door, and sat down.

"I'm pregnant," she said, without introduction. She was announcing it, she said, because it affected Hannah. The publication date for *Dreamer* would fall during her upcoming maternity leave. "You mustn't worry," she added calmly. "Everything will go as planned. My assistant is taking over while I'm away. Terrific girl. Loves your work. She'll take good care of you."

Hannah thought of the succession of deadlines she'd missed. No wonder Allison had been so persistent. It wasn't just her perfectionism; she'd known this was coming. While Hannah had been dodging her telephone calls, Allison had been trying to deal with the first trimester of a pregnancy.

"I'm so sorry," she said, ashamed.

Allison regarded her strangely. "Well, I'm not."

"I didn't mean your pregnancy," Hannah added hastily. "That's great news. I'm sorry for all the missed deadlines."

Allison waved her hands as though it hardly mattered, then settled them on her belly, which Hannah now saw had a small bulge.

"How's it going?" she asked, nodding at it. But the answer was obvious. Allison looked radiant.

"To tell you the truth, I've barely noticed it," Allison said, giving Hannah a bright smile. "I'd heard all these stories from people about nausea and dizzy spells and varicose veins, but so far"—she rapped the table with her knuckles—"I can't complain."

Hannah smiled with as much warmth as she could muster. Could life actually unfold like this? Allison March would probably be one of those mothers who got her figure back right after her natural, epidural-free delivery in the comfort of her own home. No hemorrhoids. No stretch marks. Her baby would probably sleep through the night.

Hannah knew little about Allison March outside of her work at the Word. Luc had said once that she was a former dancer who had stopped performing due to an injury, but Allison herself had never mentioned this. Nor had she mentioned a man. Hannah tried to picture her with one. He was likely rich, a successful young CEO.

"So it's done?" Allison asked.

Although Hannah had been expecting the question, it still made her breath catch. She'd told Allison she would have the manuscript finished by today. "I promise," she'd said hopefully, weeks ago. "You have my solemn word."

Hannah's spine seemed to stretch suddenly and unaccountably. Then she tipped over. It was the strangest sensation. She had no idea she would do it until it happened, then she was in motion, her torso describing a slow, ineluctable arc until her forehead touched the table.

There was a second of silence and then Allison stood up. "Hannah?" she said, hurrying to her side.

Hannah studied Allison's legs, shimmering in a pair of sheer stockings, and her burgundy pumps, low-heeled, practical, yet somehow radiating style.

Hannah sighed. "It's over."

Allison stepped in closer. "What is? What are you talking about?"

"Everything," said Hannah. It sounded melodramatic, not that Allison seemed to notice. She crouched beside Hannah and put a hand on her shoulder.

Hannah took a breath and the words flowed out at last. She declared, finally and unequivocally, that she was breaking the contract. Finishing the translation was beyond her. She could no longer bear the sight of Luc's book. He had left her, she said. She was giving up on the book, on her marriage, on the whole intricate structure of the life she had been living for the past twenty years.

The hand on her shoulder tensed and then withdrew.

She deserved this. Why should anyone stick by such a spectacle of failure? But then Allison said her name, and her tone was so unexpectedly mournful that Hannah looked up in surprise.

Allison had straightened and was hugging her arms. She shook her head. "I can't believe you and Luc are splitting up. You two always looked so solid. You're one of the reasons I decided marriage might be worth a try."

Only the seriousness of Allison's facial expression stopped Hannah from laughing out loud. She took one of Allison's hands in her own. The palm was moist, like a child's. "I'm sorry," she said, able finally to glimpse the trouble in Allison's cool grey eyes. But the truth was, she wasn't sorry. Not even a little. Love wasn't something a person ever got right. It was pure improvisation, from beginning to end. Everyone had to learn this lesson sooner or later, even perfect editors of fiction in Toronto.

24

As she reached Chatsworth Drive, the bells in the high school across the street from her parents' house started ringing. The sound was not pleasant. Several loud blasts, insistent and shrill, followed by a short synthesized tune. The students had to listen to it five or six times a day, and so did the rest of the Lawrence Park neighbourhood. Hannah shivered as she fished the small key out of her jacket pocket. Since she'd left that morning for the Word, the temperature had fallen sharply. Her fingers were so stiff that she had to jiggle the key repeatedly before the door would open.

The heat struck her. She stopped for a moment in the front hall, letting the warm air envelop her. She was grateful enough for it now, even though the previous night it had prevented her from sleeping.

Hugo's sneakers weren't on the mat, she noticed. Nor were her mother's shoes. A good sign. They were still out shopping. She removed her own shoes as quietly as possible and tiptoed into the hallway.

"Hello?" she called softly, her greeting reverberating through the house. No one answered.

"Anybody home?"

She was heading for the staircase, about to run to the refuge of her room, when the living room door opened and Irene's face appeared in the crack. "Your daddy is home," she said, smiling.

Irene was the only person Hannah knew who used the word *daddy* in reference to Alfred Stern. Hannah and her brother certainly didn't. When Benjamin was young, Alfred had made him say "sir" when addressing him. Hannah had been spared this formality, presumably because she was a girl. But even with her, Alfred had never been anything but "Father."

Irene had worked for Hannah's parents since the year they arrived in Toronto. She had a gold-capped front tooth and an easy smile. "You want to come in and visit with him?" she asked.

This was the last thing Hannah wanted. She was still feeling the effects of her encounter with Allison March, still shaken by her own admissions of failure. She had no idea what to make of those admissions, except that she had no intention of repeating them. Certainly not here, in front of her father. Laying out the shambles of her life to Alfred Stern was not on the agenda.

"He's about to eat his lunch," Irene said. "You could help him." It was not framed as a question.

Her father was in a chair by the window, wearing a checkered shirt. A tray was balanced on his lap.

"Look," Irene said to him. "It's Hannah."

Alfred looked up, unblinking and curious, the way small children do.

"You sit," Irene said, pointing at the chair opposite Hannah's father. "He will like it, I am sure." Then she disappeared discreetly out the door.

Hannah looked at the little microwavable dish on her father's tray. "Smart Ones," the wrapper said. The dish contained brilliant orange macaroni.

He was having trouble with the spoon. It took a lot of control to manipulate it with his left hand, the non-dominant one that he had never before had occasion to use. The macaroni kept slipping off. It was hard to watch.

"Here," Hannah said, sitting down. She took the spoon and gathered the fallen food. "Let's give it a try."

Her father opened his mouth wide, reminding her, as he had at the hospital, of a fledgling waiting to be fed. He liked Smart Ones, it seemed. Hannah remembered her son and his Kraft Dinner. Perhaps Connie was right. Clones.

As she scraped out the last of the noodles, the silence began to feel oppressive. "All done," she said, trying to sound cheery. Seconds later, she found herself talking about the weather, because even small talk was better than silence.

Her father didn't seem to mind. He stared at Hannah with his strange new frankness. She stopped talking, and in the stillness she heard the sound of her breath, and his. She laid the spoon down in his dish and faced him. "All right," she said, as if they'd reached an agreement. "You want to know? You sure you want to hear?"

His eyes were exactly the same shape and colour as her son's, two round black moons. And so she began to speak about Hugo, revealing the true reason for his arrival in Toronto. It wasn't a visit. It hadn't been her idea. Hugo had run away from home.

Her father's expression didn't change. The eyes were like black holes. He couldn't respond, she told herself; no matter what she said, he couldn't talk back. She was safe.

So she told the whole story, beginning with the gun.

Her father's eyes remained on hers. Did he understand that this was her child, his grandchild, who had bought a Luger? She hurried on, talking about Hugo's suspension. Still no reaction. Her father was watching her lips with great concentration. Perhaps it didn't matter in the end what was understood. The important thing was the telling.

The blind was up, and sun was streaming into the room. Hannah blinked into the brightness and described the disciplinary hearing. She no longer regretted speaking up for her son. It had been necessary. She even felt a little proud.

He was still watching, so she continued, describing Hugo's disappearance, her horror when she discovered his empty bed. The words spilled out. She was riding a runaway horse, afraid of falling off. But she didn't fall. After Hugo, she began to talk about Luc, the man whose name she had taken such pains to avoid uttering in her father's presence for nearly twenty years.

She said his full name now. She said that she had loved him. She still loved him. He was the father of her child, after all, the man whose bed she'd shared since she was eighteen. Until a month ago, she'd thought she and Luc had built something new, something stronger and more inclusive than what people had managed before.

And then she talked about Alfred himself. His closed-mindedness regarding the Québécois. She fought off the urge to run.

"You never liked him." There. She had said it. She searched Alfred's face. Not a flicker of expression.

It had been visceral from the start. In the waning hours of 1976, Luc had walked into Alfred Stern's house wearing denim. No jacket or tie. This would have been enough to provoke Alfred, who appreciated a certain decorum. But then Luc dared to speak.

"He was too different from you." Hannah looked into her father's face. It wasn't Luc she was talking about. Not him alone.

"I'm too different from you," she said quietly. Alfred Stern made a huffing noise, as if he were out of breath. He raised his good arm.

"Dad?" she said, taking him by the shoulders to steady him. "Are you okay?"

He closed his eyes and brought his hand clumsily to his face.

"Oh," she said, understanding at last, as he wiped his eyes with his sleeve.

He wept for some time. The huffing ceased, and it was just tears rolling down to his chin, where they hung in a quivering line on his stubble before falling onto his lap. She watched for a minute, then pressed her cheek to his chest to hug him.

Was it Luc, or even Hannah herself, who was too different for Alfred to love? Or was it like a series of nesting vessels within one another, rejections within rejections, until you came to the source, Alfred Stern himself? Uprooted, everywhere foreign, a boy with a red circle on his back. Hannah felt her father's heart beating fast and light against her cheek. She could hear it quite clearly. She held him close and listened.

25

The room was so hot that sweat had pooled in the dip of Hugo's breastbone. He stuck his index finger into it experimentally. It was tepid and tasted like tears. He couldn't see anything, not even the contours of his hand, which he'd raised above his chest in the darkness, stretching his fingers, making circles. The air felt like soup. He shut his eyes, picturing waves of it lapping against the dark shores of his body.

The house was stifling. His grandmother had told him she needed to keep it warm for Alfred, who chilled easily, but this was ridiculous. Hugo kicked himself free of the sheet and sat up on the cot he'd been sleeping on since his mother took over the guest room. Before the stroke, when his grandfather had still been able to climb stairs, this room had been his office. Maybe he'd climb them again. There was a feeling of hope in the house. Alfred had improved in all kinds of unexpected ways since Connie had brought him home. For now, though, the office was Hugo's.

He felt at home here. He liked the faint sweet choco-late smell of his grandfather's pipe. It had been years since his grandfather had smoked, but he still kept a pipe in the desk drawer, a memento of past pleasures. Hugo had checked out the desk's contents with great thoroughness. He was curious about Alfred Stern, and this was the man's most intimate space. There was a TV so old it had an actual dial for changing channels. There was a computer, also antiquated. But mostly there were books, shelves of them lining two walls, ceiling to floor. The lower shelves held heavy volumes from Alfred's lawyer days: *Martin's Annual Criminal Code*, *Black's Law Dictionary*, and several books on the Canadian Constitution. His grandfather had had a highly successful career. He'd been a criminal lawyer, and later a professor of law. His McGill degree was hanging over the desk. It had occurred to Hugo more than once in the last couple of days that he himself might study law.

He got up off the cot and went to the window. He was wearing white boxers, which glowed slightly in the velvety darkness. They were new, bought for him by his grandmother at the Eaton Centre that afternoon. They clung to his sweaty legs. In front of him, he could make out the contours of the venetian blind and the string at the side for opening it. He gave it a tug, but nothing happened. There was another string, so he pulled it too. Again, nothing happened. When he tugged them both together, the bottom of the blind rose up.

He opened the window and stood for several seconds in the rush of cold air. There was no moon, but in the light from the street lamp he could see his stomach, pale and hard below the jutting ridges of his ribs. Farther down was the bulge of his genitals, the pale flesh of his thighs. He stood there for several seconds, surveying himself and thinking maybe he wasn't so ugly after all.

He lowered the window a little and walked back to the desk. His grandfather's computer wasn't new, but it had an internet connection. He pressed the On button. A green light blinked and the machine began to purr. Hugo pulled the keyboard toward him. He had found his essay topic, and it wasn't Jacques Lanctôt. Lanctôt had been interviewed too many times to count. Hundreds of articles had been written about him, and by him. Monsieur Vien had even done a master's thesis on him. There was no need for any more.

It was his grandmother who had convinced him to change topic. They had been at the Eaton Centre on their underwear expedition. Until that moment, he hadn't breathed a word about what was going on, and to his relief she hadn't asked. He liked that about Connie. She could leave a person alone with his troubles, and yet Hugo didn't feel alone the way he had in Montreal. Connie was a presence, just not in your face. Lyse was sort of the same. Maybe it was a grandmother thing.

"I expect," she said, picking through samples of white cotton socks in the discount bin, "they must be missing you at school."

Hugo didn't answer.

His grandmother looked up. "You needed a break, is that it?" Her hands were still now.

"Did my mom say something?" he asked angrily. That had to be it. His mother had blabbed, and now Connie would see how mixed up and unhappy he was.

Connie shook her head. "She hasn't said a word. But it's pretty obvious you two have a secret. And neither one of you is talking." She gave him a sad little smile. "I'm in the dark, and I'm finding it pretty difficult."

That stunned him. Until that moment, he hadn't stopped to

think how Connie might feel. She was right. He was trying so hard to keep his own pitiful self a secret. Trying so hard not to upset her. Not to make her ashamed. His chin began to quiver. He tried to steady it, but that only made it worse. And then the tears came. A moment later, he was in her arms.

In the food court in the basement of the Eaton Centre, over tall glasses of bubble tea, he told her the story.

"But a gun, Hugo?" she said, after he finished. "What could you possibly want that for?"

Hugo shrugged.

The truth was, he had no answer. The moment he'd set eyes on it in Vlad's apartment, he wanted it. A Luger. He had planted his feet wide the way a soldier would, the way his grandfather Lévesque must have, and squeezed the trigger over and over again. Even now, the memory of it made his blood stir.

"My brother was like you," Connie said as they carried their glasses to the trash can. "He liked to shoot. Became a fine marksman too. In the old days, when it was summertime in the Townships, you could shoot tin cans in the woods and nobody would raise an eyebrow. And then there was my uncle Percy. He was in the Olympics before the war. Pentathlon." She counted the events on her fingers. "Fence, ride, run, swim, shoot." She looked up. If she was ashamed of him, she hid it well. They made their way up to street level and he told her about the paper he had to write as punishment at school.

"The October Crisis?" she said in surprise. "Oh, my. That's ancient history."

When he told her his subject was Jacques Lanctôt, she made a face. "But he always gets so much attention, Hugo. Why not write about the other one? The one he kidnapped." She paused, regarding him with her old blue eyes. "We knew him when we lived in Montreal."

Hugo must have looked shocked, because his grandmother burst out laughing. "Oh, it's not so surprising, Hugo. Your grandfather knew everybody. He genuinely liked Mr. Cross, though. He was Irish by birth. From a modest family. Not an obvious choice to represent the evil British Empire. Your grand-father couldn't believe it when he was kidnapped. It brought back the worst kind of memories."

The ancient computer finally booted up. Hugo logged on to his email account. There were two messages, one from Vlad, saying he was bored and hadn't found a school yet, and a spam message about getting rich quick in Nigeria.

Hugo hit New Message and typed in Serge Vien's email address. "Monsieur Vien," he began, and then stopped. He erased the name and started again.

"Cher Monsieur Vien ... "

An English construction, but it looked more complete. He took a breath. The glow from the screen lit up the room. He could make out the frame of his grandfather's law degree, although the words were a blur and the red seal in the corner looked black.

Where to start?

"Excuse me for disturbing you, but I need to know. Are there any books written about James Cross?"

He hit Send.

Half a minute later, the computer dinged, announcing an incoming message.

"Salut cher Hugo!"

Hugo was startled by the promptness of Vien's reply.

"How are you?" it read. "Where are you? I have been consumed with worry."

Nothing more, Hugo swallowed. It was strange to think of Vien thinking about him.

"I'm in Toronto," he wrote, "visiting my family." He paused and gave his armpit a thoughtful scratch. That was enough, wasn't it? Should he say he was safe? No need. It was implicit in the word *family*.

The reply from Vien came in seconds. "Why Cross?"

Hugo wrote back in kind. "Just curious."

The next answer was longer in coming. Hugo minimized the email page and began exploring what else his grandfather's computer could offer. There wasn't much, but among the icons on the left side of the screen was an encyclopedia. Hugo opened it and typed "James Richard Cross" in the search window. An entry popped up. "Born September 29, 1921, in Ireland."

Hugo reread the date. The man was certainly old. Older even than his grandfather, who was born in Austria in the spring of 1924. A vision of the bright-eyed, dark little man who kept massacring him at chess rose before him. The first time he'd done this, Hugo had dismissed it as a fluke. But the second game had been just as one-sided. And the third. His grandfather was still very much there.

Hugo went back to the entry. "James Richard Cross was a British diplomat assigned to Quebec and abducted there on October 5, 1970, by the Front de Libération du Québec (FLQ), a terrorist group fighting for Quebec independence during the October Crisis."

Hugo typed in "October Crisis." Before he could push Enter, the computer dinged.

It was Monsieur Vien. "Just like that? You just happened to feel curious about James Cross? It's not the most obvious thing for a person your age to be thinking about in the dead of night. Do you know what time it is?"

Hugo glanced at the bottom of the computer screen. Three thirty-eight A.M.

"I could ask you the same question," he wrote, and then erased it. Most mornings, Vien arrived in class looking weary and rumpled. Now Hugo knew why. "I couldn't sleep," he typed. "There's a computer next to my bed. I didn't expect you to be awake. What about Mr. Cross?"

The computer flickered. Hugo rubbed his eyes. The room was less hot now that the window was open. Did getting old mean getting cold? Hugo drained the glass of water Connie had put beside his bed. His chest was still clammy with sweat. The encyclopedia page had a photo of Cross, the same one he'd seen in Vien's folder of news clippings, taken on the day of his release. A long, pale face. Sad eyes. Greying hair. He was contemplating the image when the computer dinged.

"If it's for your paper, I don't recommend it. Cross has given two interviews in the last thirty years. The first one in 1975, the second in 1978. Both times to the CBC. That is it, my friend. There's almost nothing out there."

That was what Connie had said. Lanctôt, meanwhile, had given a ton of interviews. In Montreal, the journalists couldn't get enough of him. Hugo pecked out a response. "Maybe it's time to change that."

Vien didn't answer for some time. After twenty minutes, Hugo was ready to give up. His eyes were dry and he was getting sleepy. Just as he was about to lie down, the computer dinged.

"I'm sure people have tried. Cross is a recluse, Hugo. And he must be pretty old by now. If he's alive."

Cross had celebrated his birthday the week before he was kidnapped. On October 5, 1970, he had just turned forty-nine. Hugo paused, doing the math. He'd be eighty now.

"Can I try?"

This time, Vien wrote right back. "An interview? Let's be clear. You want to interview James Cross?"

"Yes," wrote Hugo. Why not?

After he sent the email to Vien, he pulled on a T-shirt. The room had grown much cooler. It wouldn't be all that hard to find Cross. He would be retired now, probably living in England. Or perhaps Ireland, where he was born. And if he'd died, there would be a record of it.

He opened the web browser on the computer and searched for "British Foreign Office." That was where Cross had worked all his life. They would know where he was. On the Foreign Office website, Hugo found a telephone number for their London headquarters on King Charles Street. Hugo checked the time. In London, it would be just past nine in the morning.

He navigated a string of recorded messages and a few minutes later was speaking to an actual human being with an upper-crust British accent. He explained to her what he was after.

There was a pause. "What did you say this was for?"

"A history project," he said shyly.

"Are you a student, then?"

Hugo looked up at the ceiling. The woman's voice sounded suddenly distant. "Yes," he said, beginning to regret his honesty. He would lie if she asked him his age. Monsieur Vien had done his master's thesis on the October Crisis. Hugo could easily be in university. What business was it of hers, anyway? "He was a diplomat," said Hugo, making his voice as deep as possible, "in the 1970s in Quebec." He paused. "There was an incident."

The woman seemed not to hear him. "And you say this individual is retired?"

"I think so," said Hugo. "He's eighty years old. Is there an age at which you have to stop working at the British Foreign Office?"

On the other end of the line, the woman sighed. "I'll put you through to our Records Department. Maybe they can help."

The woman at the Records Department was nicer, but had disappointing news. "I think he's deceased," she said after Hugo had spelled out the name.

There was a brief uncomfortable pause. "Is there some way for you to check?" She probably thought he was American. Pushy.

"We only keep records on current employees. Once they retire, the files are closed." Another pause. "Is there anything else I can help you with today, sir?"

Hugo stared at the notepad he had taken from his grandfather's desk drawer. The pen was ready in his hand.

"Will that be all?" the woman asked, trying to end the call.

Hugo cleared his throat. "What do you think I should do?" He was doing his best to sound as if he were thirty instead of fourteen, but his voice chose that moment to crack.

"Well," said the woman, sounding kinder, "have you tried the telephone directory?"

The operator at British Telecom gave Hugo three listings for the name James Cross: one in South Hampshire, a second in Sussex, and a third in Wales. Hugo scribbled down the numbers and hung up, elated. The one in Wales wasn't likely, but the other two seemed promising.

While he was in the middle of his second call, there was a knock on the study door. His mother's pale face appeared in the doorway. Her hair was mussed, and she was wearing a flannel nightie she must have borrowed from Connie. He put a finger to his lips. To his relief, she nodded and stepped quietly into the room.

"Thanks," he said into the telephone. He circled the hour he'd put down on his notepad and underlined it three times. "Yes, yes," he said, nodding. "At noon, then. Right. Do tell him. Yes, please." He hung up.

"Who was that?"

Beneath her nightgown, his mother's legs were bare. Ordinarily, this would have irritated Hugo. Ordinarily, he would have told her to leave, or at the very least remained silent and refused to look at her, hoping she'd take the hint and go away. But this was no ordinary day. He swivelled the chair around to face her and got up, remembering as he did so that his legs were bare too, his skinny, hairy thighs exposed. He'd been talking to England in his underwear. He had a sudden urge to laugh.

26

The street lamp outside the window was still lit. Morning hadn't yet dawned, but Hannah knew her night was over. Hugo's too, by the looks of it. He was wearing a new red T-shirt that he and Connie had purchased the day before. And he'd pulled on a pair of jeans that fit him. She could actually make out the contours of his skinny body. It was not the body of a child anymore, she noted. There was a wiriness to him that had nothing to do with childhood.

While Hannah had been sleeping fitfully in the guest room, Hugo had been telephoning England, repeatedly. He explained this once they were in the kitchen getting some breakfast. Apparently, he'd been up most of the night.

"On your grandfather's dime?" Hannah asked, alarmed.

"It's okay," he said. "Constance knows. She's the one who suggested it in the first place."

Hannah studied him. He'd hoisted himself up on the kitchen counter. Since when did her son enlist the aid of adults? And since when did he call her mother Constance?

She was making omelettes. The egg she was holding was cold from the fridge. It felt solid and smooth in the palm of her hand, more like a stone than something organic. She closed her fingers around the shell and held it over the sink. Then she shut her eyes and squeezed.

Hugo was looking at her when she opened them. "What are you doing?"

She told him about an article she'd read in a women's magazine once, explaining that an egg is impossible to break with your bare hand. It was something she had kept meaning to try. Hugo jumped off the counter, and soon they were both at the sink, squeezing with all their might.

"Cool," he said.

The egg's shape, Hannah had read, accounted for its strength.

Hugo brought his hand down with sudden force on the side of the mixing bowl. *"Par contre,"* he said, switching to French and expertly manipulating the shell so a bright yolk slipped out, perfect and intact, *"pour faire une omelette, il faut casser des œufs."*

He had learned that art—the art of breaking eggs—from his father. As Hannah whipped them into a yellow froth and poured the froth into the pan, and Hugo made toast, she knew there would never be an easy time to raise the subject that must be raised.

"Hugo, your dad and I ..." she began.

Hugo stopped buttering. "There's no need, Mom."

He was looking straight at her, holding her gaze. "I know you know," she said. "You're a smart kid." She stopped, already annoyed at herself. "Not a kid. What I mean is, you're old enough to know how people can get into trouble. Love's not an easy thing."

Hugo's face had darkened. His eyes had slid away from hers.

"We do love each other," she continued hastily, but he had turned away. All she could see was the red back of his shirt. But he hadn't left the room. She pressed on. "Your father needs space right now, Hugo. You know that place he rented? The office on Saint-Augustin Street? He's living there."

The red T-shirt still didn't move.

"For now, anyway, it's his home."

Hugo's shoulders were hunched. Hannah reached out to touch him, but he pulled away. "You'll still see him. I promise you. You mustn't worry about losing him."

He turned on her. "You really don't get it, do you? I *want* to lose him. I'd be perfectly happy never to see—"

He didn't get any further. Connie had appeared in the doorway. There was an uncomfortable silence, which Connie broke by stepping into the room. "I thought I heard voices down here. Good heavens, you two are early birds." If she noticed Hugo's distress, she gave no indication of it. She walked briskly to the kitchen table, which Hannah had set for two, and sat down.

Hannah busied herself at the stove. Hugo was in a turmoil, and there was nothing she could do about it with Connie here. Perhaps she could lead him upstairs on some pretext and continue the discussion behind a closed door. Or perhaps she should inform her mother that she'd interrupted a delicate conversation and ask her, politely, to leave. She was trying to come up with a better option when Connie started speaking again, asking about the project and about England. Hugo answered, reluctantly at first, then warming to his subject.

Hannah looked at the old woman in the pink bathrobe whom she had always thought so meddlesome. This morning, she had shown dignity and tact. And calling Cross had been her idea.

"Fantastic!" Connie said, hugging Hugo after he told her he'd managed to track Cross down. "Did you speak to him?"

"No. He was out walking. He takes his dog out on the cliffs every morning and walks for miles, his wife says."

"Barbara," said Connie.

"Yes, Barbara." Hugo nodded. "She's the one I spoke to."

"Poor, dear woman." Connie sighed.

Hannah stared. Connie was talking as if she knew her.

"She certainly remembers you," said Hugo. "Both you and Alfred. She said to send her regards."

"I must phone her, now that you've got their number." She laughed her breathy little laugh, looking thoroughly pleased with her grandson's triumph. "Will he agree to do an interview?"

Hugo shrugged. "Barbara said I would have to ask him. He doesn't usually speak to journalists, but I'm not a journalist, am I? She liked the idea of the project, and also the fact of who I am. She told me to call back at noon."

"That would be British time," said Connie. "Five hours ahead of us, right?"

Hannah glanced at the clock on the stove. "You've got ten minutes."

Hugo nodded. He didn't seem angry. He gave Hannah a quick, excited smile, hugged his grandmother, and hurried away to his room.

"Good luck," Connie called after him. She turned to Hannah. "What is it they say in French?"

"Bonne chance?"

"No," said Connie. "The dirty one."

Hannah smiled. *"Merde."*

"Right," she said, and shouted the word after her grandson.

She turned back to Hannah. "Your son is a remarkable young man. If he can get Jasper to talk—"

"Jasper?" Hannah repeated.

Her mother nodded. "That's what James's friends called him."

"You're his friend?"

"Okay," said Connie, "maybe not his closest one, but we certainly saw them socially. He and Barbara came to the house for dinner. You must have met them. You don't recall?"

Hannah shook her head. She dimly remembered parties her parents had thrown, festive affairs that contrasted sharply with Stern family suppers, but she'd stayed upstairs most of the time, hiding away.

"What they did to Jasper Cross was nightmarish. From what I heard, he never really recovered."

Hannah said nothing. They were on dangerous ground. It was the longest conversation they'd had about Quebec in twenty-five years.

"I know you don't agree," said Connie. "But he was someone we knew, Hannah. He wasn't just a symbol to treat any which way. I have to say, I don't think it's ever been properly addressed by anyone in Quebec."

Hannah found herself agreeing. Entirely. How odd that her own son seemed bent on righting this historical wrong. The omelettes were ready. She brought them to the table and put the one she'd prepared for Hugo in front of Connie. "You want some breakfast?"

Connie smiled up at her, nodding. "Good ploy to shut me up."

They ate in silence. Hannah was hungry. The eggs were light and buttery, lifting her mood. Her mind, however, kept circling back to the autumn of 1970. She remembered certain things clearly. Bomb scares at her high school. Trooping out with her class to the armoury across the street until the all-clear bell sounded. She and the other students had treated it as a joke, a lark, a welcome excuse to leave their desks. She hadn't felt a sense of danger. No bombs were ever found. "I don't remember much from that time," she said.

"You were ten years old, Hannah."

"Twelve," Hannah corrected. "I'd just started high school."

"Twelve, then, darling. You were young is my point. You're in a bubble at that age. You of all people should understand that. Your son's just coming out of it."

Her mother was gazing at her food, chewing thoughtfully. The skin around her eyes was scored with fine lines, like a sheet of paper scrunched up and then flattened again. Perhaps Hannah's bubble had lasted longer than most. Hugo wasn't the only one who appeared to be awakening.

"I overheard you, by the way," Connie said. "When you and Hugo were discussing Luc's office."

Hannah put down her fork.

"Hannah?"

She couldn't lift her eyes. Her father had predicted it. He'd said her marriage would not last.

A hand reached across the table and stopped just short of her own. It was a familiar hand, veined and sturdy. "I'm so sorry," said her mother.

Hannah took the hand. They sat for several seconds in silence, contemplating the unlikely sight.

There was a yell from upstairs. Then a second yell, full of joy. The two women were on their feet when Hugo came running into the kitchen with his news.

27

*L*uc lay on his back on the futon, listening to his pipes bang. Trapped air. He kept forgetting to bleed them, which meant not only that the heat was spotty, but that they made this infernal racket just before dawn. He squinted at the digits on his alarm clock, which he'd placed strategically on the floor near his head. Three fifty-five. *Merde.*

He'd been lying here for two hours. He got up, felt his way to the bathroom, and pissed in the dark. Then he groped with both hands like a blind man for the medicine cabinet. It contained two items: a small box of Marie-Soleil's tampons and Sweet Night, a sleep remedy he had bought a couple of days ago at a health-food store in Mile End. He flipped off the plastic cap and shook two capsules into his palm.

All week long, he'd been on edge, but tonight he'd toppled over into full-blown insomnia. It was the fault of that boy, that friend of Marie-Soleil's. What was his name? Arthur something. Saint-Cyr. That was it. The singer. Marie-Soleil called him a genius. They'd gone to the Foufounes to hear him and his band, Les Enfants Terribles.

"He can recite practically all of Rimbaud by heart," she'd said as they claimed the only remaining table in the centre of the room, within spitting distance of the stage. The lights shone directly on them, making Luc perspire. He was uneasy going out in public with Marie-Soleil, even to a big anonymous place like the Foufounes, with a crowd of people barely older than his son. All around him, he saw skinny boys with shaved heads and girls in sleeveless tops flaunting perfect flesh.

The show had been awful. Arthur Saint-Cyr did not have a voice. Or an ear. And he used a synthesizer, which Luc hated. His lyrics were plagiarized from Rimbaud, but cut up and rearranged so that what had once been poetically obscure was now meaningless.

To dull the pain, Luc had tossed down vodka shots. Three of them, in quick succession. Then things had unravelled. He'd argued with Saint-Cyr, who had come to sit with them between sets. That was why Luc was lying sleepless and alone on a Saturday night. Marie-Soleil had sided with her friend, and Luc had stalked off, his mouth dry and his head throbbing, while she stayed where she was.

He tossed the herbal capsules into his mouth and bent over the tap, slurping greedily. He couldn't handle liquor anymore. He'd never really been able to—it gave him headaches and disrupted his sleep—but these days he couldn't endure it. What had he been thinking, ordering vodka? He must have seemed pitiful.

The grout where the bathroom sink attached to the wall was black at the edges. It wasn't just dirt, he knew. Dirt doesn't grow fur. He sniffed it and made a face. Why hadn't he noticed it before he signed the lease? It wasn't as though the fat man had hidden it. And even if he'd tried, the smell would have revealed the truth. So far, Luc had no runny nose or itchy eyes, but something so ugly had to be bad for him.

When he opened his eyes again, the sun was in his face. The clock showed 11:11. Below the time was the date: October 28, 2001. Luc sat up. It was the anniversary of his father's death.

His mouth tasted like ashes. He walked to the bathroom, where he urinated prodigiously and then drank from the tap, holding his breath to block out the stink from the awful black crack.

Thirty-five years ago today, Roland Lévesque had stuck the barrel of a Luger into his mouth. Every single autumn since then, Luc had relived it. It explained his mood. Even if he hadn't been conscious of it, some part of him had remembered. His limbs were still heavy from the herbal pills. He wished he could draw the curtains and sleep some more. But he had no curtains. And sleep wouldn't return now. He'd misbehaved last night, but that was the least of it. He'd caught a glimpse of himself as an outsider might see him—an aging philanderer pretending he had something in common with children.

He took a shower, and while the water trickled down— the pressure was woeful, another thing he'd neglected to check before signing with Gagnon—he realized what he must do.

IT WAS JUST PAST ONE in the afternoon when he knocked on his mother's door. She didn't hear him immediately because she was out on the back porch, hanging laundry.

"This could be my last line of the season," she said, nodding at the clothes waving in the breeze. "The forecast is for frost tonight."

"You know what day it is?" he asked, rubbing his temples. He had a brutal headache.

Lyse nodded. "After I finish here, I'm going to the cemetery. Want to join me?"

He shook his head. After thirty-five years, she was still laying flowers at her husband's grave. *That* was love. He looked out over the rooftops, suddenly too sad for words. When he turned back, Lyse was scrutinizing him, a man's shirt bunched in her hands.

"Whose is that?" he asked.

She said Graeme White had been helping her fix something and had stained it. The shirt billowed in the wind, incongruously big among her dainty white things.

Luc had forgotten how calming his mother's presence could be. He'd barely seen her since he'd left Laporte Street, and he realized he'd missed her. After she finished with the laundry, they went back inside to warm up. She sat in her rocking chair, the one with white cushions in which she'd breast-fed him and later Rémi. For some reason, this thought affected him. Tears came into his eyes. She saw them.

"Is it your father?"

"Yes," he said. And then, "No. It's me."

She didn't say a word. She just sat, waiting for him to explain.

"The day Hugo was born, I swore to myself that I would never leave. Whatever happened, I'd stick by him. And now look. I'm almost fifty. The same age Dad was when he left."

Lyse shook her head. "He didn't just leave."

"When he died, then."

"When he shot himself," she said. "You are not remotely like him."

"Yes I am," he said quietly. "Only I used a girl instead of a gun."

"A girl?"

He told his mother about Marie-Soleil and the place on Saint-Augustin Street. She listened in silence, her face still and sad.

"It's not what you think," he said at last.

"Oh?" she said evenly. "And what do I think?"

"That it's a mid-life crisis, the tired old story of a man who can't face his own decline."

Lyse studied him.

"It isn't, Maman. You don't know. You picked someone from your own culture, someone who could understand you, someone similar to you."

Lyse took a breath and let it out slowly. "That's not true," she said.

She leaned back in the rocking chair. "I owe you this," she said quietly, and began to speak of Graeme White, the man who had been her friend and lover and soulmate for nearly thirty-seven years.

Luc stared at her. "Thirty-seven? That's not possible," he said, more harshly than he'd intended. "That's longer than Dad's been dead." His throat was hurting suddenly, his voice straining. "What are you saying? Did he know?"

His mother nodded.

Luc's stomach seemed to twist. "I don't believe it."

Lyse began to cry.

Luc shook his head wearily. Admitting this had taken courage. He put a hand on his mother's shoulder. "Don't cry, Maman. It's okay."

She shook her head. "No, it's not. You've been honest with me. I can at least return the favour. I tried to protect you and your brother, but you didn't need protection, Luc. Or maybe you did once, but not now. Not for years. It wasn't you I was protecting all this time. I was afraid you'd condemn me."

And so she told him the story, the true story, of Roland Lévesque. It was a painful telling, with no hero at its heart, no redemption, nothing remotely uplifting in its outcome. Roland Lévesque had been a failure as a husband. He'd failed to be faithful. He'd failed to be sober. He'd failed to provide, and failed, in the end, even to remain alive.

Luc remembered the drinking. Certain nights, his father's friends had carried him home from the tavern. But that was normal, Luc had told himself. It was something men of that generation did. The tavern, like the Green Spot, had been a social club.

"He was an alcoholic," Lyse said, as if answering his thoughts. "He had a problem, a serious one, and didn't have the strength to face it. He paid a high price. It cost him his marriage and his job."

"That wasn't alcoholism," Luc objected. His father had told him the story a hundred times. He'd fought for the workers. He'd defended their rights. That was why Imperial had gotten rid of him.

But Lyse was shaking her head. "He was caught drunk, Luc.

On the job. It could have been fatal, for him and for others. A
fire broke out in a basement storeroom at the plant. The alarm
went off and the firemen came, but no one was there to open
up for them. They had to smash down the door. Your father was
found asleep in the infirmary. They thought maybe he'd crawled
in there overcome by smoke, but when they shook him, he woke
up. There was a whisky bottle under the cot."

"All right," said Luc. "You can stop."

But Lyse didn't stop. "The drinking got worse after he was
fired. Once, he'd been a gentle man. He was funny and charming.
Then he turned angry and got into arguments over nothing at
all. I did what I could, paying the bills and such, shielding you
boys from the worst of it. It went on for two awful years. By
the end, we were barely talking. He wasn't home much, which
was probably a blessing. One night," she said, looking out the
window at her clothesline, "your father asked me if I was seeing
another man. Someone must have said something to him. Or
maybe it was just intuition. I hadn't been planning to tell him,
but he asked. And I told him the truth."

She sat back in her chair, hugging her arms. "They found
him that night at the Westmount lookout."

"You didn't kill him," he said, taking her in his arms. "If
that's what you thought, you were wrong. Do you hear me?"

After a while, they went to her kitchen, the same kitchen in
which he had sat as a boy, and put the ancient tin kettle on the
stove for tea. From the shelf over the sink, she took down the
stained teapot she'd used since his childhood, and the matching
bowl from which he and Rémi had stolen sugar cubes to suck
like candy.

His mother's words hadn't burdened him. On the contrary,

they'd buoyed him up. He had no idea if it would last, but he felt lighter than before. Lighter and yet paradoxically more solid.

He wanted to laugh. About what? The power of words, of stories told and untold? Luc took the steaming cup his mother handed him and breathed in the sweet, familiar aroma of tea.

28

*N*ight was falling as Luc Lévesque walked into the Green Spot. It was Halloween, and the streets were full of children in costumes. There were a lot of skeletons this year. He'd passed two of them on his way here, cheap plastic outfits from the dollar store.

He opened the door to the restaurant. Strips of protective carpet had been laid down; the snow would come any day now. It would be light at first, like the dusting of sugar on a pastry, but by the end of December it would be knee-deep. He sighed. As a boy, he'd loved winter. Even the short, dark days of November hadn't bothered him, for they meant snow was on its way. And snow meant permission to stay indoors, reading and daydreaming.

He paused on the doormat to wipe his feet, nodding a hello at the man behind the cash, who still didn't recognize him. The man winked at Luc and smiled, as he had winked and smiled at every other customer who had preceded Luc that day. Nobody knew him here. The Green Spot customers were too busy making rent to bother with books.

He patted the pockets of his raincoat. He hadn't brought anything to read. Usually, he had a book tucked away. The last one he'd read was a French translation of *Things Fall Apart* by Chinua Achebe. Translation was betrayal, as Hannah was so fond of saying, but his English wasn't strong enough to read Achebe in the original. Achebe had been criticized for writing the novel in English—indicting colonialism in the colonizers' language. At least in Quebec, novelists wrote in French.

Luc had finished reading the book weeks ago and hadn't picked up anything since. Nor had he written a word. He was dry. Frighteningly so. And when was the last time he'd walked out of the house without a book? He patted the sides of his raincoat one last time, unable to accept his lapse, and made his way to the back of the restaurant.

He sat at his favourite booth. A cold rain was falling outside, and through the streaked window he saw people scurrying along Notre-Dame Street, ducking into doorways for cover, getting lost in the blur of water on glass. One of these ghostlike beings waved an arm. A pale face paused, shimmered briefly, then disappeared from view.

Vien. There was no mistaking that hair. The front door opened and Vien burst into the restaurant, scattering the small crowd waiting by the door. He stood alone on the mat shaking himself like a wet dog. Luc watched as he started to wriggle inside his trench coat. What was he doing? Scratching himself? No, he was reaching into a pocket to extract something. A file folder brimming with his students' papers. Poor bastard. He had brought his grading with him. Luc shook his head. The teacher's life—an unending river of red ink.

Vien walked toward him. "My man," he said, with a wide

smile. He didn't seem at all perturbed about the rain or his own semi-drenched state. "Sorry I'm late. Have you been waiting long?"

Luc shook his head.

"My meeting ran longer than expected." Vien peeled off his coat. Water had seeped through at the shoulders and streaked his shirt. "Damn Tremblay." He'd spoken of this man before, a young teacher recently hired by Saint-Jean to teach history. "He wears a suit and tie every day to school. What's that about? And everything boils down to economics." Vien threw up his hands. He had met the young man to set the Christmas exam, and they had ended up arguing about politics. "'Independence is a failed dream bankrupting the province.' He actually said that. A man entrusted with the education of young minds. He doesn't even seem to regret it. 'The dream is dead. It's a new century.' Such cynicism, and he isn't even thirty."

Vien's palms were upturned, his arms stretched out. Jesus on the Mount, thought Luc. Or perhaps at the Last Supper. Only this Jesus had one eye pointing the wrong way.

"You're preaching to the converted," Luc said.

Vien paused. "Sorry. But he really gets under my skin. And the worst thing is, the kids love him." He removed his glasses for a wipe. "Go figure. A boy in a pinstripe suit."

Vien slid onto the bench across from him. Their knees touched and they both swivelled, like magnets pushing off each other.

"We're getting old."

Vien put his glasses back on and frowned. "What a thing to say."

Luc shrugged and pointed to the white hairs on his chin, then at Vien's grey stubble. "The body does not lie."

"It's not our hair that counts," Vien thumped his chest with a fist. "It's this."

Luc had to laugh. Good old Vien. He patted the teacher's hand. "They'll never take us alive, Vien."

Vien pushed his glasses up to the bridge of his nose. "You okay, Luc?"

"Could be better." Luc looked down and tapped the file Vien had laid on the table. "You planning to mark these while we eat?"

"No," said Vien, "I brought them in case you were late. But why would you be late? You live around the corner."

Luc made a face. "Not for long. I just came from a rental on Rose de Lima. One bedroom. Guess how much they want?"

"You're moving?" Vien asked, taken aback.

Luc nodded.

"But you just did that."

Luc shrugged and signalled to the waitress. The service was slow today.

"The place didn't work out?" Vien persisted. "I thought you were so pleased with it."

"It overlooks the tracks, Serge. You saw it. Ever tried sleeping beside railway tracks? Let alone working. I don't know what I was thinking."

"Well, I do," said Vien. "A writer in that house? It's too perfect for words. Gabrielle Roy's probably chuckling in her grave."

Luc folded his arms. "Let her chuckle. She's resting in peace. I haven't had a decent night's sleep since I signed the lease."

Vien grinned a little too suggestively. Luc decided to ignore it.

"It's a great setting for a novel, Vien," he allowed, "but not for a life. Really not. Trust me."

"How's your literary agent?"

Luc didn't look up. He was flipping his knife back and forth on the paper placemat. The names of the businesses printed on it started to swim.

"You're still seeing her, aren't you?"

Luc stopped flipping.

Vien's eyebrows rose, forming a quaint gable above his face. "You can't do this to me, Luc. You two looked amazing together."

The waitress chose that moment to appear with two glasses of water. Luc picked up a glass tentatively, then put it down again. Ice in November. His teeth ached just to think of it. This waitress was older than the one with the salon tan who'd served them last time. She seemed to be missing a few teeth and consequently smiled less. Luc did not need to consult the menu. He knew exactly what he wanted.

"*Un hamburger, all-dress,*" he said, in his best franglais. As the grim-mouthed waitress scribbled his order, he added a side of onion rings. For old times' sake.

Vien ordered the house salad.

"That's all you're having?" It was the first time Luc had seen anyone, let alone Serge Vien, order something green in this place.

Vien patted the bulge at his waist. "Trying to slim down."

After the waitress left, Vien asked again about Marie-Soleil, but Luc made it plain that he didn't want to talk about it. So Vien switched the conversation to himself. He had met someone, he confided. She was Ukrainian, and her name was Anya. He smiled as he pronounced it, a Ukrainian version of Hannah.

Her last name had twelve letters and was unpronounceable. He spelled it. K-u-s-z-n-i-r-e-c-k-y-j.

Anya's daughter Kateryna was in one of his classes. On the first day of the fall semester, he'd simply called her Katy K. He had met his share of difficult names over the years. Katy K's was too difficult even to attempt.

She was scoring perfect grades in the sciences and in math, but barely passing Vien's history course. It was a question of language. She'd been in Canada for only two years. She was fluent in Ukrainian, obviously, and Russian, but had only just begun to learn French.

"Her mother came to my office. It was the morning after the Lanctôt reading, actually."

When the short blonde with the electric-blue eyes knocked on his office door that day, it had seemed like fate. "I'd been with you the night before," Vien admitted shyly. "You seemed so happy with your new place and your new friend." The following day, he had driven out to Katy's apartment in the east end to offer his tutoring services. The next week, after the tutorial, Katy's mother invited him to stay for dinner as a token of thanks for all the help he'd been giving her daughter.

"The rest is history," said Vien with a wink. "She's divorced. A doctor by training, working as a nurse at Saint-Luc Hospital while they figure out the professional equivalencies. It's awful how we treat people like her. She's got qualifications coming out of her ears, and her French is quite decent."

Luc looked up, surprised.

"She's also an amazing cook," he said, flushing with something that looked like pride. He was becoming a connoisseur of Ukrainian cuisine. He sat back on the bench and they both surveyed the room, inhaling the familiar odours of coffee kept too long on the burner and reheated grease. "I should bring her to the Green Spot, don't you think? Give her a taste of Quebec?"

"It might scare her off."

Vien gave him a look. "She's pretty strong. And besides, she told me she wants to learn more about my homeland."

Luc smiled. He had rarely seen his old friend so animated.

"Maybe I'll wait until spring, though," Vien said. "Saint-Henri looks better then." He paused and scratched his chin. "By the way, I've been thinking of moving back to town. My place in Longueuil is on the market. They're turning all those old factories in Pointe-Saint-Charles into condos. Maybe I could find something along the canal. That would be a change. I could walk to work. Think of it," he said, "no more bridges to cross."

"Or burn."

Vien honked.

They fell silent. The unsmiling waitress set down their food and walked away. Vien watched Luc from across the table. His wayward eye had watched Luc during two of the most painful episodes of his life. When it counted, Vien had been there. In the years immediately following the death of Luc's father, and now, as his marriage was collapsing, Serge Vien, his very own Sancho Panza, was right beside him.

Ghosts were hovering over them. He had sat in this booth with his father forty years ago; and after that with Vien, two lonely boys finding solace in each other's company. Those moments at the Green Spot were part of him, and now this moment was part of him too. This moment, when Vien had talked about the birth of love and Luc had spoken of its death.

"Is this being fifty?"

Vien blinked.

"Seriously," said Luc. "I turned my life inside out, and for what? I still can't tell you. Don't think you're any better, my friend. You did exactly the same thing with Suzanne."

"Not exactly," said Vien, with some irritation. "I was forty-eight at the time. And Suzanne turned my life inside out, not the other way round."

"Even so," said Luc. "Mid-life. It's like being a teenager, don't you think? Disorder. Distress. Maybe worse than being a teenager. My father killed himself at fifty."

Vien gazed steadily at him. Luc knew he wouldn't turn away. Vien understood despair. He had lived through the dissolution of a marriage. He too must have faced the terrible thought *I will die alone.*

"I think I understand my father a little better now," said Luc.
Vien nodded.

Luc rubbed his tired eyes. "I got it wrong, you see, in my novels. Really, fundamentally, wrong."

He told Vien about the conversation with Lyse.

"But it's fiction, right?" said Vien amiably. "Who cares if you missed the mark? The whole point is to confabulate." He was eating one of Luc's deep-fried rings, picking the batter off delicately with his teeth the way they used to do as kids, until all that was left was the pearly, translucent string of onion inside.

To confabulate. Yes. But then, what were the layers of truth Luc had thought he was peeling back with such care and precision?

"How could you have known?" Vien went on, wiping grease from his fingers. "She kept it from you. And no one ever really knows his father."

Luc nodded. Vien had recently told him the story of his own father's death. He had received a phone call a decade ago from a government office in Maine informing him that he, Serge Vien, was the sole beneficiary under his father's last will and testament, even though he hadn't spoken to his old man since his fourteenth birthday.

Vien was probably right. Fathers were by their very nature impenetrable. Luc was flipping cutlery again, a coffee spoon this time. He missed a catch, and the spoon clattered off his saucer onto the floor before he could save it. He understood very little about Roland Lévesque. He never had, but at least he now knew just how little. The old stories had been partial truths, or simply wrong. Everything that had ever happened to him had to be revised, each memory of his childhood revisited, his father recast in a harsh new light. But even this was grossly inadequate. It was impossible to sum him up. It was impossible to sum anyone up. Luc couldn't even figure out the movements of his own pathetic heart. "What an asshole I've been," he said. "But what's done is done, I guess. Calling myself names isn't going to help. The real question is what to do."

"Go back to Hannah?" Vien offered. "She's a good woman."

Luc shook his head.

"Did you even try?"

Luc said nothing.

"You know they're back," said Vien, glancing at his watch. "Hugo's looking great, don't you think? Toronto did him a world of good."

Luc sat very still. They were back. He let the fact sink in. And of course Hugo would have seen his homeroom teacher. But he could have managed a call. At the very least, Hannah could have. Then he remembered. There was no telephone at Saint-Augustin Street. The only way to contact him was to knock on his door. It wasn't as if he'd made it easy for them.

"So, he hasn't let you in on what he's been up to?" Vien said. He was trying to cheer Luc up, trying to engage him. He didn't realize he was turning a knife in Luc's side with every word. Luc opened his mouth to say something, then appeared to change his mind.

"But I shouldn't be the one telling you this. I confess, I organized a little surprise for you both today." He narrowed his eyes as he looked at the front of the restaurant, where a small cluster of people were sheltering from the rain.

Hugo was there, looking small and wet. He was wearing his school uniform, and his old black knapsack was slung over his shoulders. Vien stood up and waved. Hugo spotted him and took a step forward, his face uplifted, happy. But then his smile faltered and he stopped short.

Vien called out his name, but Hugo had already turned. Clutching the straps of his knapsack to steady his load, he bolted for the door.

Luc scrambled to his feet. He raced up the aisle past the customers in their booths, past the waitresses, past the guy behind the counter, no longer winking as he ran by. The bell jangled as the door slammed behind him.

Rain bit into Luc's skin. As he followed Hugo around the corner to Greene Avenue, out of the shelter of the restaurant, an icy wind hit him square in the chest. The adrenalin burst was already receding and he'd started to pant. Hugo was as quick as a hare. The distance between them was widening. He had to catch up, had to tell his son that he was sorry, profoundly sorry, for everything he'd done. He had to let Hugo know that there was no reason anymore to run away.

Luc had always thought of Hugo as unathletic, a lounger without speed or endurance, yet here he was, easily outstripping his old man. The schoolbag bounced unrelentingly on his back. Running with it must hurt like hell.

He chased his son past the community garden at the end of the block, its plots bare, waiting for winter. The pavement glistened, slick with rain. Water was streaming down Luc's face. A little farther on, a bike path intersected the street. When Hugo reached it, he turned west into a grove of trees. His dark jacket, made darker still by the wet, melted into the gathering shadows. For a moment, Luc panicked at losing sight of him, but then he too arrived at the bike path. His lungs were burning now; his burger-laden stomach was heaving. His son was receding into a distant speck.

Luc's chest felt strange. For some moments, his breastbone had been tingling. He'd ignored it in the rush to catch up, but now there was pain, acute pain, ripping through his chest. He looked down, expecting to see ... what? A hole? And through the hole a poor, aging heart? He touched his leather vest and the frayed denim shirt underneath, which strained just a little these days across his chest and belly. His feet stopped their desperate sprint.

"Hugo ..."

It came out weakly. His son would never hear it. Hugo kept right on pounding, hard and steady.

Luc bent over, gasping for breath. Rain dripped down his face, turning salty and warm as it mingled with his sweat. He dropped to his knees on the bike path and bent forward, slowly,

slowly, until his forehead was in a puddle on the asphalt. He had no idea how long he knelt there in the water. Time was irrelevant in the battle to inhale.

At some point, a pair of sneakers appeared at the puddle's edge—red Converse runners just like his own, only a couple of sizes smaller, with dirty, frayed laces. Rain had darkened the canvas. Drops bounced off the rubber toes, which shone. Luc's heart leapt at the sight. The rest of him didn't move, however, remaining bent in this odd but comforting posture. His lungs were functional again, thank God, emptying and filling as if breathing were the most ordinary thing in the world.

EPILOGUE

June 7, 2002

The auditorium of the Collège Saint-Jean-Baptiste had no windows. It was a hushed, sepulchral room illuminated only by dusky yellow light fixtures appended to the ceiling and walls. Sitting here in one of the long rows of cramped folding chairs, it was possible to forget that mere steps away a bright sun filled the sky, that overnight the grass and leaves had turned a deep, luxuriant green, and that bunches of fluff from the cottonwood trees were drifting indolently through the air.

The students in the auditorium didn't need a window to know that summer had arrived. The air hummed. It was Friday afternoon. The school day was nearly over, and so was the school year. Everyone wanted to be outside. The younger boys, especially, were having a hard time sitting still. Boy energy. Hannah loved to watch it. A gang of them in the row ahead of her had folded their programs into airplanes and were pitching them in every direction. Their teachers were sitting in the first row with Monsieur Bonnaire. Occasionally, one of them would turn his or her head toward the back of the auditorium and call out a warning, but discipline had clearly relaxed.

A television crew from Radio-Canada came into the room and stood discreetly by the door. Serge Vien, who was seated a few rows behind Hannah, got up and greeted the two men, one of whom was carrying a camera. Hannah turned away from the stage to watch, grateful for a distraction. The presentations were almost over. She had been here for nearly two hours, sitting on a narrow folding seat, breathing recycled air. On the stage, a girl with a long ropelike braid was reading a prize-winning paper about the environment. Hannah tried once more to listen. The girl had developed an ambitious recycling plan for the school, with a detailed collection schedule, for the greater social good. She exhorted everyone to separate their waste plastic and paper and glass, but she wasn't a good motivator. She didn't look up from her page even once, and she ran her words together in a rapid, enervating monotone.

The Radio-Canada cameraman crouched in the aisle next to Hannah, taking a series of establishing shots. Serge Vien, who seemed to be in charge of the event, hovered at his shoulder. He caught Hannah's eye and smiled. He had cut his hair and lost weight. He looked happy, she thought, almost handsome. She smiled back at him.

The cameraman was scanning the podium with his camera. He didn't pause when he reached the girl with the braid. He swung around to take in the audience, catching a couple of paper planes in mid-glide. Then he lowered the camera and stood there, restless and half attentive like the rest of them.

Hannah was nine rows up from the stage. Lyse had chosen

the seats because Hannah had been late, buying the red roses that lay on the floor at her feet encased in clear plastic. The first time she'd received a dozen red roses was the day Hugo was born. Luc had bought them for her, an unexpected romantic gesture she would never forget.

People were clapping. The girl with the braid was finally done. Without looking up, the girl fled the stage, hugging her notes to her chest. Hugo was in the first row with the other speakers. Hannah watched him rise. In the aisle, the man from Radio-Canada rose too and took aim with his camera.

There was no common theme for the talks today. Some of them, like the one on the environment, were scientific. Others dealt with people, or the arts. Some of the speakers had just started high school; others were about to graduate. Serge Vien organized this event every year, apparently, picking the best projects across all disciplines and grades. The sole criterion was excellence.

Hugo ascended the stairs to the stage, his school shirt too big for his narrow frame. He looked younger than fourteen, so slender and small. On her last visit to Toronto, Hannah had studied the internment camp photograph more carefully. The resemblance was striking. In the photo, Alfred had exactly the same slight build, the same dark, intelligent eyes. Her father's genes had come down the bloodline intact, it seemed, skipping over Hannah but replicating quite uncannily in her son.

Serge Vien went back to his seat, from which he manned the computer for the video projection. Luc sat beside him. They had become surprisingly close over the winter, spending a lot of time in each other's company. The Radio-Canada team had spotted Luc. That, Hannah supposed, would settle the matter. The camera would stay pointed at him now, regardless of what

Hugo did or said. Heads began to turn. The boys in front of Hannah left off shooting their paper planes and swivelled in their seats to point. Hannah kept her gaze firmly fixed on her son, her mind willing the media people and everyone else in the room to do the same.

She couldn't alter things by wishing. She couldn't snap her fingers and conjure up another, less noteworthy, father for Hugo, but at least she could give him her own undivided attention. Lyse was facing forward too. Graeme White was in the next seat: her *ami de coeur*, as Lyse now called him.

On the stage, Hugo was battling technical problems. The microphone was one of those small, ultra-finicky devices, and it had been angled too high. The speakers shrieked, and Hugo, startled, dropped his cue cards. As he bent to retrieve them, a ripple of laughter spread across the hall.

Someone from the technical crew came onstage to adjust the microphone, but he had difficulty too. The boy sitting right in front of Hannah began to bounce up and down in his seat. Other boys copied him, and soon the whole row was bobbing. Paper planes whizzed again. Hannah fanned herself with her program. The lectern was too high. It came up to Hugo's nose. There was no way he could put his notes down on it.

Lyse leaned over and patted Hannah's leg. "He'll be fine," she whispered. "You'll see."

In the end, Hugo didn't even use notes. The techie gave up on the conventional mic and clipped a portable one to Hugo's collar, slipping a battery pack into his pocket. Hugo stepped away from the lectern. He paused for a second, gazing out at the room. "Whoa," he said, shielding his eyes with his arm. "It's bright up here."

His ease took her by surprise. It was as if speaking to seven hundred people came naturally to him. *Le dor va dor.* From generation to generation. Hugo had his father's gifts.

The cameraman, she noted, was no longer pointing his camera at Luc. He'd swung it around to the skinny kid in the baggy shirt, his hands in his pockets, calmly addressing the crowd.

"This project began as a punishment," Hugo said in a French that struck just the right note between conversational and formal. "When Monsieur Bonnaire proposed it, I can't say I was thrilled. That's because the idea came from the outside, from the principal and teachers at this school."

He paused, looking down for a moment at his school shoes. Then he looked up again. "But now I see how lucky it all was. It gave me a chance to find out about something important, and I'm not just talking about Quebec history, which happens to be my subject today."

He paused again. "Before I begin, there are a few people I would like to thank. And, ironically, also an institution. I'd like to thank Collège Saint-Jean-Baptiste for forcing me to do this work in the first place."

A few students laughed, but this time the laughter wasn't snide.

Hugo was scanning the auditorium. "That man over at the projector," he said, pointing, "was the instigator. I'd like to thank Monsieur Vien for his help with this project, but most of all for sharing his passion for history with me."

People started to clap, but Hugo held up a hand until the noise abated. "I also want to thank my father, Luc Lévesque, who travelled to England with me and shot most of the footage you're about to see. He had never held a video camera before. He put in a lot of time and effort. But beyond his technical support, he was just there."

This time Hugo let the crowd clap. He squinted into the room, nodding when he located Luc. "Other people were there for me too," he continued after the applause. "My *maman*," he said, shielding his eyes from the glare and finding Hannah, "and also her *maman*, my grandmother Connie Stern, who couldn't be here today, but who gave me the idea for this presentation.

"I'm not going to say much more, except to warn you that, unlike all the other speakers today, I'm not actually going to speak. It's a change from the usual rules, I know, but there is a reason. I can't use my own words here. The story isn't mine. It belongs to a man who has been silent for thirty-one years. Most of you know his name. You may even think you know his story. But in three decades, he hasn't given us his perspective.

"So, here it is, ladies and gentlemen. His voice. His words. The story of Mr. James Richard Cross, told in his own language."

He signalled to a boy standing at the light switch and the room went black. A screen above the stage lit up and white cliffs gleamed, towering over a choppy sea.

In the darkness of the auditorium, Lyse's hand reached out and squeezed Hannah's fingers. The footage was exhilarating. They watched as the camera soared, coasting like a bird on the wind, and descended, zeroing in on a lone figure walking on the cliff.

Lyse leaned over so her lips were right up against Hannah's ear. "How did they do that?" she whispered.

"With a hang glider," Hannah whispered back. It had been Luc's idea. He had noticed some local boys gliding on the cliffs and simply walked over and asked if they'd mind strapping his camera to a wing.

The figure on the cliff came into sharper focus. His back was curved, his hair white. He walked too slowly to be a young man, although there was resolve in his step. Every so often, he paused to toss a stick for a rangy Irish setter.

A narrator's voice began to speak. Her son's. In English, but French subtitles appeared at the bottom of the frame, translating his words into neat French print for those who did not understand. The man lived in a retirement town called Seaford, two hours south of London by car, and a stone's throw from the chalk cliffs overlooking the English Channel.

The man was eighty years old. He had endured, the voice told them, much as the ancient cliffs on which he walked each day had endured, withstanding storms and the pounding elements.

The next images were interiors. Now the old man was inside a cottage, pouring cups of tea from a brown teapot. There was no introduction. The man just started speaking. "My name," he said, looking straight into the lens of Luc's camera, "is James Richard Cross. My friends and family call me Jasper."

He seemed quite ordinary, sitting there in a plaid flannel shirt and corduroy trousers, talking about his life and offering Hugo, who was conducting the interview off-camera, tea and cookies. This was the man who had once dined with Hannah's parents in Montreal, the man who had played such a strange role, at once pivotal and peripheral, in the history of her family and her nation.

He spoke of his childhood in Ireland, of going away to university and eventually landing a job as a diplomat for the British Foreign Office in India and Malaysia. Some decades later, when he was nearing fifty, he was stationed in Canada.

He introduced Barbara, his pleasant-looking wife, who stood at the threshold of the living room, not venturing to step over it, watching the interview proceed with round, attentive eyes. He talked in loving tones about their daughter, an only child, who had been a student in Montreal at the time of what he referred to as "the incident." She now lived in London, making the drive south to Sussex to see her parents at least once a month.

He described the events of October 1970 in detail, as if they had just occurred, and spoke about the effect his abduction had had upon him. Every time he read about a kidnapping in the news, he said, regardless of where it had taken place or who the perpetrators were, it brought him right back, forcefully and viscerally, to October 1970 in Montreal.

He described the room on Avenue des Récollets in the city's north end where he had spent fifty-nine days in captivity. He described how he had been forced to sit with his back to his captors. How he had been forbidden to look at them. If he turned reflexively at a noise, say, or an unexpected movement behind him, they panicked. The woman in the group, whom he knew now to be Jacques Lanctôt's sister, Louise Cossette-Trudel, would scream threats and cock the gun. He had been convinced that he would die.

The scene changed again, and Cross was back on the cliffs. But this time, the camera was at ground level, pointing directly at him. The day was clear and bright. He was walking, shoulders hunched into the wind coming off the water. He recounted how, for the two months of his captivity, he had travelled in his mind back to Ireland, all the way back to his boyhood, anchoring himself in memory. This was how he had survived. Every day, he set himself the task of retrieving a piece of his past. It did not have to be anything spectacular. The pink and grey bark, for instance, on the trees around his family's home. He did not know the trees' name, but he could picture them, clear as day, with their disturbing and beautiful skin-tone colours. His favourite way to pass the time was thinking about a walk he used to take every day when he was young, from his childhood home to the school-house a mile or so away. It was a form of mental gymnastics, he explained. A discipline to keep him sane, a distraction from his plight, from the soiled mattress on which he was forced to sit, patterned with thin black lines that made him think of prison bars. He got very good at it, picturing, eventually, every turn in the road, every house that bordered it, every memorable rock and tree. Hour after hour, he played his game, reconstructing the private, inviolable world of a lived past.

Hugo never once entered the frame. He was only a voice, interjecting discreetly when Cross had finished with a given subject. Hannah pictured him sitting across from the old man, watching intently, encouraging him with his intelligent brown eyes. His English was perfect, not betraying any hint that he had been raised and schooled in French.

The subject of conversation had switched to politics now. How did Cross see his role in Quebec's history?

The old man joined his fingertips and pressed them to his lips. After a moment's thought, he lifted his head. "I've been a pawn," he said, looking at the camera. "A pawn in your history. Maybe now, I'll be a face. Not the British diplomat, not the imperialist, but a man. A husband. A father. A human brother."

The picture froze as he finished this sentence, and then the credits started to roll. Cross's name came first, right in the middle of the screen, and floated up slowly over his head.

Hugo's name came after it. Luc was listed simply as "the cameraman."

When the lights came up, Hannah sat blinking at the screen, which was once again an unassuming blank square suspended above the stage. At the front of the auditorium, someone stood up. It was Monsieur Bonnaire. He held up his hands and began to clap. The teachers started applauding too, and soon everyone was on their feet, hooting and whistling and stamping.

Hannah looked behind her, trying to locate Luc, but there was a commotion around his seat. People were standing up, blocking her view. Hannah recognized a columnist from *La Presse* trying to nudge her way through the crowd. A younger man in jeans, probably from one of the local arts weeklies, bumped the *La Presse* woman aside, and for a second Hannah caught a glimpse of Luc's startled face. The Radio-Canada man was in there too, elbows out, jostling for position. Did the film signal a shift in Luc's politics? the *La Presse* woman asked shrilly. How had he managed to locate James Cross after all these years? How had he convinced him to talk? They were shouting their questions, clearly audible now that the applause was dying down. Had Luc given up on the nationalist dream?

Luc did not answer. He'd stood up and was trying to make his way to Hugo, but he couldn't push through. The journalists blocked him. He got as far as the aisle and stopped in exasperation.

"Look," he said, loudly enough for Hannah to catch it. "I have nothing to say. This isn't my project. It's my son's."

The *La Presse* woman was the first to head for the podium. The Radio-Canada man was next. Soon the others followed, moving in a pack to the front of the room, where Hugo was standing.

"Nice," said Hannah, walking over to her ex-husband. "Set the jackals on him."

Luc straightened his jacket, which seemed baggier than usual. He had taken up jogging over the winter. He looked youthful, she thought, and not just because he'd shed a few pounds. There was a new tentativeness about him. He kept looking into people's eyes as if he wasn't sure what he would find there.

"He's got to learn to deal with it sooner or later," he said, shrugging. Then he noticed the flowers in her arms.

"For Hugo," she said.

"They're spectacular."

She shrugged. "He was the spectacular one."

Luc was looking at her in that odd, uncertain way he'd acquired. How funny they were together, she thought. You'd hardly guess they'd spent so many years sleeping in the same bed. It was ridiculous, but she felt shy in his presence, as if they'd only just met.

He was back on Laporte Street, although not living with them, exactly. He slept downstairs in the first-floor flat with Rémi, who was home from the Plateau. For the first time since Hannah had met him, he wasn't writing. He didn't seem too upset about this fact. He had enjoyed his stint as a cameraman on Hugo's film, although "cameraman" hardly covered all the roles he'd played, first in England, then after their return. He had bought editing software and spent hours reading manuals, and more hours reviewing the vast amount of footage he and Hugo had logged. More recently, he had put together a promotion package and mailed it to every contact he had in the media. No one had expected any reporters to show up at the school today, but now that they had, he was in no position to complain.

Eventually, he would get back to his desk, he had confided to Hannah, but for the time being he was taking unexpected pleasure in the break.

Hannah checked her watch. She, on the other hand, was busier than she'd ever been. She had to get home right now. The Word was supposed to call, and for the first time in months, she could offer them good news. *Death of a Dreamer* was done.

She had already called Allison March, who was home on maternity leave. Not that Allison seemed to care much anymore about translations or any other book-related matters. All she could talk about was her baby.

She'd had a son, not the daughter her doctor had confidently predicted. He was napping when Hannah had last spoken with her, in the pink room that Allison had so meticulously prepared for a little girl. The birth had not taken place at home, as Allison had hoped. Despite the Lamaze baths and massages and ethnic lullabies sung by her doula, all of which Allison described to Hannah in great detail over the telephone, Allison had ended up having a C-section in an operating room of Toronto's largest hospital.

"Nothing went the way I'd planned," Allison had reported, laughing with what sounded like genuine mirth. "But you know what? That's just fine."

Hannah could have said the same. Her parents were still struggling in the aftermath of her father's stroke, but she felt closer to them than she had in years. Luc's departure hadn't been such a disaster either. It had led her to Manny Mandelbaum, initially for Hugo, but then to help her sort out her own confusion. He had helped her understand that her career as a translator was over. In October, this had seemed like a calamity, but now, nearly nine months later, it was a simple fact. Translation no longer interested her. On Manny's counsel, she had kept her contract with the Word Press but farmed out the last chapters of *Dreamer* to a young woman who had just graduated from the translation department at Concordia University.

And she had started to read fiction again. Not searching for books to translate, but the way she had read years ago when she was young, eclectically and for pleasure. She had found her old copy of *Bonheur d'occasion*, dog-eared and marked up, from her days at Dawson College. What she found in its pages surprised her. It wasn't anything like Luc's novels, despite what the critics claimed. The setting was Saint-Henri, as in Luc's books. And the characters were working class, like Luc's characters. But the similarities ended there.

What struck her in *Bonheur* were the voices. Weary Rose-Anna and her dreamer of a husband, Azarius. Flighty, self-involved Florentine Lacasse and her equally self-involved lover, Jean Lévesque, all of them so closely observed that it was easy to forget they were fictional. Gabrielle Roy's emotional antennae picked up frequencies missed by most people and transmitted them whole and true in her writing. Hannah had forgotten how she had once known each member of the Lacasse clan as intimately as the members of her own family. She told all of this to Manny Mandelbaum, whom she was still visiting periodically, and whose expensive Westmount office rent she was now helping to subsidize. She wasn't sure she would call it therapy—it felt more like chatting with a friend—but it was helping.

The young translator's work on *Dreamer* had been excellent. After Hannah finished the edits, she had no more excuses. At the Bureau en Gros, she bought a Hilroy notebook with three subject dividers and a pack of econo-brand ballpoint pens. And she began. This also had been inspired by Manny. His definition of adulthood could be applied to other types of people—writers of fiction, for instance. It was all about telling someone's story, getting under the skin, catching the intricate truth of personal history.

Hannah still wasn't sure what it was that she had begun, or what shape it might eventually take. But she knew she wanted voices. More than one, and each of them telling a story. She wanted a character, based loosely on Alfred Stern, whose voice would be extinguished. She wanted a boy like her son at this precise moment, age fourteen, daring to speak out. She wanted a writer like Luc, with his bright eye and his oh-so-human heart. And she wanted a woman facing the difficulties she had faced, a translator who for reasons she didn't understand found herself unable to translate.

Eventually, she would have to let Luc know about the project. He had been dropping by with increasing frequency, supposedly to help finish the film, but occasionally staying on after the work was done and joining her and Hugo for dinner. So far, she had kept her writing a secret, but she couldn't keep it from him forever. Every day, she sat a little longer at her desk in the pantry, filling the spiral notebook with words. This book, or whatever it would turn out to be, was no longer inside her. Quite the contrary. It had swallowed her up, and she knew that sooner or later Luc or Hugo would ask about it. By that time, she hoped, she would have figured out what to say.

BOOKS, FILMS, AND WEBSITES
REFERRED TO IN THIS NOVEL

"The British Diplomatic Oral History Programme," 1996,
www.chu.cam.ac.uk/archives/collections/BDOHP/Cross
.pdf.

Fanon, Frantz. *The Wretched of the Earth*. Translated by
Constance Farrington. New York: Grove Press, 1963.
Reprint, London: Penguin Classics, 2001. Originally
published as *Les damnés de la terre*, 1961.

Kaufman, Fred. *Searching for Justice: An Autobiography*.
Toronto: University of Toronto Press, 2005.

Leblanc, Carl. *L'Otage* (The Hostage). Ad Hoc Films, 2004.

Rosenberg, Marshall B. *Nonviolent Communication: A Language
of Life*. Encinitas, CA: PuddleDancer Press, 2003.

Roy, Gabrielle. *The Tin Flute*. Translated by Alan Brown.
Toronto: McClelland & Stewart, 1980. Originally
published as *Bonheur d'occasion*, 1945.

Vallières, Pierre. *White Niggers of America: The Precocious Autobiography of a Quebec "Terrorist."* Translated by Joan Pinkham. Toronto: McClelland & Stewart, 1971. Originally published as *Nègres blancs d'Amérique: Autobiographie précoce d'un "terroriste" québécois*, 1968.

ACKNOWLEDGMENTS

First of all, I am indebted to Carl Leblanc for his fine, probing film *L'Otage* (The Hostage), which filled me with questions and inspired this novel.

Véronique Boscart of the E.W. Bickle Centre for Complex Continuing Care and the late Electra Risacher offered generous assistance while I was researching strokes and aphasia. Archivist Phil Gold of Sunnybrook Hospital provided invaluable historical details about that Toronto institution. Michael Rudder took me on a personal tour of Laporte Street in Saint-Henri, and the Saint-Henri Historical Society helped me research the novel's setting. Its "Gabrielle Roy Tour" pamphlet and map were particularly useful. For research about English-speaking Montreal families and the October Crisis, I extend my thanks to Sheila Goldbloom and Fred Kaufman (who also provided editorial input on the manuscript). For research about the anglophone exodus, I thank Collin Mills.

I am deeply grateful to my agent, Samantha Haywood of the Transatlantic Literary Agency, and to her associate Shaun

Bradley, for buoying my spirits at key moments in the creative process and, more generally, for handling all the real-world issues that arise as one turns an idea into a manuscript and a manuscript into a book. Shima Aoki of Penguin Canada, with her delicate, probing questions, and sharp-eyed Alex Schultz, helped me arrive at a final draft. I thank my partner in life, Arthur Holden, for the attentive care he bestowed on this book at various stages, and—just as importantly—on its author.

Finally, I want to express my gratitude to the Canada Council for the Arts, provider of the generous grant that financed the first draft of *My October*.